CRIME SCENES

CRIME SCENES

JOSEPH S. WALKER

LEVEL BEST BOOKS
LEVEL SHORT

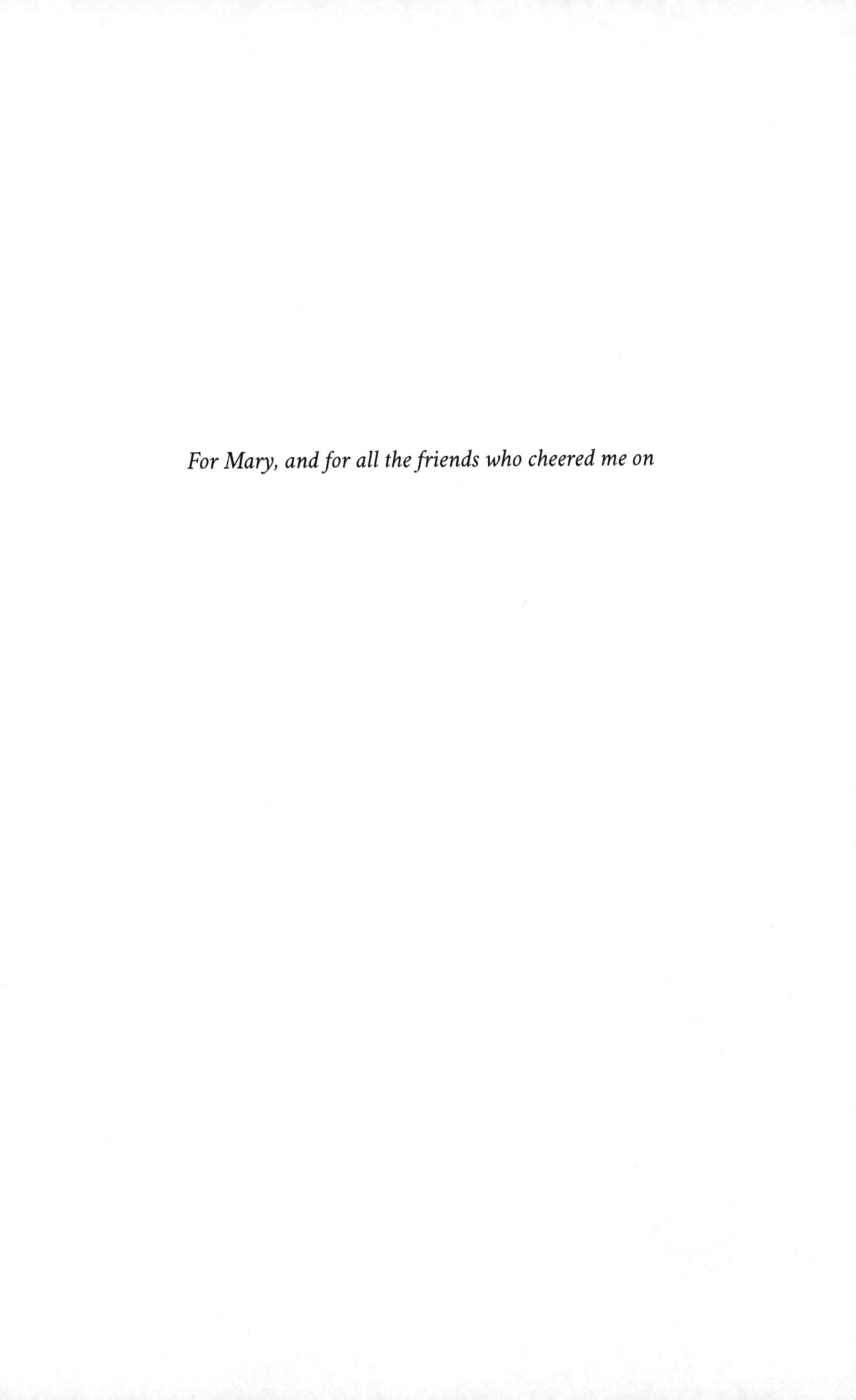

For Mary, and for all the friends who cheered me on

Contents

Praise for CRIME SCENES

"I have been reviewing mystery short stories for sixteen years. Joe Walker has made my Best of the Week list AND my Best of the Year list more than any other writer. The selfish jerk should leave some talent for the rest of us. If you don't love this book you don't love crime fiction."—**Robert Lopresti**

"*Crime Scenes* is the finest crime fiction collection I've read in quite a long time. Thirteen of the stories in this remarkable collection have won or been shortlisted for major industry accolades. Every story seamless, every story memorable, every story riveting, these are absolute gems that have earned Joseph S. Walker a place on the Mount Rushmore of living short crime fiction authors."—**Avram Lavinsky**

"If you've not read Joseph S. Walker's short fiction before, you're in for a treat. These twenty stories of crime and deception—they range from bars to ballparks to back alleys to movie sets—will grab you right away and hold you until the end, with no wasted words and no dull moments. Walker's style is both fast-paced and easy to read, and is only one of the reasons he's among the best crime/suspense writers working today. I truly enjoyed this book!"—**John M. Floyd**, Edgar nominee and Shamus Award winner

"If crime fiction was baseball, Joe Walker would be the league's MVP. In *Crime Scenes*, he knocks the ball out of the park again and again. I don't know any other living writer who hits a home run every time he steps up to the plate...."—**Josh Pachter**

"Sure, you'll come for the twisty plots and wonderfully drawn characters in

Crime Scenes, but you'll stay for the heart and humanity. Joseph S. Walker is a short story pro's pro!"—**Alan Orloff**

"Joseph S. Walker does for the short story what Jeff Beck did for the guitar. He is a master of technique but never uses it to show off. He uses it to pull his readers into the action and experience it along with the characters. He's a true virtuoso, and every time I pick up one of his stories, I learn something new."—**Steve Liskow**, Edgar and Shamus Award finalist, two-time winner of the Black Orchid Novella Award

"One of the most striking things about Joseph S. Walker's work as a short story writer is how refreshingly original his ideas are. Whether the germ of the story is a trivia contest, a lost chance in a baseball game, qualifying for the Olympics, a solar eclipse, a horror movie, urban exploration, the scene of the Kennedy assassination, or reality TV, he never fails to develop it in an unexpected way. The styles of this author's stories vary; when he's in classic noir mode he could rival Chandler for similes that hit the mark and stay in the brain. Every fan of short crime fiction will find something to enjoy in this volume!"—**Janet Hutchings**

"Joseph S. Walker is arguably the best short crime fiction writer on the scene today, and I expect his stories to be read, studied, and enjoyed for many years to come. His collection, *Crime Scenes*, showcases a breadth and depth of talent that places him in the pantheon of Stanly Ellin, Doug Allyn, and Peter Lovesy. There is no scene or locale here that he is not intimately familiar with and cannot present to you as your own land. There are no situations, however mundane or exotic, that he does not turn into an unforgettable tale. You have only to read, and he's even made that so easy that all have to do is begin. You'll forget everything else once you do."—**David Dean**

"One of the heavyweight champions of short story writing today."—**Alec Cizak**

"Although I kept seeing Joseph Walker's name associated with various "Best of" story collections and other honors, I had only read his excellent Sherlock Holmes pastiches. Now, with this new collection, I further understand why he is so well regarded, and all the writing skills that he displayed as a Holmes pasticheur are also demonstrated on the wider stage of *Crime Scenes*."—**David Marcum**

"First published in 2011, Joseph S. Walker soon became one of the 21st Century's best writers of short crime fiction. His multiple awards, award nominations, and appearances in annual best-of-year collections attest to the overwhelming quality of his work. *Crime Scenes* gathers together many of his best short stories, and you'll find it difficult to stop reading once you've opened the book. Highly recommended."—**Michael Bracken**, Anthony, Edgar, and Shamus nominee

Etta at the End of the World

After she left the truck stop south of Jacksonville, Etta kept passing signs with names she'd heard all her life from TV and people with the time and money for vacations. Orlando. Tampa. Daytona Beach. It all felt imaginary, but then Florida felt imaginary, like a giant billboard for itself. She passed a lot of palm trees before she accepted that they were real. She couldn't always see the ocean off to her left, but she knew it was there, knew it by the wind and a smell that would never touch Iowa. The sky was big and blue and untouched until the late afternoon, when mountainous clouds started to rise up out of the east. It was like driving into a 3D antidepressant commercial, but she felt an itch at the back of her neck all day. She was cutting herself off. There was only one direction to go now, and if they found her, no place else to run.

Of course, running wasn't really the idea.

She pulled off in Boca Raton. It was still light out, but she had no chance of making Key West before sunset, and her back wouldn't take another night in the car. She found a run-down motel, not one of the big chains, a few blocks away from the beach. The Sandcastle Lodge. It was a long L, two stories high, sheltered from the main drag by a mini-mall and backed by a big, abandoned lot full of scrub pine trees. She'd put up with roaches for the sake of a desk clerk who wouldn't find cash strange.

Her room was on the first floor, near the swimming pool tucked into the elbow of the building. A man in the pool was drinking a can of beer and roughhousing with a couple of kids, while a plump woman perched on one of the deck chairs made dismayed noises every time one of them went under the water. The only other person near the pool was a teenaged girl, sleeping on her stomach on a lounger, wearing sunglasses and a red swimsuit that said she thought her body was a little slimmer than it actually was. Etta only glanced at her as she walked by, but the clearly defined bruises on the girl's upper arm jumped out at her like they were lit up in neon. She'd seen their match often enough in her own mirror. Four angry purple blemishes perfectly staking out the shape of a man's hand. The girl's arm was the most real thing she'd seen all day.

* * *

The room was as bad as she expected, but the sheets were clean and the water in the shower hot enough to satisfy. She let it pound onto her aching shoulders for more than half an hour. There was a time when she could have driven for four straight days and then partied all night, but fifty was creeping up on her a lot faster than she'd like. She dried herself with the surprisingly adequate towel and fell across the bed, intending to get up in a few minutes and go in search of some kind of dinner.

The next thing Etta was aware of was a heavy thud that shook the whole bed. She jerked upright, with no idea for a moment of where she was or what was happening. She was nude, sprawled across the bedspread, shivering with cold. She could see the outline of the window behind the drapes, but the room was pitch dark. Heart pounding, she tried to figure out what had woken her.

There was a yell from behind the headboard, a deep man's voice. She couldn't make out the words, but the anger was clear. It was cut into by another voice, a female voice, this one pleading and tearful. The second voice got out only a few words before the initial thud happened again: something heavy being thrown up against the wall. She remembered now—the imprint of those fingers on that arm.

She sat still for the next ten minutes, listening to what could have been the soundtrack of most of her life. At some point, she noticed the faintly glowing dial of the clock beside the bed. If it was remotely accurate, it was just past three in the morning.

When the noises ended, she still did not move, unable to decide if she could still hear crying from the room next door or if her mind was filling that in. Eventually she stood, moving as quietly as possible to the chair where her backpack rested. A t-shirt and shorts were the closest thing she had to sleeping wear, and she pulled them on. Then she stuck her hand back in the bag and felt the grip of the gun. She held it for a long minute, biting her lip, then went back to the bed and crawled under the blankets. She brought the backpack and put it next to her pillow and stared into the darkness, willing the room next door to stay silent.

* * *

Shooting Tyler had been like a power outage. That instant when everything falls dark and all the hums of a house, the ones you don't hear until they're not there to hear, end. She put the barrel against the base of his skull and pulled the trigger, and he simply dropped, first face forward onto the table and then rolling to the floor. He didn't flop or gasp for breath or spit out bitter final words. He didn't even bleed that much. He just...stopped. Twenty minutes later, Etta was on the Interstate outside Davenport, deciding where she would stop to steal a different car. Tyler taught her how to steal cars. He taught her about guns, too. He was a good teacher. That didn't come close to making up for all the things he was bad at.

* * *

The knock at the door the next morning was so light that Etta wasn't sure she'd heard it. Just dressed after another shower, she was looking out the bathroom window at the wild tangle of trees and vines that ended about ten feet from the motel, picking out all the plants she'd never seen before.

Surely the cops wouldn't knock?

She looked through the peephole and wasn't really surprised to see the girl. For a moment she just stood with her hand on the knob, trying again to project silence, but the girl must have heard something because she knocked again.

Etta opened the door a few inches. "Can I help you?"

"Um, yeah," the girl said. She was wearing the sunglasses again, but with jeans and a t-shirt with sleeves long enough to obscure the bruises Etta had seen. "I lost my ID? And I was wondering if I could give you some money to go to the liquor store for me." She pointed at the mini-mall. "There's one right at the road there."

"Lost your ID," Etta said. "Clerk didn't believe that either, right?"

The girl stared blankly at the door.

"It's a little early in the day for a beer buzz," Etta said. She was about to add "dear" and bit it off, horrified to be talking like an old woman.

"I don't need beer," the girl blurted. She shifted from foot to foot. "Ma'am, it's not for me. Honest. Tone…the man I'm with…he wants me to get him a bottle of Jack. I tried yesterday and…look, he's gonna be real mad if I don't get it again today."

"The man you're with," Etta said. "Not your husband."

"I ain't married," the girl said forcefully.

Etta sighed. She wanted to close the door. She wanted to crawl back on the bed and just wait until somebody found her. Instead, she said, "Is there a place to eat around here?"

The girl cocked her head. "There's a restaurant next to the liquor store."

Etta nodded. "I'll make you a deal. Come have breakfast with me, and I'll buy you the liquor."

* * *

The restaurant was a diner where everything was coated with a thin layer of grease. All the employees were slender young dark-skinned men who shouted Spanish at each other and seemed perpetually annoyed by the customers wanting attention. The girl left her sunglasses on and kept touching the bottle of booze in its plain brown bag as if to assure herself it was real. She insisted on going to buy it before eating, though she had waited outside.

Etta ordered eggs and toast and watched the girl work on a stack of pancakes. "So, Tone," Etta said carefully. "Is he underage, too?"

"No, ma'am," the girl said. "He's old. In his thirties."

This definition of *old* made Etta decide she'd been ma'amed enough. "Call me Etta," she said. "So why doesn't he buy his own whiskey?"

The girl shrugged. "He's real busy."

"Too busy to go into a liquor store right outside his door?"

"He's supposed to be meeting a guy." The girl pushed her food around a little. "He's gone all day waiting for him."

Etta nodded as though that made sense. "But what does he expect you to do if they're carding?"

The girl didn't say anything. She stared down at her plate.

"Let's try this again," Etta said. "My name is Etta, and you are."

"Grace," the girl said quietly.

"It's nice to meet you, Grace." Etta took a sip from her coffee and waited.

Grace finished the pancakes. She put the fork down, took off the sunglasses, and looked Etta in the face for the first time. Etta carefully didn't react to the black eye she had known she would see.

"He gets off on making me do stuff. He told me to shoplift," Grace said. "Only I tried that yesterday, and they caught me. That's why I waited outside. So then he told me." She looked out the window. "He told me to offer to blow the clerk."

A waiter came up and slapped the check down on the table, where part of it immediately turned translucent with grease. Grace put her sunglasses back on. Etta dropped a twenty on top of the check. "Do you have to stay at the hotel all day?" she asked.

Grace shook her head. "Tone won't be back until late."

"I thought I'd walk down to the beach," Etta said. She stood up. "Join me?"

* * *

They went back to the hotel first, so Grace could drop off the bottle and Etta could pay for another night. She got directions to the beach from the clerk, who warned her not to go into the lot behind the hotel. "Snakes back in there," the man said, in an accent Etta didn't even try to identify. "Gators."

"I think he was putting me on," she told Grace as they walked.

The girl shrugged. "He told us the same when we checked in," she said. "Then, a couple of days ago, a gator ate some lady's dog a few blocks from here."

Unreal Florida again. Etta tried to imagine scaly monsters strolling around in Davenport and people just accepting it.

The beach seemed unreal, too. They sat a few yards above the water line, Etta propped up against her backpack, watching the waves come in and dead-eyed gulls scurrying down onto the wet sand as the water receded. It was still early in the day on Monday, and there were only a few other people around, mostly just watching the water themselves.

Etta thought she could watch it all day. "I've never seen the ocean before," she told Grace. "I've spent my whole life in Iowa."

Grace idly traced a line in the sand with a piece of driftwood. "Tennessee," she said. "I never saw it either before a few days ago."

Etta dug her hand into the sand, looking for shells. *Souvenirs*, she thought, then wondered when she expected to ever enjoy such a thing. She'd always thought of sand as light, but this was heavy, shifting, hard to walk through. The breeze from offshore kept the sun from being too hot, and she was mesmerized by the perpetual motion of the water.

"Just think," she said. "It's been doing that since before we were born, and it'll keep doing it until the end of the world."

There was no answer. Grace was sleeping. Etta kicked her shoes off and buried her feet in the warm sand. There was nobody in the world who knew where she was or what she was doing. Nobody in the world to tell her to do something different.

She dozed some herself and was startled when Grace suddenly spoke. "You just here on vacation?"

"Sort of," Etta said. "I'm on my way to Key West. Thought I'd make it today, but there's nothing wrong with tomorrow."

"What's in Key West?"

"The end of the world," Etta said. She dug up a scalloped white shell, no bigger than her thumbnail but exquisite and perfect. She turned it over in her fingers. "It's the last island in this group of islands that hangs off the end of Florida. It's where the road ends. Where all the roads end. My parents honeymooned there, sixty years ago. My mother said until the day she died that if you haven't seen the sun set in Key West, you haven't lived a complete life."

"That's nice," the girl said. "Now you're finally gonna see it."

"That's the plan," Etta said. She dug into her backpack and found a rolled pair of socks and carefully put the shell inside them. She tucked the socks back into the bottom of the bag, next to the pair concealing what had been Tyler's emergency stash of hundreds and twenties. "What about you?" she asked. "You said Tone is here for business?"

Grace was quiet for so long that Etta was sure she'd fallen asleep again. "Sort of business," she finally said. Etta waited.

"His name is Tony," Grace said. "He makes people call him Tone because he thinks it makes him sound tough. Gangster."

"And is he a gangster?"

"He wants to be." Grace rolled over on her stomach. "He works for my daddy. Now my daddy, *he's* a gangster. Runs meth labs around the whole state."

Etta wanted to ask if Grace should be talking about this, but she bit her tongue.

"Daddy wants to branch out," Grace said. "So Tony is down here to buy coke. He set up a deal where a guy is supposed to meet him at a spot a couple of miles out on the water, but the guy says he has to wait for a day when he's sure it's clear. So Tony's been going out and waiting for the last four days. He's in a pretty bad mood when he gets back to the room."

"And he takes it out on you," Etta said. Grace didn't answer, but it wasn't really a question. "Grace, why are you with this guy? What do you see in him?"

Grace barked out a laugh. "See in him? Jesus. I hate him." She pushed her fingers roughly into the sand. "Daddy *gave* me to him. Said I'm a useless shit like my mother, but maybe I can make a grandson to carry on the business."

Etta sat silently for several minutes. She thought about patting the girl's shoulder, making comforting noises, but that would have taken something she didn't quite think she had. She thought about all the ways the girl might be playing her, about the fact that she could go back to the hotel right this second and leave. Eventually, she surprised herself by speaking.

"You've got better taste than me," she said. "My husband Tyler was like Tone. A crook, somebody who wanted everyone to know how tough he was. My parents tried to warn me about him, but I fell for it. God, I thought he was everything." She stared out at the water. "I thought I must deserve the things he did." She didn't look, but she knew Grace was listening.

The waves came in, the waves went out. They were doing it long before Etta was born. They'd be doing it long after she was gone.

Etta stood up. "I passed a library yesterday," she said. Grace looked up at her, and Etta held out a hand to help her up. "Come on. I want to show you something."

* * *

The library, a couple of blocks off the beach, was a low-slung stucco building with pastel awnings and red terracotta tiles on the roof. Etta couldn't help but wish it was just a plain old concrete block. *Jesus, Florida*, she thought. *We get it already.*

The few people inside were dressed as casually as those on the beach. Etta found the computer stations and chose one in a private corner. Grace stood next to her, hip cocked against the desk, looking around from behind her pitch-dark shades. Etta had the feeling she didn't spend much time in libraries.

It took her only a few minutes to find the article she was looking for in the online version of the *Quad-City Times*. "Here," she said. She stood up and steered Grace into the chair. "Read this."

Grace took off the sunglasses and began scanning the article. After a few seconds, her eyes opened wide. Etta didn't need to look; she read it at another library, in Georgia, two days ago. Local man Tyler Hession found dead in his home of a single gunshot wound. Troubled history. Grand theft, domestic abuse. Wife, Etta, missing and being actively sought by police as a person of interest. If you have any information…

"Holy shit," Grace hissed. She looked up at Etta. "Did you do that?"

"Yeah," Etta said. She pulled over another chair and perched on the edge, leaning forward. "Tell me something. Does Tone shower when he comes back at night?"

* * *

That night Etta sat in the chair in her room. She'd cleaned and reloaded the gun, every step reminding her of Tyler's impatient lectures, his warnings about a gun that jams at the moment when you need it. As though he'd ever done anything with a gun other than wave it around. She put the gun on the nightstand and forced herself to leave it alone. She turned on the TV with the volume all the way down to have something to look at. She nibbled on cookies and drank soda to stay alert. A hospital show. Lots of very earnest, very serious young men and women in scrubs, frowning at helpless-looking people in beds.

After a while, they were replaced by the local news. From what she could tell without any sound, it was exactly the same as the local news in Iowa. She'd come here because Florida felt like the end of the world, but there were people who lived here every day. They'd probably find a few miles of unbroken corn fields as bizarre as Etta found the beach.

The talk show host who came on after the news was on his second guest when Etta heard a door open and the mumble of voices through the wall behind her. She turned off the TV and listened. She still couldn't make out words, but it didn't sound like he was hitting her this time, though he still sounded angry. Probably pleased to have his Jack. She listened to the two voices rising and falling, the indistinct movements around the room. It was hard to be sure what was happening. Was that Tone throwing himself onto the bed? Grace moving around to get him a drink? What was she going to do if Tone decided not to shower tonight? Grace said he always did, that he couldn't stand sleeping coated in the sweat and sunscreen of a long day out on the water, but now, sitting alone in her room, Etta didn't think that sounded like much to base a plan on. Maybe they should have gone with their first idea, having Etta hide under the bed, but she hadn't been able to stand the idea of being under there in God knows what filth for God knew how long.

The bedsprings in the next room creaked again. Tone said something that had a nasty edge to it and laughed loudly. Then footsteps, then a moment of silence, and then a pipe somewhere creaked to life, and three soft but distinct knocks came against the wall.

So this was it. Etta seemed to watch herself from a distance as she picked up the gun with her right hand and covered it with a folded towel held in her left. Moving quickly, she went out the door and turned and came to the door of the next room, which was cracked open. She pushed through. Grace was on the other side, her eyes wide. She closed the door behind Etta and put the chain on, just as they'd rehearsed, and Etta dropped the towel and walked to the bathroom, seeing nothing but what was immediately in front of her.

The shower curtain was not quite closed. She could see Tone, facing away from the door, scrubbing at his crotch. He was a small man, shorter than Etta, but his frame was wiry and muscular. He had more body hair than any man she'd ever seen.

He must have heard something or caught a glimpse of something, because he started to turn and raise his hand and the shot Etta had intended for the back of his head, the same place she shot Tyler, instead hit the corner of his jaw. His head jerked back and his eyes widened, and she shot him two more times, both in the head, and now he dropped, and she saw the tile behind him spattered with blood.

Tyler always said she was a good shot.

She kept the gun raised and watched him not moving. There was quite a lot of blood, but the running shower was swirling most of it away down the drain. She replayed the three shots in her head and thought about the people in adjoining rooms, imagined them jerking awake or suddenly looking up from the TV, wondering about the bangs. They'd sit still, like she had after the thud last night, waiting to see what else would happen, convincing themselves that it was a car or something equally meaningless. Nothing they needed to be involved with.

After she had counted off five minutes in her head and heard no sirens, she lowered the gun to her side. There was no new blood coming from Tone, and the one eye he had left was milky and unfocused.

She stepped out of the bathroom. Grace was sitting cross-legged on the bed, clutching a pillow to her chest and shaking. "It's over," Etta said. "Go get the stuff." Grace nodded, jumped from the bed, and ran outside. In a minute, she was back with the plastic bags holding the supplies they bought that afternoon. Cleaning solution, paper towels, plastic bags, duct tape, flashlight, and, just because Etta had damn well wanted some, Oreos.

"You don't have to look," Etta said.

Grace shook her head. "I didn't have the balls to do it," she said. "Least I can do is look at it." Etta stepped aside and Grace dropped the bags on the bed and walked into the bathroom. Etta let her take her moment, let her make it whatever it needed to be for her, as she thought through a list of everything that needed to be done. Clean up the bathroom. Use the duct tape and plastic bags to cover any part of Tone that might leave a blood trail. In a few hours, when it was the deadest part of the night, shove his body through the bathroom window, then go around the building and move him as far as they dared into the wooded lot. If there were gators, they were in for a nice breakfast. Then, hopefully just before dawn, take off. They would leave Etta's stolen car in a parking lot with the keys in it. Tone's Mustang would be a safe ride for a while. It wasn't like Grace's father was going to file a missing person report on his drug mule.

Grace came out of the bathroom. For the first time since Etta had met her, she looked completely composed. "Thank you," she said. "Let's get started."

* * *

The sunset in Key West was everything Etta's mother had promised, fantastic bands of pink and orange remaking the sky continuously, the colors edging into the impossibly vibrant. Seemingly just to keep living up to the postcards, Florida was even kind enough to provide a couple of magnificent sailboats perfectly silhouetted against the spectacular sky. Etta couldn't even bring herself to resent it.

She and Grace watched from a restaurant on a boardwalk thronged with tourists and street performers. They seemed to be the only people actually watching the sky, as opposed to filming it on their phones. Etta had left hers in Iowa, and Tone had never allowed Grace to have one. It was hard to feel they were missing anything. Between Tyler's stash and Tone's unspent coke money, they could always get a burner phone if they needed to. Or a dozen.

When the sky was finally dark, she lifted her margarita glass and clinked it against Grace's diet soda. "I have to say that was worth the trip," she said.

"It was fantastic," Grace said. She was still looking out over the water, but now she turned to look at Etta. "So what were you going to do after the sunset?"

"I hadn't decided," Etta said. She leaned back in her chair. "I was either going to blow my brains out on the beach or walk into the water and wait to drown."

Grace looked shocked. "You wanted to die?"

Etta shrugged. "I thought that's what you came to the end of the world to do."

"And now?"

"Why rush?" Etta said. "It'll happen sooner or later. Might as well go for later. Why, do you have any plans?"

Grace looked down at the table. "I thought maybe we could go see my daddy."

Etta smiled, drained the last of her drink, and set the glass down.

"Why the hell not?" she said.

Bonus Round

Cary Grant was born Archibald Leach.

Woody Allen's real name is Allan Stewart Konigsberg. In a written contest, you need to be careful about the spelling of "Allan," which could well be a tiebreaker.

Of course, Lewis Carroll was Charles Dodgson, and the real Alice's last name was Liddell.

This is all basic stuff. If you don't have this nailed, you'll never get past a first round.

So ask me something I *don't* know.

* * *

Here are some facts I pretty much know by heart.

At 6:45 AM on June 17 of last year, Felix Garcia, 57, arrived at a construction job on the north side of West 118th Street near Amsterdam Avenue. The site was a two-story pit surrounded by a chain link fence. Garcia unlocked the gate and climbed a long ladder to the bottom. When he turned on floodlights to illuminate the site, he noticed that a blue vinyl tarp, which was supposed to be covering a grader, had apparently blown off and was resting at the base of one of the pit walls. He grabbed a corner to pick it up and uncovered a bare human foot.

Patrol Officer Hamza Balik, 27, in his fourth year on the job, was the first member of the NYPD to arrive on the scene, at 7:08. Wearing gloves, he moved the tarp aside just enough to determine that it concealed the body of a Caucasian female with short dark hair, age roughly 20. She was wearing only a yellow sundress, which had been pushed up around her upper torso. There was considerable bruising around her throat, and her flesh was cool to the touch. Balik took Garcia's identification, directed him to prevent any of his coworkers from entering the site, and placed a priority call for additional uniforms and crime scene investigators.

* * *

Here are some trivia facts, which is to say, some facts about trivia.

During an average week in Manhattan, forty-four bars, restaurants, and other venues host trivia contests. Some are for teams, some for individuals. Some are written quizzes, others held out loud like game shows. Many are neighborhood fluff, with no entry fees or prizes beyond a free round of drinks, and a casual, joking atmosphere. Other places cater to players who take the games as seriously as the chess hustlers in Washington Square. Teams are carefully built and rigorously defended against defections. Rivalries develop. Titles and trophies are celebrated, losses mourned. There are teams that move from bar to bar all week long, their members every bit as committed as the most rabid fantasy sports addicts. They spend their days mainlining Google and Wikipedia, stocking up names and dates and places.

I'm one of them. Three years ago, I wandered into a bar having a trivia night and, simply by virtue of having read a lot of books, won second place. I went back the next week, and the week after. I looked for other contests in my neighborhood, discovered a lot of them were for teams, and started recruiting. I work in the Records Division of the NYPD, so hard-core infogeeks were not hard to come by. Some of them got bored and fell away, but I haven't. It's a rare week when I don't play in at least four contests. I've broken up with more than one girl who thought it was fun at first, but couldn't understand going back week after month after year.

Am I obsessive? If so, I've got plenty of company. Sift the population of this city through the right filters, and you'll find a lot of subcultures exhibiting this degree of obsession. Ferret owners meeting in Central Park for playdates. Knitters making colorful yarn sleeves for trees. Harley riders taking over Wall Street early weekend mornings. Walking clubs trying to cover every block on the island. A thousand varieties of harmless fun, each bringing together people who would otherwise never meet.

There are worse things to be obsessed with.

* * *

By eight AM, the case of the Jane Doe on 118th Street had been assigned to Detective Karen Byers, 36, in her eighth year as a member of the NYPD and third as a detective. She arrived at the scene at 8:35 and learned that uniforms had found a place at the back of the lot where the fence had been cut. A trace of blood found on one of the cut wires had been taken for analysis. Crime scene techs had collected the tarp and recorded identifiable footprints in the hard-packed dirt of the pit. The victim's hands had been bagged to preserve possible evidence, and hundreds of photographs had been taken. After interviewing the site foreman (Harlan Denver, 41), Byers crouched and examined the body. Looking for additional wounds, she rolled the victim away from the wall she'd been shoved against.

There was a wallet underneath her.

* * *

The biggest county in New York state, at over 2,800 square miles, is St. Lawrence.

The geographic center of the 48 states is just outside Lebanon, Kansas.

The state that borders the most other states? Trick question, because it's a tie: Tennessee and Missouri each border eight. Likely bonus question: Kentucky is the only state that touches both Tennessee and Missouri.

* * *

Jane Doe was young, white, and showed every sign of having been sexually assaulted—just the kind of victim the media would go crazy over. One Police Plaza put her murder at the top of the priority list, starting with an immediate postmortem conducted by Dr. Jonas Mills, who had 27 years of experience and a flawless reputation. Mills quickly determined that Jane Doe's windpipe had been crushed, and that there were indeed signs of sexual trauma, though he recovered no semen. Skin cells scraped from underneath her nails suggested that she had fought her attacker.

The victim's fingerprints were not in the system, but x-rays showed that at some point in her life she had broken her left arm. There were surgical pins in the bone with serial numbers that could be easily traced. By two in the afternoon, the NYPD had identified Jane Doe as Jessica Osman, 22, a waitress, temp worker, and wannabe singer. She had moved to New York two years previously from her childhood home in Concord, New Hampshire. She lived in an apartment near the corner of Claremont Avenue and Tiemann, a little more than eight blocks from where her body had been found.

* * *

The first Oscar winner for best picture was *Wings*.
The first Tony winner for best musical was *Kiss Me, Kate*.
The first Grammy winner for album of the year was *Peter Gunn*.
The first Emmy winner for outstanding drama series was *Pulitzer Prize Playhouse*.

* * *

The wallet underneath Osman's body contained $33 in cash, two credit cards, an expired Delaware driver's license, and an employee ID card from Columbia University, all in the name of Raymond Thiel, 51. The Columbia card said he was a custodian. Uniforms were dispatched to the campus, but Thiel's supervisor told them he hadn't reported for his shift that day or called in sick. The address on file with the University's HR department was a PO Box.

Tracking Thiel through the system, Detective Byers learned that he had been arrested twice on domestic violence complaints and once for sexual assault, all in Delaware. He'd served three years on the final charge and been out for eighteen months, but was still on parole. Half an hour of phone calls to Dover finally turned up a harried and defensive parole officer who said that Thiel had requested and received permission to move to New York City in order to avoid accidentally violating a restraining order taken out by his ex-wife. He was supposed to have been transferred to a Manhattan parole officer, but apparently the paperwork had never gone through. The Delaware officer did, though, have an address for him, on 139th just off Broadway, in what would turn out to be an illegal sublet.

Byers and two uniforms pulled up outside the building, armed with an arrest warrant, at 1:10 in the afternoon, and met Thiel as he was walking out the front door.

* * *

Elizabeth Taylor's husbands, in order: Conrad Hilton, Michael Wilding, Mike Todd, Eddie Fisher, Richard Burton (twice), John Warner, and Larry Fortensky.

Hedy Lamarr held a number of patents, including one for a frequency-hopping system to help torpedoes evade radio jamming.

When he was starring on "Wanted: Dead or Alive," Steve McQueen, later to die of lung cancer, shot dozens of ads for show sponsor Viceroy cigarettes with the tagline "thinking man's filter, smoking man's taste."

* * *

Jessica Osman's two roommates, Evelyn Williams and Hanna Bright, were stage actresses with a handful of off-off-Broadway credits. Two hours after Osman had been identified, uniforms pulled them out of a tap-dancing class they were taking together, telling them that Osman had been involved in a crime. They left it to Byers to break the news of just how involved she had been.

The previous night, the three girls had gone together to One And The Same, a neighborhood bar two blocks from their apartment. In recent months, they had frequently participated in the bar's weekly trivia contest, which was conducted in a single-player, written-answer format. Osman had been particularly enthusiastic about the contest, and in fact had twice won the top prize of fifty dollars in bar credit. On this night, however, she was distracted and performed poorly. She'd had a fight that day with her parents, she was bored with her current temp position at a food packaging plant, and she still had not fully recovered from a bad breakup the previous month. She was drinking heavily, far more than her usual practice, and gave up on the quiz halfway through the list of questions being read over the bar's sound system.

One of the other players was Sean Kenyon, a boy Williams had dated off and on. When the contest ended, Kenyon invited the girls to go with him to a party in his apartment building. Williams and Bright were willing, but they decided that Osman was too drunk to get home by herself. Accompanied by Kenyon, they walked her the two blocks back to their building and put her in the elevator. They then went on to the party. When they returned several hours later, Osman's bedroom door was closed. It was still closed when they got up after a few hours of sleep and left for a hectic day of auditions and classes. They assumed Osman was sleeping off a hangover and thought no more about it until a rather brusque policeman interrupted their halting efforts at a tricky version of "Shuffle Off to Buffalo."

The second time Byers walked the girls through this story, she pressed them hard on trying to come up with the precise time they had last seen Osman. Closing her eyes to visualize the scene, Hanna Bright remembered texting with a friend as they stood in the lobby, making plans to attend an upcoming audition together. Just before Osman got on the elevator, Bright took a selfie and sent it to the friend. She pulled the exchange up on her phone and passed it to the detective.

There's a copy of the picture in the case file, clear and sharp enough to fill my computer screen. Williams and Bright are close to the camera, smiling with a lot of teeth. Between their heads and farther away is Osman, leaning against the frame of the open elevator doors and looking off in another direction. She seems, to me, dazed and exhausted. She's wearing denim shorts and a black and white patterned top.

The time stamp on the picture is 11:05 PM, just under eight hours from when the young woman would be found eight blocks away, wearing completely different clothes.

* * *

The most famous hijacker in history was listed on his 1971 passenger manifest as Dan Cooper. The name "D. B. Cooper" was a reporter's mistake that stuck.

John Adams and Thomas Jefferson both died on July 4, 1826, exactly fifty years after the signing of the Declaration of Independence.

Fitzgerald's original title for *The Great Gatsby* was *Trimalchio in West Egg.* "Trimalchio" is a character in the Roman work *Satyricon* by Petronius.

* * *

When Raymond Thiel walked straight into the arms of the cops who had come looking for him, there were a number of recent scratches on his neck and forearms. Detective Byers had these photographed when he was taken into custody, then let him stew in an interrogation room for hours until the search of his apartment was complete. Thiel, like a lot of people who had done time, had learned at least one lesson: the only thing he said to anyone was that he wanted a lawyer.

Stuffed deep into the pillowcase on his narrow bed were a pair of panties and a bra, both white, both decorated with a pattern of bright red cartoon strawberries. Before questioning Thiel, Detective Byers called Evelyn Williams, who said that Osman did own such garments. She and Bright had already confirmed, before leaving the station, that Osman owned a yellow sundress, though they hadn't seen her wear it recently.

* * *

The last single by the Beatles to reach #1 in the US was "The Long and Winding Road."

The longest song to reach #1 in the US was Don McLean's "American Pie." The shortest was "I'm Henry VIII, I Am" by Herman's Hermits.

The first American artist to reach #1 with a posthumous record was Otis Redding, with "Sittin' on the Dock of the Bay."

* * *

Detective Byers sat down for her first interview with Raymond Thiel and his court-appointed lawyer at 7:23, a little over twelve hours after Osman's body had been found. At first, Thiel refused to address her questions, but on the advice of his counsel, he stated that he had spent the previous night competing at a team trivia event at Jungle Jim's, a bar in Greenwich Village. The bar was several miles from Thiel's apartment, but Jim's hosted one of the most popular contests in the city, and Thiel's team, the Beer Barons, competed there regularly. They came in third place and left the bar around midnight, he thought. He caught a cab home, paying cash for the ride. The next morning, he overslept and missed his morning hours at work, but he was leaving to report for the afternoon when the cops outside his apartment stopped him.

Asked about his wallet, he said it had been stolen from him at some point during the evening, after he left the bar but before getting home. He suggested forcefully that pickpockets in the city were running wild due to the incompetence of the NYPD.

Asked about the underwear found in his apartment, he insisted that he had never seen them before and that the police were planting evidence.

Shown pictures of Osman, from both before and after her death, he said he had no idea who she was.

I've listened to the recording of the interview many times. Byers is good, pressing her points hard, trying to make Thiel believe that he has a glimmer of hope if he just tells the truth. He never comes close to buying it. His denials are flat, monosyllabic, almost bored. Byers would later describe him, from the stand, as seeming to lack all affect.

An hour after the start of the interview, Byers informed Thiel that he was being formally arrested on suspicion of homicide. She recorded his response in her notes: a shrug.

Byers had known about Jungle Jim's before beginning the interview, thanks to the most recent charge on Thiel's credit card. Back at her desk, she began reviewing the security footage she'd sent two uniforms to request from the highly cooperative establishment. There was clear video from several well-placed cameras, confirming at least part of Thiel's story: he and his teammates met at the bar shortly before seven. They played through several rounds of the trivia tournament, ultimately coming in third place. They shared a final pitcher after losing and walked out the front door at 11:52.

Byers called the bar and verified that their camera system was set to the correct time. Thiel had left Jungle Jim's forty-seven minutes after Jessica Osman had gotten on the elevator at her apartment building, several miles to the north. I often look at the page from her notes where Byers has circled the two times and drawn an arc connecting them, with a question mark halfway between.

* * *

By the way, here's a key strategy tip: if you want to get serious about the team events, you need a sports guy. You'd be surprised how many people roll right through general knowledge or history questions and then have no idea if Jim Brown was a halfback, a relief pitcher, or a goalie. The best sports guys, combining a head for stats with an interest in the histories of the games, are in high demand. I was on a team a while back with a great sports guy, but he got poached by another team that offered to pay his rent every other month. He still works two offices down from me, but we don't talk much.

Raymond Thiel was a sports guy. He was strongest on football.

* * *

On the basis of his previous criminal record, his parole status, and the viciousness of the crime, Thiel was denied bail. He was taken to Riker's to be held until trial, arriving there just after noon on June 18, about 24 hours before Jessica Osman's body was turned over to her parents to be taken back to New Hampshire.

The brass had the headline they wanted. There would be no panic about Osman's killer being on the loose. But the pressure was still on Byers to make sure the case would stick, and her case notes from the following weeks circle back, again and again, to those 47 minutes between Jessica Osman getting into an elevator and Raymond Thiel walking out of a bar. By all rights, there was no way the two of them should have met that night. How had Osman ended up in completely different clothes? Why had she even left her apartment? Was it possible Thiel had gone there and somehow enticed her out?

Crime scene techs scoured Osman's apartment for any sign that Thiel had ever been there, and came up empty. The clothes she had been wearing when her friends last saw her were stuffed into the top of the laundry hamper in her room. The small purse she had been carrying that night was nowhere in the apartment and was never found. Byers was sure Thiel had tossed it, and whatever shoes Osman had been wearing, in a dumpster. Thiel's apartment was similarly barren of a single fingerprint or strand of DNA pointing to Osman's presence—except for the underwear.

Osman's phone was on her dresser, plugged into a charger. Williams and Bright agreed it would have been tremendously out of character for her to go out without it. There were no contacts in the phone's history that matched up with Thiel. Thiel himself didn't seem to have a cell phone of any kind. Byers couldn't find any traffic camera footage from near any of the involved locations that clearly showed either of them on the streets. The cab driver who'd given Thiel a ride, if he existed, never turned up.

In short, there was only one slim connection between Osman and Thiel: both had played in trivia contests in the months prior to June 17. But then, so had thousands of their fellow Manhattanites. Byers spent weeks on the case, going through credit card bills line by line, interviewing everyone she could find who knew either the victim or the suspect, looking in vain for a shred of evidence that they had ever been in the same place at the same time. For all her efforts, she was unable to identify a single establishment that both had been in separately, let alone simultaneously. Expanding the search to include the other Beer Barons and more of Osman's friends was no more successful. None of their orbits seemed to touch in any way she could find.

The DA's office was trying, all this time, to convince Thiel to take a plea deal. If he didn't, Byers was worried there were going to be questions at the trial she wouldn't know how to answer.

* * *

The largest pumpkin-producing state, by a wide margin, is Illinois.

Chuck Berry's only #1 hit was "My Ding-A-Ling."

Jimmy Stewart was an accomplished pilot who flew dozens of bombing missions in Europe during World War II.

* * *

I've never been to One and the Same, the Upper West Side neighborhood joint where Osman and her roommates played trivia. Too small-time, too far from my orbit. We all carve small local towns for ourselves out of the big city. But I do know Jungle Jim's. It's not part of my regular cycle, but I've been in the team events there several times. Once was in May of last year.

I was filling the fourth chair for the Cracked Eggs, a team of kitchen workers with a regular member having gall bladder surgery. It was an odd experience, playing on a team I'd often played against, with their different rituals, their different shared jokes. The atmosphere that night at Jim's was charged, with several of the top teams in the city playing. Single-elimination format, fifteen-minute rounds. The bar was even posting video of the rounds live to their website. Playing as a fill-in had me feeling loose and confident. Anything I contributed would be a bonus, as far as the Eggs were concerned. I did well that night, answering a lot of entertainment and literature questions. I even earned a round of applause by jumping in spectacularly early on one question to correctly identify Shel Silverstein. Some nights are like that. You get on a roll where you almost feel like you've seen a list of the questions ahead of time, like you know exactly what's coming the minute a category is announced. Other nights, you get inside your own head, ringing in late on the buzzer and second-guessing everything you want to say.

In the quarter finals, we went up against the Beer Barons. Jim's was their home turf, but they were never a top-tier group. They were really just four random guys who drifted together because they never caught on with any more successful teams. I don't remember much about the match itself, but I know we rolled over the Barons pretty easily, on our way to what would turn out to be a tight, exciting title match where we would come up just short.

Truth to tell, I don't remember the title match very well either. What I remember is the final buzzer going off in the quarter finals, with the Eggs up by five points. We slumped back into our chairs momentarily, letting the tension of the round ease away, and slapped each other on the back. Then, as protocol required, we stood up to shake hands with the vanquished foes.

There's no reason I should remember shaking hands with Raymond Thiel. He was the fourth Baron, I was the fourth Egg. By the time we got to each other, everybody was just anxious to hit the head, get another drink, get to the next set of questions. Thiel wasn't famous, yet. The nametag with his team affiliation said "Ray," but I wouldn't learn his last name until the rest of the city did. He was just one more guy in the bar. A lot of people would assume that the memory of him is something I've constructed, a way of injecting myself into a drama that doesn't really touch me.

And yet I do remember. His hand was small and very dry, offering no response at all to my brief grip. His thin lips were pressed together in a tight, perfunctory smile, which I took to be a reaction to his team's loss. His eyes were narrow and dull grey and aimed over my right shoulder. As we shook, they swept across my face like a searchlight, pausing for a fraction of a second to meet mine.

I said, "Good match." He didn't say anything.

* * *

You start out by memorizing state capitals, stirring dormant memories from grade school. Then world capitals. You practice identifying African nations by the shape of their borders on a map. You stand in your shower, chanting the names of the eleven men who walked on the moon after Neil Armstrong. You read lists of British and French monarchs over and over again, creating increasingly arcane and personal mnemonic devices. You scroll through webpages listing the opening lines of the 100 most important novels written in English.

Lately I've been working on a list of popes going back to the tenth century. They don't come up as often as presidents, but when they do, it's often in a bonus question with a lot of points on the line.

* * *

Against all legal advice, Thiel refused to accept a plea deal. His trial started in early December and lasted only a few days. The prosecution's case was a broadside, a series of body blows obliterating reasonable doubt. The wallet. The blood on the fence and the skin under Jessica Osman's nails, both a match for Thiel. The scratches on Thiel's neck and face when he was arrested. The underwear in Thiel's apartment, by now confirmed by DNA testing to be Osman's. The defense was hobbled from the start. Thiel couldn't afford a lawyer other than the inexperienced duo assigned by the court. They tried without much enthusiasm to poke holes in the prosecution's narrative.

Perhaps the wallet had been stolen, the underwear planted, the scratches the result of a fight separate from Osman's later murder. None of it was very convincing, and the defense called no witnesses of their own, probably afraid that they would open the door to making Thiel's previous crimes admissible evidence. To Byers's relief, the time discrepancy which had been haunting her for months never came up in her questioning. The outcome of the trial was never really in question.

Two weeks ago, three months into his sentence, Thiel was found dead in his cell, the back of his skull caved in. The official explanation is that he committed suicide by perching on his cot and then flinging himself backwards against the edge of his toilet bowl. Maybe so, or maybe he made an enemy once he was inside. I don't mourn Thiel. But I mourn the destruction of the brain that held something unique in the world: the story of what happened between him and Jessica Osman in the early hours of June 17.

Everybody else in the city seems to have forgotten. I sit in my office at work, the Osman file permanently open in one window, no matter what else I'm working on. I must have read the thing a hundred times, looking for the connection that never reveals itself. I sometimes think about calling Karen Byers, the only person who might understand, but I've never met her, and the truth is I've broken some rules by looking at her case so much. The bottom line is, she has no answers for me, and I would have none for her.

* * *

The empress Mumtaz Mahal died on June 17, 1631. Her grief-stricken husband spent the next seventeen years building her resting place, the Taj Mahal.

The Battle of Bunker Hill was fought on June 17, 1775.

O. J. Simpson was arrested on June 17, 1994, following the nationally televised pursuit of his white Ford Bronco.

* * *

I often relive shaking hands with Raymond Thiel, that moment of perfunctory courtesy, utterly unremarkable as it happened. Every time I revisit that instant in my mind, I find myself recalling, as well, a piece of Hanna Bright's testimony from the trial. She said that as she and her friends were walking out of the lobby that night, she glanced back and saw the elevator doors closing on Jessica Osman's face. She thought Jessica was starting to raise her hand to wave, but the doors finished closing, and she was gone, and a moment later Hanna was out on the street, young and excited and on her way to a party in the hot city. Six months later, she said on the stand that she had dreams about that glimpse of Jessica almost every night. The hand just starting to move. The face vanishing between the closing doors.

Raymond Thiel's eyes passing briefly over mine.

Flicking away.

* * *

J. R. Ewing was shot by Kristin Shepard, his sister-in-law and mistress.

The Skipper was Jonas Grumby. The Professor was Roy Hinkley.

The one-armed man most often used the alias Fred Johnson. His real name was never definitively revealed.

* * *

The jury (seven men, five women) was out less than two hours before finding Thiel guilty on all counts. I was in the courtroom when he was sentenced to life without parole. Judge Margaret Palmer asked him if he had anything to say before the sentence was carried out.

Thiel just shrugged.

And Now, An Inspiring Story of Tragedy Overcome

It was past two in the morning by the time Lonnie Walsh found the right private waiting room on the seventh floor of the hospital. His mother, Helena, stood at the window, staring over the parking lots stretching toward the expressway. Brant Simmons, Lonnie's brother-in-law, was curled up in a fetal position on a couch. Lonnie's stomach lurched at the sight of him.

"Where have you been?" Helena asked, without turning around.

"I had a thing," Lonnie said. "At the place with the guy about that stuff."

Helena stiffened. "Make your jokes," she said. "Your sister died in childbirth two hours ago."

Lonnie did a couple of years in college, back when he was pretending he might be something different than what everybody knew he was. At the phrase *died in childbirth* he had an immediate, visceral memory of the books from some of his lit classes, thick black paperbacks with *USED* stickers and cracked spines. Dying in childbirth was a thing out of those books. It was a thing that happened to Dickens characters.

"That still happens?" he said.

"You have a niece." Helena's voice was like a pencil scratching at rough paper. "Her name is Kayla."

From his spot on the sofa, Brant groaned.

"Stop that noise," Helena said. "Sit up."

Brant rolled himself into a sitting position, his head hanging down near his knees. He wasn't crying, but his face was red and twisted. "Go easy," he said. "I just became a widower."

"Don't talk to me about your loss," she said. "Alonso."

Lonnie, his vision swimming with watery images of his little sister, was slow to reply. "Ma."

"I'm telling you this in Brant's presence so there's no confusion. This family takes care of its own. Anything that girl needs, for the next twenty-one years, you will provide for. Tuition, medical bills, clothing."

None of this would, in other words, come from Ma's bankroll. No surprise. "Yes, Ma."

"Family is everything," Ma said. "Brant. You need money for my granddaughter, you go to Lonnie."

"I need money now," Brant said. "I have to hire someone. I can't take care of a newborn by myself."

"Do what you need to do," Helena said. She still had not turned from the window. "If it's for Kayla, Lonnie will pay." Her voice got stronger. "But if one dime of his money goes to the track, or a bottle you can pour down your throat, or a shiny new car so you can impress some tramp, I will see it taken out of your hide. Understand me, Brant. I'll put my men to work on you, and I will watch it and enjoy it. Do you believe me?"

"Yes," Brant said. The voice of a child caught misbehaving, surly but resigned. "I just want to bring her up the way Sophie would have wanted."

"Take Lonnie to see his niece," Helena said. "I need to say goodbye to my daughter."

At the words, Lonnie felt his stomach contract as though he'd been hit, hard, in the gut. None of this seemed real. He wondered if he would have a chance to see Sophie, to say his own goodbye, but when Ma was this way, there was no use asking questions. He beckoned to Brant, turning away from his mother's rigid frame. He didn't even know where Sophie's body was.

Brant stood, moving like a man underwater. The two men were at the door when Helena spoke again, still giving them her back.

"Don't say Sophie's name in my presence again, Brant. I don't care for the way it sounds in your mouth."

* * *

Easy enough for Ma to talk about putting money in Brant's pocket. All she had to do was sit on the porch of the big house outside Annapolis, looking out over her infinite green lawn as the money flowed in. Tribute, still owed because of who her husband, Lonnie's father, had been.

Things were tougher for Lonnie, in the West Baltimore scrapyard that was his base of operations. Everything was harder than it used to be, more complicated than when his father was the local boss. Take girls. These days, hookers could set up their own dates online without ever leaving the house or showing themselves on a street corner. They could do a background check on the john in minutes. No need for a pimp to collect eighty bucks out of every hundred they made, kicking twenty up to Lonnie. The only women left on the corners were too stupid or too old or too strung out to realize the twenty-first century was leaving them behind.

Everything was like that. How do you put money on the street when you're competing with payday-loan storefronts? Run a book when legal sports betting was spreading across the country? Put together a heist when everybody uses plastic for everything? These days, if you wanted to rob a bank, you started by hacking their website, and the hackers didn't need a boss any more than the whores needed a pimp.

Some days, Lonnie wondered if it wouldn't be simpler to get an actual job.

In the years after Sophie's death, though, Lonnie managed to provide what was needed whenever Brant came around. He knew better than to break a promise to Ma. Brant knew better, too. He provided a detailed accounting of where every penny went. There were a lot of medical bills, especially in the first year. Nannies. Clothes. Formula, then baby food. Day care, as soon as the girl was old enough. Brant insisted he couldn't miss time at work, as though there was nobody else in the world to sell used cars. Lonnie thought it would be cheaper and simpler for him to quit the damned job and take care of his kid himself, but he never said so.

He didn't see his niece more than two or three times a year. It killed him, Sophie's eyes looking out from Kayla's tiny face.

* * *

Kayla was five when Lonnie got a frantic call from Brant in the middle of a cold December night. He got dressed, drove to a hotel down on the water, rode the elevator up, and knocked lightly on the door of 1712.

Brant opened the door, wearing a half-buttoned shirt and a pair of boxers. Sweat beaded his face, and his eyeballs vibrated in their sockets. "Lonnie," he said. "You gotta help me, man. I didn't know what else to do."

"Start by getting out of sight." Lonnie pushed past Brant down the short hallway into the bedroom. The woman lying on top of the comforter was young, nude, and very obviously dead. Her eyes pointed up into a corner of the room, but she wasn't seeing it—or anything else.

"It wasn't my fault," Brant said from behind him.

Lonnie spun on his heel. The back of his right hand, moving with all the force he could muster, caught Brant at the hinge of his jaw. Brant stumbled backward, hit the wall, and fell to his side. Down on the floor, he wrapped his arms around his head as though expecting Lonnie to begin kicking him.

"I ought to kill you right now," Lonnie said.

Brant's voice was a choked sob. "Think about Kayla, Lonnie. I'm begging you."

"You think Kayla needs this kind of father?"

"At least I *am* her father." Brant pushed himself into a seated position, his hands still raised to ward Lonnie off. "Where would she go if you kill me, Lonnie? You gonna raise her?"

"Ma would take her."

Brant shook his head. The right side of his face was already swelling, and blood dripped onto his shirt from a cut from Lonnie's ring. "Come on, man. You know better than me that Helena is done playing mother. She was never cut out for it."

Lonnie turned back to the woman on the bed rather than agreeing or disagreeing. "Who is she?"

"Her name's Rachel something. I met her at the bar downstairs. She's in town for the sales convention."

"She hawks cars?"

"In Pennsylvania somewhere, I think."

"Okay, you met her downstairs. I guess you hit it off. This her room?"

"Yeah. We came up and did a bump and, you know, fooled around some. Then she pulled out a syringe and said she wanted to really party. I told her I didn't do that, but she should go ahead. Then I went to the john. When I came out, she was like this."

Lonnie's whole body was tense with disgust. "I don't know what the hell my sister ever saw in you."

"Jesus, Lonnie. If Sophie was alive, I wouldn't be here."

"I wish I believed that." Lonnie squatted and grabbed Brant's chin, forcing him to look directly into his face. "Think. Did anybody you know see her with you?"

"I don't think so. It's almost all out-of-towners. But there are cameras in the bar."

"Of course there are." Lonnie shoved Brant's head back against the wall and held it there. "Shame they were out of order."

Brant tried to twist out of his grip, but Lonnie held him forcefully against the wall as he thought. Something substantial had to go to the house dick to get that footage lost. A deep cleaning of this room, enough to get rid of any DNA Brant might have left behind. Two or three guys to get Rachel Whoever out of the building and into the Chesapeake Bay. "You got no idea what this is going to cost me," he said.

"I'll pay you back." Brant tried to pry Lonnie's hand away.

"No, you won't." Lonnie let him go and stood. "Where's your car?"

"Parked in the garage around the corner. I can be home in twenty minutes."

"Don't try to drive. Go to your car and wait. A couple of my guys will find you. One of them will drive you home."

"Thanks, Lonnie." Brant pushed himself to his feet. "No hard feelings about smacking me, man. I probably deserved it. This never happens again,

I swear it."

"Just put your pants on and get out of here," Lonnie said. "And for Christ's sake, put them on right. Your damn boxers are backwards."

* * *

Not long afterward, a new item started appearing on Brant's reports of his expenses with Kayla: ice-skating lessons. "She saw some movie about a blind chick who skated," Brant said. "Wouldn't shut up about it until I agreed to let her try. She loves it, man. You ought to come see her go at it."

"Nah," Lonnie said. "Next month she'll be into archery or something, right?"

Kayla wasn't. The ice-skating expenses kept appearing, inching up year by year. Practice time on rinks rented by the hour. Coaching fees. Club dues. High-quality, fitted skates, outgrown as fast as they could be made. Costumes. Music. Entry fees for competitions. Who knew you had to pay to have skates sharpened? Who knew you had to do it so often? Lonnie wondered if Kayla was using the blades to carve wood when she wasn't on the ice.

After a few years, Lonnie was curious enough to show up at a juvenile competition being held at an arena out in the suburbs. He sat in the back row of the lower bowl and watched kids, all somewhere between eight and twelve, warming up on the ice, most of them seeming more like they were playing—goofing around, laughing at falls—than really working at it. Even to Lonnie's untrained eye, Kayla stood out. She was easily the fastest child on the ice, even faster than older boys already beginning to put on adolescent muscle. Her routine was crisp and polished, and she did more jumps than any of the other girls in her level.

He didn't see Brant anywhere.

Lonnie left right after Kayla's routine, knowing she was going to win. Driving back to the scrapyard, he kept seeing her long black hair whipping out behind her as she flew around the rink.

Sophie's hair streamed back like that when she and Lonnie took horse-riding lessons one summer, part of their father's efforts to cultivate a respectable image. He remembered his sister, always out in front of him, bent down close to her animal's neck, shouting with delight when it jumped.

* * *

When things were slow, Lonnie liked to sit by himself in a lawn chair up on the roof of the scrapyard office. He drank beer and contemplated the big buildings downtown. Hotels and offices. Banks that stole more money in a single day than his whole family had stolen in the last century. He appreciated the sense of perspective.

He didn't appreciate being interrupted by Brant clambering up the ladder and slouching over to him, with the look of a puppy who knows he shouldn't have pissed on the rug. "They're gonna fire me," he said.

Lonnie reached into the cooler beside him and held out a bottle. Brant shook his head. He crossed his arms and turned to join Lonnie in looking east, squinting in the glare of the late afternoon sun bouncing off acres of glass.

"I'll bite," Lonnie said, easing the beer back into the cooler. "Why are they going to fire you?"

"They think I turned back some odometers."

Lonnie took this to mean *I got caught turning back odometers.*

"I've lost track," he said. "This is, what, the sixth dealership that's shitcanned you?"

"It's not my fault."

"You should have those words tattooed on your forehead. It would save time."

"I don't want Kayla seeing me out of work. I thought you could talk to my boss."

"You did, huh?"

"Or let me borrow a couple of those guys hanging around down in the yard. Put a little scare into him."

"Great plan," Lonnie said. "Your boss is a civilian, you idiot. I'm not getting a couple of my guys put away just because he hurt your feelings."

Brant rolled his shoulders. "Maybe I should ask Helena."

Lonnie laughed out loud. "Go for it. She'll more likely have a couple of her guys put a little scare into you."

"You gotta do something for me." Lonnie hated the whine in Brant's voice. "For Sophie's sake."

"You know what?" Lonnie said. "I think I'm with Ma on this one. Don't say my sister's name to me again."

Neither man spoke for a few minutes.

Lonnie sighed. "There's a trucking outfit up in Pikesville. Stevens Freight. Go there and tell Mick Stevens I said to give you a job."

Brant's shoulders relaxed. "Thanks, Lonnie."

After Brant left, Lonnie took the beer he'd offered his brother-in-law from the cooler and knocked the cap off, but the pleasure had been drained from the day. He poured the beer out onto the pebbled roof, watching it foam and puddle. He had to call Mick, warn him not to put Brant near anything that mattered. And then he had to figure out where he was going to unload a couple hundred crates of cigarettes that had fallen off a truck somewhere. And then he had to check over the books from a downtown strip club, a place where trusted customers were invited to do coke off the bodies of the dancers. He didn't understand why anybody wanted their coke cut with glitter and sweat, but plenty of people seemed to enjoy it. And then he was due in Annapolis to give Ma her monthly update on the business. And then, and then, and then.

All he really wanted to do was watch Kayla skate. He'd seen her five times now, never sitting close enough to the ice to be spotted. She won every time, and Lonnie hadn't yet seen her fall.

He hadn't yet seen Brant come to watch his daughter, either.

* * *

Kayla was twelve when Brant said she needed a new coach who was going to cost three grand a month. "Alicia Petkov. She's the real deal, Lonnie. Her

35

mother was an Olympic gold medalist."

"That's thrilling as hell," Lonnie said. "I don't care if her father was Secretariat. For that kind of money, I want a sit-down."

They met at a coffee shop near Petkov's home rink in Roland Park. Lonnie was the last to arrive. He found Brant sitting on the patio with a blond woman in a pastel pantsuit. She wore her hair in a short, severe cut. From the fine lines around her mouth and eyes, Lonnie guessed she was in her early fifties.

Brant stood to make the introductions. "Alicia, this is Lonnie Walsh. Kayla's uncle."

Lonnie sat without shaking hands. "I'm not here because I'm the uncle. I'm here because I'm the money."

"I understand that," Petkov said. Lonnie was expecting an accent, but Alicia Petkov sounded like she'd grown up in the dead center of America. He approved of the way she looked straight at him.

"Brant, go get a coffee," Lonnie said. "Then sit down somewhere and drink it. I want to talk with Ms. Petkov alone."

Brant opened his mouth, closed it, and left the table.

"I found a clip of your mother skating in the Olympics," Lonnie said when he was gone. "Didn't seem all that impressive."

"Impressive is defined by context," Petkov said. "My mother nailed routines beyond what anyone else was capable of at the time. Today, any talented junior could skate rings around her. It's an entirely different sport."

"Let's talk about Kayla in that sport. For what you're asking, I want to know if she's actually any good."

"Have you seen her skate?"

"Yes. But I don't know anything about it. She goes fast, and she doesn't fall. That's about all I could tell you."

"Going fast and not falling is a lot of it." Petkov sipped her coffee. "She has the legs. The musicality, the grace. More important she has the mind. She understands putting in the work. I believe she's the most talented skater her age on the Eastern Seaboard. She should zoom through the Novice level and be competing as a Junior within eighteen months."

"You mean, assuming I pony up the money for you."

"Of course. I am the most talented coach on the Eastern Seaboard."

"Three-grand-a-month good?"

"A bargain at twice the price, Mr. Walsh. You're buying many hours of my attention and experience. But you should know there is more expense to come. She needs ballet lessons, for one thing. Better costumes. Better equipment."

"There aren't a lot of poor people in this sport, are there?"

"Not many. There are grants she could apply for, support from the national organization or local clubs. But that's a great deal of time and work that would be better spent on the ice."

"All right, we'll try it. See where we are in a year."

"Excellent." Petkov shifted in her seat. "There is one more thing we must discuss, Mr. Walsh, but I'm rather hesitant to risk offending you."

Lonnie spread his hands in a go-ahead gesture.

"I assume you've watched the Olympics on occasion," Petkov said.

"Sure."

"Then you know the way they talk about the athletes. Particularly the American athletes. Before almost every event, they show profiles of the ones they really want you to pay attention to or root for. Inspiring stories of tragedy overcome, those are the ones they like best. Those stories matter, Mr. Walsh, to the networks, to the Olympics, but especially to the national organization that decides which skaters will represent the US."

"You're telling me Kayla needs an inspiring story."

"She has an inspiring story. I'm sorry to be blunt, but your sister's death is too perfect an angle for them to ignore." Petkov put her coffee down. "Unless they find one that knocks Kayla out of the competition."

"Like, for example."

"Like, for example, the talented young skater backed by the mob. Forgive me, Mr. Walsh. I'm only referring to the context in which your name has frequently appeared in the news."

"People use that word, *mob*." The rest of Lonnie's explanation wouldn't come. He glanced down the street. "You're telling me to stay away."

"I'm telling you it's very possible that at some point, a group of people in a small room will decide who to send to the Olympics. When they have that discussion, we want Kayla to be the girl with the saintly dead mother. Not the girl with a gangster in the family."

* * *

Lonnie stopped going to watch Kayla skate, but he kept up with her results. As Petkov had predicted, her move through Novice level to Junior, just one level below the top, was almost immediate. Kayla kept winning, meet after meet, for almost three years.

Then, like a switch had been flipped, she started being listed in second place. Three competitions in a row. The name listed above Kayla's was the same every time: Wendy Brockton.

* * *

"Her family just moved from the West Coast," Brant said. "Alicia thinks they came out east looking to rack up some fast wins and move up the rankings."

They were back up on the roof. Down in the yard, Lonnie's guys played three-on-three basketball under the hoop riveted to the side of the building. Their grunts and shouts rose into the quickly gathering dusk.

"What's Kayla say?" Lonnie asked.

"What she always says. That she can beat her. No doubt in her mind."

"But there's doubt in yours. Why, you see something in Brockton?"

Brant shrugged, chewing on a nail. "I've never seen her skate."

"Jesus, you still don't even go?"

"Alicia says Kayla doesn't need distractions."

"Sure. I bet that's the reason."

"This isn't the point." Brant pulled his chair closer and turned to face Lonnie, lowering his voice. "You gotta do something. The sooner the better. Wendy could really cost Kayla, set her move to the Seniors back a year."

"So I've got to do something. What did you have in mind?"

Brant tilted his head in the direction of the noises coming up from the game, raising his eyebrows.

"You're suggesting I kneecap a teenage girl?" Lonnie said. "Why stop there? You want me to kill her, Brant?"

"Jesus, no. Just get her off the ice for a few months, that's all I'm saying." Brant smiled. "You gonna try to tell me you haven't done things just as bad for worse reasons?"

* * *

Lonnie stood to one side of an entrance tunnel at the practice arena, where he wouldn't be easily seen from the ice. Except for amateur cell phone videos posted to YouTube, it was the first time he'd seen Kayla skate in years. She'd gotten faster, but her movements were also smoother, with a new elegance in the way she moved her arms. When she jumped, she seemed to explode from the ice, twisting into the air with such speed that Lonnie had trouble counting the spins. He had never learned to tell the difference between the various kinds of jumps, but the sheer distance she was covering in the air made him catch his breath.

Alicia Petkov paced at the side of the rink, arms crossed. Her pantsuit today was blue. Every few minutes, she called Kayla to the railing, gesturing to make some point. Even from across the rink, Lonnie could see his niece listening closely, nodding.

He watched for half an hour before Petkov happened to glance his way. He lifted his hand to catch her eye, and jerked his thumb over his shoulder. She nodded. The next time Kayla glided to the rail, Petkov spoke to her for a few minutes. Then one of her assistants started strapping Kayla into the lift they used to help practice jumps. Petkov walked in his direction, and Lonnie went farther back into the tunnel to wait for her.

"The money shows its face," Petkov said. "You know, I never meant that you couldn't even be in the audience."

"Better to be safe," Lonnie said. "Brant is worried about Wendy Brockton."

"I'm very much aware. I've got twenty voicemails documenting his worry in wearisome detail."

"Should he be?"

"No. I have explained this to him at some length. Wendy Brockton is a talented amateur who has reached her peak, a peak above where Kayla is at this moment. In a year, Wendy will be exactly where she is now, if not beginning to decline. In a year, Kayla will have a quad. In three years, barring injury, she will be on the Olympic podium."

"You're that sure."

"Mr. Walsh, I've spent my life in these rinks. I could skate almost before I could walk. I've watched hundreds of skaters' careers, from juvenile all the way through to retirement. If I didn't know Kayla was a champion, I wouldn't be here. Wendy Brockton will spend decades trying and failing to convince strangers that she once won against the great Kayla Simmons."

"But you can't get Brant to see that. Do you think he might do something stupid?"

Alicia Petkov folded her arms. "Well, let me ask you this. Have you known him to do stupid things before?"

* * *

Helena Walsh had taken up painting. Several thousand dollars' worth of high-end paints and supplies filled neatly organized bins on her sun porch, where she spent five hours a day applying brush to canvas. The results were, invariably, abstract swirls of muddy color. Lonnie could never understand how Ma decided a painting was finished, ready to be added to the stacks in the cellar she never looked at again.

She painted and listened without comment as Lonnie talked about Kayla and Wendy Brockton.

"I have Kayla to dinner once a month," she said when he finished. She didn't look away from the painting or stop working on it. "By today's standards, she's a remarkably well-behaved and self-possessed young woman. I must admit I've paid little attention to her talk of her hobbies. Is she honestly so good?"

"She could be an Olympic champion," Lonnie said. "That's what Brant's counting on. He wants to be around for the Wheaties box and the endorsement deals."

"Hmm." Helena picked up a new brush and began covering the blue she'd just laid down with an orange that was neon bright. "There was a young woman skater several years ago whose husband assaulted one of her rivals."

"Tonya Harding."

"What happened to her?"

"Nothing good."

Helena put her brush down. She backed several feet away from the canvas, her head cocked to the side. Keeping her head at an angle, she drifted back to it and began using a small blade to scrape lines into the block of orange. She worked at it for several minutes before speaking. "I'm not sure why you're still here, son. Surely your course is clear."

"I thought so. But you always say that family is family."

"Do I?" Helena drove the blade deeper. "I think you're misremembering, Alonso. I believe what I actually say is that blood is blood."

* * *

Lonnie sat on the roof, watching on his tablet as Kayla, halfway around the world, took the ice with five other girls for a last few minutes of warm-up before her first Olympic program.

"I bought that outfit," Lonnie said out loud. There was nobody else on the roof. He'd had more than a couple of drinks, waiting for Kayla's group. "Damned expensive for half a yard of cloth and a fistful of sequins."

The camera tightened on Kayla's face. She looked a lot calmer than Lonnie felt. The announcer said something about her long journey, and the network's biographical package started. It was an inspiring story of tragedy overcome, scored with suitably somber music and interspersed with shots of Kayla looking at family photos. The mother she lost in the very first moments of her life. The devoted single father whose disappearance, fifteen years later, baffled law enforcement and threatened to derail Kayla's career.

The dedicated coach who stepped up in the hour of need, first fostering Kayla and eventually, alongside her supportive wife, adopting her.

Lonnie could only imagine how happy the segment's producer had been to learn that Alicia Petkov was a married lesbian. Tragedy, mystery, triumph, *and* progressive cred? America was about to fall in love with Lonnie's niece. They wouldn't have a choice.

Damn shame Brant wouldn't be around to see it. Much later that night, on the chance the dead could hear, Lonnie would stand near the several tons of rusted iron atop Brant's final resting place and tell him that his daughter was in first place after the short. On the chance the dead could feel, he'd then take a leak on the compacted ground.

That would be later. Right now, the pre-taped story was ending. Kayla spiraled into the center of the ring. A hush fell as she took her opening position, waiting for the music to start. Lonnie Walsh held his breath, waiting along with her.

Give or Take a Quarter Inch

Ryan Vargas had been home for ten minutes when his phone buzzed with an incoming text. Tina, no doubt, with an explanation of why she wasn't there. When a man gets home after three weeks on the road, he has a right to assume his wife will welcome him. It's nice to feel you've been missed. Ryan took a deliberately long swig from the soda he'd opened before picking up the phone to see what her excuse was.

The message was from Tina's number, but it wasn't text. It was a picture of Ryan's wife in a chair. There was a strip of wide silver tape across her mouth, and more wound around her arms and legs, holding her firmly in place. Her hair was unkempt, and her wide eyes had a pleading expression as she stared into the camera.

Ryan put his drink down. He was very aware of the sound of his pulse in his ears. He brought his hand up to the phone, but before he could begin typing, new messages began scrolling up the screen.

3CY3YOUNG3. WE'RE WATCHING YOU.

"3CY3YOUNG3" was the password for the security system, installed just last year. With the password and Tina's cell phone, whoever this was had access to every camera in the house. Ryan forced himself not to look at the one, mounted over the fridge, that covered the entire kitchen.

TWENTY MINUTES. GLEN OAK PARK. LOWER DIAMOND.

COME ALONE. CALL NOBODY.

Glen Oak Park was just a few blocks away. Ryan had donated the funds for its professional-grade baseball fields, where he played host to Little League tournaments played under banners with his name. He had money, plenty of money. He could pay a ransom. But the message didn't say anything about a ransom, and twenty minutes wasn't enough time to gather any cash. He stared at the screen, uncertain, and after a few seconds, a new text appeared.

YOU'RE NOT MOVING, RYAN.

He moved.

* * *

There were four baseball fields in different parts of the sprawling Glen Oak Park, all, thanks to Ryan, fully equipped with ample bleachers, real dugouts, and banks of lighting for night games. The lower diamond, at the bottom of the long, wooded slope on the park's north end, was the most remote from the park entrance. There'd be a game there almost any weekend day and many nights during the week, but now, on a crisp Tuesday morning a month into the new school year, only one other car was in the parking lot. It was a dark blue Honda sedan, the rear end starting to go to rust. Ryan got out of his SUV and started toward the field. As he passed the sedan, he used his phone to snap a picture of the license plate.

A row of tall pines divided the parking lot from the field. He followed a paved path through the trees and came out behind the bleachers on the first-base side. A man sat on the edge of the dugout roof across the field, swinging a bat idly back and forth in front of his legs as though practicing golf swings. He was wearing track pants and a sleeveless black t-shirt, with a red baseball cap pushed far back on his head and a disheveled beard. His arms were thick with muscle and densely covered with tattoos, a web of symbols and words Ryan found incomprehensible. The man watched him coming across the diamond, his expression blank, the bat a metronome in front of him.

Ryan stopped ten feet away. "Where's my wife?"

"She's safe," the man said. Up close, he looked a little older than Ryan had thought at first. Close to his own age. He held up a cell phone. "She's with a buddy of mine. As long as he gets the calls he's expecting from me, and I say the things he's expecting me to say, she'll be fine."

"I want to talk to her," Ryan said.

"You know what they say about folks in hell and ice water. What you want isn't part of the game right now." The man's voice was deep, with just a trace of some kind of accent. Something southern, maybe, but barely there.

Ryan crossed his arms. Absurdly, he wished he had a prop, like the bat the man was swinging. Something to do with his hands. "Then let's talk about what you want. How much?"

"We'll get to what I want," the man said. He tilted his head back, inviting scrutiny of his face. "You remember me?"

Surprised, Ryan looked more closely. "No. Should I?"

"I'll give you a hint. My name's Mickey Loch."

Ryan's mouth went dry. He'd never been through a kidnapping before, but he was dead sure kidnappers didn't generally go around announcing their identity. "Why would you tell me that?"

"Thought it might spark something. I'd be surprised if you did remember, though. It was nineteen years ago. 1997. Your second Cy Young year."

"That's ancient history. What does this have to do with my wife?"

"I told you we'll get to it." Loch pointed into the dugout with the bat. "You want to sit down?"

"No," Ryan snapped. "I want you to tell me whatever the hell it is you brought me here to tell me."

"Man's in a hurry, I guess," Loch said. "Okay, we'll start the wayback machine. It was about this time of year, a game in Oakland that didn't mean a damn thing. You boys had already locked up your division, and Oakland was just trying to avoid losing a hundred games." Loch hopped down from his perch, put the bat on his shoulder, and swiveled into a batting stance. "Maybe you remember me better like this."

Ryan frowned. "I don't remember a Loch on the A's."

"I was only with them for one game," Loch said. "That game. Phil Jacobs was on bereavement leave, and Hector Ruiz was nursing a sprained thumb. They just needed somebody who could stand in left field and look semiprofessional."

"And I suppose I was pitching."

"You were. I don't know why. You should have been resting up for the playoffs."

"I was trying to get to twenty-five wins. I had a bonus clause." He hadn't made it, but there was a big bonus for the Cy Young, plus playoff pay. 1997 was a good year. A bought-my-parents-a-house year.

Loch grunted. "Shoulda guessed. Anyway. I came up to bat three times that day. Three at-bats, three strikeouts, nine pitches total. My career in the majors."

"Am I supposed to apologize?"

Loch kept going as though Ryan hadn't spoken. "Next day, I was on my way back to Triple-A. And the day after that, I was out on a run and landed in a pothole wrong. Broke my left leg in three places, shredded my ACL. X-ray looked like a damn jigsaw puzzle."

"Tough break. Are we getting to where my wife is anytime soon?"

Faster than Ryan would have thought possible, Loch darted forward, grabbed him by the front of his shirt, and shoved backwards, at the same time sweeping his leg sideways to cut Ryan's feet out from under him. Ryan's back slammed into the ground. Before he could move, Loch was standing over him, holding the fat end of the bat forcefully against his throat.

"I been waiting to tell you this story for nineteen years," Loch said. "You mind shutting up for a minute and letting me do it?"

Unable to catch his breath, Ryan nodded. Loch stepped back, lifting the bat. Ryan, wheezing, rolled to his side and managed to sit up. He didn't try to stand.

"Team cut me, of course," Loch said when Ryan was breathing more easily. "First, though, they sent me to a doc who gave me pain meds. They were handing that shit out like candy back then. Cut forward six months, and I'm unemployed, still limping, and hooked. Couldn't pay my dealer, so he told me I could work it off making some deliveries." Loch got into a batting stance again and took a couple of casual half-speed swings, staring out over the field. "I fell in with disreputable characters, is how my lawyer said it. Word of advice, Mr. Vargas. If you ever commit a felony, don't do it in Arizona. The guards are mean as snakes, and they don't believe in wasting

AC on criminals."

"I'll keep that in mind," Ryan said. It took him two breaths to say it.

"Now, Oregon, they got some nice jails," Loch said. "But I guess I'm digressing." He crouched down to look Ryan in the eye. "Bottom line is, I want my fourth at-bat."

Ryan looked from Loch to the pitcher's mound. "Here? Now? You're kidding."

"You saw the picture I sent," Loch said. "Seem like I'm kidding?"

"You kidnapped my wife so I'd, what? Lob one over the plate so you can say you went yard against a Hall of Famer? You're insane."

"Maybe. But I don't want any damn lob. I want you to try to get me out." Loch straightened and walked toward the dugout. "Doesn't mean anything if you're not trying."

"It doesn't mean anything either way," Ryan said. "For the love of God, man, I'm forty-five years old. I haven't thrown a pitch in ten years."

"That ain't exactly true." Loch stepped down into the dugout. He bent over and came up with a duffel bag and tossed it up onto the grass. "I was at that old-timers game in Cooperstown back in July. You threw two scoreless innings, and you can still break 90 when you put your mind to it."

"Come on. That was against a bunch of other relics."

"Think I look like a spring chicken?" Loch bent again for a three-gallon bucket filled with baseballs. "So we've both lost a few steps. Just makes it a fair contest. I was in Indianapolis a couple of nights ago, too, where you did that appearance at a minor league game. Watched you working with the pitchers. I'd say you've still got something."

"I'm a scout," Ryan said. "That's what they pay me to do now. Just how long have you been following me around?"

"Long enough," Loch said. He came up out of the dugout with the bucket. "On your feet, Vargas. One at-bat. A real one. After that I make a phone call, and this is all over."

Ryan pushed himself to his feet. "I'm not really dressed for this."

Loch nudged the duffel bag with his toe. "Tina picked out a few things from your closet."

Ryan felt the anger he'd been holding down surge. "Don't say her name."

"Whatever, chief." Loch bent over and unzipped the duffel. He pulled out a batting helmet and put it on, tossing aside his cap. "Get yourself ready. I'll wait out at the mound." He picked up the bucket and carried it out onto the field, along with the bat he'd been holding since Ryan arrived.

Ryan knelt by the duffel bag. He recognized it now, a relic from his playing days. It had been sitting on a shelf in his closet for years, untouched. Inside, he found cleats and a cap and some of his workout clothes. His second-best glove was in the bottom of the bag. His best glove was in a glass case in Cooperstown. He pushed his left hand into the glove.

There was a gun inside.

The tiny .22 Tina bought last year, at the same time the security system was installed, after she saw a strange man lurking around the yard and got nervous about Ryan's weeks-long scouting trips. It occurred to Ryan to wonder if the strange man had been Loch. Had he been planning this for more than a year?

Ryan felt the cool metal of the small gun with the tips of his fingers, imagining the scene. Loch getting into the house somehow, forcing Tina with a gun or a knife to get this bag together, telling her it was stuff Ryan would be using. Tina somehow finding a way to slip the gun in.

But what could he do with it? Loch said his buddy was expecting phone calls at specific times. If Ryan shot him and he couldn't call, what would happen to Tina? Even if he just held Loch at gunpoint while he called, what code word would or wouldn't be said?

"Let's go, Vargas," Loch yelled. "Sooner this is over, sooner everybody gets to go home."

"Coming," Ryan said. He tipped the glove so that the gun fell into the bottom of the bag. As quickly as he could, he changed his shoes and traded his jeans and button-down shirt for a loose pair of shorts and a t-shirt. He shoved the clothes he had been wearing into the bag, on top of the gun. Pulling a cap on, he picked up the bag and walked onto the field.

Loch was standing just to the third-base side of the mound. The bucket was between his feet, and the bat rested in the grass. He was tossing a rosin bag from hand to hand. As Ryan got close, he lobbed it to him. Ryan dropped the duffel in the grass and caught it.

"Forty warm-up pitches sound fair?" Loch asked.

"It's your carnival," Ryan said. "You tell me."

"I want this real," Loch said. "No excuses. I don't want you thinking later that your arm was stiff, and I don't want you hanging one over the plate in slo-mo. I want the best you can give me."

"Fine," Ryan said. "Forty's fine."

Loch nodded. "Go to it," he said. "I'll feed you."

Ryan climbed the mound. He kicked at the rubber, stretched his arms over his head, and bounced the rosin bag in his hand before dropping it to the back of the mound. "You bat left or right?"

"Right," Loch said.

Ryan nodded. Loch reached into the bucket and underhanded a ball to him.

Ryan toed the rubber and fell automatically into the stance he learned from his father four decades ago and had refined by the best pitching coaches in the world. Time slowed down. He felt as he always did with the ball in his hand. At home.

He lifted his left leg, still able to bring the knee nearly to his chest, and swung it down as his arm came whipping around at three-quarter speed. The ball split the plate in two, but was chin level as it crossed.

"High and slow," Loch said. "You can do better than that."

"Gotta wake the arm up," Ryan said. He held up the glove. "Gimme another. This would be a lot easier with a catcher."

"I'll try to arrange more accomplices next time." Loch lobbed the next ball.

Twelve pitches in, Ryan could feel the blood stirring, the muscles growing loose and warm. Twenty pitches in, he started to work on location. For the twenty-fifth, he kicked into gear, unleashing a full-speed fastball that tore right down the pipe and, hitting the chain-link barrier between the plate and the stands, wedged itself into one of the squares and stuck there instead of bouncing back toward the infield.

Loch whistled. "That broke 90, sure," he said.

"Gimme another," Ryan said.

Loch tossed it. "Lemme ask you something, Vargas," he said. "You ever watch the Hartman at-bat?"

"I've seen it a few times," Ryan said. It was the first clip they showed at his Hall of Fame ceremony, the clip they would show on *SportsCenter* when he died. Game seven, bottom of the ninth, two out, bases jammed, and his team, the Tigers, clinging to a one-run lead. Sal Rodgers brought Ryan out of the bullpen on two days' rest to face Jace Hartman, who'd won the triple crown that year. It was the only relief appearance Ryan made in his entire career. His shoulder was on fire before he threw the first pitch, and fifty thousand rabid Pirates fans were howling for his blood. It took eleven pitches, but he struck Hartman out.

Thinking about it now, he threw the cutter that Hartman had missed for strike three and held out his glove for another.

Loch tossed it. "That second pitch," he said. "The one Hartman fouled straight back. You remember?"

Ryan grunted. He remembered. The crack cutting right through the crowd noise, the momentary sense of an abyss of despair before he realized where the ball was heading.

He stepped off the rubber and stretched his arms, feeling the fine sheen of sweat he'd built up.

"I figure he missed that one by about a quarter inch," Loch said. "Bat's a quarter inch higher, that's maybe a grand slam. No parade in Detroit, no third Cy Young. One-fourth of one inch. You ever think about that?"

"No," Ryan lied. He got back on the mound and threw. The ball skipped off the dirt two feet in front of the plate.

"Yeah," Loch said. "I guess not."

Ryan held out his glove. "Gimme another. Shouldn't you be warming up?"

"Spent most of the morning at a batting cage," Loch said. He tossed the ball. "Two more pitches and it's go time, chief."

Ryan turned his back to the plate and looked out across the field, rubbing the ball between his palms. The fence seemed a lot farther off in the old days. He turned back toward the plate and uncorked a beauty of a slider.

One more pitch—a fastball he deliberately put high and inside—and Loch nodded. "Okay," he said. "Batter up. Just remember, Vargas. You're not going to like what happens if I think you're teeing it up for me." He picked up the bat and walked toward the plate. "And if you're thinking about beaning me, remember I'm due to make a call soon."

For the first time, watching Loch walk away, Ryan noticed the minuscule catch in his stride, the whisper of a limp favoring his left leg. The ghost of one bad step, one moment of looking the wrong way. Off by a quarter inch, maybe.

He shook his head. He wasn't here to feel sorry for the man.

Loch got to the plate. He kicked aside the balls that had rebounded into the box, turned his shoulder toward Ryan, and screwed his back foot into the dirt. His stance was compact. Coiled. Ryan felt a distant tickle of memory. Maybe he did remember Mickey Loch.

He peered over the top of the glove for a second, picturing Vic Kelly, his longtime catcher, holding out a target. He dropped his hands to his waist, spun into his delivery, and gave Loch the best fastball he'd thrown in years, sizzling in just over the inside corner. Loch tensed as it came, lifted his left foot a fraction of an inch, but couldn't pull the trigger.

"Strike one," Ryan said. Loch stepped out of the box, looked like he was going to argue for a second, then nodded. Ryan got two more balls from the bucket, dropping one just behind the mound. He felt good. Loose. The way he had always felt on the good days. The ball was itching in his hand, begging to be thrown.

Ryan had always been a fast worker. Keeps the batter off balance. The Vic Kelly in Ryan's mind shifted slightly to the outside, dropped two fingers between his thighs. Ryan nodded to nobody, went into his windup, and produced a curveball that broke three laws of physics on its way to the backstop. This time, Loch swung, but he didn't come within a foot of the ball. He stepped back from the plate, cursing.

Ryan didn't say *strike two* out loud. He turned and picked up the third ball, rubbed it up, and got set. If Loch had said anything about Tina at this moment, it would have taken Ryan a beat to remember what he was talking about. He was entirely absorbed in the feeling he'd had all those thousands of times, the feeling he'd almost forgotten, the sense that he was ten feet tall and bulletproof. He was gonna strike his man out.

The phantom Kelly held down a single finger. Back to the heat. Ryan nodded again, dropped his hands, and sent the ball screaming in.

He didn't see Loch swing. He didn't have to. The sound was enough, the solid, sharp concussion of wood meeting leather. Ryan let the momentum of his delivery carry him around to face the outfield, already knowing what he would see: the ball hurtling toward the wall in center right, a solid line drive, fast and straight. The apparition outfielders weren't even trying to catch it, just head it off. The ball bounced once, hit the wall halfway up, and spun back onto the grass.

In the silence he heard Loch's footsteps clearly. The man came and stood beside him, and they looked out together at where the ball had landed.

"Double?" Loch said.

"Probably," Ryan said. He didn't look at Loch. "I don't know how fast you were before you caught that pothole."

"Fast enough," Loch said. He took off the batting helmet and dropped it and the bat in the grass. He walked over to where he had tossed his hat, picked it up, put it back on, and walked back to the mound. Ryan was still staring out at the wall, his hands on his hips.

Loch pulled a keycard from his pocket and held it out. "Residence Inn," he said. "Room 327."

Ryan finally broke his gaze from the wall. He looked at Loch and slowly took the card. "327," he said. "What about your buddy waiting with her?"

"Isn't one," Loch said. "Oddly enough, I don't actually know anybody willing to commit a felony so I could get my lifetime average to .250."

"But she's all right?"

"I imagine she's pissed," Loch said. "Scared. But yeah, otherwise fine." He crossed his arms. "For what it's worth, Vargas, I didn't say anything to her about the woman in Indianapolis. The one who shared your taste in bourbon."

Ryan clenched his jaw. "You want me to thank you? Or, what, not call the cops?"

Loch shrugged. "Doesn't matter. I'm already wanted in five states. Car I came in was stolen this morning. An hour from now, I'll be in a different one and across a state line."

"So that's it," Ryan said. "This really is all you wanted."

"It's all I've wanted for nineteen years," Loch said. "Guess I'll find something different to want now." He turned to face Ryan fully. "I don't suppose you'd shake my hand."

"No."

"All right. Goodbye, Vargas." He turned away. Instead of heading straight for the parking lot, he trudged out to center field, where he picked up the ball he had hit and stuck it in his pocket. Ryan watched him every step of the way. He might have been imagining it, but Loch's limp seemed a little more pronounced as he turned toward the right-field line and eventually disappeared through the pines.

Chasing Diamonds

"I've never gotten used to this place," Grainger said. "It's like watching baseball in a damn warehouse."

Grainger has been to games in 28 of the 30 major league parks, so I suppose his opinion carries some weight. His goal, as he'll tell anyone willing to listen, is to finish the list, with visits to Seattle and Miami, and then start checking off Triple-A fields. He calls it chasing diamonds.

Since we live in Houston, he sees a lot of Astros games under the retractable roof at Minute Maid Park. It's true that when the roof closes, with the towering wall of windows out beyond left field and the steel beams running across the sky, there's something sterile and overly sleek about the place. The field seems jammed in at a cramped angle, instead of being the reason the building exists in the first place. Grass under glass.

I wasn't paying much attention to the players warming up. Even if I hadn't had other things to think about, I didn't care about baseball. Grainger's been to hundreds of games, but this was only my second. The first was yesterday, a kind of dress rehearsal to give me the feel of the place.

Today was showtime.

Not that you'd know it to look at Grainger. He was writing down the lineups in his scorecard, reading glasses perched on the end of his nose, seemingly unconcerned with anything else. I tried not to notice the tremor in his hand, the way he had to clamp down on the pencil to keep it controlled. My fingers itched to snatch it away and finish the task for him, but I wouldn't offend his pride that openly. Stupid, I suppose, given the much deeper betrayal that was coming.

The stands were filling in. We were on the aisle in the back row of section 215, close to home on the third base side. It was ten minutes before the first pitch when Jorge Baptiste walked into 214, to our left, and took a seat several rows closer to the field. He was wearing a red cap, distinctive among the orange gear of the Houston faithful, along with khakis and a buttoned shirt that concealed his tattoos. Anyone looking at him would have seen a working man who decided to ditch his tie and take in a game.

Anyone looking at us would have seen a man just slipping into his twilight years, at the game with his daughter, or possibly his granddaughter. Grainger was wearing casual slacks and a completely nondescript blue shirt. I was dressed the way I usually was for working: denim shorts and a t-shirt, both a size or two snugger than they might have been. It was one of the first things Grainger taught me. A young woman showing a little skin can get close to a mark, even press up against him in a crowd, and he'll be thinking about things other than her hands and what he has in his pockets.

"Baptiste is here," I said.

"I know," Grainger said, though I hadn't seen him look up from his scorecard. "Relax. Nothing's happening until the seventh." He took off the glasses and watched the Astros run out onto the field. "Don't watch Baptiste. Watch Altuve. He's oh for his last twelve, might be breaking out today."

"Riveting," I said.

We stood with everybody else for the National Anthem, performed today by some guy with a saxophone. Yesterday, it was a high school acapella group. I guess Beyoncé was already booked.

"You know, this place was called Enron Field when they first built it," Grainger said as we sat back down. He snorted. "And people think I'm a crook."

* * *

I met Grainger when I was eighteen. I was living in a youth shelter then, for reasons I don't talk about. I lifted a tourist's purse from one of those hooks under the table at an upscale brewpub and, because I didn't really know what I was doing, got caught. Grainger was sitting a couple of tables over and intervened, telling the woman I was his niece and suffered from kleptomania. He sweet-talked her into letting me go and walked out of the place with me. I figured he planned to have me express my gratitude in the back seat of his car. Instead, he showed me the cash he'd lifted from the purse and asked if I wanted to learn how to do what I was doing the right way.

That was five years ago. Today I could walk off with that tourist's purse without breaking a sweat. Hell, I could get her bra, and she'd never know I had been in the room.

Grainger was a hell of a teacher. Until I noticed that minuscule tremor starting in his hands a few months ago, and the new hesitation in his steps, I would have said he was a hell of a partner. Now I worry. I'm not sure I'm ready for my turn to pull his ass out of the fire.

* * *

The game dragged into the middle innings. The crowd was drowsy compared to the night before, when there had been a lot of home runs and errors on both sides to keep them jumping. I tried not to fidget, focusing on doing finger exercises Grainger had taught me and not looking at Baptiste too often.

"Jesus," I said. "Could we get a bench-clearing brawl or something? This is like an experiment in treating insomnia."

Grainger shook his head. "Both pitchers have no-hitters going into the fifth," he said. "Can't you feel the players getting keyed up? Look at the way they set themselves for every pitch. One hanging curve, one grounder that skips just past the end of the glove. It could be any tiny thing that decides this one, and they're waiting to see what it is."

"Whatever," I said. "I just wish this swap was happening at a wrestling match or something."

"I've always wanted to be at a no-hitter," Grainger said. "This game is all about patience, kiddo. Letting the tension build until something snaps."

"Wake me when the snap comes," I said, but of course I was too keyed up to sleep.

* * *

There's a man named Norton with a storefront on Washington Avenue, downtown, offering both payday loans and bail bondsman services. Grainger says it's a profitable mix of legal loan sharking and legal kidnapping. The back room is where Norton engages in his other activities, the ones that don't even pretend at being legal. Grainger and I don't exactly work for Norton, but we pay him tribute for the privilege of operating around Houston, and a few times he's had us take on specific jobs for him.

Three days ago, he called us in for another.

We sat across the desk from him. *Norton* is an Anglo name, but Norton himself is Hispanic, though he seems to have less of an accent every time I see him. Grainger says he owns a house in River Oaks and sends his kids to the Fusion Academy. Today, he was wearing a silk suit in a shade of blue that seemed to slide right out from under my eyes. The slick image was undercut somewhat by Baptiste, who was parked in a corner wearing cargo shorts and a wifebeater, his torso and upper arms dense with ink.

Norton put a thumb drive on the desk in front of him. It was neon orange and about two inches long. "Say a man has this on him," he said. "Could you take it without him knowing?"

Grainger does the talking when we meet with Norton. He had his arms crossed, I thought to disguise any trembling. He shrugged. "If it was in one of his pockets, and we knew which one, sure. If he sticks it in his shoe, no. If we don't know where he's carrying it, maybe. It would help if it was bigger, more prominent."

Norton grunted. "Yeah, I figured. This is about the biggest they make them these days. Some of them, you can put a whole library on something the size of your thumbnail."

"You say where and when, we can take a shot."

"Tuesday. Astros game." Norton nodded at the tattooed man. "Baptiste is making an exchange with a rep from some gentlemen up north. One thumb drive for another."

Grainger frowned. "I go to the park all the time. I've never worked there. I don't like fouling the waters where I drink."

"I don't give a shit," Norton said. "We picked the meeting place because of you, because you know it inside and out. I wanted to give you the best possible shot at it."

Grainger started to speak, thought better of it, nodded assent. I shifted uneasily in my chair, wondering what would happen if our best possible shot wasn't good enough.

"Baptiste is supposed to be there for the whole game, in a red hat, I guess so they can scope him out," Norton said. "Home half of the seventh, somebody wearing a white cap will sit down next to him. They make the exchange, and then you follow White Cap and take this," tapping his finger heavily on the drive, "back from him."

I couldn't stop myself. "Why not just give them a blank drive, if you don't want them to have whatever's on it?"

Norton glared at me. Grainger answered. "Because if we miss, a blank drive means that Mr. Norton was double-crossing them. If we take it, though, it's White Cap's fault. He'll look either incompetent or dishonest, and then it's his problem, not Mr. Norton's."

"Right," Norton said, pointing at him. "Bright boy."

"What's on the drive?" I asked.

Grainger answered before Norton could even start to scowl. "We don't need to know."

* * *

Three days later, as the game ground into the sixth, I was still wondering. "What would you guess is on the drive?" I whispered.

"I don't need to guess," Grainger said. He was a little peeved because both teams had gotten singles in the fifth, wiping out his no-hitters. "It's an encryption key that opens a bank account with three million dollars in it."

I couldn't help gaping at him. "How the hell do you know that?"

Grainger shook his head. "What have I been telling you for five years? You keep your ears open and your mouth shut, you'd be surprised what people will tell you. Everybody who works for Norton knows old Grainger."

"So what's Norton buying for three million dollars?"

"Information," Grainger said. "Distribution routes, dealer contacts, friendly cops. He's expanding. I hear he wants to be operating in Chicago by this time next year."

"I don't understand why he's doing this," I said. "He can afford the three million. Why not just let them have it?"

Altuve chose that moment to break out, lifting a towering home run to left. Everybody in the stands stood to cheer, and we stood with them, Grainger trying to cover the momentary trouble he had levering himself out of his seat. The train engine on top of the left field wall blasted a whistle and trundled down its truncated track. I stood and continued to clap so I wouldn't have to watch Grainger carefully lowering himself back down.

"Men like Norton don't let go of a dime if they can see a way to hold it," he said when the crowd had settled down. "That's how they get so many of them."

But I wasn't thinking about the drive now. I was thinking about the fact that Grainger had quietly stopped trying to keep score a couple of innings ago, evidently unable to make the tiny symbols in the scorecard boxes.

* * *

The day before, after the game we went to as a dry run, Grainger stopped me as I was about to go into my apartment building.

"You're going to have to be the worker on this," he said.

It was the first time he said anything that even hinted at what I'd been seeing. It was also exactly what I'd been thinking, so I don't know why I argued. "No, you should take it, boss. I've never handled a job for Norton."

"You're ready," he said. "Tomorrow you'll have the bag." The bag was a big, ugly purse the two of us had doctored, covering it with buttons and patches to obscure its shape and putting hidden pockets in the lining. Slip a wallet or a piece of jewelry in, and it would take a patient, determined search to find it. "I can run interference if I need to. But you're gonna do the lift, Alice."

My name is Maria. Grainger calls me Alice sometimes because he says I followed him down a rabbit hole. It's his way of telling me that I'm really still just a visitor in his world. I'm not sure if he knows that I hate it. Surely by now I've earned my seat at the tea party.

"Fine," I said. "I'll meet you at the gate tomorrow." I went inside without saying goodbye.

If I hadn't still been fuming, I would have known they were there before I closed my apartment door behind me. But I was fuming, and I did close it, and then I flipped on the light, and Norton was sitting at my table. Baptiste was in the living room, leaning against the wall and looking out the window. I screamed and gave a little jump, clawing behind me for the knob.

"Settle down," Norton said. "If we were here to hurt you, you'd be hurt. Sit. We got business."

I slid into the seat across from him, my heart in my throat. He folded his hands on the table, leaned toward me. "This thing tomorrow," he said. "You think Grainger is up to it?"

"Of course," I said. "Grainger's the best."

"Was, maybe," Norton said. "Don't treat me like an idiot, girl. Don't think I haven't seen those old hands starting to shake." He tilted his head. "By the way, this how you treat guests? You gonna offer me a drink?"

I started to get up. "I'm sorry, Mr. Norton. Can I get you something to drink?"

"No, I don't want a fucking drink. Sit down." He grinned as I sank back into my chair. "You know he was in the hospital last week?"

"Who? Grainger?"

"No, Ted Cruz. Of course Grainger. Fell down a flight of stairs while he was working a wedding crowd at the Astorian. He said he just tripped, but his medical file says some kind of blackout." I didn't bother asking how he got the file. "That's a story with no happy ending, girl. Maybe he gets caught, and some DA asks him if he's got anything to trade. Or maybe his brain turns to mush, and he ends up in a home babbling about his old friend Norton. Either way, I can't have it."

Norton might not have wanted a drink, but I did. My mouth was dry. "What are you telling me, Mr. Norton?"

"I'm telling you tomorrow is your audition. Kind of a make-or-break thing for you, understand? Either way, though, it's the end of the line for your partner."

"I won't—"

"I'm not asking you to pull the damn trigger. That's what Baptiste is for." He stood up. "I'm just telling you the play so we start this thing on solid footing. Starting tomorrow, the org chart is gonna be a little simpler. You kick straight up to me. We clear?"

"Yes, sir," I said. "We're clear."

* * *

"Here we go," Grainger said. "White Cap."

I pulled my own Astros hat down lower so I could cut my eyes left while seeming to still watch the game. Most people were still settling back into their seats after the seventh inning stretch. The man in the white hat trundling down the steps toward Baptiste was either a little fat or very muscular. It was hard to tell under the loose, billowing Hawaiian shirt he was wearing over cargo shorts.

"I've got the backup man," Grainger said. Guy in the black shirt at the top of the aisle."

"Check," I said, after a glance. White Cap sat next to Baptiste, who had left the aisle seat open for him. There seemed to be a few seconds of talk, and then White Cap dipped his right hand into his front pocket. A second later, the hand went back in, and I caught a hint of orange. "There," I said. "Right front pocket."

"Right," Grainger confirmed.

White Cap stood up.

"Damn," Grainger said. "I thought he'd at least stick around for a whole inning." We stood up as the big man started back up the stairs. "Go. I'll block out Black Shirt if I can."

"Right," I said. "Meet up in front of the right field restrooms." I moved, not thinking about anything now except White Cap's pocket. It was a relief to be moving, with a simple task to focus on.

The area immediately behind our sections was walled in and carpeted, basically a long corridor with souvenir shops and various concession stands. Clumps of people were strolling along or eating together at chest-high tables, but it wasn't crowded.

White Cap had turned right, which would take him to the main exits out on Texas Avenue. It was also the direction opposite where Grainger and I had been sitting, so there'd been no chance to box out White Cap's partner. They were walking together, neither rushing nor dawdling. I put myself about twelve feet behind them and kept pace, holding my phone out in front of me and scrolling through pictures. I wasn't looking at the phone. I was looking past it, getting the rhythm of White Cap's walk, the slight dip and swing of his arms.

We went through a set of glass doors onto the concourse proper, concrete and open to the stands to our right, coming up on the ramps that would take us down toward the exit. Just past the doors, White Cap and his companion had to slow down for a group of older fans heading the same direction, clustered around a woman using a walker. As White Cap tacked to the right, intending to go around them, half a dozen young men, carrying the two beers apiece they'd just bought before alcohol sales were cut off, were coming the other way, boisterously joking and bumping each other to make the beer slosh to the ground. White Cap stutter-stepped and turned sideways, trying to slip past them without bumping the woman with the walker.

I'd seen the chance coming and closed the distance. I was just behind White Cap as he pivoted, and I made my own clumsy attempt at a pirouette to get around one of the beer boys, in the process knocking solidly against the bottom of another's cup with my shoulder. A spray of beer popped straight up into the air. The guy holding it and I both yelled out at the same moment, his "Hey!" blotted out by my high-pitched "watch my phone!" I jerked the phone up and out of range of the splash, and the eyes of everyone in the tangled little knot flicked to it for a moment, including White Cap's, and in the split second he was looking up at my phone and simultaneously leaning away from the spray of beer, it was done.

Like I said, Grainger's a hell of a teacher.

The young man I bumped started apologizing, his friends turning to watch. The old folks stopped to see what was happening and get their bearings. White Cap shook his head impatiently, slid between two of the old folks, and walked on, moving a little faster than before. In two minutes, he'd have forgotten all about the near collision.

I assured the beer boys I was fine, and they turned back onto their original route. I ducked into a woman's room and opened my hand. The orange drive was there. I felt the usual surge of exhilaration—there's no rush quite like getting away with something—but it was colored by a prickle of concern for Grainger. I hadn't really believed until this moment that I was ready to work without him, which meant that I hadn't really believed until this moment that his road was coming to an end.

I had to warn him.

I slipped the drive into the hidden pocket in the lining of the bag and left the bathroom, heading back the way I had come. Our rendezvous point was the right field restrooms, on the far side of the massive building from our seats and from the logical exits White Cap might use. It took me four minutes of brisk walking to get there.

The game was almost over, and there were more people in the walkways, aiming to beat the traffic. Grainger hated people like them. He always said that when he paid for a ticket, he damned well meant to see every pitch. This might well be the first game he'd ever left early himself.

It took me a second to spot him. He was leaning against a pillar behind the right field bleachers, watching the game. I came up behind him and put my hand on his elbow. He started and looked at me, his eyes wide. He seemed to be trying to catch his breath.

"Jesus, are you okay?" I said.

"Fine," he gasped. He waved his hand dismissively. "Just had to hustle to get here. Are we good?"

"We're good. Let's get out of here. We need to talk."

"About what?" he asked. He turned away from the pillar, and his feet seemed to get tangled underneath him. I reached to grab his arm again, but his knees buckled. He was reaching for me as he fell, and there was a heavy thud as he hit the concrete.

Two ushers materialized beside us. I sensed other people turning to watch as I dropped to my own knees beside him. His breathing was fast and shallow, and as he rolled onto his back, his hands groped out blindly, one clutching at an usher's jacket, one at my bag. The ushers were making soothing noises at him.

"I'm fine, dammit, I'm fine," he panted. "Just let me sit up, will you?"

We got our hands behind his back and propped him into a sitting position. "I just tripped," he said. His breathing was evening out, and I realized he was angry, as angry as I'd ever seen him. "Just give me some room, will you? Can you give a man some room?" He held his hands up in front of him. "Ah, look at this crap," he said. His palms were scraped, blood welling at a few places from where he'd caught himself.

"Is this your father, miss?" one of the ushers asked.

Grainger spoke before I could decide how to answer. "No, I'm not her father. She's the damn nursemaid my family sends along to keep an eye on the old man." He sneered at me. "Fine job she makes of it, isn't it?"

I dropped automatically into the role. "I'm doing my best, sir, but you have to work with me."

"Sir, can we get you to the first aid station?" one of the ushers asked.

"I don't need any damn first aid," he said. "Just let me go wash my hands off. Help me up."

They got him to his feet. His breathing seemed normal now, but his hands were shaking, worse than I'd seen them before. One of the ushers kept a hand on his elbow. "Can I help you to the restroom, sir?"

"Fine, fine." Grainger looked at me. "You wait here, Alice. I'll be back in a few minutes, and then we can get out of here."

I nodded. I was looking at his face to keep from staring at his shaking hands. All I could hear in my mind was Norton's voice, talking about Grainger in a home, wasting away. For the first time, that seemed more of a threat than Norton himself.

I rested my bag on the condiments table next to a hot dog stand in the process of closing down, watching as Grainger shuffled around a corner, the usher at his side. I don't know what I was thinking about. I still had to warn Grainger about Norton. Maybe he could hide out somewhere while I took the thumb drive to Norton's storefront. I could claim ignorance of Grainger's whereabouts, but I doubted Norton would buy that for long. I was sure Baptiste wouldn't. For the first time I wondered where Baptiste was, and I looked around, but didn't see him or anyone else I recognized. The departing crowds were getting thicker. It sounded like the game was over. I thought about asking somebody the final score. I was sure Grainger would want to know.

As I was thinking about this, I realized that the tinny version of "Take Me Out to the Ball Game" I'd been hearing for the last thirty seconds was coming from my bag. I opened it, frowning, and found a phone I'd never seen before, the screen displaying an incoming call from a blocked number.

I think I knew right then. I felt like I was going to fall down myself. I picked up the phone, but instead of answering immediately, I pushed my other hand into the hidden pocket.

The drive was gone.

His hands groped out blindly, one clutching at an usher's jacket, one at my bag.

I answered the call. "Grainger," I said.

"Hello, Maria," his familiar voice said. "I guess you've figured out I have the drive."

I gripped the table. "Why?"

"Why do I have it?" His voice was strong, assured. "Three million reasons. Or do you mean why am I calling you? I figured you deserved as much of a head start as I could give you. If you've been listening to a word I've said for the last five years, you've got a panic bag stashed away somewhere. Go get it. Now. Toss your old phone and don't go near your apartment. You've probably got about an hour before Norton starts hunting."

"Why didn't you tell me?" I said. "We could have done this together."

"Ah, kiddo," he said. "What can I tell you? Nobody becomes a thief because they like sharing money."

"We were partners," I said. "You taught me everything."

"Not everything," he said. "I never quite got around to teaching you the shaking hands or the phony ER visit. A few other things." His voice softened. "You'll be fine, Alice. You'll have a good life. But I'm not kidding when I tell you every minute counts. Run."

The call ended.

I spun from the table, dropping my old phone into the nearest garbage can. Grainger, I think, would have been happy to know that I had been listening to him. There was a storage facility two miles from here with a locker containing enough cash to keep me going for several months. By the time I got to the street, I was half jogging, planning my route there and then the fastest way out of town.

Grainger had a ten-minute head start. All he would need. I had no idea where he was. But I knew where he was going. I knew he wasn't going to stop chasing diamonds. He was going to Miami, and he was going to Seattle. I flipped a coin in my head. Seattle. I'd wait for him there. I'd find him.

What I haven't decided yet is if I'm going to kill him.

Wednesdays at Ten

Physician, heal thyself.

That's a good one. A knee-slapper.

Even better: therapist, treat thyself. Explain the scarf biting into the sides of my hands. Explain my muscles knotting in effort. It can't really be as simple as wanting to get rid of Nolan, can it?

I demand a second opinion.

All right: I'm also probably an alcoholic.

* * *

9:57 on a Wednesday morning. My least favorite time of the week.

I squared and centered the notepad on my desk, the pen on top of it. I put my hands flat in my lap, closed my eyes, and tried one of the quicker calm-breathing exercises I teach some of my patients. It didn't take any of the tension out of my shoulders.

I reminded myself I'd have two free hours after Nolan left, and allowed a fleeting thought of the bottle in the bottom drawer. I no longer offered appointments Wednesdays at eleven, and twelve to one was my daily lunch break. All I had to do was get through an hour. Really, just fifty minutes.

Precisely at ten, I opened the door to the waiting room. Nolan August pushed through like he'd been standing on the other side with his nose pressed against the wood.

"She's really pushing me, Doc," he said. He fell into the black leather chair opposite my desk. There's a sitting area in the other half of the office that's more casual, but Nolan has never expressed any interest in moving his sessions there. "I don't know how much we can get done today. I'll try, but I'm seeing red."

"Good morning, Nolan," I said. I walked around and took my seat behind the desk, uncapped the pen. "I thought we might start with some meditation this week."

He shook his head. "There's no way I can be still that long. I'm seething. That woman will not see reason. I shouldn't even say *woman*. Veronica is simply a *child*."

And he was off.

* * *

Nolan August first came to my office at ten on another Wednesday morning, three years ago. He shot the cuffs of his conspicuously well-tailored suit and looked around the room, letting me take in the shaved head, the meticulously trimmed goatee, the patterned socks which landed just this side of acceptably eccentric. He mentioned a friend who recommended me, a banker I nursed through a standard-issue midlife crisis. I said I was pleased to be of help and asked him to talk about why he was considering therapy himself.

Nolan crossed his legs and clasped his hands around his knee. "I suppose I need to start by telling you about Veronica." He said the name the way other people in that chair said words like *cancer* and *addiction*. His mouth twisted. "My stepmother."

Nolan's father had been Anthony August, known to the readers of New York tabloids as Double A, a real estate developer and landlord who reshaped chunks of the city while engaging in a range of very public feuds and a shamelessly indulgent private life that wasn't very private. Late in his sixties, Double A married his third wife, Veronica Knapp, a marketing executive forty years his junior and eight years younger than Nolan, his only child. Less than a year later, and about two years before Nolan came to my office, Anthony August was shot dead in the parking garage outside his office. The newspapers called it a mugging gone wrong, and the resulting hysteria cost a police commissioner and three precinct captains their jobs.

I knew all this before Nolan's first session. I could hardly avoid knowing it. Even if the senior August hadn't been a regular presence in the news, I was reminded of his existence every month when I wrote "August Properties" on the rent checks for both my office on the east side of Manhattan, a few blocks from the Met, and my apartment across the park and farther uptown. I didn't, of course, have any personal connection with the family, or else I never would have agreed to meet with Nolan when he called to make an appointment.

Lord, how I wish I'd had a personal connection with the family.

* * *

Three years after that first session, Nolan was still talking about Veronica.

I picked up the notepad, where his name and the date were already written at the top of the page, and jotted down the letter "V." Many weeks, it was the only note I had to make, though I tried to look like I was writing more. Usually, I put checkmarks every time he mentioned her name so I could watch the line of them marching across the page. I don't know why I bothered feigning real notes. For all the attention Nolan paid to me. I could just as well have been slowly pushing the pen through the palm of my hand.

"We've talked recently about some negotiating strategies," I tried.

He snorted. "You can't negotiate with someone entirely irrational," he said. "All she cares about is lining her own pockets."

Anthony August's will had been prepared by some of the best lawyers in the city, and it was ironclad. According to its terms, both his son and his widow had lifelong seats on the board of August Properties. Neither inherited any money from the multimillionaire directly. Instead, they each had access to a generous trust fund, contingent on actively maintaining a presence on the board. In effect, the will required the two of them to continue working together for the rest of their natural lives.

As far as I could tell, this was Double A's way of guaranteeing that if he had to be dead, nobody else would get to have any fun either.

The origins of Nolan's antipathy for Veronica were easy enough to understand. Double A's decision to marry a woman younger than his son would have been provoking enough, but when he followed up the engagement announcement by boasting to the *New York Post* about Veronica's skills in the bedroom, you didn't have to be Freud to see the warning lights flashing. From Nolan's perspective, she was an obvious gold digger, an embarrassment, a tarnishing of his father's reputation and legacy.

A lot of people would have laughed at that. Double A's name was hardly unblemished to begin with. Longstanding rumor spoke of deep ties between the senior August and New York's crime families. He was tried for money laundering twice in the last decade of his life, going free both times because jurors simply couldn't track the byzantine trails of evidence. Some of the news stories about his death openly speculated that Double A had outlived his usefulness to people who didn't believe in retirement plans. The idea that his involvement with Veronica was the more serious stain on his memory was one that only Nolan seemed to hold, but he clung to it fiercely. At least his mother and his first stepmother had themselves come from old money. Veronica had grown up in an anonymous Long Island commuter town with two blue-collar parents carrying three mortgages. Nolan would sometimes grudgingly acknowledge the hard work she did to put herself through school, but invariably insisted in the next breath that it had only been part of a plan to entrap some wealthy husband.

"She's still fighting August Gardens," he said. "She won't even authorize more money for updating the plans." His hands were clenched on the arms of the chair so tightly that the knuckles were white. I nodded and pretended to write a note about this while making a crude sketch of one of his fists. "She's completely indifferent to father's wishes."

I made a halfhearted effort to take advantage of this reference and steer the session in a new direction. "You're very invested in your father's intentions for the company," I said. "What would happen if you made your own plans? Decided on what you want yourself?"

He clucked his tongue and waved this off. "This is what I want. There's no other point to maintaining the company at all."

At the time of his death, Double A had been in the early stages of planning August Gardens, an ambitious—Nolan would have preferred *audacious*—scheme to remake several blocks of the upper east side into a virtually self-contained community within the city, a miniature Eden using cutting-edge technology and abundant green spaces to allow thousands of people to live and work in comfort with, if the promotional materials were to be believed, no carbon footprint at all. A model for the future of urban development in the era of climate change. From what I read, few people thought there was any chance it would work. *New York Magazine* ran a lengthy piece examining what was known of the scheme and concluding that it was "the final, grotesque joke of a man who was never as entertaining as he believed himself to be."

As far as Nolan was concerned, though, the vision for August Gardens might as well have been brought down from a mountaintop on divinely graven tablets. Completing the development would be his tribute to the father he both worshipped and loathed, a final bid to earn the approval he'd spent his life aching for. Veronica's apathy was all the evidence necessary that her own love for Double A had never been anything more than a sham. For her, to hear Nolan tell it, August Properties had three functions: to collect rents, to raise those rents whenever possible, and to make the proceeds available to her.

Every Tuesday afternoon, the board met and the impasse continued. For reasons I'd never been able to get Nolan to address, he seemed unwilling or unable to push the conflict to any kind of final resolution, a showdown that would end the debate one way or another. Instead, every Wednesday morning, he came to me to rage about the latest skirmish.

And the checkmarks kept moving across my page.

* * *

In my darker moments, I couldn't help but hold Nolan partly responsible for the collapse of my own marriage, which was probably unfair.

Well, let's call it mostly unfair.

True, Daniel and I were fighting about a number of things before Nolan first came to me. Daniel went through a period of unemployment that strained our finances. Our daughter, Sharon, had some troubles in school that neither of us knew how to deal with. I continue to think that Daniel may have had an affair. It couldn't have helped matters, though, when I started becoming sullen and snappish on Tuesday nights, dreading the newest episode in Nolan's endless, droning, never-changing saga, and then withdrawn and irritable on Wednesdays, as my sense of frustration grew. I began drinking more, something Daniel watched with concern that developed into scorn. There were a lot of nights when I wanted nothing more than to sit in a darkened room with a glass in my hand.

These days, I was writing checks to August Properties for an apartment that felt much too big and much too empty. Daniel had moved to Brooklyn, and Sharon, old enough to make the decision herself, chose to live primarily with him. I'll confess that hurt.

I should probably have been in therapy myself. Most therapists are, for the same reason dentists don't do their own root canals. But the therapist I'd seen since graduate school retired to Florida shortly before I started seeing Nolan, and what with one thing and another, I never quite got around to finding a replacement.

My problem was considerably easier to diagnose than Nolan's. I was angry—angry at Nolan, angry at Daniel, angry at myself. Childishly, I wanted to hang on to that anger. I didn't want to work on myself. I wanted to take a sledgehammer to the world.

I did sincerely try to help Nolan. I deserve some credit for that. I spent the first year of our sessions diligently, then desperately, trying to shift his focus away from the conflict with Veronica. There were certainly other things he needed to deal with, starting with his obsessive need to live up to the name of the dominating father whose affection he'd never truly gained. The friction between them may have originated with Nolan's homosexuality, something Double A insisted, to the day he died, on seeing as a personal affront. That rejection probably played a role in Nolan's inability to maintain a relationship for more than a few months, something else he had no interest in exploring with me. For him, our sessions were exclusively about Veronica, and he didn't want tools to help him accept her presence in his life placidly. He just wanted to destroy her or, failing that, rant about her.

When a year's effort had failed to make a dent in his fixation, I gently suggested, near the end of a session, that he consider finding someone else to work with. Nolan knit his eyebrows, looking at me as though I'd told a joke he didn't understand but found mildly offensive.

"I'll keep working with you," he said. "You understand me."

All too well, I thought. "I'm not cutting you off this instant or anything, Nolan. But you shouldn't stay with me out of inertia. I obviously haven't been able to help you deal with your frustration over your stepmother's disagreements with you."

"But you do help," he said. "I always feel better when I leave here."

"I'm happy to hear that, but it doesn't seem to be making a difference in your actual circumstances."

"I see," he said. He cocked his head and looked slowly around the room. "You haven't had a rent increase since you took this office, have you?"

I capped my pen and set it on the desk. "I don't think that's relevant to this discussion."

He ignored this. "Nor at your apartment."

At this, I almost rose up out of my chair. We had never talked about where I lived. "Nolan, you can't force me to keep treating you just because you're my landlord. I can always move to a new office, a new apartment."

He shrugged. "Sure you can. At certain expense. And, of course, with letters of referral. We landlords do talk to each other, you know. Who's a good tenant, who's a bad tenant. Not a lot of people realize how cooperative with each other we can be, behind the scenes."

Just the day before, I had talked to a divorce lawyer for the first time. What would it do to my hopes for custody if I suddenly couldn't get a decent place to live?

He stood up. "Let's both take a week to think about our options. Next Wednesday?"

Neither of us ever brought the topic up again.

***

I got him to try meditation, grudgingly. He didn't like it and would rarely tolerate more than ten minutes of it in a session, his fingers ceaselessly drumming against his knees the whole time.

He wouldn't keep a journal. He seemed to find the very idea of writing about his feelings distasteful, as though the result would be the mental equivalent of soiled toilet paper.

Any attempt to talk about his father invariably circled back around to complaints about Veronica.

Any attempt to talk about his birth mother would cause open jeering. *"Zo, tell me about your muzzer,"* he intoned in a cartoon German accent. She lived in Florida. He saw her twice a year and found her paralyzingly boring.

He had no children, nor any desire for any. He considered this lack of desire to be eminently reasonable and refused to see a connection to his troubled relationship with his own father.

He saw his series of short-term romances, with men invariably younger, fiercely attractive, and usually financially dependent on him, as evidence of an evolved understanding that "love" was simply a doomed attempt to discipline biological urges.

In some ways, he might have been the most well-adjusted patient I ever had. He knew precisely what he wanted—to build August Gardens—and precisely what he hated—Veronica.

I knew precisely what I wanted, too.

I wanted him to shut the hell up about Veronica.

***

I suppose this all sounds trivial. So I had a patient I didn't like. At least he was paying good money for the privilege of annoying me. Here's a dirty little secret: most therapists have patients they don't like. It's an occupational hazard. Learning to set those feelings to one side and offer the same level of help you'd give anyone else is a big part of the training. And when all else fails, you can always send them to someone else.

Usually. Usually, you can send them to someone else. If you can't do that, and you can't help, where are you?

Nolan was an itch I couldn't scratch. He was a splinter under a fingernail, poking straight into a nerve. For three years.

* * *

"Just walk away," I said. "You must have some savings. Start your own company."

He looked down at his hands, rubbed his thumb lightly across his fingers. "If only it was that easy," he said. Before I could ask why it wasn't, he glanced at his watch. "I see our time is up." He rose fluidly to his feet and held his hand across the desk. "I'm not sure if you're aware, but it's been three years this week. Happy anniversary."

I stood and took the hand, hope flickering. *I appreciate all you've done*, I imagined him saying, *but I think it's time for me to try something else.* "Three years," I said.

He nodded and dropped my hand. "See you next week," he said, and turned for the door.

* * *

That night I made myself eat a frozen dinner and then wandered through my echoing apartment, a tumbler of vodka in my hand. In the silence, the creaks and groans of the old building were constant, a slammed door two stories down sending a ripple through every joist. The hall closet never had closed correctly, and had a tendency to swing open on its own as you walked toward it, which could scare the living hell out of you in the middle of the night. Maybe I should present Nolan with a list of needed repairs in our next session.

At some point, I found myself in Sharon's room. I'd dragged in one of the kitchen chairs and was staring at her bed, which was a bare mattress, the sheets and blankets and pillows tumbled in a pile in the corner. I stripped them all off after one too many times jerking awake in the morning to find myself sleeping in my daughter's room.

I raised my glass to the bed. "Happy anniversary," I said. I was never going to have another anniversary with Daniel. Nolan August had become the steadiest relationship in my life.

I don't know how long I sat there before it became suddenly, vitally urgent to know when Sharon would next be staying the night. I would need to make the bed back up before then. There was a calendar showing my visitation days stuck on the refrigerator, but instead of looking at it, I went into my bedroom to get the phone off the charger and called Daniel.

It rang five times before he answered, his voice slurred.

"Sally?"

"Hello, Daniel," I said. I was careful to speak calmly. "Can you tell me when my next night with Sharon is?"

There was a long silence. "Jesus," he breathed. "Do you know what time it is?"

I didn't. I leaned over and looked at the alarm clock. "2:35," I said.

"In the morning," he rumbled. "How the hell much have you had? Christ, Sally. It's the middle of the week." He hung up.

I put the phone back on the charger. Middle of the week. He was right. I'd seen Nolan that day. I had six days before I would have to see him again. That sounded like cause for celebration: being as far away in time from Nolan's next hour as I could get.

Of course, I was closer to it now than I had been a few hours ago. Or a minute ago. Nolan's next hour, the start of his fourth year, was hurtling toward me. Nothing to celebrate in that.

I was miserable the next day, partly hungover and partly afraid that Daniel might take the call as an excuse to revisit our oh-so-civilized shared custody plan. After my morning sessions, I screwed up my courage and texted him an apology, saying it wouldn't happen again and asking him to confirm that

I could come pick Sharon up Saturday morning. It was the long Labor Day weekend, and I'd have her until I took her to school Tuesday morning.

He didn't text back for two hours. When he did it was one word. "Fine."

I resolved not to drink that night. By the time I got home, though, I decided all that was really necessary was to prevent problematic impulse calls. Before I poured my first drink, I got out one of my suitcases, put my phone inside, and then locked it shut and put it back on the floor of the linen closet.

That's the kind of plan years of higher education will help you come up with.

* * *

By Friday night, I was sick of myself. I couldn't take another night of brooding over sloppily poured drinks and counting the bare spaces on the walls where family pictures had hung. I knew what I would tell a patient to do. Get out of the house. Get moving. A change of scenery. Take a walk.

I got myself dressed up just a little, a favorite black skirt and a blue top that I knew worked well with my eyes. There was an Italian restaurant five blocks away that Daniel and I had loved. I hadn't been there since he left, but why not? Why should I lose that, too?

As soon as I was outside, I felt better than I had in weeks. The city was at its late-summer best, the heat of the day giving way slowly to breezes that promised the coming fall. The streets were lively with students and tourists and just plain people. Most of them were staring at their phones, but the mood was buoyant, with snatches of conversation and music everywhere. I hadn't realized just how dank I'd allowed my apartment to become. I would need to open all the windows tonight, let it air out, not give Sharon a reason to hate coming back to her first home. Remembering that I would get to see her tomorrow made the night even more pleasant. I could almost believe I was on a holiday.

I held myself to a half bottle of wine with dinner, lingering over rigatoni and gelato while I read a magazine. There had been a time when I wouldn't have dreamed of eating out by myself, but if this was something I was going to have to get used to, it didn't seem so bad. At my table by the window, I could glance up to watch the life of the city rolling past, listen to the murmurs of the other diners. I felt I'd stepped beyond myself, disengaged from the concerns that had been consuming me. I was distantly aware of problems, but I held them at bay, keeping up the delicate balancing act of not actually thinking about them.

I wanted to keep the feeling after I ate. Going home would mean returning to practical concerns, getting Sharon's room ready, setting the alarm clock. Instead, I started wandering, turning corners at random. Dusk was settling in. I'll go home in an hour or so, I told myself, but then I ran into something that ended the balancing act and brought everything crashing back down.

It was a poster outside one of the lecture halls at Columbia. A round table discussion, being filmed tonight for an educational series, with a business professor interviewing five high-ranking female executives from different fields. The topic: Has The Glass Ceiling Shattered?

One of the executives was Veronica Knapp.

* * *

I'd seen pictures of her before, of course. One from Double A's funeral, with her standing impassively by his casket in a black veil and Ray-Bans, still popped up on the news when August Properties did something noteworthy. As I slipped into a seat near the back of the lecture hall, though, it felt like I was seeing something mythical, something I'd heard about for years without ever quite believing in. Veronica certainly didn't look like the ogre of Nolan's stories. She was the youngest woman on the stage and the only one wearing a dress, a striking but professional red number set off by a black scarf. I scanned the audience for Nolan, but there was no sign of him. Apparently, his obsession with his stepmother did not extend to attending all her public appearances.

The panel had been going for twenty minutes when I arrived, and I watched as it continued for another hour. Veronica spoke less than the other women, but when she did talk, she was confident and poised. If she felt any embarrassment at having achieved her position through marriage, she concealed it well. Her argument was that the glass ceiling would never go away, and that it was up to every woman in every office to break through it herself, using any means necessary.

"That's how we level the playing field," she said. "By being just as nasty and selfish and greedy as every mad man who ever slapped his secretary's ass and sent her for coffee."

This got a laugh, and some resistance from the other executives, who spoke of the nobility of women helping each other to advance the sisterhood. Veronica nodded respectfully, but was unmoved. "My sister's a stone bitch," she said. "If I waited for a hand up from her, I'd starve." Another laugh. The audience didn't exactly like her, but they were amused by her.

Nolan might have a point about her disinterest in negotiation.

Eventually the session ended, the professor thanking the participants and offering an idealistic summation that pointedly omitted Veronica's point of view. "There's no formal q and a tonight," she concluded. "However, there is a wine and cheese reception being held in the atrium upstairs, and our participants have all graciously agreed to stick around for a while. Can we thank them again for sharing their time?"

I was tempted to leave. Watching Veronica longer might give me some new insight into Nolan, and she was interesting enough in her own light, but it felt risky to be engaging with his life outside the confines of my office. I hesitated, but it was clear most of the audience was sticking around, and I let them sweep me along upstairs.

The atrium was spacious, with tables and chairs scattered around and waiters wandering through to offer glasses of wine and bites of cheese. I took a glass and hovered in a corner, waiting for the panelists to appear. They came in to another round of polite applause and dispersed through the crowd, shaking hands and posing for occasional pictures.

Veronica was the most physically attractive of the panelists, but it quickly became clear she was the least in demand for conversation. Much of the audience was made up of young women, probably either entering their final years at the school or just recently finished. Given the choice between four women who spoke earnestly of their obligation to help create a new generation of feminist leaders, and one who proclaimed it was every girl for herself, they didn't have to think hard about who to talk to.

Veronica drifted around the big room from group to group, mostly talking to the clusters of older people, many probably faculty. I drifted along in her vicinity, usually getting close enough to catch a snatch of the empty pleasantries being exchanged. She kept looking around, and for a few minutes I thought she had noticed my frequent proximity, but eventually I decided she was looking for someone else.

I was busy enough trying to keep track of Veronica that I lost count of the number of glasses of wine I picked up. After an hour or so, with the crowd just beginning to thin, I realized that I needed to go find a restroom, and also that I had gotten considerably tipsier than I had intended. The virtuous half bottle at dinner had become something more like two, and while I'd built my tolerance over the past couple of years, the edges of the room were starting to tilt dangerously.

A waiter directed me to the ladies' restroom. After I attended to business, I leaned on the sink and examined myself closely in the mirror. Definitely showing some signs of wear. I was having a little trouble focusing, my eyes had a reddish tint, and I couldn't disguise the slack movements and posture that had so often disgusted Daniel. At least I hadn't made the mistake of wearing heels, which would have made the several blocks between here and home a true obstacle course.

When I left the restroom and saw a room across the hall labeled "Faculty Lounge," I decided having a quiet place to sit and rest for a few minutes might not be a bad thing. The door was unlocked. The room on the other side was large and thickly carpeted. In the dim light from streetlamps outside, I could make out clusters of chairs and tables and sofas scattered around. I chose a sofa in the far corner, facing away from the door, where I might be left alone even if someone else came in. I kicked off my shoes and eased myself down onto it. The room wasn't exactly spinning, but it was definitely engaging in a bit of pitch and yaw. I closed my eyes, just for a moment.

* * *

"What in the hell are you *doing* here?" someone snapped.

I started awake, nearly falling off the couch. I had no idea how much time had passed or where the voice had come from. A woman, I thought. My heart thudded as I tried to orient myself, the dark room confusing and unfamiliar.

I was about to sit up to try to answer when someone else spoke, this time a man. The second voice was low, and taut with restrained exasperation. "I texted you," he said. "I said I wanted to see your talk."

"And I told you not to come," the woman said. "What did you tell *her*? What kind of flimsy excuse did you come up with?"

Something moved in the dim corner in front of me. I nearly yelped, then realized there was a display case there, with books by faculty members. The movement was the reflection in the glass of two people behind me, standing just inside the door to the lounge. The man was a blur of dark blue, but the vivid red of the woman's dress was unmistakable. It was Veronica.

"I said I was meeting some guys at the Yankees game and then going bar hopping," he said. "She won't expect me for hours. We could go to your place."

"Sure," Veronica said. "So you can go home in the middle of the night smelling like my perfume instead of beer and hot dogs. What a bright boy." In the glass, the blue shape moved toward the red and was pushed away. "We made rules, remember? Only during the day. Only when she's at work. Christ, I nearly walked out when I saw you in the audience."

"I'm glad you didn't," he said. "You were the smartest one up there."

I thought I could hear Veronica's eyes roll from all the way across the room.

"Whatever," she said. "Go home. Or better yet, go to the damn game. At the very least, you ought to be able to bring back a program."

"C'mon," he said, barely a notch above rather pathetic whining now. "I came all this way."

"Well, now you can go all the way back. The last thing I need is a bunch of headlines about Double A's treasure hunter also being a homewrecker." Veronica shifted gears, and I heard the effort she put into softening her voice. "It would be nice, baby, but it's just not smart. I'll see you Wednesday, like usual, okay? I'll be extra nice to you."

Now the red shape moved to the blue. For a moment, there was near silence, with a few muffled rustles. "Get on out of here," she said, eventually, more quietly.

"All right," he said. "I'm sorry. Are you leaving too?"

"I'll stay in here for a few minutes," she said. "Secrecy, remember?"

Another minute of muffled kissing, and he finally left, the door easing shut behind him.

Veronica sighed. The red shape in the glass moved, and I heard her settling into a chair. After a moment, a new light appeared across the ceiling, and I realized she was looking at her phone. Moving with infinite care, I peered over the back of the couch.

She was in a plush armchair with her back to me, the edges of her hair haloed with the light from the phone. The obvious thing to do was to wait quietly for her to leave, but then I saw the black scarf still around her neck. As soon as my eye hit it, the urge was in my head like it had always been there, like it was the reason I'd ended up in this room. I'd spent three years failing to solve Nolan's problems. Here, finally, was a way to do it, decidedly and permanently.

And surely if Nolan's problems were solved, mine would be as well.

I rolled to the floor and got up, thankful for my bare feet. The carpet was thick and soft, absorbing any noises I made as I went softly around the end of the couch. I think I expected her to catch me, to see a glimpse of movement reflected somewhere or hear the whisper of my breath. I crossed the dozen feet between us one quiet step at a time, waiting for her to look around. I'd jump and stammer a little and apologize for accidentally overhearing her scene, and then rush from the room. She'd never know who I was, and nobody need ever know I'd met her, including Nolan. I'd be able to forget, for the rest of my life, the moment when I had become this person.

But she didn't hear. She didn't see. She didn't turn in startled surprise.

She was absorbed in her phone. I got close enough to see the text window over her shoulder, her thumbs flying across the keys. I watched my hands reaching out for the ends of the scarf.

It was luxurious, expensive silk, soft but strong in my fingers. I grasped the ends firmly, took a breath, and yanked back brutally, leaning away to put all my weight and strength into it. Her head snapped back, and she made a panicked gurgling sound. I heard the phone drop to the floor. Her hands clawed at the fabric, trying to pull it away from her neck. I felt the strain in my arms and went down on one knee as she waved her arm frantically behind her. She couldn't reach me. She couldn't get enough leverage to turn or push herself over the back of the chair. Even in the soft light from outside the windows, I could see the skin of her ears getting darker.

It took a long time. Longer than you'd think.

When it was over, I was exhausted. I could have collapsed right onto the carpet and gone back to sleep. Instead, I went back across the room and slipped into my shoes. I didn't look at the chair. I used the hem of my skirt to open the door and walked out into the hallway, trying to act as though I belonged there. There was no one in sight. I ran the hem around the outer knob, having no idea if it was doing any good, and walked toward the staircase. I didn't think about Veronica or Nolan or anything else. Just my feet. One at a time. Taking me home.

* * *

I'm afraid Sharon didn't have much of a weekend. I was, just barely, on time to pick her up Saturday, wearing a baseball cap and dark sunglasses, glaring at Daniel and daring him to say something. Once I had her, it was a challenge figuring out what to do with her. She was twelve, just hitting the age where she found her childhood interests painfully embarrassing but hadn't yet found her adult self. I had planned for the zoo, but it was raining, and at any rate, she had become a budding animal-rights activist who would have only bristled at the cages. Instead, I took her to Times Square and let her pick a movie at a big multiplex, then loaded her down with popcorn and candy.

As soon as the film started, I slipped out to the bathroom to check the local news on my phone. Still nothing, just as when I checked from the apartment and multiple times on the train. I refreshed the page three times with no change. I was starting to feel like I wasn't getting enough air. Could I have been wrong? Had Veronica stirred after I left, staggered out for help, described the woman who had assaulted her?

It was early evening before the news broke that her body had been found by a maintenance crew. By that time, I was a nervous wreck, unable to sit still or focus on anything other than the news updates on my phone. We were back at the apartment, resting for a bit before going out for dinner. Sharon, clearly alarmed and alienated by my jumpy behavior, had retreated to her room and closed the door as I bounced off the walls, keeping myself away from the liquor cabinet only out of a desperate sense that I might soon need all my wits about me.

I fell into a chair and scrolled through the story, my whole body numb. There were few details as yet. The police indicated that it was definitely murder, though the means had not yet been made public. Nolan was on his way back to New York. He was in Denver at the time of Veronica's death, at a conference for the solar panel industry. It was only when I read this that I realized one thing that had been worrying me: that I might have unwittingly framed my own client.

Nolan apparently had an alibi, though, so I could go back to worrying about having incriminated myself.

The story developed over the next two days as I took Sharon to her favorite restaurants and treated her to lavish shopping sprees, none of which could blind her to my obvious agitation and distraction. I couldn't maintain a conversation or focus on anything. My arms and shoulders ached as though I'd overdone a workout, however forcefully I told myself I was imagining it. I couldn't sleep. Every time I closed my eyes, I saw the back of Veronica's head, again, the tips of her ears turning an ugly purple. Miraculously, I kept myself from drinking, partly for Sharon's sake but mostly because not surrendering to the safe oblivion of the bottle felt like a punishment

I deserved. After she was in bed, I paged through the textbooks from my old classes on pathological disorders, but the words blurred together and I found nothing that seemed to describe those moments when my hands were on the scarf.

While I was falling apart, the Veronica Knapp murder case was coming together, news bulletin by news bulletin. The initial stories made pointed references to the long-standing rumors of the August family's engagement with the mob. Late on Sunday, however, the police took a man named William Deloft into custody. Deloft, a city construction inspector frequently assigned to August Properties projects, had been recognized by an associate in the audience at the Columbia round table. His wife told the police that she had long suspected Deloft of having an affair with Veronica Knapp. Despite their warnings, she also took an apparently vindictive pleasure in sharing this suspicion with the press.

By the time I dropped Sharon off at school Tuesday morning (to her obvious relief), Deloft had been essentially convicted by the press, not only of Veronica's murder but of having accepted sexual or financial favors from her for favorable inspections. A formal charge was expected at any moment. I should have been absorbed in his fate, my guilt warring with my self-righteous disdain for a man cheating on his wife, but in fact I could barely bring myself to think about William Deloft. There were only two things on my mind: finally allowing myself the drink I'd craved for three days, and my next meeting with Nolan.

For the first time ever, I couldn't wait to see him. He would tell me that, with Veronica out of the way, he was finally able to take control of his father's company, which would now demand all his attention. His problem had been solved, and there was no need for us to continue our work. He would thank me for all my efforts and shake my hand and walk out of the office, and I would never have to see him again. Sometimes. in my visions of this moment, he graciously told me that the rent on my office would be covered as long as I cared to remain. I didn't really care about that, though. I just wanted to see his back going through a closing door. Maybe after that, I'd spare a thought for Deloft or Veronica. Maybe I'd be so giddy that I would never need a drink again.

But I was going to need more than one to get me there. In the taxi back to my place, I emailed my Tuesday clients, telling them I was sick and would see them next week. I asked the driver to wait while I ran up to my apartment and shoved a change of clothes into a bag, along with two bottles of vodka and a loaf of bread. Then I had the taxi take me to a hotel down the block from my office and got a room for the night, leaving a wake-up call for the next morning.

I hung the do not disturb sign on the knob and, to be sure, shoved a table up against the inside of the door. My cell phone and purse went into the safe, and then I turned my back to it and punched buttons at random to lock it. I unplugged the TV and turned it face down on the dresser. I got the plastic cup from the bathroom, set it on the nightstand, and filled three-quarters of it with vodka.

I was tired of Nolan, tired of Veronica, tired of myself, tired even of Sharon and Daniel. I needed a day of oblivion, and I knew how to get it. I lifted the cup to my lips, and that's the last thing I remember from that day.

* * *

The wake-up call dragged me out of nothingness. At some point, I had thrown up, but, thankfully, into the garbage can. I took a shower and brushed my teeth three times. I pulled the table away from the door so somebody from the hotel could come open the safe, which they were happy to do for a thirty-dollar convenience fee. My phone had died, but I didn't much care. I made it to my office by 9:30, looking at least moderately respectable. My head was pounding, but I'd expected that. It was more than compensated for by the excitement of knowing I was about to see Nolan for the last time. When I heard the outer door of my waiting room open seven minutes before ten, I couldn't wait any longer. I went to usher him in.

It wasn't Nolan. It was a young woman in a rather severe blazer, carrying a briefcase. She stood up when I came out of the office.

"I'm sorry," I said. "I see new patients on Fridays. I'm fully booked today."

"I'm not a patient, Dr. Moss," she said. She held out a card. "My name is Audrey Fowler. I'm a junior partner at Rodgers and Ingram. We're representing Nolan August. Can I have a moment of your time?"

I took the card. She was going much too fast. "I'm sorry—you're a lawyer? Is Nolan suing me?" I couldn't imagine any other reason he would send a lawyer to his appointment.

Audrey frowned. "Of course not. Should he be?" Seeing my expression, she held up a hand. "I'm sorry, that was a poorly timed attempt at humor. Can we please go in your office and start over?"

Still confused, I ushered her in. She took the seat Nolan always chose, and I went behind my desk, setting her card on top of the notepad with Nolan's name and the date. "I really don't understand what this is about."

She had taken out a notepad of her own. "To be honest, Dr. Moss, it might be nothing. If it becomes something, you'll be seeing someone far more senior than me. I'm basically here to get a sense of your willingness and ability to testify on Mr. August's behalf."

"Testify?" I wondered if this would be clearer without the hangover. I didn't think so. "About what?"

She was staring at me. "Dr. Moss, are you not aware that Mr. August has been arrested?"

My eyes widened. "Arrested? But I thought he was in Denver when—when Veronica." I couldn't finish the sentence.

"He wasn't arrested for that," she said.

I shook my head. "I'm sorry, Ms. Fowler." I had to glance at her card to get the name. "I'm afraid I haven't seen any news since Monday. I have no idea what you're talking about."

She tapped her pen against the notepad. "Well," she said. "Normally, I'd say it wasn't my place to tell you this, but it's all been leaked to the press anyway. Ms. Knapp had left instructions with her attorneys that, in the event of her sudden or unexplained death, they were to open a safety deposit box at her bank in the presence of law enforcement. That was done yesterday, after the holiday weekend. Inside the box was a gun."

"A gun," I repeated, numbed.

"Yes," she said. "It appears to be the gun that killed Anthony August, and Nolan August's fingerprints are on it. The police are operating under the theory that Ms. Knapp had been using it to blackmail him for some years. He's been arrested for the murder of his father, and—" Audrey Fowler broke off, looking at me in stark surprise. "Dr. Moss, may I ask why you are laughing?"

Awaiting the Hour

Although he was awake most of the night, obsessively checking and rechecking weather reports, Monday morning found Matthew feeling wired with energy he couldn't contain or direct.

How do you behave on the day you've waited decades for?

Without really thinking about it, he went to the closet in the spare bedroom where he hung his old suits when he retired, each sheathed in its plastic dry cleaner bag. It felt right to present himself formally for the occasion. He chose the light blue and adorned it with a yellow tie and matching pocket square. He'd lost weight, and he had to cinch his old belt in two extra notches, but when he looked in the mirror he was satisfied with what he saw. His hands might tremble slightly, but they had not forgotten how to make a neatly executed knot. Matthew nodded to himself. On his way out of the bedroom he raised his hand and briefly touched Alex's face in the picture hanging near the door. Today was for him.

There were hours yet to fill. He sat on the porch for a time, nursing a cup of coffee and watching the familiar neighborhood stir itself awake. Over the years this had become a sleepy little corner of town. Most of the children had grown and left. Matthew raised his hand politely as the parents left behind passed by on morning walks or drove off to work. He knew their faces, even if he had grown uncertain of names. The truth was that he felt little association with them. When he and Alex moved in all those years ago, there had been a distinct frostiness. Two men living together was still a novelty in those days, particularly in Kentucky. By the time the neighbors decided that they were, after all, just two more guys mowing the lawn and taking out the garbage, the chance for real connection had passed.

He was in the kitchen rinsing out his coffee cup when he heard the front door open and close. He turned off the water and cocked his head. There was a murmuring voice, the creak of shifting weight. Someone was in the house. Still carrying the dishtowel, Matthew walked around the corner.

There were two of them, standing just inside the front door, hovering like they were trying to decide where to sit. The man was wearing khaki shorts and a white t-shirt, his blond hair hanging shaggily to his shoulders. The woman was in jeans and a halter top with dark hair cut almost to her skull. Both had tattoos on their arms, and Matthew was looking at these when he realized the man was holding a gun, a revolver with a two-inch barrel.

For a moment, they all looked at each other. The man made a move as if to raise the gun, seemed to think better of it.

"Do you remember me?" he asked. *Old man* hung in the air. He hadn't said it, but he might as well have.

"No," said Matthew.

"I was here last year with the crew that redid your roof."

Matthew nodded as if this explained something. "What do you want?"

The man chewed his lip. "Is there anybody else here?"

"No."

"Sit down," the man said.

Matthew pulled out a chair and sat at the dining room table. He began folding the dish towel.

The man nudged the woman. "Look around," he said. "Make sure he's telling the truth."

The woman looked at Matthew. "Sorry, mister," she said. She moved off toward the bedrooms.

Matthew put the folded towel on the table and rested his hands on either side of it as the man came and sat across from him.

A thought struck the man, and he leaned back in the chair and yelled over his shoulder. "Close all the curtains!"

There was a rattling noise from the other room as curtain rings slid into place, and the light in the hallway got slightly dimmer. It startled Matthew more than the couple had, or even the gun. He knew from the sound exactly where the woman was standing, exactly how hard she had pulled. You get to know the sounds of your own home, each as distinct as a different bird's call, and you know without looking what door has been opened or closed, what faucet is running, where someone is walking. Then you go a few years without hearing any of those sounds, because there's nobody to make them but you. When you hear them again, your mind will do strange things. For a fraction of a heartbeat, when he heard the curtains, Matthew felt Alex's presence. Remembering that he was gone was a punch of grief behind his ribs.

"You're all gussied up," the man said. "You going somewhere? Is somebody coming here?"

"No," Matthew said.

"Listen," the man said. He put the hand with the gun on the table. "We're not here to make any trouble. If you don't give me any reason to hurt you, I won't. But lying is a reason."

Matthew nodded. "I'm not lying to you, young man."

The man stared at him for a long minute. The woman came back through the room, walked into the kitchen, and closed the drapes. Matthew listened as she opened the basement door and went down and almost immediately came back up. She leaned against the wall. "Just storage in the basement. There's nobody else here."

Matthew looked at her. "My name is Matthew Shaw, young lady. What's yours?"

"Don't answer that," the man said immediately.

Matthew looked back at him. "I take it you're planning to be here a while. I have to have something to call you."

"Sir and ma'am will do fine."

Matthew shrugged. "What do you want?"

The man chewed his lip again. "The car out front is yours?"

"It is. I'll give you the keys."

"Got any cash?"

"Very little in the house. A few hundred dollars, maybe."

"We'll come back to that."

"Hey, Bonnie and Clyde," the woman said.

They both looked at her. "What?" the man asked.

"He can call me Bonnie and you Clyde. That fits, don't it?"

Matthew couldn't help himself. "You know what happened to them, don't you?"

She looked interested. "No, I never saw that movie. What happens?"

"They die," Matthew said. "Gunned down like dogs." He and Alex had gone to the movie on one of their first dates, just a few months after Matthew got back to the States. Neither of them would have used the word *date* at the time, of course. Things were so much more difficult then, all the wary circling until you were sure you both wanted the same thing. Today, Matthew knew, you could just walk through the world telling everybody you met exactly what you wanted.

"Whatever," Clyde said. "Everybody fucking dies." He seemed to reach a decision. "Here's the deal, Matt." Again, Matthew heard the *old man*. "We need to be out of sight for a little while. So we're just going to hole up here until nightfall, and then we'll take your car and your money, and it will all be over with. You'll have an exciting story to tell at the bingo hall."

Matthew picked up the towel, opened it, and began to refold it. "I'm too old to bullshit," he said. "What you mean is that you're going to keep me around today in case it turns out you need a hostage. Then tonight you're going to kill me and take whatever you want."

"Aw, no!" Bonnie cried out. She moved beside Matthew's chair and put her hand on his shoulder. "We wouldn't hurt you, mister, honest."

"Sure," Clyde said. "We'll just tie you up when we leave. Get a little more of a head start."

It was simpler to pretend to believe him. "Fine. You won't have any trouble out of me." He leaned forward. "Except one thing. I need to be out in the backyard at twenty past one. Just for five minutes."

Clyde snorted. "What the fuck? That when your neighbor comes out to water her rosebushes or something? No fucking way. We're all staying inside."

Matthew shook his head. "You can kill me tonight. I don't give a damn. But I need those five minutes."

"Forget it."

Matthew held his gaze. "You refuse an old man this one thing?"

Clyde grinned, mocking. "Yeah, old man," he said. "I refuse."

Matthew nodded slowly. "Okay, then," he said.

Let it not be said he hadn't given the boy a chance.

* * *

They moved into the living room. Clyde had Matthew sit in a recliner in the corner farthest from the front door. Bonnie lounged on the couch. Clyde sat beside her at first, but he was too jumpy to stay in one place. He drifted around the room, sometimes peering around the edges of the curtains, asking Matthew when the mail was delivered and if cops ever cruised down the street. Matthew's answers were terse but polite.

Bonnie dozed off for twenty minutes, waking when Clyde stomped past her again. "Whyn't you watch TV?" she moaned, stretching. "You're driving me nuts."

"TV puts me to sleep," Clyde said. "We'll watch the news at 11:30, though." He stopped in front of a framed picture on the wall near a built-in bookcase. "This you?"

"That's what they tell me," Matthew said. The man in the picture seemed impossibly young to him now, many years younger than Clyde. He was wearing fatigues, grinning as he sat at the gunner's port in a Huey and gave a thumbs-up. The photo was on a black velvet backdrop, surrounded by a cluster of medals. Matthew hated the display. It felt like bragging, bragging about something he didn't want to remember at all. It was Alex who insisted on putting it together and hanging it where anyone who visited the house would see.

It's part of you, he said. *And I won't have you denying any part of yourself.*

Clyde moved on to the next picture on the wall: Matthew and Alex in their matching tuxes on the beach at Cape Cod. "Hey man, what's this?"

Matthew's throat was dry. "My wedding."

Clyde barked out a laugh. "Get this, Lizzie. We got the world's oldest fruit with us."

"Who's Lizzie, *Clyde*?" the woman said.

Clyde grimaced. He turned to Matthew. "You were a fruit when you were in Vietnam?"

"Yes."

"Well, where's this guy now? Your *husband*?"

Matthew held his gaze. "He died."

Clyde grunted and turned away.

"I'm sorry to hear that, mister," Bonnie said drowsily from her nest on the couch. Matthew nodded at her tightly.

Clyde hunched his shoulders and leaned against the wall, looking at the front window and chewing his lip. Matthew had seen the look on his face before, on soldiers before battle, on cops at the marches Alex asked him to go to. It was the look of a man wondering what he was capable of doing.

* * *

When Bonnie got restless, Clyde sent her to search the house. Matthew told her where to find the small amount of cash he kept on hand, but Clyde said she should search anyway, and bring anything of value she could find. "And make sure he doesn't have a gun."

The two men sat in the living room, listening to her rummage through the bedrooms and office. Clyde's right foot bounced up and down, and he shifted the gun from hand to hand. He had not put it down or even slipped it in a pocket since Matthew had been watching him. It was a small gun, but even a tiny weight gets burdensome with time.

"You don't have to stare at me," he said. Matthew shrugged and let his gaze drift to the ceiling.

"I don't know what made me think of this place," Clyde said. Matthew couldn't tell if he was trying to chat or just talking to fill the silence. "I mean, I noticed it was a real quiet neighborhood when we were doing your roof last year."

Matthew had long since gotten comfortable with silence. He didn't say anything.

"You're retired, right?" Clyde leaned back on the couch, his foot still bouncing. "What did you do?"

Matthew sighed. "I was an accountant."

"Man, I couldn't hack that. All those fucking numbers. Weren't you bored out of your skull?"

"I don't mind numbers."

Clyde gestured with the gun. "What about your *husband*?" He was incapable of saying the word without making it sound like something that tasted bad. "What did he do?"

Matthew didn't want to talk about Alex. "Dentist."

"No fucking kidding. Jesus, the most boring gay couple in the world."

There was nothing to say to that. Maybe it was true. Matthew didn't think it sounded like such a bad thing to be. So he was surprised to hear himself talking again. "Alex wasn't boring. His real love was astronomy."

"What, you mean horoscopes?"

Matthew shook his head. "That's astrology. It's bullshit. I mean the real science. Planets, stars, galaxies. We took vacations to the world's great telescopes."

Clyde snorted. "Oh yeah, I take it back. Sounds fucking fascinating."

Bonnie came back into the living room before Matthew had to think of an answer to that. One of the pillowcases from Matthew's bed dangled from her right hand. She handed Clyde a little stack of bills, and he glanced at it and tucked it in his breast pocket without counting it. Bonnie perched on the edge of the couch and dumped the pillowcase out onto the coffee table. The small chest with Alex's collection of silver dollars. A couple of watches and some cufflinks. Matthew's laptop computer and the cell phone he rarely bothered to charge. Prescription drug bottles from the bathroom. She poured it all out as casually as a child emptying out a toy chest, and Matthew winced as the items bounced and skittered, scratching up the surface of the table.

"There's not much here," she said. "Didn't see no gun."

Clyde grunted and scrounged through the pile. He picked up the drug bottles and tucked one—the painkillers, Matthew assumed—in his pocket.

"Shove it back in the bag," he said. "Might be a few bucks in there."

The most expensive thing in the house was the telescope mounted on its tripod in the office. Matthew wasn't surprised that she'd paid it no attention. He wouldn't have looked twice at it either before meeting Alex, before going out on hillsides with him and listening to him talk about the first time he'd seen Jupiter's moons with his own eyes. Some doors have to be opened for you.

* * *

At 11:30 Clyde had Matthew turn on the local news. The three of them sat and watched the familiar cycle—traffic accidents, local politics, sports, weather. Matthew had never lived in or visited a town with interesting local news. The inevitable lighter story at the end of the half hour was about the eclipse that would be visible in the area that afternoon.

As the program went on, Clyde grew more and more agitated, eventually pacing back and forth in the small space between the couch and the coffee table. When a soap opera started, Matthew flicked off the set.

"Fuck!" Clyde exclaimed. He flopped down on the sofa and stared at the set in wonder. "I really thought we'd be on there, babe."

"What exactly did you do?" Matthew asked.

Clyde looked at him slyly.

Matthew shrugged. "Tell me or don't. I can't imagine what it will change."

Bonnie nudged Clyde's shoulder. "Oh, just tell him."

Clyde looked down at his gun. "Killed my parole officer."

Matthew cocked his head. "Yes, I would think that would be on the news."

"Maybe they haven't found him yet," said Bonnie.

Clyde nodded, looked up at Matthew, half grinning. "See, I robbed this gas station last night? And then he had to pick this damned morning to come around for one of his surprise visits. Fucker was always trying to nail me.

Well, I couldn't have him finding a bunch of cash I couldn't account for."

"So you shot him," said Matthew. "And just left him in your house?"

"Yeah," Clyde said. "Then we took off, but I figured they'd be looking for my car, so we ditched that and just started riding a bus around. And we were a couple blocks away when I remembered working on your place."

"And you decided to hole up until nightfall," Matthew said.

"Well, yeah," Clyde said. He looked at the gun again, uncertainly.

Matthew closed his eyes. He was dealing with the world's dumbest criminal, and the time he had to do something about it was running out.

Clyde was apparently tired of explaining himself. "I'm getting hungry. What kind of food you got around this place?"

"Basic stuff," Matthew said. "Pasta. Fish sticks."

"Fish sticks," Clyde said. "Jesus, I haven't had a fish stick since grade school." He pushed Bonnie's shoulder. "Go make us all some fish sticks, babe."

She pushed back at him. "How long you known me, *babe*? I don't do kitchens. Make him cook for us."

"Sure," Matthew said. "I can make us lunch."

"Fine," Clyde said. "But you go with him, make sure he doesn't sneak out the back or call anybody."

Matthew stood up from the chair, trying to make standing look harder than it really was. He had been starting to think he was going to have to bait Clyde close to the chair. Being upright was a step in the right direction. He started to shuffle toward the kitchen.

"Hey," Clyde said. "Toss me the clicker before you go. Maybe some other channel has it."

Matthew reached back, picked up the remote, and flipped it onto the couch. Clyde picked it up and switched the set back on, settling back against the cushion as he began to flip. He paid no mind as Matthew and Bonnie walked to the kitchen.

Once there, she jumped up on the counter and crossed her legs. "Don't expect any help from me, mister," she said. "My mom spent half her life trying to get me to cook. I fucking hate kitchens."

"I don't need any help," Matthew said. He turned on the oven to preheat and turned the knob for one of the front burners as high as it would go. He got a baking sheet from the drawer under the oven, a box of fish sticks from the freezer, and a pouch of linguine and set them on the counter. "Tell me something. How much did he get from the gas station?"

Bonnie was chewing on a nail. "Like a hundred and fifty bucks. Everybody just uses their cards these days."

"So for that, he killed a man."

Bonnie shrugged. "If he goes back up, it'll be for at least fifteen years. He's no good at doing time."

Matthew started to open the food. Since Alex died, he'd been doing time of a sort himself. Waiting.

"Can't believe it's only lunchtime," Bonnie said. "It's gonna be forever before he wants to leave. Hey, you got any soda?"

"Diet Coke."

"Lemme have one."

He got a can from the refrigerator and passed it to her. Clyde bellowed from the living room. "Nothing on the other channels either. Everything okay in there?"

"Fine!" Bonnie yelled back. She stuck her tongue out in Clyde's direction and winked at Matthew. He smiled at her weakly and arranged the fish sticks on the baking sheet.

"He can be a pain, I know," she said. "Hey, tell me on the level. Why did you want to be outside at one?"

"Twenty after one," Matthew said automatically. He glanced at the clock on the wall. Fifty-seven minutes from now. He got the big pot from under the sink and put it under the faucet to fill. "I need to be out there to see the eclipse."

"Oh yeah, I heard about that," she said. She took a swig from the can. "It's supposed to be some big deal."

"It's the first eclipse in centuries to cross the entire American continent," Matthew said. "It will be the last total solar eclipse in America in my lifetime, and quite likely in yours." He took the full pot of water and set it on the hot burner. "The vast majority of people will never see one."

"So what's it gonna look like?"

Matthew crossed his arms and watched the stove. "It will look like a black disc sliding over the sun," he said. "If you're in the path of totality, it will cover the sun completely for a moment, and you'll be able to look directly at the solar corona. Then it will slide off the other side. The whole thing will last just a few minutes."

"Huh," she said. "And are we in the, what'd you say, path of totality?"

"We are," Matthew said. He kept his voice carefully controlled. "We are in it very precisely, as a matter of fact. That's why we bought this house forty years ago."

"Say what?"

"Alex took the long view," Matthew said. He was no longer talking to Bonnie, not really. "He plotted out the exact course the eclipse would take and found us a house damn near right on the center line. He said we would watch it together in our old age."

The water in the pot was beginning to bubble slightly.

"He didn't know he wouldn't be here," Matthew said. "He liked to talk about how on the day of the eclipse we'd be out in the backyard with our filtered glasses on, and the shadow would be racing toward us, all the way from Oregon, coming faster than the speed of sound."

The oven beeped, indicating that it was done preheating. The water in the pot was bubbling fiercely now.

"It should really be him here," Matthew said. "It was his dream."

"Hey," said Bonnie. "Shouldn't you be putting them noodles in?"

"But I'm here," Matthew said. He stepped forward, grasped the handle of the pot, and turned to fling the boiling water in Bonnie's face, past the arms she was raising too late to stop him.

There was a sickening hiss that was immediately lost in her screams. His own hand was burned from the handle, but he ignored it. He dropped the pot and stepped forward again. Bonnie was off the counter and falling to the floor, screaming hysterically, and he could hear Clyde yelling and feel the floor registering fast-approaching steps. Matthew reached over the convulsing girl and pulled the biggest knife from the rack on the counter where she had been sitting.

Too slow, he was thinking.

He was turning back to face the corner of the room as Clyde came around it, his mouth twisted in rage and surprise, the gun held straight out in front of him. Matthew saw the muzzle flash and felt something punch him hard in his right side, and then his left hand closed over Clyde's gun hand, pushing it off to the side, and the knife was coming up. He felt the shock of the gun going off twice more travel up his arm, and then the knife was past Clyde's defensive arm, and for a moment Matthew was back in basic, fifty years ago, learning about the things that a determined man can do with a blade.

The next thing he was aware of was being on the floor, with Clyde underneath him and an enormous dull pain from his right hip to his shoulder. He rolled away from the younger man and, with some difficulty, sat up. It was impossibly quiet. The knife was in Clyde's chest and a pool of blood was spreading out beneath him. He looked at Bonnie and saw that one of Clyde's panicked shots had caught her in the back of the head. It was a mess, but he'd seen worse.

He explored himself. The bullet had hit him high on the right side. The entry wound wasn't bleeding much. He couldn't tell if there was an exit wound. Breathing was tough, so he was guessing Clyde had done some damage to his lung. His hand was blistering where he grabbed the pot handle. Overall, he didn't think he was going to die. At least not immediately, and in—he looked at the clock—forty-four minutes he wouldn't give a damn anyway.

Remembering something, he leaned forward. It sent a twist of agony through his side, but he found the bottle of pills Clyde had shoved in his pocket. He transferred them to his own. He couldn't take any yet. He wasn't going to risk falling asleep.

It took him a solid ten minutes to get his feet securely under him. Much of his blue suit was now dark with blood, most of it Clyde's, but there was no time to do anything about that. He pulled his belt out of its loops and used it to secure a clean dishtowel over the entry wound. On his way to the back door, he got a cold can of soda and held it in his burned hand. No time for anything else. He'd been listening for sirens or cries outside but heard nothing. There was nobody around in the middle of the day on a Monday to hear a brief scream and a few muffled pops.

He stumbled down the three steps to the backyard. For a moment, he thought he'd gotten the time wrong after all and it was starting, but then he realized the darkness creeping in at the edge of his vision was his alone, not the world's. He shook his head and willed it away. The big two-person lounger was waiting in the middle of the yard. On the cast-iron table beside it were two pairs of dark glasses and another picture, he and Alex at the solar observatory in Arizona.

It seemed to take much longer than it should have to reach the chair. He half collapsed into it, remembering to put the glasses on before he looked up. There wasn't a cloud in the sky, and the sun was whole and round and perfect. He was on time.

"Alex," he said out loud.

Afterwards, there would be time, plenty of time to take the pills, to call the police, to go to the hospital, to answer questions. Or perhaps there wouldn't. Matthew was no longer thinking of Bonnie and Clyde. He was thinking of *Bonnie and Clyde*, the first tentative touch of hand to hand, all the years that followed. He was on time.

Above him, a section of the sun's perfect unbroken circle bulged inward and broke, and as the world grew dim, the great black circle made its steady progression into place.

Haven

I was sitting with Jess and Angie on the front porch at Haven, waiting for Mason Barnes to come try to kill his wife. He was running later than we'd expected, and my attention was wandering.

"If my legs were a little longer," I said, "I could put my heels up on the porch railing and tilt the chair onto its back legs and pull my hat down over my eyes."

Jess and Angie were sitting together on a bench swing a few feet to my right. Angie, focused on the long driveway leading down the hill, ignored me. Ignoring me was one of Angie's favorite pastimes. Jess snorted. "Only if by *a little longer* you mean ten inches," she said.

"It would look cooler when Mason shows up," I said. "Just sitting here in an old kitchen chair with all four legs on the floor makes it seem like I'm waiting on him."

"We are waiting on him."

"Sure, but why give him a big head about it?"

"Why do you want to look cool to a wife-beating drunk?" Angie asked.

"General principle of the thing," I said. "Better to look cool than not."

"You forgot how you're dressed," Jess pointed out. "It's a lost cause."

I was trying to think of someone who looked cool in a deputy's uniform when a cloud of dust lifted into the air down where the long gravel drive met the highway. A second later, we heard an engine coming.

"Here we go," Jess said. She stood up and cracked her knuckles, stretched her neck back and forth. She was wearing a tank top and a pair of denim shorts, and her arms and legs showed a lot of hard, defined muscle. The left side of her head was shaved down to a light blond fuzz, and a curtain of neon-purple hair hung down on her right. Sometimes people get distracted by the hair and miss the muscle. That's a mistake.

"Go easy, champ," I said. "We've got fourteen different charges to hang on him."

"He'll walk," Angie said. "They always walk."

That wasn't true, but I let it go. Angie's earned the white-hot anger that keeps her moving through the day, from one crisis to the next. That anger turned the sprawling compound her family had owned for a century and a half into Haven, a shelter for battered women and kids. The house we were sitting in front of had been built by men who got rich when Goldwood was one of the centers of Maine's lumber industry. From what I knew of them, their women and their children were essentially trophies. Every time I came out here, I wondered what they would think of what their fiery lesbian progeny has made.

A fairly new blue pickup I'd never seen before came through the trees where the driveway pierced them, barreling along a little faster than was probably prudent on the loose, dry gravel. I might be able to tack grand theft auto onto Mason's laundry list of recent felonies. The truck sliced around the curve and slid to a stop about ten yards off, with the driver's door facing us. It flew open before the truck was completely still, and Mason stepped unsteadily out. He hadn't slowed at the sight of my cruiser parked alongside the barn, and he didn't seem bothered by my uniform now. He certainly showed no signs of thinking I looked cool, so apparently the vote on that was unanimous. A tire iron dangled from his right hand as he slammed the door and peered up at the three of us, his eyes red and sunken in his pale, bearded face.

"Looking good, Mason," I said. "A credit to your family and upbringing. You're under arrest."

"Fuck you, Wade," he said.

I nodded. "Eloquently expressed, but you're still under arrest." I hadn't moved from the chair, but I'd popped the strap at the top of my holster. Mason was just the kind of slow-thinking asshole to show you a tire iron and then suddenly remember a piece tucked under his shirttails.

"I wanna see Brenda," he said. He took a step toward the stairs. Out of the corner of my eye, I watched Jess start to bounce a little, shifting her weight from foot to foot.

"Not a chance," Angie said. "You put her in the hospital last time you saw her, you inbred piece of shit."

"Fuck you too, you dyke bitch," Mason said. He raised his voice to a holler. "Brenda, baby, you in there? C'mon out, honey."

"Honey," Jess said, giving me a look.

"You like that?" I asked her.

"Classy."

"Well, you know, Mason's a classy guy. Always has been."

"That's just what I thought when I saw Brenda's X-rays," Jess said. "Mason, that classy, classy guy."

Mason was staring at her, his lip curled. Now that he'd been out of the truck for a minute, I could smell him, even at this distance. Old clothes, dip, spilled beer, unwashed hair. I'd been looking for him for four days, ever since he took the frustrations of his dimming world out on his wife and then ran off into the humid night. From the reek of him, he'd spent those four days in backseats and shallow ditches. A couple of hours ago, he turned up at the body shop where he worked and beat the living hell out of the owner, telling him Brenda was next. His next stop had been the small county hospital, where he broke a nurse's nose and a security guard's arm before being convinced Brenda was no longer there. Mason didn't have much of an IQ, but he'd lived in Goldwood County all his life, and he knew where a woman in Brenda's situation would probably end up. Haven.

Now that he was finally here, he stabbed a filthy finger in the air at Jess. "You don't know me, bitch."

"Actually, she does, Mason," I said. "She went to school with us, remember?"

"I'm gonna be real fucking hurt if you don't remember me, Mason," Jess said. "I'm the chick who broke a chair on your face one day in the lunchroom."

"It's that shoddy damn furniture they put in the public schools," I explained, directing my comment to Angie. "Shameful."

Angie shook her head, but didn't take her eyes off Mason. She'd moved to the front door of the house and was standing with her back to it and her arms folded across her chest. "Would you please just arrest him and end this?" she said.

Mason didn't like all three of us talking. He had to swivel his head back and forth, and he didn't know which of us to threaten. He settled for yelling again. "Brenda! Get your ass out here!"

"Don't forget 'honey,'" Jess said. "Get your ass out here, *honey*."

"Oh, fuck you, cunt," Mason said. We'd just about exhausted his vocabulary. He started forward, only a little unsteady, heading directly for the steps up to the porch.

"Last warning, Mason," I said.

"Gonna shoot me, fucker?" He was almost to the stairs, looking at me.

"No need," I said.

Jess vaulted over the porch railing, swinging her legs around in a quick, compact arc. Focused on me, Mason saw the movement too late. He started to raise the tire iron, but Jess's foot in its steel-toed work boot caught him in his left temple, and he staggered several steps to his right, fighting for balance. Jess landed easily and followed him, and as he righted himself and started to swing the iron wildly at her, she stepped inside his reach and brought the heel of her hand up sharp and fast under his chin. The blow crossed his eyes, and he fell backward, sprawling into the grass.

I was standing now, at the top of the stairs. My right hand rested on the butt of my gun. "Stay down, Mason," I said. "She kicked your ass twelve years ago, and that was before she enlisted and really went pro."

Mason was on his hands and knees and didn't seem to be hearing me. Whatever he was flying on was keeping him conscious. Jess stood seven or eight feet back from him and waited as he shook his head and worked his way painfully upward, wobbly as a newborn colt. He still had the iron, and as soon as his feet were under him, he roared and charged her, raising the iron back behind his head and swinging it in a long circle. Jess caught the iron and stepped to the side as he came, twisting it out of his hand and sticking out a leg to trip him and send him windmilling wildly back to the ground. I winced at the sound of the hard-packed earth knocking the wind out of him. Jess tossed the iron behind her and watched him struggling to get up again.

"I can do this for hours, asshole," she said.

"I can't," I said. "I'm gonna have a shitload of paperwork to fill out when I haul him in. Wrap this up, would you?"

Jess grinned. "You never let me have any fun." She tucked her purple hair behind her ear, walked over to where Mason had gotten to his hands and knees, and brought her boot down hard on the fingers of his right hand. I heard several small snaps, and Mason let out a howl of pure agony and rage, rolling to his side and pulling the injured hand tight against his chest. Behind me, Angie sucked in her breath. Jess crouched behind Mason and put her hand almost tenderly on his shoulder. "Be a while before you hit anybody with that hand again, right?"

Mason's yowl settled into anguished sobs. "Bitch," he moaned. "My fucking hand."

"Jess," I said. "Enough."

She looked up at me. We've been best friends since fifth grade, and I've seen every mood and thought she's ever had in her life play itself out in her eyes. The way she looked now, I seriously thought for a moment I would have to pull my gun on her to keep Mason alive.

She saw me thinking it and shook her head. "He's not worth it," she said. She held out her hand, and I tossed her my cuffs as I started down the steps. She rolled Mason onto his front, not gently, and against his protests pulled his hands back around and cuffed him. Three of the fingers on his right hand were swollen and bent at ugly angles, and though he swore viciously again as the arm was bent behind him, all the fight was gone.

Jess and I hauled him to his feet, but the second we let go, he dropped back to his knees, letting his head hang down almost into the dirt. "Bitch crippled me," he said. He sounded like he was about eight years old and whining for justice on the playground. "You saw it, Wade."

I fought down the impulse to pull him up again, this time by his hair. "Gee, Mason, all I saw was you resisting arrest and then Miz Hendrick here graciously stepping in to assist an officer in completing his duty." I looked up at Angie, who'd come down to the foot of the stairs. "That what you saw, uninvolved bystander?"

She nodded. Behind her, the curtain in a front window twitched, and I saw Brenda Barnes looking out at us. The entire left side of her face was still the purple and red of deep bruises, and there was no emotion on her face that I wanted to put a name to.

I was pretty sure she didn't think any of us looked very cool.

* * *

Before I could even get to the shitload of paperwork, I had to take Mason to the hospital, where the entire staff was all too aware of the damage done on his previous visit. They didn't seem to be in any special hurry to get his hand taken care of, or to find the painkillers he kept screaming for. I'm not sure he ever did get the painkillers, actually. They finally got around to setting the fingers and wrapping his whole hand in a cast that made him look like he had a softball at the end of his arm. When they were done with him, it was off to the county lockup and then, finally, inevitably, back to the office, well past what should have been the end of an honest working day.

"New postcard on your desk, Wade," Sally said as I came into the building.

"Good evening to you, too, Sal."

"Don't shoot the messenger," she said. Sally's been working the reception and dispatch desk for the county cops since my earliest conscious memories. My father used to say that the first settlers in the area came across her sitting in a field one day and built the police station around her.

My father, William Finch, became a deputy in Goldwood County the day he turned eighteen, and was sheriff by the time he was thirty. He was forty-seven when he responded to a 911 call from the house of Sean Kelly, a bar owner my dad had known since they were on a Little League team together. Inside the house, he found Kelly sitting nude on the couch, drinking straight from a bottle of Jim Beam. Kelly's wife, his teenaged son and daughter, and the daughter's boyfriend were on the floor in front of him. All four of them were naked, hog-tied, and shot in the head. Kelly still had the gun in his right hand, held against his naked thigh. The barrel was warm enough that the skin of his leg had blistered a little.

Dad played it by the book. He took the gun away from an unresisting Kelly, cuffed him, and checked the victims for signs of life, though I'm sure he knew that was futile. He found a robe and a pair of sweatpants and put Kelly in them and waited for backup. When three deputies arrived, he had them watch and record him while he recited the date and time and read Kelly his rights straight off the Miranda card in his wallet. He put the wallet back in his pocket and squatted in front of Kelly, still sitting on the couch.

"Do you understand the rights I've read to you, sir?" he asked.

"Sure," Kelly said. His eyes were clear and alert, the deputies all agreed later.

"Did you shoot these people, Sean?"

"Yep," Kelly said. He didn't hesitate.

"Why'd you do that?" my father asked.

Kelly smiled. "Never liked any one of 'em," he said. "Cocksuckers talked too much."

There's thirty-seven seconds of silence then. I've timed the recording. It doesn't sound like much, but it's a long time to sit through ambient noise. Finally, there's the sound of my father letting out air through his nose and the squeak of his gun belt as he stands.

"Secure the scene," he said. "Call the coroner and have Sally ask the state for a forensic team. I'll take Mr. Kelly in."

He put Kelly in his car and drove off, and for the next seventy-two hours, that was the last anybody knew. The two of them simply vanished.

I'd been on the force a year at that point. Like every other cop in the county, I spent the next three days scouring the twenty-three miles between the Kelly house and the county jail, looking for any trace of my father, Kelly, or the car.

It was a state cop who finally found the car in an abandoned sawmill, fifty miles and two counties away. Kelly had been tied to a beam and shot six times. My father's uniform was neatly folded on the hood of his car, next to his badge and emptied sidearm. A page from his notebook was skewered on the pin of his badge.

"I quit," it said, followed by his slashing, incomprehensible signature.

* * *

Now, seven years later, I was at my desk in the sheriff's office looking at the same signature at the bottom of a postcard, inside a clear plastic evidence bag. The picture side of the postcard showed some kind of stork standing on one leg in a swamp. The lower right corner said "Greetings from the Everglades!" in flowing yellow script. The other side was postmarked three days ago in Grand Rapids, Michigan. In blue ink, my father had neatly printed the address of the sheriff's office and then, in the space reserved for the message:

Kelly's son was probably going to be trouble in a few years. I busted him a couple of times for vandalism and underage drinking. Maybe he would have grown out of that. I did. Or maybe by now he'd be in prison.

The first postcard showed up a month after the deaths, after the APBs and the national media frenzy and the county's decision to hire a new sheriff from someplace as far out of town as they could manage. It was a confession, a few sentences confirming that he'd killed Kelly and acted alone, and it was mailed from Texas, though the picture was of the St. Louis arch. I thought that was going to be the last we ever heard of him, but the postcards kept coming, sometimes once a month, sometimes three or four in a week. Never the same postmark twice, never an image that matched the postmark. Never any kind of salutation or greeting. Just a few brief sentences, always about Kelly or his family.

"This one makes forty-seven."

I looked up. Cheryl Hernandez, the sheriff, was leaning against the desk next to mine.

"I don't keep count," I said. "Appreciate you letting me see them."

"A man deserves to know about his father," she said. Cheryl had been a homicide detective in San Francisco before Goldwood County hired her away. We'd never discussed the fact that she'd plainly been hired because she was as unlike my father as possible. "We're done with it, so just get it off to the FBI once you've looked at it."

"Sure," I said.

Cheryl shifted her weight a little against the desk and looked around. Zeke Robbins was the only other person in the big squad room, and he was down at the other end, fooling around with the coffee maker and making hushed, urgent noises into his cell phone. She looked back at me. "I hear Mason Barnes had a rough afternoon."

"Wasn't a lot of fun for me, either."

"I bet it was fun for Jess Hendrick."

I didn't say anything to that.

Cheryl sighed and stood. "She's gonna need to come in and sign a statement. Angie, too."

"I'm expecting Jess tomorrow morning, Angie probably later in the day. You know they won't both leave Haven at the same time."

"What about Barnes's wife?"

"I don't think she saw anything. I'm dead sure Angie's gonna make sure she stays put out there until Mason's breaking up rocks."

"Christ, Finch," she said. "How fucking long do you think it's been since Maine put prisoners on chain gangs? You need to freshen up your references." She rapped her knuckles sharply on the edge of my desk. "And you need to get that lunatic Hendrick on a short leash before she crosses the line."

I wanted to promise her that Jess would never cross that line, but I couldn't. It's what I would have said about my father, right up until he picked up the phone one day, put on his badge, and drove out to Sean Kelly's house. Who the hell was I to make promises?

* * *

I got home after dark and found that Ronnie had come by and taken the last of his stuff, mostly winter clothes and the final crate of his treasured vinyl collection. The note he left on the kitchen table was brief and chilly. I crumpled it up and threw it in the trash. Then I pulled it out of the trash, folded it neatly, and stuck it in the drawer where I kept my utility bills and bank statements. I poured myself a shot of bourbon and sat on the living room sofa.

The TV was tuned to a reality show about a group of people competing to find a hidden idol on some island. I didn't have the energy to change the channels, and I kept losing track of the rules. After a while it seemed like I was on the island and Mason and Ronnie were taking turns chasing me around. I gave it up and pulled out my phone.

Barrelhouse? I texted Jess.

She must have been awake. It was less than a minute before the screen lit up with a little picture. Thumbs-up.

* * *

Twenty minutes later, I was at a picnic table on the back deck at the Barrelhouse, looking out over the dark waters of Three Pine Lake. The building had been a bar for generations, under a dozen different names and twice that many owners. Once upon a time, Sean Kelly had owned it. I was trying to remember what it had been called then when Jess came out the back door. She had a metal pail filled with ice and six bottles of beer.

"What was this place called when Kelly owned it?" I asked.

She sat down across from me and handed me one of the beers. "The Scuttlebutt."

"That's right." I took a pull. "Stupid damn name. Angie asleep?"

"She's in bed, anyway. She doesn't sleep much."

"I get that," I said.

We looked at the lake for a while and the big clear sky. There was a full moon bright enough to read by. We were the only ones out on the deck.

"I feel like there were more lightning bugs around when we were kids," I said after a while.

"Maybe," Jess said.

"Ronnie picked up the last of his stuff today," I said. "Left a note."

Jess blew some air out of her nose. She touched her nearly empty bottle to mine, drained it, and pulled another out of the pail. "That sucks. It's gonna suck for a while. But there will be somebody else."

"Sure," I said. "Gay guys are lining up to date a cop in the middle of nowhere, Maine."

"I found Angie," Jess said. "And everybody loved the cop in the Village People."

I slapped the table. "There it is," I said. "I knew there was somebody who looked cool dressed as a cop."

Jess laughed. I took a drink and thought about telling her about my father's latest postcard. I swear that's what I meant to say, but it's not what came out when I opened my mouth.

"Was there a moment today where you were ready to kill him, Jess?"

She looked down at the bottle and rolled it back and forth in her hands. She was quiet for a long time. I listened to an owl announcing itself from somewhere around the lake off to the left.

"You know what really scares me about assholes like Mason Barnes?" she said finally. She didn't wait for an answer. "It's that on some level I get them. Stuck out here a hundred miles from anything, no money, no real jobs, no hope, nothing to do but drink and fuck around and feel your life going away a day at a time." She took a swallow. "Get to a point where you want to feel like there's somebody on the rung under you. Somebody you get to shit on."

"No excuse."

"I fucking know it isn't." She put the bottle down. "Yeah, I wanted to kill him. There have been a bunch of them I've wanted to kill. You wanted to kill him, too. Don't think I didn't see that."

I half shrugged. I felt like that was as close as I could get to admitting it.

"Yeah," she said.

"So why didn't you do it?"

She interlaced her fingers behind her neck and looked up into the sky.

"Man, I thought you were just going to be crying in your beer about Ronnie. If I'd known you were going to be getting all touchy-feely on me, I would have stayed in bed with my woman."

I held up my hands. "Okay. Question withdrawn."

"No, listen," she said. "I'm not going to give you any bullshit about law and order or tell you that if I sink to his level and kill him, he wins." She brought her head back down and looked me in the eye. "You were there. Angie was there. And I don't want to end up in a place where all I can do is send the two of you postcards."

I didn't say anything. I looked at her.

"We didn't kill him today," she said. "Take the win."

We sat for a while after that, mostly just looking at the lake and listening to the strange, disconnected sounds of insects and birds and distant splashes. We didn't drink anymore.

Eventually, Jess stood up and picked up the pail. "I should get back to Haven," she said. "Hey, how about you and me drive down to Fenway this weekend?"

"You're just looking for an excuse to stop at Bob's Clam Hut."

"Guilty as charged," she said. "But you get a game out of it."

"Sox are in Anaheim this weekend," I said. "But we can go get you your clam cake anyway."

"God. You are so fucking easy." She punched me on the shoulder and walked away.

I stayed out on the deck until the bartender came out to tell me they were closing. Walking the ten minutes home, I wondered how long it would be before Mason Barnes had his next beer. I didn't think he'd ever lift one again without feeling an ache in his fingers that he'd never really get used to. That was fine with me. At least I didn't kill him today.

When I got home, I took Ronnie's note out of my paperwork drawer and burned it in the kitchen sink. If I dreamed that night, I have no memory of it.

Golden Lives

I knew Officer Whitney Lewis would be waiting for me when my flight got into Sacramento. I didn't know she'd be one of the most beautiful women I'd ever seen. Neither her uniform nor her severe buzzcut could disguise the lithe way she moved, or how the light found her cheekbones. Seeing her should have been diverting, but it just made me angry. Ike would have been awed by her, would have elbowed me in the ribs, thinking he was being subtle. Ogling hot women: just one more item on the endless list of things my little brother would never do again.

Standing at the gate, she noticed the curves of plastic and steel where my right foot used to be and then immediately switched her gaze to my face as she came forward. "Private Annalee Lincoln? Whitney Lewis. We spoke a couple of days ago. I thought I'd give you a ride into town and we could talk. Do you have more luggage?"

"Just this," I said, lifting the roll-on bag I'd been living out of for the last three months.

She hesitated for half a beat. "Are you okay for a short walk?"

"Sure. I'm a wonder of modern science."

"All right," she said. She started off, and I fell in step beside her. "I didn't know you'd been wounded."

"I never came within a thousand miles of combat," I said. "I was working in the motor pool in Frankfort and a faulty jack dropped an armored Humvee on me."

"Jesus. When was this?"

"About four months ago. Spent a month in the hospital, got a medical discharge. Since then, I've been kicking around Europe trying to figure out what to do next. And then you called. Officer, what the hell happened to my brother?"

"Let's talk in the car," she said.

Her city cruiser was parked in a security lot near baggage claim. Lewis put my bag in the trunk, nodding me into the passenger seat. She pulled into traffic, driving smoothly and confidently. "I've got your uncle's address."

"I want to see Ike first," I said.

Again, there was the barest pause. Whitney Lewis liked to think before she talked. "I'm sorry, Private Lincoln, I assumed you knew. Ike has been cremated."

I snapped my head around. "Cremated? I thought I was going to make it in time for his funeral. It's only been, what, three days?"

"Your uncle said that that's what Ike wanted. No ceremony." Lewis kept her eyes on the road, sweeping her gaze back and forth across the lanes in front of us.

"What *Ike* wanted? Bullshit. The old bastard just didn't want to lay out any cash."

"I can't claim to know Mr. Lincoln's motives," Lewis said carefully.

"I just told you his motives." I looked out the window at the city I hadn't seen in almost three years. Except for the trees, and that big open California sky, we could have been anywhere in America. All the same signs. All the same cars. All the things I hadn't wanted to come back to. "That miserable prick never gave a damn about either of us. He just had to take us to get what little money our parents had when they died. He pissed that away quick enough. What he didn't drink, he gambled."

"Are we talking abuse, Private? Or just general neglect?"

"Call me Annalee," I said. I leaned my head back and closed my eyes. "I'd call it abuse, sure. We both got more than our share of bruises. He broke Ike's arm once." I opened my eyes and looked at the roof of the car. "I'm not here to talk history. You need to help me understand what happened."

"That's what I was hoping you could do for me." Lewis signaled, and the police car glided onto an exit from the freeway. "On the surface, it's clear enough. A security guard found Ike trying to break into a storage unit. He ran, so the guard chased him, and he went into the street and was hit by a bus."

I don't know what to call the sound I made when she said that.

"I'm sorry. I don't mean to be insensitive. For what it's worth, it was quick. I don't think he knew what happened."

"That's not Ike," I said. We were in the old neighborhood now. Del Paso Heights. A lot of it looks calm, middle-class, maybe even suburban. You have to look closer to notice the fences, the vacant lots, the graffiti. You have to live here to know which blocks you shouldn't walk after dark. "You know this place. You know there are gangs here. Easy money, if you want it. Ike could have gone that way. He never did."

"I know." Now that we were on the surface streets, Lewis was even more alert. She was calm, but her head was on a swivel, and she drove slowly. "I've talked to his teachers, his friends, his coworkers at the pizza place. They all say the same thing, and he had no record at all."

"So one day he just decides he's a thief?"

"It doesn't track," she agreed. "I was hoping he'd said something to you."

That stung. "I didn't call as often as I should have," I said. "I was trying to get away. Stay away. I thought he'd leave too, when he could." I let out a long breath. "I should have been here."

"Don't," Whitney Lewis said. "Whatever this is, it isn't on you."

My palms were itching. I needed out of this car. We turned a corner, and the sign up ahead looked like deliverance. "Christ, the Night Owl is still open?"

"Oh yes," Lewis said. "I spend a lot of time parked outside it. 911 calls more nights than not."

"Drop me there," I said.

"You're kidding."

I undid my seatbelt. "I can't face Uncle Ty right now. I'd probably assault him, so think of this as crime prevention. We can finish this conversation over a beer, can't we?"

"I can't," Lewis said. "This is my lunch break. I'm back on duty in twenty minutes. But I'll come in with you."

The Night Owl hadn't changed since I'd left. In some ancient past, it had been a family diner. Now there was plywood over the windows and dim lighting and a pool table with a long scar down one side of the felt. The few customers sat alone, staring into their glasses. A bartender I didn't know gave me a beer and a shot of Jack and Lewis a bottled water. If he was bothered at having a uniformed cop in the place, he didn't show it. We sat at a table in a back corner, and I took a long pull on the beer and made a face.

"I forgot about American beer," I said.

"You've been away a while," Lewis said.

"Not as long as I was hoping," I said. I drank again. "I feel caged here."

"How so?"

I looked around the room. I would have sworn that the same bulbs were burned out. I'd fallen down a gravity well back into the past, back into my own personal hell.

Except now it was worse. Ike was gone.

"I said Ike wasn't a thief," I said. "So let me tell you what he was. After our folks passed, Ike started trying to map out our family tree. At first, he was just looking for somebody other than Uncle Ty to take us, but he got into it. Spent hours at the library, over the years. He was so damned smart."

Lewis sat very still, listening.

"One of the last times we talked before I left for basic, he told me he found our great-great-whatever-number-grandfather. A guy who came to California in a wagon train in the 1850s. I said we live in a cesspool, and the guy should have stayed where he was. But Ike said that California used to be the dream, the place where people would go to live golden lives. That was what he said, *golden lives*. I laughed, but he was serious. And he said that the reason everything sucks now, the reason there are so many people shooting each other, and so many people like Uncle Ty just wallowing in sad, messed up lives, is because we ran into the ocean and all that momentum and energy died, and now we don't have any frontier. No place to go. Nothing to do but rot away." I picked up the beer glass, found it was empty, and downed the shot. I know most people drink the shot first. I'm contrary that way.

"You found someplace to go," Lewis said.

"I thought Ike would too," I said. "That brain of his. I thought any day he'd be calling to tell me…tell me something. Something he'd come up with."

Lewis stood up. "I have to go on duty. Will you be all right here?"

"Why are you doing this?" I asked.

She cocked her head. "What do you mean?"

"I've been around a little," I said. "Uniforms don't investigate. There should be somebody in plain clothes with a gold badge talking to me, and Ike shouldn't have been cremated so quick. There isn't actually an investigation going on, is there?"

This hesitation was a little longer.

"No," she said. "The department doesn't know I've been talking to people. As far as they're concerned, Ike's a petty thief who died in an accident."

"But you think there's something more."

"I do," she said. "I can't say why. Some cases just stay with you. Some people. Ike's one." She took a card out of her breast pocket and put it on the table. "My personal cell is on the back. Please call me after you see your uncle. Or if you think of anything else."

I put the card in my pocket and nodded.

As soon as Lewis left, the bartender came over.

"Let's do the same again twice," I told him. "But skip the beers."

I was on the second shot when I remembered that Lewis still had my suitcase.

* * *

I cracked my eyes open and light pounded my brain with sledgehammer force. My mouth tasted like something had died in it, and from the way my stomach felt, I'd swallowed the corpse. The rough fabric under my cheek suggested a couch rather than a bed. I propped myself up on my elbow and forced my eyes open wider. A vague shape across the room wavered, shifted, and resolved itself into Whitney Lewis. She was sitting in an easy chair a few feet away, wearing a t-shirt and shorts and watching me over the rim of a coffee cup.

"Aw, hell," I breathed.

"Well," she said, "I guess that answers the question of whether you're happy to see me."

I waved my hand. "No, no. It's just I was hoping I dreamed it all, and Ike was okay." I sank back onto the sofa, realizing I was under a blanket. "Jet lag and Jack don't mix," I said. "Is this your place? How did I get here?"

"The bartender called me near the end of my shift," she said. "He saw you take my card. He got it out of your pocket somehow and told me that he wanted you out. Apparently, you were alternating between threatening to assault anyone who came near you and trying to recruit people to go beat up your uncle."

"Nice of you not to arrest me," I said. I took a peek under the blanket. I was still dressed.

"Relax," she said. "I don't molest drunks."

"That's kind of a shame," I said without thinking. Immediately, I felt my face go warm. "Can I get some of that coffee? Maybe an aspirin?"

"Sure," she said. She got up and walked around the corner, and I levered myself into a sitting position. In a moment, she came back and handed me a mug and a couple of pills.

"Thanks," I said. "You took off my foot."

"I assumed you'd be more comfortable. I hope it wasn't an imposition."

"Not at all. It just makes most people squeamish."

"I'm a cop. We don't squeam."

"Good point," I said. I saw my suitcase against the wall. "You've been very kind. If I could maybe use your bathroom and change, I'll get out of your hair."

"No rush. I'd like to know what you're planning to do."

"Been thinking on it. I can't put off seeing Ty forever. Maybe he can tell me something that will make sense."

Lewis put her coffee down. "He wasn't much help to us. Frankly, I think both times I talked to him he was half wasted."

"I'd be surprised if he wasn't."

"How are you going to get around?"

I lifted my hands in a half-shrug. "I assume the buses still run. I guess I could rent a car. I've got some savings from the last few years."

"No need." She picked up a ring with a couple of keys on it and tossed it to me. "Don't expect luxury. It's a little green Civic with rust spots."

"You're trusting me with your car?"

"Am I going to see it parked outside the Night Owl later?"

"No. I'm just going to talk to Ty. And then maybe go see where it happened. Where is this storage place?"

She told me where to find it, out by the Interstate. "It's pretty new," she said. "Fully automated, three stories of units. There's a machine like an ATM in the lobby, and you just use it to rent a unit, a month at a time. They have one of the local private security firms do a walk-through several times a day."

"What would have happened if Ike actually got into the unit?"

"The security crew would have called us," she said. "It's standard procedure if they even find so much as a broken lock. That takes it from misdemeanor trespass to felony B&E."

Ike with a felony. Unimaginable.

"Okay," I said. "I can't thank you enough for all this."

"We both want to know what happened, and you can spend time on it that I can't," she said. She glanced at a clock. "I've got to get dressed and go. I'm working a double today. Take whatever time you need here, and feel free to use the shower. Lock up when you leave and call me when you can."

* * *

Two hours later, I was feeling almost human as I parked Lewis's car in front of the house where I spent several miserable years. Unlike the Night Owl, Ty's house was changed, and not for the better. The chain link fence around the yard was sagging, and the yard itself was an explosion of uncontrolled weeds. The paint was peeling off the siding, and some shingles were missing. A few of the houses on the block looked recently renovated. Ty's neighbors probably weren't thrilled with his impact on local property values.

I was at the porch steps when the door opened, and my uncle stepped out, looking even rougher than the house. He had always been scrawny, but now his thin frame was stooped inside his unbuttoned plaid shirt. He'd lost a couple of teeth, and the ones left were an ugly shade of brown. He hadn't shaved in several days and hadn't shaved cleanly in years.

"Annalee," he said. "Ike told me about the leg. Hope you got paid on it."

"I'm touched by your concern," I said. "The get-well card must have gotten lost in the mail."

He didn't seem to hear me. His gaze wandered out over the street, and he was swaying a little. It's never too early in the day as far as Ty's concerned.

"Guess you'd better come in," he said. He turned and disappeared into the dim hallway. I took a deep breath and followed.

Even as a kid, Ike had kept the house clean. Ty didn't give a damn how it looked, and I was too angry to care, but my brother couldn't stand a mess. He'd been gone four days, and already Ty's natural chaos was overtaking the order Ike had imposed. Empty bottles and food wrappers were scattered around the living room, and there was a smell that spoke of some deeper rot beyond Ike's reach. Ty shuffled to the battered recliner he'd always favored and reached for the bottle on the stool next to it. The TV that had once been in the room was gone.

I leaned against the wall. The place was bringing back my nausea.

"Do you have Ike's ashes?" I asked.

He shook his head. "Haven't gotten to it," he said. "I gotta pay first, for the cremation and the little vase I picked out for him."

"Well, there's a bill I'm going to end up paying," I said. I didn't really mind. If they gave the ashes to Ty, he would lose them or throw them away.

Ty scowled. "You don't gotta be so nasty," he said. "You oughta be nice to me. I brought you up."

"If that's what you want to call it," I said. "I mostly remember you beating me down. Me and Ike both."

"Had to toughen you," he said. His gaze caromed off my face every few seconds and veered away. "Wasn't nothing to the way my old man was to me."

"You're a saint," I said. "You need to tell me what happened to Ike."

Ty shrugged violently. "Got hit by a bus," he said. "Bad luck. That's all."

"Like hell." I thought about the missing TV, the house falling apart despite Ike's efforts. "You having money problems, old man? Aren't you still on disability?"

"Ain't enough," he said. He looked up into the corner of the room. "I'm a little behind with Alton."

He didn't need to say a last name. Alton, the neighborhood bookie and loan shark, was a bald, barrel-chested sociopath with a worse temper than any drill sergeant and a seemingly limitless supply of sadistic sons and nephews to collect debts and impose stiff late penalties.

"How much is a little?"

"None of your concern."

"We both know you're going to tell me. Save us some time."

He shifted. "Ninety K."

I reeled a little. "How in the *hell* did you get that deep in a hole?"

"Bad bets," he said. "Loans. Interest. You know how Alton works."

"Sell the house," I said.

He laughed. "Bank owns the house. Has for years. I'll be out on my ass one of these months pretty soon."

"So what's the plan, Ty?"

He shook his head and looked away.

"I know you've got some kind of scheme." A dark suspicion dawned on me. "It wouldn't have anything to do with robbing a storage unit, would it?"

He bit his lip. The hand holding his bottle shook. I came off the wall and in two steps was on him. I yanked the bottle out of his hand and hurled it against the wall, pulled him up out of the chair, and shoved him chest-first to the floor, twisting his arm up behind his back. He cursed and tried to squirm away, but there was no real fight in him. I wasn't the little girl scared of his belt anymore. "Talk," I said. "Or swear to god, I'll break it."

"Lamar," he gasped out.

"Lamar Jackson?"

He nodded frantically.

Jackson was one of Ty's few friends. He was a little younger, a little smarter, a little more capable of actually acting on his wild visions. When I was seventeen, Jackson came into my bedroom one night, and I put the steak knife I kept under my pillow into his thigh. He didn't come to the house again while I was there, but I knew from Ike that he'd been around since I left.

"Okay," I said. "Tell me about Lamar."

"He's got a contact in Mexico," Ty said. "Oxy. Tons of it. He showed me the storage unit where he keeps it."

"So your master plan to save your pathetic life was to steal from your best friend."

Ty was crying now, his nose running onto the carpet. "Had to do something. You know Alton. He'd take me to Death Valley, damn it."

Legend had it that Alton and three of his sons once grabbed a man who owed them too much money for too long, threw him in a trunk, and drove overnight to Death Valley. There, they stripped the man nude, staked him out in the rising sun, and spent the day sitting in the shade, drinking bottled water and watching him fry. I thought it was bullshit, but lots of people who knew Alton repeated the story as gospel.

"So you sent Ike." I pushed his arm up further. Ty screamed and clawed at the floor.

"He wanted to do it! He wanted to help me!"

"No," I said. "You're just too chickenshit to do your own dirty work." Suddenly disgusted at touching him, I pushed myself up and stepped back, resisting the urge to kick his ribs. Ty curled into himself, clutching his shoulder, moaning.

"Tell me the unit number," I said.

His eyes opened. "You gonna help me?"

"Sure, old man. I'll help you."

* * *

The storage place was easy to find. The units on the ground floor had outside doors you could drive right up to, but the second and third floors were interior corridors lined with smaller units. I went in and walked around. There were padlocks on the doors of the rented units. I opened an empty one and looked inside. Just a cinderblock box the size of a closet with an overhead light. 257, the number Ty had given me, had a padlock. There were cameras, but they were only in the lobby and at the entrance to each floor. None of them had a view of 257.

On my way out, I read the directions at the rental station. You had to scan a driver's license, then pay with cash or credit card. Two hundred bucks a month for one of the small upstairs units.

The whole time I was there, I didn't see another person. I went outside and sat in Whitney Lewis's Civic across the street and waited. Waiting is one thing the military will make you expert at.

After ninety-three minutes, a car with a security logo pulled into the lot and drove the perimeter, hugging the building. It parked by the main entrance, and a man in a tan uniform got out of the passenger side and went in.

I wondered if he was the man who chased Ike into the street.

He was inside for eight minutes. He came out and the car drove away, off to whatever their next checkpoint was. I marked the time.

In exactly an hour and forty-five minutes, they came back and did the same thing.

Okay.

I got onto the Interstate and drove until I saw a Home Depot. I paid cash for two padlocks, the strongest pair of bolt cutters they had, a small flashlight, a package of plastic gloves, a pair of canvas work pants, and a big windbreaker with the store's logo on the back.

I was back across the street from the storage in time to confirm another hour and forty-five-minute cycle. It's nice to see that kind of discipline. After that, I had some time to kill. I found a sports bar attached to a mall and sat there for a while, working my way through chips and salsa and several glasses of soda. They were showing basketball games on the big screens.

I wondered how much money was passing through Alton's hands as the scores mounted.

When it had been dark for a while, I drove to Del Paso Heights and parked half a block from Ty's.

The key I had still worked. Wearing gloves, I eased the front door open and listened. As I'd expected, Ty's foundation-shaking snores were coming from the living room. He'd always been dead to the world once he went to sleep, most often simply passing out in his chair. I shielded the flashlight with my fingers and made my way to the kitchen. Ty still kept his wallet in the second drawer. I rifled through it and found his driver's license and put it in my pocket. On my way back to the front door, I picked up three of his empty bottles.

Back to the storage place. I waited twenty-seven minutes, and the security men showed, still on schedule, exactly three and a half hours after the last time I'd seen them. As soon as they left, I put on the windbreaker and flipped the hood up to cover as much as my face as possible. The work pants would mask my mechanical foot, and I put on another pair of the gloves. I used Ty's license and some more of my rapidly dwindling cash to rent unit 233. I went up to the unit and put Ty's empty bottles in a corner and one of my new padlocks on the door. All told, I was there less than fifteen minutes.

Back to Ty's again. I was exhausted, but I was almost done. Ty was still out cold. I replaced his license and took the windbreaker to the bedroom he almost never used and dropped it on the closet floor. He'd never notice it, and if he did, he'd just assume he picked it up somewhere and forgot about it.

✳ ✳ ✳

Whitney's double shift ended at two in the morning. I was dozing in a rocker on the front porch of her little bungalow when her cruiser glided to a stop at the curb. She came up the steps, looking tired but still better than anybody had a right to look at that hour.

"You never called," she said. "I've been a little worried."

"I'm sorry," I said. "I thought I'd tell you about it in person."

"You could have let yourself in," she said. "You didn't have to wait out here."

"Seemed like it would be an imposition."

The smile she gave me was the best thing I'd seen in months. "It wouldn't."

"Well," I said. I stood up. "If you think you can put me up for another night."

We sat in the living room, me on the couch, her on the chair, both of us with glasses of wine. I told her about Ty, and his debt to Alton, and Lamar's stash. She was a Sacramento cop, so she knew about Alton. She even knew the Death Valley story.

"I don't know how much pressure Ty had to put on," I said. "Ike was too damn nice for his own good. He hated Ty like I do, but he wouldn't want to see him killed. He would have felt obligated to do what Ty wanted."

"I guess it explains things," she said. "Of course, there's nothing we can prove. So what are you going to do next?"

I rolled my glass between my palms. "I'm thinking on it."

"I don't want to hear that you're going to kill him."

"No. That's letting him off easy."

"All right," she said. "I've had a long, hard shift. I need a shower and bed. You're welcome to the couch." She put the glass down and stood up. "You're also welcome to come join me."

My mouth went dry, and I was very conscious of my breathing. Whitney Lewis was doing a hell of a job of making me feel like a teenager. I made myself finish the wine before I looked up at her.

"If it's not an imposition," I said.

* * *

At ten the next morning, I was under her sheets, watching her put her uniform on. The mood of the last eight hours was a lovely thing, hanging delicate and alive between us, but I had to say something before she left.

"Your patrols," I said. "Can you more or less decide where to go while you're driving around?"

She looked at me, curious. "Within reason. I mean, I can't just take off for Disney World."

"Right," I said. "Listen, I'm going to say something now, and I hope it won't make you kick me out, and I hope you won't ask any questions."

Her smile faded. "Okay."

"It might be a good idea if, around two this afternoon, you happened to be the patrol car closest to the storage place."

She looked at me for a long time.

"It occurs to me," she said, "that I don't really know much about you."

I met her eye. "I'm hoping you know enough."

She finished pinning the badge to her chest. "I'm thinking on it," she said, and she left the room.

* * *

I wore the work pants and gloves again, and a Sacramento Kings hoodie I bought at a gas station. I parked at the office complex next to the storage facility, screened behind a row of shrubs. I got there in time to watch the security men make a stop at a quarter past noon. At twenty after one, I got out of the car and started moving as fast as my foot would allow.

Once again, there was nobody around. I went to 257 and pulled the bolt cutters out of my pants and snapped the padlock. Ike hadn't been able to do it, but I was stronger and had a better tool. I slipped inside, closed the door, and turned on the light.

There were several cardboard boxes stacked inside. The one on top was filled with old paperbacks, and for a minute I was afraid that Ty's addled brain had given me the wrong number. In the fourth box down, I hit it. Four huge bottles of Oxy, packaged for pharmacy use, with labels almost entirely in Spanish. I had no idea what the street value would be, but Ty had seemed sure there was enough here to cancel out his debt. I trusted his criminal instincts.

I took the ruined padlock off the door and replaced it with a new one. I carried the box to 233 and put it in the corner, in front of Ike's empties. I unscrewed the top of one of the Oxy bottles, spilled a few of the pills out, making sure that some went into the corridor, and put the bottle on its side on the floor. I left the door half open with the broken padlock on the floor next to the spilled pills. Short of hanging a neon "Botched Robbery of Illegal Stash Here" sign, I couldn't think of anything more to do. By 1:40, I was back in the car.

At two on the dot, the security car showed up.

I watched the guard go into the building and held my breath. Maybe he wouldn't do a full walkthrough. Maybe he'd try to take the pills for himself. Maybe I'd let Ike down. Again. The minutes dragged agonizingly by and then Whitney's cruiser pulled into the lot and the driver got out of the security car. The two of them conferred for a few minutes and headed inside.

I started to breathe again.

* * *

It was just after midnight when Whitney got home and found me again in the rocker on the porch. She sat down in the other chair, and we looked at the street together.

"The only thing I haven't figured out," she said, "is how you got Ty's prints on one of the Oxy bottles."

"Lamar took him there to show off," I said. "He must have picked one of them up. I take it Ty's been arrested."

"He has," she said. "If you scatter around enough Oxy for a captain to pose with on the news, you will get people moving. We had a search warrant in under an hour and an arrest warrant thirty minutes later. He's got two prior felony convictions, and he'll have a court-appointed lawyer with no time for conspiracy theories. He's going away for a long time."

"Not long enough. But I'll take it."

"Were you telling me the truth when you said he once broke Ike's arm?"

"Ike was twelve," I said. "He brought home a stray dog because he felt sorry for it. Ty chased the mutt off and might have beaten Ike to death if I hadn't come home."

She didn't say anything for a few minutes. Always thinking before she talked. I might start to get irritated by that. In sixty years or so.

"I think," she finally said, "that a good kid died, and the man most responsible is going to prison. I suppose I can live with that." She stood up and held out her hand. "Will you come inside with me?"

It hurt that Ike would never know her.

I took her hand and stood up.

"If it's not an imposition."

Mercy

Before our father set it on fire, my big brother, Stevie, amassed what was possibly the largest collection of 45 singles in our town. He started buying them when he was seven. By the time he was twelve, he was nearly obsessive, funneling the money from a paper route and his grudgingly tendered allowance directly to the local record shop. When he was fifteen, he scrounged scrap wood from around the neighborhood and built shelves of his own design to hold the hundreds he'd collected and lovingly maintained, allowing me, his worshipful little sister, to touch or play them only in his presence. At sixteen, he brought home "Penny Lane," with "Strawberry Fields Forever" on the flip side, and spent one blissful Saturday listening to the two songs over and over again.

At eighteen, his number came up in the draft lottery.

I sat on his bed and watched him pack. By then, we'd started to hear about boys who ran off to Canada rather than risk Vietnam. I knew Stevie wouldn't, but watching his slender fingers fold shirts, I was heartsick at the thought of him in uniform. To distract me, I think, he made me promise I would take care of the records while he was gone. He said I could choose one of them to have as my own as payment for being their guardian. He probably expected me to pick one of the new songs, a mind trip from the Beatles or a grinder from the Stones.

I ran my fingers along the alphabetized rows, letting the corners of the paper sleeves rustle under my nails. When I chose, it was a record he'd had for more than five years, one of the first ones I remembered loving. I handed it to him shyly.

"Monument 851," he read. "'Oh, Pretty Woman' by Roy Orbison and the Candy Men. B side 'Yo te Amo Maria.'" He looked at me. "How come?"

"I like the way he says *mercy* at the end of the first verse." As I said the word I tried, without much success, to imitate Orbison's teasing delivery, the playful lasciviousness layered over something that wasn't play, something I didn't yet understand. "And then the growl after the second verse." I didn't even try to replicate that.

Stevie laughed. He picked up a pen and turned the record over.

He had written his name on the back of the sleeve of every single in his collection. In later years, when I worked in a record store myself, I learned this reduces their value. I don't think Stevie would have cared about that, if he'd known. He didn't want the records for money. He wanted the records for the records.

On the back side of "Oh, Pretty Woman," he wrote, under his name, "Traded to Lila Benson for services rendered." He signed and dated it and handed it to me, grinning.

Five months later, I came home from school and saw the telegram from the Army on the kitchen table. Dazed, I walked to the window and saw our father in the backyard. He had stacked Stevie's records in a pile and poured the gasoline from the shed over them, and now he stood there while they burned, not even seeming to watch as the sleeves darkened, came apart, and drifted away, black scraps edged with fading red embers.

* * *

For years, I tried to feel some sympathy for my father. He was widowed when I was born, left alone with an infant daughter and a two-year-old son. It must have been hard in ways beyond my comprehension. I couldn't use it to explain or justify, though, the ease and speed with which he reached for his belt, or the feeling of the back of his hand across my face. It couldn't undo the jolts of pain or erase the ugly purple welts everyone at school looked away from.

Stevie intervened when he could, often accepting bruises meant for me.

After Stevie was killed, my father's cold rage filled the house, seeking a target, finding one, as often as not, in his strange, quiet daughter. It grew all the stronger as he started to suspect what I'd discovered for myself years earlier. My complete disinterest in the boys on the football team. My not-quite-casual-enough ogling of Mary Ann on *Gilligan's Island* and Goldie Hawn on *Laugh-In*. There would be no strapping, beer-guzzling son-in-law to take me off his hands.

I hid the Orbison single, the last remnant of Stevie's collection, under a floorboard in my closet, alongside the lurid paperbacks about fallen women I shoplifted from The Book Emporium. I started spending as much time as I could manage anyplace else but the house where I'd grown up. On a good day, I didn't have to see my father at all.

* * *

A couple of years after Stevie died, I was out of high school and working on being out of the house for good. I clerked part-time behind the counter at Music's Last Stand, the record store where they remembered me as the little sister of their all-time best customer. I crashed on friends' couches when I could, slept at home when I had to, took a couple of classes at the community college, and spent a lot of time in the town square, hanging around in what was half a homeless camp and half a permanent protest against the war. There was a lot of pot, a little bit of LSD, and always music, but we didn't think of ourselves as hippies. Altamont had happened by then. Manson had happened. We had lurched into the '70s. It felt like the hippie thing was over, but we still had Nixon, and we still had the war, and we sensed it was still our duty to hold up the signs and chant once in a while. A lot of towns would have run us out, but the police chief had lost his youngest son during Tet. As long as we didn't panhandle or hassle people going about their business, he let us be.

One May morning, I was perched on the low wall circling the square. I hadn't been home in a couple of weeks. I'd saved a little bit of money, and I was wondering if I could manage the rent on my own apartment and who to ask to be my roommate. I stopped thinking about all of that when a woman I'd never seen before walked around the corner.

I forgot to breathe. The world reoriented itself around her, like loose playing cards returning to order as you tap them against the table, edges all lined up. In that instant, I understood everything about Roy Orbison's growl.

Her short, jet-black hair was swept up into an Elvis pompadour. She wore a leather jacket over a white T-shirt and tight jeans, her eyes hidden behind sunglasses blacker than Spiro Agnew's soul. She carried no purse, wore no jewelry, but her mouth was outlined with neon-red lipstick, one corner turned up in the barest hint of a smile. Her clothes clung to her in a way that made Goldie Hawn drop clean out of my mind, but it was her walk that slayed me, smooth and confident, moving fast while barely seeming to move at all. A guy would have said she walked like she owned the place, and he would have said it with a bit of a sneer, but that wasn't it. She didn't walk like she had a claim on the world.

She walked like it had no claim on her.

I had ten seconds to look at her after she rounded the corner and before she was past me. I didn't turn my head, because I didn't want to watch her disappear around another corner. I wanted to save her, whole in my mind, always coming toward me. I closed my eyes, and a voice spoke, right at my elbow. "Hey, pretty girl."

It was her. The corner of her lip had lifted a little more, and her head was tilted. I had the feeling she knew everything I'd just been thinking, and I felt my face flush.

"You look like you know what's what," she said. "Where can I get a good breakfast around here?"

I had to swallow a couple of times before I could answer. "McCoy's Diner. A couple of blocks."

"Cool. You want to come have breakfast with me?"

"Yes," I managed. I had just enough dignity not to add *please*. I stood up and nodded in the direction she'd been going. "It's this way."

"Lead on."

We started down the sidewalk together, my heart hammering. I felt like an oaf next to her. I had on a Monkees T-shirt I pretended to wear ironically and a flowered skirt that already seemed like some kind of costume, a pretentious bit of Woodstock playacting. I tried desperately to think of something to say that wouldn't make me seem like the clueless dolt I was. I couldn't come up with anything. We covered a block in silence, my humiliation growing with every step.

Halfway to the diner, we were passing the mouth of an alley when she put her hand on my elbow and pulled me into the opening. She spun me up against the bricks and put her forearm against the wall next to my head and leaned toward me. Her right hand slipped casually under the hem of my T-shirt, and there was the electric touch of her warm fingertips against the bare skin of my side.

"What's your name?" she asked.

"Lila," I got out.

"Lila," she said. "I don't want coffee on my breath the first time I kiss you."

It was slow and sweet and warm, and when it was over, she pulled back, tipping the dark glasses down, and for the first time I saw her blue eyes.

"My name's Mercy," she said.

*　*　*

Mercy had a green VW Bug she'd been driving around the country for two years, working odd jobs and waitressing, moving on whenever she wanted. She had a set of tools to keep the Bug running and a switchblade to keep overly helpful men at bay. She had a rock she picked up on a Key West beach that she worried with her thumb when she was thinking. She had a dream of settling down and running a little bookstore, somewhere in Arizona. She had an atlas she hardly ever looked at, a box full of *Green Lantern* comic books she reread constantly, and parents in New York City who had made it clear they never wanted to see her again.

I didn't learn all this at that first breakfast. I learned it, and much more, over the course of the week we spent together, starting right then. I had to work a shift at Music's Last Stand, so she sat on a stool next to mine behind the counter, swinging her legs and teasing the customers, one hand resting on my thigh. When the shift was over, I took her to the back room of the house where I was crashing. I won't talk about that. There are moments that are only for the people who are in them.

Mercy took her time revealing herself to me, sharing her stories. I took my time, too. It was five days before I told her about Stevie. I thought I had cried all the tears I had for him, but telling Mercy made it new and raw again, and she held me as I found there were a lot more.

When I was all cried out, we held hands, lying on our backs and looking up into the sky. It was the wee hours of the morning, and we were on the roof of Music's Last Stand in a big sleeping bag she kept in the Bug. She liked being under the stars, even though we couldn't see very many of them with the town's lights in the way. It's why she wanted to end up in Arizona. Out there, she said, there were hardly any lights at all, and you could see the whole Milky Way, spread out just for you.

"So the record's still there," she said, after a time. "Hidden in your old closet."

"Yes. When I have my own place, where it can be safe, I'll go get it. I don't want to risk carrying it around. It's all I have of him."

"Well," she said. "We'd better go get it soon."

I took a moment to savor the *we* and then looked at her silhouette in the darkness. "Why?"

"I'm about ready to move on. And you can't leave it behind."

"You want me to come with you?" I didn't know how to think a thought that good.

Mercy laughed.

"Oh," she said, "pretty woman." And she rolled and reached for me.

* * *

We went to the house two days later, at a time I was pretty sure my father would be at work. He was a warehouse foreman, and his shifts sometimes

135

got moved around, but early afternoons had generally been a safe time to be at the house, even back before Stevie left. I thought the house looked smaller than I remembered, shabbier. As far as I was concerned, the place was already receding into my past.

The inside was a mess. I'd given up cleaning for him months ago, and there was a smell I didn't remember, a combination of dirty laundry, empty beer bottles, and full trash cans. I opened a window to get some air circulating and led Mercy to the back of the house, resisting the urge to hurry. I wasn't trespassing. This was my home too, and if this was going to be my last time in it, I wasn't going to sneak.

My room felt hollow, staged, and I realized it had been a long time since anyone had really lived there. It was like a museum exhibit of what a girl's room might have looked like in an unimaginable past. Mercy drifted along, looking at old school portraits and sketches from my high school art class. I could tell she sensed it too.

I remembered a cheap suitcase I'd had for sleepovers in grade school, still under the bed. "I'll get the record," I told Mercy. "Will you pack some clothes?" I showed her the drawers where she would find things that still fit. In the closet, I knelt and did the tricky push and slide, the only way to move the loose floorboard.

The record was still there. I realized I'd been afraid he would have found it and started another fire. I set it by the door and looked at the other treasures-in-hiding. A glass piggy bank full of pennies. A doll my father had called ugly and threatened to throw away. A journal I'd written two entries in and then stopped, lacking the language to express the things I was feeling. And then three paperbacks that had expressed them too well, paperbacks I had slipped into the waistband of my skirt and smuggled past the bookstore register, heart pounding. I picked up the top one. The title was *Private Rooms*, and the blurb on the cover asked, "What mad delusions send normal women down the twisted paths of lesbian lust?"

I turned to show the book to Mercy and saw my father standing in the doorway.

* * *

Mercy was folding my underwear, her back to the door. I dropped the book, and at the sound, she looked up at my face and then spun to see him.

He was still a big man, but the hard muscle that had defined him was beginning to soften, and his stomach bulged a little against his shirt. The tight buzz cut was iron gray now. I'd known these things, known he was getting old, but seeing him now, with Mercy there, was like seeing him for the first time.

He didn't look at me or Mercy. He looked at the record.

"Guess I missed one," he said. Somebody who didn't know him might think he sounded mild, thoughtful.

"It's mine." I picked up the record and stood, my back to the wall. "Stevie gave it to me."

"It wasn't his to give," my father said. "Everything he had became mine when he died. If I want that record, you'll damn well give it to me."

"I won't. It's mine." I was breathing hard, but I made myself think of Mercy and of Stevie. "I'm leaving. For good."

He shook his head and, for the first time, looked at Mercy. "Who the hell are you?"

"My name's Mercy." She sounded calm. Resolved. "I'm in love with your daughter."

For a second, I forgot to breathe again.

My father's face distorted. "Don't be disgusting. You're not going to bring your sickness into *my* family."

"We're just here for a few of Lila's things. Then we'll be leaving."

"You will be. Not her." He looked back at me. "Give me that record."

I put it behind my back. "No."

"You think I can't take it? I'm not that old yet." He took a step forward. Immediately, Mercy glided between us. She held up her left hand in a *stop* gesture and, with the right hand, pulled her switchblade from her jacket pocket and flicked it open.

He stopped, staring at the knife and then her.

"I don't want to hurt you," Mercy said. "But we are leaving, and we are taking the record."

I find myself back in that moment, all the time, in my dreams. The three of us, frozen in place, all of us waiting to see what would happen.

After a second, I stepped away from the wall and stood right behind Mercy, putting my hand on her hip to let her know I was there. My father watched me do that, looked at my hand, then turned his back and walked out of the room.

Beneath my hand, I felt the tension in Mercy marginally ease. "Hurry," she said. "Before he comes back." I went to the bed and put the record in the suitcase and closed it. She hadn't gotten to all the clothes, but I didn't care. I wanted out of this room, out of this house.

I took her hand. "Let's go," I said.

We walked down the hall. Maybe everything would have been all right if we'd gone into the garage and left by the back way. But we went the way we'd come, into the living room, and my father was sitting in the chair he always sat in, and in his hand was a gun.

He lifted it and pointed it at us. "Sit on the couch," he said. "Right now."

Mercy hesitated, just a beat, and he pulled the trigger. There was the loudest bang I'd ever heard, and I swear I heard the bullet pass through the space between our heads. We both jumped.

"Couch," he said again.

We moved to the couch and sat. I put the suitcase between my feet.

"Don't do this," I said. "Where did you even get a gun?"

"I'll let you know when you can talk," he said. "Toss the knife on the table here in front of me."

Mercy tossed the knife gently. It came to rest on the coffee table a foot and a half in front of my father. I saw he was sweating.

"Did you know that they're less likely to take only children?" he asked.

Mercy and I looked at each other, confused.

"The draft," he said. "They'll try not to take an only child." He looked at me. "First, you took my wife. She died trying to bring you into the world. Then you took my son. If he'd stayed an only child, I'd still have him."

I could hear Mercy's breathing. I wanted to take her hand, but I was afraid. I would die before I let him hurt her. What terrified me was, I was sure, entirely sure, she was thinking the same thing.

"You took *everything*," he said. "And now you're going to, what, shame me? Take my good name, too? Make sure everyone knows I raised a pervert?"

"Dad," I said.

"Don't call me that."

"Just let us go," Mercy said. "We'll never come back. Nobody will know."

"I'll know," he said.

"We love each other," I said.

"Oh, I can see that," he said, his lips tightening. "If you call that love."

"Yes," Mercy said. "We do."

He shook his head. "You took everything from me," he said again. "So now I'm going to take everything from you."

I pulled my feet back and leaned forward, preparing to jump at him, to put my body between the gun and Mercy, but instead of lifting the gun, he picked up the phone on the little side table by his chair. Working left-handed, he dialed 0.

"Operator," he said. "Give me the police. This is an emergency."

Now he did lift the gun, pointing it at us.

"Police," he said, his voice rushed, panicky. "My name is Tony Benson. I live at 435 Sycamore. I just came home and found a woman here with my daughter. Her name is Mercy, and she's robbing the place. She has a knife. A switchblade—yes, she is threatening me. Listen, I think she's brainwashed my daughter. She's some kind of sick pervert, and my daughter says they're in love, but I think this Mercy woman has her all turned around. She's a good girl, she's not like that. Please come. I think this Mercy wants to hurt me. I've got a gun, and I fired a shot to scare her, but I only had the one bullet. Please come fast. I think she's going to—"

He broke off and dropped the phone to the floor. For the first time, I saw he had a handkerchief. He leaned forward with it and grabbed Mercy's knife. She understood a second before I did and jumped for him, too late. Looking at me, smiling for the first time I could remember, he brought the knife up and cut his own throat.

* * *

I told my story, again and again, to everyone, even when I knew they weren't listening. I told them Mercy tried to save him, that she was covered in his blood because she tried to hold it in him with her bare hands. I told them he was lying, we weren't robbing the place, we didn't threaten him. None of it mattered. The police dispatcher who took his call cried on the stand as she recalled his words, and as soon as she said *brainwashed,* Mercy's trial was as good as over. The prosecutor was happy to remind the jurors of the women who sat outside the courthouse during Charlie Manson's trial, proclaiming their love, making up alibis, still willing to kill for him. Now our little town had its very own lesbian Manson, and a martyred father who had tried to save his little girl. Every cop and reporter in town preferred that story.

So did the jury.

* * *

The one saving grace turned out to be the gun. Because my father had it, the lawyer appointed to Mercy's case argued there was an element of self-defense and got murder reduced to manslaughter. With good behavior, Mercy will be out in June of 1983.

Five years down. Six more years to wait.

I visit every week. The guards have gotten used to me. They let us hold hands across the table. At first, Mercy told me not to wait for her, that I was throwing my life away. Now she holds my hand, and we count the remaining days together.

I sold the house and everything in it. I still have Stevie's record. I live in a tiny apartment, work at the record store, and save every penny, except what it takes to keep Mercy's Bug running. In my spare time, I go to the library and read up on possible places to live in Arizona and the economics of running an independent bookstore.

One of the things everyone loves about "Oh, Pretty Woman" is the irresistible opening guitar riff, a stuttering, immediately repeated rendition of the opening notes of the progression that drives the rest of the record. Record store legend says it sounds like a mistake because it was, the guitarist not quite getting the full riff right the first time through. Orbison decided to keep it, and that gleeful little false start became the key to the record. That's how I think of the week Mercy and I had together. A little false start before the real music begins.

I'll be there in 1983, with the Bug fully gassed and ready for the road, a route to Arizona marked out in that same old atlas. The door will open, and there she'll be, a few lines at the corners of her eyes, a touch of gray in the pompadour, but that same gliding step that every guard will turn to look at. I'll hold out my arms, and my Mercy will come walking.

Back to me.

Pillbug

The jeep slid to a stop in the dry scrubland, the driver gaping out the front window and fumbling for his sidearm as Frank Kellner and Adam Nelson jumped from the back. Both men wore faded combat fatigues and carried M1 carbines. They began firing into the air, aiming at the top of a telephone pole twenty yards away, the sound of their weapons oddly muted. In front of them, a ruggedly handsome scientist and his perky reporter fiancée half-carried, half-dragged a semiconscious man in a Colonel's uniform toward the jeep, the scientist firing wildly over his shoulder with the pistol he'd taken from the Colonel's holster. They stumbled past the soldiers and shoved the Colonel into the front passenger seat of the jeep. The woman climbed into the back as the scientist turned and fired.

"Go, go now!" The scientist yelled. "We'll never stop them with bullets!"

He and the two soldiers leapt to claim their places, clinging to the side of the jeep. The driver floored it, sending a spray of sand and dirt into the air before friction took hold and the vehicle jumped forward, passing within a few feet of a dozen men clustered around a big camera on a roughly built platform.

Immediately past the platform, the jeep slowed and stopped. The one man near the camera wearing a suit—thin around the elbows though it might be—spoke in a deep, accented voice. "And now we tilt up," he said, "and hold for a few moments on the sky, please." He waited a beat, as everyone looked at him.

"And cut," he said. "Print that, please."

The man in the suit turned to a canvas chair behind him and picked up a script, ignoring the burst of activity as men started adjusting and moving equipment. In the jeep, the Colonel straightened in his seat, running his hand through his hair and pulling out a pack of cigarettes. The perky reporter fiancé swung her legs out onto the sandy ground and stood up between Kellner and Nelson, patting each of them on a shoulder. "That's it, boys," she said. "You're now officially in the pictures."

"That's it?" Nelson asked. "I thought they always did everything twenty-seven times."

"Only in real Hollywood," the girl said. "They have a thing called money. This is an Eagle Productions feature, my lads, and that means we shoot once and move on, unless somebody keels over and dies in the middle of a scene. The whole thing will take about two weeks. Lemme have one, Pops?"

The Colonel handed her a cigarette and stood up out of the jeep himself. The scientist and the jeep's driver had gone over to the film crew and were listening to their chatter, arms crossed, waiting to see when they'd be needed again. "So you're the replacements," the Colonel said to Nelson and Kellner. "Welcome aboard." He held out his hand. Nelson shook it, then nudged Kellner with his elbow. Kellner hadn't moved since the director spoke. He was staring at the man, his lips moving silently. When Nelson nudged him, he started, looked around, and took the offered hand mechanically.

"I'm Adam Nelson, this is Frank Kellner. I didn't realize we were replacing anyone."

"Oh yes," the girl said. "We had a couple of guys playing the soldiers the first three days, then yesterday they just didn't turn up."

"Found a better job or an even better bottle, I imagine," said the older man. "I'm Roy Prine, by the way."

"I think I saw you in a Western," Nelson said.

"I've done about three dozen of the damn things. Can't stand horses."

"Susan Reid," said the girl. She didn't put out her hand. She was watching Kellner, who had walked over close to the film crew and now stood about two feet away from the director, staring at him intensely. "What's your friend doing? He seems fascinated with Victor."

Nelson shook his head. "Don't ask me. I've only known the guy a couple of weeks, since I moved into his boarding house. We've been drunk together a few times, but I wouldn't call him a pal."

"Korea," Prine said. Not quite a question.

"Yes, sir," Nelson said. "Both of us."

"Tough coming home sometimes."

"Tougher for some than others," Nelson said.

"These uniforms are the wrong color," Frank Kellner said. None of them had noticed him coming back.

"They have to be," Prine said. "They come out looking right in black and white."

"Must be the same with this," Nelson said, lifting his rifle. "It probably looks good on the screen, but up close it's a little off. A little too short, a little too heavy."

"They ought to do the uniforms right," Kellner said.

"What matters is how they come out looking, Frank," Nelson said. "Like Roy said."

"Is this your first movie?" Susan asked.

Nelson nodded. "Buddy of mine tipped us to it just this morning. We showed up, and they stuffed us in these outfits and tossed us in the jeep. I figured we'd have to do a screen test or something, but they just hustled us on out here."

"Screen tests cost money," Susan said. "Money and time. I'm sure they were just relieved to see somebody walk through the door."

"Well, it's fifty bucks a week to look like grunts. I figured we could handle that."

"We could, in the right uniforms," Kellner said.

"You definitely have the right look," Prine said. "Mutt and Jeff."

"What's this picture called, anyway?" Nelson asked.

"They didn't even tell you that?" Susan said.

Nelson shook his head. Prine snorted and dropped his cigarette butt.

"You tell them," Susan said to the older man. "I can't stand it."

Prine shrugged. "Gentlemen, you now have the pleasure to be forever and after part of *They Came For Our World*, an Eagle motion picture."

"Catchy," said Nelson. "Who are they? Them? Who were we just shooting at?"

"Pillbugs," said Susan. "You know, roly-polies? Those little black bugs that curl up in a ball when you touch them?" She pointed at the man playing her boyfriend, who was now leaning against a stack of crates, talking to the man who'd been driving the jeep. "Will Joplin over there is my love interest, a scientist trying to invent new tunnel drilling weapons. Or mining tools or something, I forget. Only instead, he discovers an underground colony of these giant pillbugs, and they come swarming out and try to take over the world."

"I hope you've got your Oscar speeches ready, boys," Prine said.

"Okay, everybody," one of the men by the camera shouted. "We're going straight into scene 34, please. Susan, Roy Prine, and Will Joplin over here. If you are not in scene 34, please clear the area."

"See you later, boys," Susan said. She and Prine walked away. Nelson looked around. Kellner was back over by the film crew, again standing just a couple of feet from the director, who was now engaged in animated conversation with some of the technicians. None of them paid any attention to Kellner, and once again Nelson hadn't noticed him leaving the little group by the jeep. He walked over and pulled at Kellner's sleeve.

"Come on, Frank," he said. "Let's get some coffee."

Kellner turned and followed Nelson immediately, but he kept casting glances back over his shoulder. "We oughta leave, Adam," he said. "I don't like this."

"What's not to like? Fifty a week, and I bet we just sit around most of the time. We don't even have lines to memorize."

"I don't like working for commies, is what."

"The director?" Nelson looked back. Victor was positioning the three actors, walking them through the upcoming scene. "What are you talking about? What do you know about commies anyway?"

"I know enough to spot a Russian," Kellner said as they reached the tent the production was using as a mess. For a moment, he stood in the doorway as Nelson held the flap open above him. "I seen plenty."

"What, in Korea?" The inside of the tent was dim, but not much cooler than outside. The two men drew cups of coffee from a huge vat and found seats away from the door. People were scattered around the big tent at different tables, smoking and reading. "That was a little bit different, Frank. Those weren't Russians."

"It don't sit right. Why ain't there an American running this picture?"

"Maybe he is American. What did your grandparents sound like when they talked? Don't get worked up, Frank."

"I'm not worked up."

"You're gonna blow this job. For both of us. Have you taken your medicine today?"

Kellner hung his head and shrugged.

"Tell me again what the doctors say?"

Kellner didn't look up, but his right hand slipped into his pocket and came out with a small glass bottle. He shook two white and two green tablets into his palm and popped them into his mouth, swallowing them dry.

"That's the way," said Nelson.

"I did see Russians," Kellner said, surly.

"In Korea? Chinese, maybe."

"These were white men," Kellner said. He leaned forward, clasping his arms around his stomach. "It was a misty morning. Low visibility but patchy, you know? You were there, you know what it could get like. They were a half mile off. Ten, maybe twelve of them. Russian uniforms. I saw them through my scope."

"Okay, Frank, but who else saw them?"

Kellner looked off. "I'm enough."

"What did they do?"

For a long time, Kellner didn't speak. His head shook slowly from side to side. "I don't remember," he said in a low rasp. He rubbed at his temple. "I saw them, I know I did. I can see it as clear as I see you. But then—" He gave up, and his shoulders slumped.

Nelson pushed Kellner's coffee cup closer to him. "It's okay, Frank. I believe you. Anyway, it doesn't have anything to do with this guy, does it? Victor Whoever."

Frank's lips were moving, but Nelson couldn't hear if he was actually saying anything. They sat quietly for twenty minutes, Nelson watching Frank's lips working, until an assistant director came and fetched them for another shot.

* * *

By their third day of work, when they moved to interior sets, it was clear that Victor—Victor Evans was the name he used when he finally introduced himself—was pleased with his new extras. As Prine had said, the contrast between them—Nelson, blond and lanky and constantly grinning, and Kellner, smaller and dark and twitchy—was visually interesting. "The two of you are America," Evans said, moving them around in the background of a scene. He clapped Nelson on the shoulder. "A nation takes up arms, yes?" His English was slow and thick, but carefully and correctly used.

"Yes, sir," Nelson said, allowing himself to be positioned. Kellner shied away from Evans's actual touch and had yet to say a word to the man, but he, too, moved where he was told. Once he had them in place, Evans didn't give them many actual instructions, so Nelson had developed his own secret of acting and shared it with Kellner: listen to what people are saying, and don't look at the camera.

"Wonderful." Evans turned to his primary actors. "So, Will, here you are explaining how the pillbugs multiply, and how easily they will take the city. You are confident, you know what you speak of. Roy, you must be angry here, right? You want the air strike, the bombardment. And Susan, this is all very frightening. Perhaps you take Will's arm? Yes, good." Evans walked backwards out of the laboratory set, holding up his hands to frame the scene as he walked. "We will try to get this in one so all have a long lunch today, please?"

They'd only had to do multiple takes on a couple of scenes, once when Susan Reid burst out laughing when she was supposed to be kissing Joplin

147

and once when Kellner simply wandered away in the middle of a shot. Nelson followed him, then told Evans the two of them had misunderstood the timing of the scene and made Kellner take an extra pill before the reshoot. Mostly, though, Kellner did exactly what he was supposed to do: stand around and look worried. He did it again, now, as Evans called for action, and Nelson found himself trying to copy him, dredging up things from his own life and history to be upset about. None of them seemed as bad as giant bugs tearing apart the country, but he did his best. It was good enough, apparently, since Evans shot the scene once and immediately announced lunch.

Kellner started for the door and turned to see that Nelson was not with him, but hanging back, talking to the Reid woman as she leaned against one of the ersatz lab tables, smiling at him. Nelson caught Kellner's eye and held up a just-a-minute finger. Kellner looked away as though he'd seen something foul and walked blindly through the nearest door. Prine had told him and Nelson yesterday that there was nothing real between Reid and Will Joplin, the actor playing her scientist boyfriend, the one who looked more like a quarterback than any scientist Kellner had ever seen. Prine had laughed, in fact, and said that Joplin lived with Mike Hughes, the guy who had been driving the jeep on their first day. Kellner hadn't understood why that mattered, but then Prine had said *you know, live together*, and then he understood and felt queasy sick. Nelson had been happy to hear about it, though, and had spent all last night talking about how he was going to ask Reid out, and maybe Kellner could ask out one of the makeup gals, and they could all double.

Kellner hadn't been with a woman since he'd come back, and the thought of it made him feel like he was clawing at the inside of his own skull. He couldn't remember the last time he'd been physically excited. The doctors told him it was the pills, a side effect, just another side effect, like the way he couldn't sleep more than a couple hours at a stretch, or the cotton taste in his mouth all day, or the constant need to rub his head or scratch at his eyes. He needed to get off the pills. He told himself that every day, but somehow every morning when he put on his clothes, the bottle in his pocket was full.

He had to ask the doctors about it, but when did he see the doctors? He had to see them sometimes. He remembered them, three of them, gaunt men, all with the thinning grey hair and the serious looks. Or maybe there were only two of them? He remembered at least two, strapping down his arms so they could run their tests, the bright light in his eyes. He remembered them talking to him continuously, though he couldn't really remember all they said. It was just clear he was very sick, and he felt sick, he knew they were right, he needed to be strapped down for his own good, and theirs too, he might do something. And pain, he remembered pain. Still, the pills were too much. There had to be something else they could give him. He tried to remember when he was seeing them again and when he'd seen them last. He could see the office so clearly, the light shining off the cold white tile and the silvery tables, the light getting brighter and brighter until he was blinded and the light shaded into mist, like the mist he'd seen the Russians through—

"Frank!" someone yelled, and Kellner felt his arm being pulled back, and he turned and swung his fist.

"Whoa!" Nelson yelled, barely ducking the blow. He held up his hands. "Take it easy, Frank, it's just me!"

Kellner looked down at his hand, still balled into a fist. Slowly, it relaxed. He was two hundred yards down the road from the warehouse Eagle had rented for interior scenes, walking the opposite direction from the commissary. "Sorry," he said.

"It's okay, Frank." Nelson tentatively patted his arm. "Lose your way?"

Kellner rubbed his temple. "Yeah," he said. "Guess so."

"Well, come on back. We'll get some lunch," Nelson said. He took Kellner by the elbow and started him moving back up the road. They walked silently for a few minutes.

"Listen, Frank, you might have been onto something about Evans," Nelson said.

"Evans?"

"I guess you know your commies after all. Susan says he's a defector." Nelson waited, but Kellner said nothing to this. "He was a big deal over there, too. His real name is Victor—what did she say? Mishnev, something like that. She said he was supposed to be the next Einstein and I said Einstein didn't make pictures and she laughed."

Kellner kept walking.

"I guess that was a joke or something. Anyway, he made all these big pictures about how swell communism is and how they were going to wipe the floor with America, and then right after Stalin died, he snuck over here to make pictures about how swell we are. Except, of course, as a card-carrying commie, he's blacklisted, even though everybody says he's a genius. Eagle was the only studio that would hire him, and he still has to use the fake name and make this giant bug picture."

They'd reached the door to the commissary. "So you were right about him being a commie, but he's a good commie, okay? A white Russian." Nelson was amused by this. "That's good, huh? Like a white hat in a Western. So maybe you can be a little nicer to him, right? We blow this, and we'll have to get real work."

"I'll try, Adam," Kellner said mechanically.

"That's all I can ask, Frank," Nelson said. He walked through the door.

Three. Kellner was certain there had been three doctors. They'd told him exactly what was wrong with him and exactly how to fix it, if he could just remember.

* * *

Nelson and Kellner weren't in the next day's last scene, in which the scientist pleaded passionately with his fiancé to take the last plane out of the city before the Army bombed it in a last-ditch effort to stop the pillbugs. She, of course, refused, explaining tearfully that she had a job to do as well. Kellner left as soon as he was allowed to, but Nelson changed out of his off-color uniform and hung around to watch them film. He was expecting the usual single take, but for once, Evans seemed actively engaged, shooting the exchange between the two several times from various angles, experimenting with different lighting schemes. His interest sparked something in Joplin and

Susan, and they were better than Nelson had ever seen them. He would have almost believed they were a couple. Evans stopped only after the eleventh take, when one of the assistants said something sharp about how the price of film stock must have dropped. His eyes closed, Evans slumped back into his canvas chair and called day's end.

Nelson went out the main doors of the makeshift studio and hung around by the dozen or so parked cars, smoking. Most of the cars were gone within fifteen minutes. Joplin and Hughes drove off together in a sporty little two-seater, laughing at some private joke. Nelson was looking after them, wondering if he was part of the gag, when someone spoke behind him. "My blond soldier, good evening."

It was Evans. He was standing only a couple of feet away, taking a cigarette out of a cheap-looking case that he quickly tucked back into a breast pocket. "Can you give me a light?"

Nelson pulled a book of matches out of his own pocket and held one up. Evans leaned into it carefully and inhaled.

"My thanks," he said. "Are you waiting for a car?"

"For Susan," Nelson said. "Miss Reid. We're going to dinner."

"Hm. I was going to tell you that you're doing very well for your first film, Mr. Nelson, but apparently you're doing even better than I was aware."

"I'm glad you think I'm doing a good job."

"I'm thinking of giving you your own death scene," Evans said. "It's not in the script, but one more horrific death would not hurt. Would you enjoy being eaten by a tremendous *Armadilidum vulgare*?"

Nelson laughed. "Why not? How will that work? Has Eagle been breeding real giants this whole time?"

"Sadly, no. For the most part, I'm afraid, the visual spectacle in this film will be provided by common pillbugs crawling about on picture postcards of Los Angeles, and that is precisely what it will look like when it is shown. Eagle lacks the resources of the major studios."

"Well, that's lucky for me. If they could pay real wages. they'd have real actors."

"That's true." Evans took a long drag on his cigarette. "I am told that the carpentry division, whoever and wherever they may be, has prepared one full-sized monster made of wood and leather, which is said to be moderately convincing. No doubt we will still need to shoot it in low light and at oblique angles. It will be on the set tomorrow."

"That should be fun," Nelson said. He hesitated. "I suppose it isn't much fun for you, though. Miss Reid told me this was the only film work you could get in America."

"And why?"

"Yes, and why."

Evans nodded. "And will you be reporting me, Mr. Nelson? Will you have the film blocked from release because it was made by an enemy sympathizer?"

"Why would I? It's 1955, Mr. Evans." Nelson emphasized the name. "Nobody's paying any attention to McCarthy anymore. Everybody I know thinks the blacklist is a joke."

"Then I devoutly wish everyone you know was everyone I knew."

"It's tough enough that you have to work on dreck like this."

Evans shrugged. "It beats digging ditches, Mr. Nelson, and I say this as someone who has known many ditch diggers. I have faith that someday I will be able to tell the stories I wish to tell about my new country. In the meantime, I can at least save it from the pillbugs."

Nelson laughed. "I suppose someone has to."

"Exactly." The door behind them opened, and they turned to see Susan Reid approaching. "And now here is our young lady. Very lovely."

"Can we offer you a ride?"

"Thank you, no. My car is on the way." He took Susan's hand and bowed over it shortly, then kissed her once on each cheek. "Have a wonderful evening, you two, but not too late an evening. We have a world to save tomorrow."

* * *

Several hours later, Nelson, after a very satisfactory evening, parked his car down the street from the rather ramshackle boarding house he shared with Frank Kellner and half a dozen other vets. Most of the men spent their days smoking, listening to the radio, and counting the hours until their next benefit check arrived. Over the last two weeks, Nelson and Kellner were the only ones who'd held any kind of job. The other men in the house had responded with a combination of bruised disdain and open mockery. After their second day of filming, they'd found star-shaped cutouts from a nudie magazine tacked to their doors.

Walking down the street, Nelson glanced into the window of the nameless bar all the vets frequented and wasn't surprised to see Kellner at a back booth by himself. He picked up his pace, but he'd only gone another ten feet when he slowed to a stop, stood for a moment, and sighed. He squared his shoulders, turned, and walked back to the bar.

It was a small place, a former hardware store with the shelves removed and a few tables scattered around. There was a jukebox, but Nelson had never seen anyone try to play it. This late on a weeknight, there were only a few men in the bar, all sitting by themselves and doing the kind of drinking that actively discourages company. Nelson nodded to the bartender, who looked at him without expression, and walked back to Kellner's booth.

"Hello, Frank," he said, sliding in opposite the smaller man.

Kellner was rubbing the side of his head. His lips were moving soundlessly. His pill bottle was on the table in front of him, along with five empty glasses. He gave no sign of noticing Nelson's presence.

Nelson walked back to the bar. "How long he been like this?"

The bartender's shoulders rose and fell about an eighth of an inch. "Been here since around seven. Gave him his last shot and beer an hour ago, just been sitting there since. Hasn't bothered anybody, so I haven't bothered him."

"Glass of water."

The bartender's eyes narrowed. "I'm closed in half an hour."

"Yeah, I got it. Water."

He took the water back to the booth and set it down in front of Kellner, then lifted Kellner's right hand and wrapped it around the glass. Nothing happened for a moment then, like a mechanical toy catching its gears, Kellner's arm lifted, and he drank half the glass straight down.

Nelson sat again. "That's the boy, Frank. Finish it up."

Kellner's eyes found him. "I saw the Russians, Adam." He spoke with the exaggerated correctness of the long-since drunk.

"Sure you did, pal."

"I know they weren't supposed to be there. I get it." Kellner's eyes dropped.

"Let's get you back to your room, boy. Get some sleep."

"I been taking my medicine."

"That's good. Sleep's good too."

"I wish I could remember my doctor's name," Kellner said. He'd picked up the pill bottle and was turning it over and over in his hands. "Shouldn't it be on here?"

"I don't know, Frank. Different places do it different."

"It should be on here." Kellner closed his eyes. "I can see him. Except it's them. Three of them. Older guys. Not much hair. They don't smile often."

"Well, you know, doctors. They spend all day giving bad news."

"I can't remember what's wrong with me." He opened his eyes and looked at the pill bottle. Nelson took his other hand and put it on the glass. Once again Kellner's arm seemed to move without him being aware of it, and he finished the water.

"You're just nervous, Frank. A lot of us are nervous since we got back."

"That's another thing. When did I get back? I don't remember getting back, Nelson, I swear to Christ I don't." He closed his eyes and concentrated. "I remember the plane over there. And I remember hills and tents. And the Russians I saw in the mist. But then it's like the floor drops out and it's just the doctors talking to me."

"Do you remember what they said?"

Kellner's eyes squeezed tightly. "No. Christ, how I want to. There's something I'm supposed to do. It's important. There were needles…I think. Bright lights, all the time." He opened his eyes and looked at the bottle again. "I must still see them. Where else do the pills come from?"

"Sure you see them, Frank. Every three weeks. I took you last time, remember? I waited outside for you."

Slowly, Kellner nodded.

"It's that place over near the ocean. We're going back next week. You remember, Frank. You can see the ocean from the waiting room."

"That's right. We saw lifeguards on the beach."

"Sure."

"You're a good buddy, Adam. You'll take me back there when it's time again, right?"

"Sure I will." Nelson stood up. "Let's go home now, okay, Frank? Big stars like us need our beauty rest, right?"

Kellner nodded, taking the question seriously. He pulled himself to his feet, swaying only slightly. "Okay, Adam. Thanks."

"That's what I'm here for, Frank."

They walked out together, the bartender calling for last orders as the door shut behind them.

* * *

The carpentry division had outdone themselves. When Nelson and Kellner got to the laboratory set the next morning, it had been transformed, half of it turned into a cage to contain the bulbous leather form of the pillbug. The thing was about a dozen feet high in its middle and almost twenty long, with shiny black leather arranged in sections to simulate the creature's armored segments. Nelson was expecting eyes or antennae or something, but somehow the smooth, unbroken leather was much more disquieting. He couldn't say it looked like a giant pillbug, exactly, but it certainly looked like something nasty. Something to avoid.

"How the hell did they get it in here?" he asked out loud.

"It breaks into sections," a nearby crewman said. "The cage walls, too." He handed Nelson and Kellner their screen rifles. Nelson swung the strap of his across his shoulder without conscious thought, watching Evans consulting with the technicians, explaining how the giant bug worked.

Kellner held his rifle uncertainly. He tested the trigger gently, remembering the noise the fake weapons made. Nothing at all like the real things. If you knew.

Susan Reid walked onto the set. Nelson winked at her, and she blushed and walked over to run her hand over the leather hide of the thing. When she saw him watching her and grinning, she blushed harder and turned her back to him completely.

"Mr. Nelson, join us, please?" Evans said.

Nelson walked over to the group clustered around the new cage wall, which now included Will Joplin and Roy Prine. "Morning, Mr. Evans," he said. "This is quite a toy you've got here."

"Isn't it? I'm really quite pleased. It will look ridiculous on screen, of course, but any reaction is better than none."

"Tell him the gag," one of the techs said.

"Thank you so much for the suggestion," Evans said. "Mr. Nelson, I'm afraid the moment has come for your tragic death."

"That's a shame. I was so young."

"Full of promise," Joplin put in.

"We all had our eye on you," said Prine.

"All eyes will indeed be on you," said Evans. "However briefly. Now, here are the details of your gruesome demise. Mr. Prine and Mr. Joplin will be in the foreground of the shot, discussing Mr. Joplin's attempt to find a poison that will kill the captive pillbug as an alternative to bombing the city. Miss Reid will be at the table behind them, taking notes. Your colleague, Mr...."

"Kellner," Nelson provided. Kellner was on the edge of the little group now, still holding his rifle uncertainly. Susan had also come closer, and everyone on the set was now listening to the dapper Russian.

"Mr. Kellner, thank you, will be by the door of the lab, armed, of course. You, Mr. Nelson, will be standing here, immediately in front of the cage, you see, with your back to it."

Nelson stood on the spot.

"Precisely, thank you. Now, the pillbug is mounted on wheels, you see, and we will have some men behind it prepared to push it suddenly forward. The cage wall is made to break apart in the middle—you see the joints here, and here—as the creature surges against it. The men will push at the moment Mr. Joplin says his line—" The director pointed at Joplin.

"None of the mixtures have any effect at all," Joplin provided.

"Precisely, thank you, perhaps a bit angrier, but good. At this point, Mr. Nelson, as the cage breaks behind you, you will turn, give me your best scream, and fall backwards as the creature overwhelms you. There is a clearance of eighteen inches at the front. It will simply roll over you, and to the horror, or perhaps the amusement, of our audience, it will appear to be devouring you whole."

"Either that or having its way with me," Nelson said. There was some laughter.

"You and I envision very different types of film, Mr. Nelson. At any rate, after your disappearance, Mr. Kellner and Mr. Prine will oblige me by shooting their weapons as many times as possible at your killer, while Miss Reid screams her beautiful head off and Mr. Joplin pulls her offscreen to safety." The director clapped his hands. "We cut, we pull you out, and then we reset the camera to shoot some close-ups. Does everyone understand?" He seemed satisfied with the nods and general grunts of assent from all directions. "Very good. To your places, all."

Technicians began to scatter around the set. Kellner was already by the door, at the far side of the set from the cage. Nelson stood on the spot Evans had indicated. He would have liked a rehearsal, just to get a sense of how quickly the thing moved and exactly how the wall would break, but he'd been told several times that Eagle's accountants were allergic to rehearsals. He bounced slightly on his feet, visualizing how he would fall and watching as Evans moved Joplin, Prine, and Susan into their places. He didn't want to fall on his back with the rifle under him. But of course, he would be reaching for the rifle, trying to shoot the thing as it came for him. All right.

He was distracted from his preparations by the realization that Kellner was no longer in his place by the door. He felt the start of a surge of anger. Everything was ready to go, and now he'd have to stop everything so they could get Kellner back in position. He'd probably need more pills before they'd be able to go.

Evans was already backing away from the set, his hands rising in the now-familiar gesture to frame what he was seeing. Nelson was about to step forward to stop him when he saw Kellner behind the director, stepping toward him, holding the screen rifle by its barrel over his shoulder, like Musial tracking a curve coming right down the middle.

Nobody but Nelson was looking, but everyone in the big room heard the sound like an ax sinking into lumber as the stock of the weapon connected with the base of Evans's skull. He dropped forward, his arms uselessly limp at his sides. Nelson broke forward into a run, knowing it was too late to do anything that would mean a damn. Somebody screamed. Kellner spun the rifle upwards, holding it now like a sledgehammer, and brought the stock down with all his strength on the top of Evans's head. This time, the sound was lost in the explosion of voices and shouts as three people tackled Kellner from different directions.

* * *

It was almost two in the morning, three days later, when Nelson walked back into the bar down the street from his boarding house. The same bartender was reading the sports page. There was one customer, a man near sixty, sitting at the end of the bar nearest the street. Nelson took the stool farthest from him. "Beer," he said. He closed his eyes and listened to the bartender put the paper down and draw the drink, then set it on the bar in front of him.

Nelson was tired. There'd been the frantic surge of activity three days ago, slipping in the pool of Evans's blood, the useless ambulance, the techies taking turns socking Kellner in the jaw. By the time the cops collected him, Kellner's face was turning purple, and he'd lost three teeth. He didn't try to defend himself. The whole time, the only thing he said, over and over, was "I killed a commie. Ain't that what I was supposed to do?" When the cops took him away, Nelson asked them to be sure Kellner took his medicine. He didn't think any of them had really been paying attention, though.

Then the hours with the detectives, in groups and singly, explaining over and over where and when he'd met Kellner, how they'd gotten on the film. And the men from the State Department in the expensive suits. And the trip back to the boarding house to show them Kellner's room. And then, when it should have been all over. The men from Eagle insisted they had to complete the film. Roy Prine slapped one of them across the face pretty good, but in the end, there was no getting around it. A lot of money—at least by Eagle standards—had been sunk into the movie, it was almost done, and nobody was getting paid unless they finished the thing.

The only one who refused was Susan.

Eagle brought in a new director—a bald guy in his sixties who never got out of his chair, never learned anyone's name, and never stopped sipping from his flask—and a girl with Susan's height and hair color who kept her back to the camera. They shot the remaining scenes in two days, moving from one to the next as quickly as possible. Evans's bloodstain was still on the floor. Everyone took care not to step on it.

As soon as the last scene was done, Nelson went looking for Susan. Her roommate said she'd gone back to her hometown. She wouldn't tell Nelson where that was.

He heard coins hitting the bar and realized he'd been half asleep. He opened his eyes. The other drinker was gone. The bartender folded the paper, put it under the bar, and came down to where Nelson was sitting.

"Nice job," he said.

Nelson didn't say anything.

"They told me to say that. They don't tell me to do that very often," the bartender said. "They figured it would take you at least another few days to get him there."

"He was on a hair trigger," Nelson said. "Another few days and I could have had him taking a run at Eisenhower."

"You don't want the pat on the back, no skin off my nose. I'm just the messenger boy."

"I know that."

"Well then." The bartender picked at something under his nail.

"They'll open him up," Nelson said. "A month without the pills and he'll tell them everything."

"Maybe. Maybe not. That's not our problem, is it?"

"It'll be somebody's." Nelson drained the last of his beer. He got up, walked around the bar, found a bottle and a glass, and brought them back to his place.

"They know what they're doing. He'll get called a nut. Probably won't even go to regular jail. In a few years, he'll get released, and somebody will scoop him up and prime him again. Maybe he'll take a run at Ike then."

Nelson had filled the glass. He set to work emptying it. "What did Mishnev do, anyway?"

"Now that is really not our problem," the bartender said. "You could get into some trouble, if I even mention that you asked."

"Mention away."

"You don't ever ask why. You know that."

"Sure."

The bartender moved his feet. "Who the hell knows. Maybe he knew something he wasn't supposed to know. Maybe he screwed somebody's wife, and that's why he ran in the first place. Or maybe they just want the next guy thinking about coming over to remember that the last guy got beaten to death by a psychotic ex-GI, and God bless America."

"You don't ever ask why," Nelson said. "I heard that somewhere."

"Screw you."

Nelson drank the last of the glass and stood up. He looked the bartender in the eye until the smaller man had to look away.

"You know," Nelson said, "I actually liked the guy."

The bartender picked up a napkin, refolded it, put it back down. "Which?" he asked. "Mishnev or Kellner?"

"You've got a message, messenger boy. Let's have it."

The bartender cracked his knuckles, but he still didn't look Nelson in the face. "Houston," he said finally. "There's a bookstore across the street from the main bus station. A man named Lewis works there afternoons. You're to make contact within the next ten days."

"Houston, bookstore, Lewis," Nelson said. "It's been a goddamn pleasure working with you."

***

Six months later, the man no longer named Adam Nelson was in Columbus, Ohio, working at a shipping company, diverting a couple of trucks a month to unscheduled destinations. One day, the local paper told him *They Came For Our World* was playing as the B feature behind *The Sea Chase* at a downtown theater. He went every night for two weeks.

He had to admit it: the uniforms came out looking damned good.

Herb Ecks Goes Underground

Tobin was playing solitaire in his office when Casey stuck her head in. "You expecting a guy named Herb Ecks? He's asking for you."

Tobin flipped over three cards and moved a red jack onto a black queen. "Never heard of him."

"Well, he's heard of you," Casey said. She watched him turn over more cards. "You know, you can play that a lot faster on the computer."

"Fast isn't the point. Where is this guy?"

"Stuck him in the Yaz room. I'm heading back up front."

Tobin played for another few minutes, got stuck, and swept the cards back into a deck. Ecks was probably selling something. Tobin managed the Scarlet Mallard, a pub in downtown Boston. Somebody was always trying to sell him something. Coasters. Glassware. Japanese vodka. Last week, stickers with pictures of flies for the urinals, so guys could try to kill the bugs with their streams of piss. Tobin passed.

The Yaz room, its walls covered with Carl Yastrzemski memorabilia, was one of the small, private spaces at the back of the Mallard. The guy sitting at the table, staring at his phone, was younger than Tobin expected. He was small and wiry, with stringy blond hair and a patchy beard. Dense swirls of abstract, colorful tattoos covered his arms, and both of his earlobes were stretched out around thick black rings.

Microbrewery, Tobin thought. Kid wants me to buy the beer he's been making in his basement.

"You Ecks?" he asked.

The kid looked up, confused. "Ecks?"

"I'm Mike Tobin. The girl said Herb Ecks wanted to see me."

The kid frowned, then something clicked. "No, she misunderstood. I told her I do urbex."

Tobin sat down. "What the hell is urbex?"

"Urban exploration," the kid said. At Tobin's blank look, he waved his arm to take in their general surroundings. "It's a hobby. A sport, kind of. Exploring the hidden parts of cities. Abandoned buildings, old steam tunnels, deserted subway lines, whatever."

"Sounds like a great way to get hauled in for trespassing."

"It happens," the kid said. "You've gotta stay up on your tetanus shots, too."

"Okay, so you're not Herb Ecks. Who are you, and what can I do for you?"

The kid hesitated. "You know what? Maybe I should just keep being Herb for the moment."

Tobin pushed back from the table. "I don't play these games."

"Wait a minute." The kid grabbed Tobin's wrist. Tobin looked down at it, his expression stone, and "Herb" let go. "Give me five minutes. Please. I promise it'll be worth your while."

Humoring the kid would probably be faster than fighting with him. "Fine. Make it quick."

"Okay." Herb—Tobin couldn't stop thinking of the kid as Herb—visibly gathered his thoughts. "About a month ago, I was in this restaurant that went out of business. I won't tell you where, exactly, but it's near Faneuil Hall."

"You were just in this restaurant. You weren't, like, breaking and entering or anything."

"I said that's part of it. Anyway, the restaurant was only there a few years, but the building is pre-Civil War. I squeezed in behind the walk-in freezer and found a little door in the wall. It was boarded over, so long ago that the boards were half rotted through. I pried them off and found a shaft. I think maybe once upon a time it was a dumbwaiter."

"Great work. You going around the city telling everybody about this, or am I lucky?"

Herb ignored the interruption. "I went down the shaft and ended up in a subbasement that I don't think anyone's been in for decades. There was a stack of empty crates in one corner, and an access hatch behind them."

"And you went through that. I get it. Pick up the pace."

"I'm not telling you the whole route anyway. But you wouldn't believe how complex it gets down there. People have been living in Boston for hundreds of years, digging tunnels, building basements, laying in utility lines, storm drains, emergency access points to sewers and power cables. And of course, you're trying to figure this all out in the dark. It takes time. I've been exploring this route for a month. And last week, I ended up here."

Herb put his phone flat on the table, and a video started to play on the tiny screen. It showed flickering views of a cramped, narrow passage between a slab of cement and a brick wall. The floor looked like dirt, and as the camera moved slowly along a few rats scurried away. After a minute, the camera turned to the brick wall at a place where a few bricks had fallen away. The camera refocused. Through the gap in the bricks was some kind of metal, scarred and stained. The video ended on a close shot of it.

Tobin shrugged. "So?"

"So." Herb leaned forward, excited. "I've been mapping as I go, very precisely." He tapped the screen. "That brick wall is the northern end of the basement of New England Federal Trust, the big branch. The original one downtown. And the metal is the back of the safety deposit boxes."

Tobin's mouth tightened. "You can't be sure of that."

"I'm sure. Two days ago, I rented a box so I could go down there. When the guy opened my box, he was standing about three feet from where I was when I shot that."

"Let's say you're right. Why tell me?"

Herb bit his lip. "Because I don't know anyone else who's done time for bank robbery."

Tobin stiffened. "You don't know me either, punk. You sure you want to go down this road?"

Herb held up his hands in a calming gesture. "I don't mean any offense."

"I don't care what you mean. Where you getting this about me?"

"I had a cousin who worked here, five or six years ago. He told me about you, said you were a good boss. He was surprised when another bartender told him about your record."

"Some people need to learn to keep their mouths shut." Tobin stood up. "Goodbye, Herb. Stop up front and tell Casey I said to give you a beer on the house."

Herb jumped to his feet. "Mr. Tobin, I'm not trying to cause any trouble. I just thought you would know someone who could help me."

"Help you," Tobin said flatly. "Help you commit a federal crime."

"I can't do it alone," Herb said. "It'll take a few men with tools hours to get through that wall and peel back the metal. But once they do—hundreds of boxes, Mr. Tobin. Jewelry, bonds, art, who knows what. I wouldn't know what to do with that stuff, how to turn it into cash."

"And you think I do."

"I looked up the old news stories. You were part of a crew, but you were the only one who got caught. I figure that means you didn't give up any of your partners. I figure it means you still know people who would listen to you."

"You've been watching too many movies, kid." Tobin turned to leave.

Herb grabbed his arm, this time not letting go. "All I'm asking for is an introduction. Sir, I'm desperate. I won't stand here and give you a sob story, but I need this. It's a once-in-a-lifetime chance." To Tobin's shock, he fell to his knees. "Please."

Tobin closed his eyes. He'd always liked the fact that in these back rooms you couldn't hear any street noise, not even anything from the busy bar up front. The walls were thick, solid, ancient compared to the crap buildings they threw up these days. The building was old.

Tobin was old, too.

"Call me Wednesday night," he said. "Don't talk to anybody else. Don't come here. Just call. I'll either give you a time to come back or just say no, and if it's no, that's it. I don't want to see you in here again."

He didn't wait to see what Herb had to say to that.

* * *

A week later, Tobin was waiting in front of the bar when Herb came around the corner. He was practically skipping as he came down the sidewalk, a grin on his face, and Tobin resisted the impulse to smack him.

"Calm down," he said when Herb came up to him. "You go in there like some kid at Disneyland, and this ends ugly. Act like a professional."

Herb nodded, his expression calming. "Yes, sir."

"You gotta understand, a meeting ain't anything. People have meetings all the time, and nothing happens. There ain't a dime in your pocket yet, is there?"

Herb was visibly shrinking. "No, sir."

"There won't be at the end of the night, either. Just remember, your name is Herb."

He led the kid down the stairs and through the main barroom. Casey, working the tap, gave them a look. Tobin ignored it.

Two men were waiting for them in the Yaz room. The one about Herb's age, sitting at the table with a bottle of beer, was wearing a black tracksuit and bobbing his head to something playing in his earpods. The older man, leaning against the wall next to the door, could have played linebacker for the Patriots. He was wearing a suit that strained against his shoulders.

"Herb," Tobin said, "this is Al."

Herb stuck out his hand. Al, tucking his earbuds into an inner pocket, ignored it. "First thing that's gonna happen, Herb," he said, "is that Big G here is gonna take you to the men's room and watch you strip."

"What?" Herb looked at the impassive giant. "Why?"

Al shook his head. "If you really gotta ask that, you're too stupid for me to stick around for anything you got to say."

Herb swallowed, but nodded and followed Big G from the room. Tobin sat down across from Al. "Don't think you're gonna scare him off," he said. "Kid really wants this."

"I don't give a shit. I'm here as a courtesy."

"So be courteous."

Al shot him a look. "You teaching me manners now?"

Somebody should, Tobin thought about saying. It wasn't worth it. He looked up into the corner of the room while Al scrolled through something on his phone.

In a minute, the other two men were back. "You should see this guy, Al," Big G said. "He's got more ink than anybody I've ever seen."

"I'll take your word for it," Al said. He made an exaggerated gesture at the seat next to Tobin, smirking. "Won't you be so kind as to join us, Herb?"

The kid's energy had drained some, but he took the seat. "Thank you for coming."

"Yeah, yeah. We'll skip reading the minutes. Let's just get to it."

Herb took out his phone and started his spiel. Al glazed over at the explanation of urbex, but his attention sharpened when Herb mentioned the bank. He had Herb play the video of the wall twice, then tapped his fingers on the table, thinking.

"Say I believe all this," he said. "What makes you think nobody else knows about it?"

"Explorers tag their routes with spray paint," Herb said. "Partly so they don't get lost and partly so they can claim credit for new trails. There isn't a single tag anywhere on this path except mine."

"Okay," Al said. "So what exactly do you have in mind?"

"I figure it'll take three or four guys, including me," Herb said. "They'll need to be small, because there are tight spaces along the way. We'll have to carry in tools, plus food and water. And I guess a bucket for, you know, necessaries."

"Food and water?" Al frowned. "How long you figure this to take?"

"A while," Herb said. "We can't use power tools because of the noise. That brick wall is crumbling, but it's still going to take time to pry the bricks out and move them out of the way. Then we need to peel the metal, and then we'll need to pop the boxes open and take whatever's most worth taking, because there's no way to carry that many boxes back out."

"You've been thinking about this," Tobin said.

"I've hardly thought about anything else," Herb said. "Memorial Day is coming up in a few weeks. If we go in Friday afternoon, we can be in position to start working Friday night. We'll be long gone by the time they open up

Tuesday morning."

Al rubbed his chin. "So you're saying, like, Big G couldn't go."

Herb shook his head. "No way," he said. "There are a couple of spots along the way that I can barely get through."

Al looked at Tobin. "That lets you out, too."

"I was never in," Tobin said. "I'm too old and tired to be crawling through rat shit. Back in my day, the finder's fee on something like this would be five percent."

"Still is," Al said. "How about you, Herb? What you looking for?"

"Half," Herb said.

There was nothing remotely friendly in Al's smile. "Try again."

"You need me," Herb said. "You'd never find your way there on your own."

"So I don't go. I've got plenty of other ways to make money, Herb. Seems to me you're the one needs us."

Herb crossed his arms. "Thirty percent."

"Fifteen," Al said.

"A quarter."

"Twenty. That's it, or Big G and I are leaving right now."

Herb grimaced but nodded. "All right. Twenty."

Tobin stood up. "I suppose that's all you need from me," he said. "I'll leave the details to you two."

To Tobin's surprise, Herb stood up and held out his hand. "Thank you, Mr. Tobin. I'm very grateful that you listened to me."

Tobin shook his hand. "You really want to thank me?"

"Of course."

"Don't come in my place again," Tobin said. He looked at Big G. "Come on out front," he said. "I'll treat you to a drink while the brain trust gets to work."

*　*　*

It was past midnight, but the stifling heat that had been punishing Boston all through July hadn't let up. Thanks to some quirk in the design of the building, the heat in the Scarlet Mallard gathered and focused in Tobin's office, so he didn't spend much time there.

He was sitting at a table in the corner of the front room, playing solitaire and periodically tipping a little rum from a bottle into a glass. Casey was behind the bar, reading a magazine. Every few minutes, she fanned herself with it. A man sat alone at the bar nursing the last beer of the day, and three women dressed for a funeral were at a table on the far side of the room. The place was otherwise empty.

The door to the street opened, and Al and Big G came in. Al spotted Tobin and said something to Big G, who nodded and went to the bar. Al headed for Tobin's table and sat across from him.

Tobin kept his eyes on his cards. "Don't recall asking you to sit," he said.

"Black nine on the red ten," Al said.

Tobin narrowed his eyes, peering through the haze the rum had been pleasantly drawing across his sight. He watched his hand sluggishly move the card. He didn't know how he'd missed it.

Al looked around. "Guess you do a little more business when it isn't two hundred degrees out, huh?"

"Don't you read the papers? Climate's changing. This is how it's gonna be from now on."

"Nah, I don't buy that," Al said. "You watch. Couple years from now we'll have a snowstorm in June or something."

"Me, I read the papers," Tobin said. He put down the cards and poured himself a slug. "Saw a story a couple weeks ago about a body found in a basement. Lots of tattoos and two bullets in his head."

Al grinned. "Yeah, I saw that too."

Tobin took the glass of rum in one swallow. "Haven't seen any stories about safety deposit boxes, though."

Al picked up the bottle and took a swig. "We hear they're trying to keep it quiet," he said. "Bad publicity. And it's not like the customers have any proof of what they lost. Hell, some of them won't want to own up to what was in those boxes. Lots of lawyers having lots of talks behind closed doors."

Tobin pushed the cards into a deck and started to shuffle. "Convenient."

"Works out for us. All of us." Al pulled a plain white envelope from his hip pocket and pushed it across the table.

Tobin didn't touch it. He started dealing out a new game.

Al looked at the envelope, then back at Tobin. "You gonna count it?"

"Nope." Tobin moved an ace. "Guess you let him carry some of the shit out before you capped him."

"Somebody wants to do you favor, you gonna say no?"

"Not how I would have done it," Tobin said. "Not how your old man would have done it."

Al had gotten very still. "I could have sent some errand boy. I'm here myself out of respect. That has to work both ways."

"Sure, sure," Tobin said. He turned over more cards without seeing them. "There was something I wanted to ask you, though."

"Yeah," Al said. "What's that?"

Tobin looked him in the eye for the first time. "You think your father is proud of you?"

Al's face turned red. He leaned forward, knuckles white on the arms of the chair. "You want to say something direct, old man?" he hissed. "I spent three miserable days underground shitting in a bucket to get you this." He tapped the envelope. "I haven't heard a thank you."

"Thank you," said Tobin. He pushed the cards together and began dealing a new game without shuffling.

Al shook his head and stood up. "I grew up on stories about you," he said. "This is just damned sad now."

"Yeah," Tobin said. "Sad."

"Don't call us again," Al said. He headed for the door. Big G met him there. Al stormed out, while Big G held the door for the three mourning women to file out before him. The other man at the bar was already gone. Big G looked across the room at Tobin, who didn't meet his eyes.

When the door closed behind the big man, Tobin was left alone except for Casey, across the room, putting glasses and plates from the women's table into a big plastic tub she carried into the back.

Tobin made four piles of cards on the table in front of him in a rough square. He started dealing cards onto them one at a time, moving from stack to stack at random. He took his time. If he could hold himself to one card a minute, he'd kill almost an hour just getting through the deck once.

He didn't hear Casey coming up to the table. "What's that game called?" she asked.

"It's called Tobin," he said. "I'd teach you the rules, but there aren't any."

Casey gave a half chuckle, not understanding if he was kidding. "I'm about to take off," she said. "Anything else I can do for you?"

"Two things," Tobin said. He nodded at the bottle. "Pour that out and toss it."

Casey picked it up. "It's half full," she said.

"Get rid of it."

"You're the boss. What's the second thing?"

Tobin put the eight of diamonds on the bottom right stack. He picked up the envelope, feeling the thick stack inside, and gave it to her. "This is yours."

She took it, peeked inside, and made a noise Tobin hadn't heard before. "Are you kidding me? You want this in the safe, right?"

"No," Tobin said. "It's your severance pay."

Seven of clubs. Upper right.

"Wait a minute," Casey said. "You're firing me?"

"Yeah," Tobin said. "If I see you in here again, I'll hurt you."

She stood staring at him. When she didn't move, he looked up into her face. "Leave now, Casey," he said softly.

When she was gone, Tobin locked the door behind her. He got a fresh bottle of rum from behind the bar, sat at the table, and drank directly from the neck. He put the three of hearts in the lower left.

Half a block from the front door of the bar, there was a stop for one of the hop-on, hop-off tourist buses that clogged every downtown street. Tomorrow he'd get on one, for the first time. He'd sit on the top deck, sipping from a hidden flask. He'd feel the punishing sun and the rum-scented sweat pouring from him, and he'd listen to stories of revolution recounted through scratchy speakers.

King of hearts. Lower right.

Crime Scene

When Adler got back to his private dock, Melanie Phelps was sitting at the end, legs kicking in the air over the water. Her Stevie Ray Vaughan T-shirt and khaki shorts made her look like the kid she'd been when they first met, thirty years ago. Adler hadn't seen her in more than a year. He cut the engine and let the little boat drift in, tossing her a line. As she tied it off, he climbed up onto the planks beside her, carrying his pole and a small cooler.

"Catch much?" she asked, nodding at the cooler.

"This is for beer," Adler said. "These days, I let the ones I catch go. Too much trouble cleaning them." In truth, he hadn't wet a line in months. When he went out on the lake, he mostly just drifted, staring out over the water. "How's your father?"

Melanie shook her head. "No change. Wish I could say different."

Lamar Phelps had spent decades as the country's top criminal talent scout, hooking crooks up with jobs from coast to coast for a slice of the proceeds. When a stroke cut him down five years ago, Melanie took over the family business. Adler went to Denver once to see his old friend, but found nothing of Lamar in the chair being wheeled from one sunny spot to another. Given the things Lamar knew that would be of interest to prosecutors, the fact that he was completely nonverbal was, Adler supposed, a blessing in disguise. It was one bitch of a disguise, though.

"I was going to grill a steak," he said. "You want one?"

"You cook now?"

"Beats the hell out of driving an hour and a half for a Big Mac."

He grilled on the cabin's back deck. Melanie sat at the picnic table. He tried to remember how old she was while she chatted, mostly gossip about people Adler had long forgotten or never knew. She had to be in her forties, but she didn't show it. There was maybe a whisper of gray, barely detectable, in the blond hair at her temples.

By the time he served the food, she was lapsing into a silence to match his own. He'd seen it before. The spell of this place. When a V of geese came overhead, close enough to hear not just their honking but the velvet sound of their wings cutting the air, she looked at them with an open delight that took her right back to childhood.

She finally pushed her plate away. "I can't remember the last time I had a steak and baked potato."

"I'm a simple man," Adler said. "Gonna talk about why you're here?"

"A job," Melanie said. "But you knew that."

He opened another beer and waited.

"One target," she said. "Your cut is a hundred K, twenty now, and the rest after."

"Something with that kind of number attached has to be hairy."

"There are some complications. The target is locally prominent, and the customer wants him to get it in a very public place at a very specific time."

"Hold the pickles, hold the lettuce," Adler said. "Special orders don't upset us." He waved a hand at her confused look. "Before your time. Give me the details."

"Ever been to Dallas?"

"Passed through a few times. Never worked there."

"All the better if nobody local can make you." Melanie took an eight-by-ten from her bag and slid it across the table. It showed a silver-haired man in an expensive suit, his arms crossed. Some kind of publicity shot.

"Alex Lersch," she said. "Sixty-four years old, net worth a couple hundred million. Never married, no known children."

"Gay?"

"Don't know. Could be he's just allergic to sharing the pile. He got his start in real estate and software, but he's so diversified now that you couldn't really say what he does. Active in local politics and charities, mostly leans left, which isn't easy in Texas these days. Has a reputation as shrewd but basically honest."

"Who'd he piss off?"

"Don't know," she said again. At Adler's look, she raised a hand. "Honestly. This one came through deep back channels. The money's real, but I don't know who the client is."

"I'm hearing warning bells, kiddo."

"I get you, but show me the cop who can put out this kind of cash just on the chance of netting somebody."

"What about the time and place?"

"You're gonna love this. Dealey Plaza on November twenty-second."

He gave her a flat stare. "You drove one hell of a long way for a joke."

"No joke. Lersch is an assassination buff, an obsessive. He's supposed to have the largest private collection of Kennedy materials in the world. Funds an annual conference that's a mix of legitimate historians and tinfoil nutjobs. One of the activities is a visit to Dealey Plaza that he leads himself on the anniversary. That's where you're supposed to tag him."

"Somebody's got a sick sense of humor."

"If you've got the money, I think it just counts as an eccentric sense of humor. Anyway, there it is. You in or out?"

* * *

He gave Melanie the extra bedroom to spare her the two-hour drive to the nearest hotel. After she went to bed, he sat on the dock, under the stars. It was too late in the year for lightning bugs, but the woods and the water were buzzing with the constant small sounds of living creatures.

Adler had done a lot of jobs in fields of work where nobody writes a résumé. He started in explosives, blowing safes for crews on the West Coast, then learned to hack alarm systems. He hired on for a handful of kidnappings, which always seemed to go screwy. There had been some hijacking, some smuggling. Eventually, word got around that he didn't mind eliminating people under the right circumstances, and Lamar started steering hits his way. By his count, Adler had done thirty-four. If he thought hard, he could remember all their names.

Lately, he'd been remembering them a lot, drifting around on the lake. It was always easiest to assume they all deserved what was coming. It was starting to bother him that for some of them, he didn't know. He didn't know why somebody in their lives wanted the hammer dropped.

The money from this Dallas job would be nice, but he didn't need it. He took it because maybe this time he could know why. Even thinking the question was breaking some rules, but he was too old and tired to care. November 22 was almost a month off. The way Adler figured it, how he spent that time was up to him.

He was going to spend it figuring out why somebody wanted Alex Lersch dead.

* * *

Two weeks later, Adler set foot in Dealey Plaza for the first time. The Rangers ball cap pulled low on his forehead and the heavy black sunglasses covering half his face would complicate facial recognition programs that might be running on any one of the dozens of security cameras on an average American city block. The Cowboys jersey and the camera around his neck marked him as a tourist. He'd barely crossed the street into the plaza when a tall Black man with a canvas bag slung over his shoulder offered him a "personal tour" for a hundred dollars. Adler got away by giving the man twenty bucks for a reproduction of the November 23, 1963, edition of the *New York Times*. He held it loosely at his side as he wandered, letting it ward off the other hustlers.

On a pleasant Saturday afternoon, with the anniversary approaching, there were plenty of tourists for the hustlers to prey on. Some were rolling through on buses, the rehearsed patter of the guides echoing through tinny loudspeakers, but many were just walking around. Adler drifted among them, occasionally snapping a picture. In part of his brain, he held a sketchy biography of this version of himself. *Midwest. Retired schoolteacher. Middle-grade science. Widowed?* Mostly, though, he focused on getting a feel for the setting, finding the lines of sight, the obvious entry and exit points, the less obvious maintenance and structural features.

It was an odd place. The plaza itself was just a rough triangle of patchy grass, with the base along Houston Street to the east and the point at the west, where the streets defining the two sides swept under railroad tracks. All the energy and interest was along the north edge, where the former Book Depository squatted at the corner of Houston and Elm, Oswald's window clearly marked. Two big white Xs in the middle of Elm showed the exact places where Kennedy had been hit.

In an hour and a half, Adler saw at least fifty people, most of them young men, stroll out into the road to take a selfie on an X, usually with the Oswald window in the frame behind them. They seemed oblivious to active traffic on the street, and he wondered how many got hit over the course of a year.

He heard at least twenty-five people, most of them slightly older men, looking back and forth from the window to an X and proclaiming it an easy shot. "He was right on top of him," they usually said.

He heard at least fifteen people, most of them middle-aged men, saying that their lawn back home was bigger than the grassy knoll.

They were inane, but they weren't wrong. The place had the aura of a backlot recreation, a three-quarter-scale model that didn't quite convince. It was the field of myth, the pressure point where the American century shattered. The most devastating rifle shot in history shouldn't be so short. The grassy knoll should at least be large enough for everyone mentioned in the conspiracy theories to stand on. If it wasn't for the sheer weight of the names, Dealey Plaza would look like what it was: a stunted, inconsequential green space tucked into an odd margin of a big city.

None of this mattered. He wasn't Lersch, trying to solve some riddle for the ages. He was a professional, here to do a job. He watched where the cops strolled and what they were looking at. He watched the traffic lights, timing them in his head. He walked five or six blocks in every direction, noting parking garages, bus stops, and buildings with multiple access points. He verified what he already knew: that from every corner of Dealey Plaza he had a clear, unimpeded view of the neon red shirt he'd hung in the window of his room on one of the upper floors of the big hotel a couple of blocks to the southwest.

* * *

Before coming to Dallas, Adler spent a week in another hotel in San Antonio, buying the things he would need at several different stores using credit cards under several different names. One of the things he bought was a laptop. At night in his room he used it to read everything he could find about Alexander Malcolm Lersch—interviews, profiles, news stories, the last few years of the available records on his various businesses and charitable funds.

He found nothing that provided an obvious motive for the man's murder. Lersch had no living relatives. Upon his death, half his fortune would go into a trust for the "perpetual funding" of a Center for the Study of Assassination and Political Violence at the University of Texas at Arlington, which would also be the recipient of his personal Kennedy collection. The other half would be distributed to various local charities focusing on voting rights and hunger. In his business dealings, Lersch was aggressive, but not ruthless, leaving no ruined rivals to dream of revenge. Even reading between the lines, Adler saw no evidence of scandal. No mysterious payoffs to former employees. No trace of money laundering or obvious bribes. From all appearances, Lersch was an upstanding citizen. The only unusual thing about him was his hang-up about the Kennedy hit.

Ideally, Adler would have shifted from research to surveillance once he was in Dallas, but keeping eyes on a multimillionaire around the clock wasn't a realistic proposition. He could hardly hang out in the reception area of Lersch's offices, which occupied several floors in a downtown skyscraper. Sitting in a coffee shop across from the entrance to the attached parking garage, he did verify something mentioned in almost every profile: despite his wealth, Lersch still drove his own car, arriving at the office at nine every morning and making it a firm practice to leave at five. He spoke in many interviews about the importance of maintaining a balance between work and the rest of life, and of resisting overwork on one hand and unnecessary luxury or indulgence on the other.

Adler was grateful that Lersch's distaste for "unnecessary luxury" did not extend to buying some anonymous sedan or SUV. He drove a silver Rolls-Royce that was easy to follow. For several days in a row, Adler trailed him from the office just after five, hoping to be led to something that would give him a thread to pull. A mistress. An underground sex club. A poker room. Every night, though, Lersch drove straight to his estate in Highland Park. Adler's research told him that the place was worth in the neighborhood of ten million dollars, and that Lersch lived there alone. Here, too, he couldn't just sit on the street and watch the place. In a neighborhood like that, the cops would have been on him in twenty minutes. He made several passes a night, though, and never saw any other cars go near the place or anything remotely suspicious.

Driving back to his hotel, Adler drummed his fingers on the wheel. He was starting to wonder if somebody had just pulled Lersch's name out of a hat, or if maybe this was some kind of elaborate sting. He was tempted to call Melanie to try to track the back channels she'd spoken of, but asking questions like that in the middle of a job would set off every alarm she had. Melanie was fond of him, but she would assume he was either going soft or had flipped on her. Either choice meant that she would be visiting another one of her subcontractors soon, and sliding a picture of him across the table. Adler was on his own.

* * *

He briefly considered registering for Lersch's assassination conference before rejecting the idea as too conspicuous. The schedule was online, though. There was nothing for him in the scheduled sessions on bullet trajectories and Cuban diplomatic archives. On the night of the twenty-first, though, there was a three-hour formal banquet, with a keynote address by Lersch himself. "Living in the Echo of Gunfire: The Continuing Legacy of

Assassination Studies."

Poetic, Adler thought.

Lersch's estate backed onto a creek that, two miles away, ran through the grounds of a country club. An hour before the banquet was scheduled to start, with dusk gathering, Adler parked in the employee lot of the club. He walked to the creek and began following it, sticking as close to the edge of the water as he could. Most of the creek's path through the whole area was still heavily wooded, and along much of the way he was completely out of sight of any structures. He stopped occasionally to check his exact position on his phone's GPS. There was heavy undergrowth in many places, and the wet ground made for slow progress, but in forty minutes he was at the low wall marking the rear boundary of Lersch's property. Ten minutes after that he was at the patio door at the back of the house.

The security system had been installed by one of the big national firms. Several years back, keeping his skills up to date, Adler used one of his dummy identities to go through the firm's hiring and training programs. There had been some updates since then, of course, but people in the security business are every bit as inefficient as people everywhere else. They couldn't always be bothered to, for example, check their systems for legacy backdoors left by a previous generation of programmers.

He had the door open in twenty minutes. It took him another thirty to find the security system's central drive, disable the cameras, and wipe the last two hours they'd recorded.

* * *

The speech went well, Alex Lersch thought. Perhaps a little dry, but he hoped his sense of urgency came through. He had spoken at length of the coming establishment of the Center at UT-Arlington, urging his fellow enthusiasts to unite their scholarship and investigative powers around its banner. The time had come to set aside petty squabbles and ensure the security of future inquiries. Had he persuaded them? Time would tell.

Tomorrow would tell.

When he got home, he went into the office, intending to make a few final notes before the tour in the morning. The sconce in the hallway cast a long, canted column of light across the room as he crossed to the desk. He was reaching for the lamp, thinking that something seemed odd without being able to put his finger on what it was, when a calm voice came from behind him. "Don't turn around," it said. "And don't turn on the light. I have a gun."

The chair, Lersch thought. The chair that normally sat in the middle of the room was missing. Pulled into some corner for this man's comfort, no doubt.

Lersch put his hands flat on the desk and waited.

* * *

Adler gave Lersch credit for not panicking. He seemed perfectly calm.

"There was a revolver in your upper right-hand desk drawer," Adler said. "There isn't now. Go behind the desk and turn the chair to face the wall and sit down."

Lersch did as he was told. "I don't suppose you'd believe me if I said there's not much here worth stealing," he said.

"No, but it doesn't matter. That's not what I'm here for."

"And what are you here for?"

Adler could just make out the curve of Lersch's head above the top of the chair. "You and I have an appointment tomorrow morning."

Lersch was slow to answer, the extra beat confirming what Adler already knew. "I have an appointment with a lot of people tomorrow morning," he said. "I'm leading a tour."

"Our appointment isn't about an old murder."

Rich people always have the quietest homes. Adler knew the air conditioning was running, but it didn't keep him from hearing Lersch's breath getting shallow as he answered. "I don't know what you mean."

"How long have you got, Lersch?"

The answer came with a touch of acid. "I guess that's up to the man holding a gun on me."

"I've seen your medicine cabinet. I'm no doctor, but I've had plenty of time to Google the stuff you're taking. It's not for lowering your cholesterol."

For a time, he thought Lersch wasn't going to answer.

"Two months," he finally said. "Probably a little less."

"You put the hit on yourself."

"I've spent my entire adult life studying assassination," Lersch said. "I knew the kind of people to get in touch with. The professionals."

"Very flattering," Adler said.

"But not very professional," Lersch said. "This is not what I paid for."

"I've been trying to figure out why anybody would want you dead," Adler said. "That's why I came here tonight. I wanted to know the reason."

Lersch made a noise in his throat. "I've bought many things and services in my life. I've never before had anyone demand to know why I wanted them." He made the noise again. "Not professional."

"I'll report myself to the union when this is over," Adler said.

"And now that you know? Does my motive meet your exacting standards? It's rather late for me to seek alternate arrangements."

"Now that I know? There's no reason you have to bleed out on dirty pavement, Lersch. I can do this right now. I can make it quick. Painless."

"*Not what I paid for.*" For a moment, Adler thought Lersch was going to come out of the chair, but he brought himself under control. "Please. Follow the directions you were given. Tomorrow, at the plaza."

"Why?"

"Why, why, why. You're certainly consistent in your curiosity, Mr. Whoever You Are."

"You're not answering."

The outline of Lersch's head dipped, came back up.

"Because I want what they have," he said.

"They?"

"Kennedy. Oswald. Two paths crossed, and more than half a century later, we don't fully understand why or how. You know what lasts, Mr. Killer? A mystery. A riddle. We'll talk about the two of them forever because there is no final piece to the puzzle. And me?" Lersch gave a low whistle. "One of the foremost experts on the assassination, cut down in exactly the same place by an unknown assailant for unknown reasons. There will be books about me. Podcasts. I'll be part of the story forever."

"Very pretty," Adler said. "Is it from your speech?"

"It's from my life."

It was Adler's turn to be quiet, for so long that Lersch finally stirred. "Did I put you to sleep?"

Adler stood up. "No, but you should go to bed yourself, Mr. Lersch. You've got a big day tomorrow. I'll leave the gun on your back patio."

* * *

A little over twelve hours later, a bus adorned with the logo of the conference made the tight turn onto Elm and parked at the curb directly in front of the former Book Depository. The plaza was already crowded with more people than Adler had seen there before. He was across the street watching, back in his tourist gear.

Lersch was the first person off the bus, followed by about two dozen men and women. He had a small megaphone with him, and he led the group along the sidewalk, gesturing at the street and occasionally the building. Adler couldn't hear the speech. What looked like a rather old-fashioned hearing aid in his right ear was playing the police radio band, at a volume high enough to drown out most of the noise around him.

Lersch led his group along Elm, taking them to the spot where Abraham Zapruder's 8mm camera caught the only footage of the assassination, then on to the grassy knoll. He was using the megaphone less, and seemed to be getting drawn into conversations with one or two individuals at a time. Adler shifted from foot to foot, seeming to stare at his phone while actually keeping track of the group's progress. Finally, Lersch led the entire bunch across to Adler's side of Elm and started bringing them the right direction. He was focused on the building now, gesturing at Oswald's window. When he was ten feet away, Adler dialed the first of two preprogrammed numbers on his cell phone.

Four blocks east, the burner cell he'd dialed triggered a device in the base of a sidewalk garbage can. Adler always enjoyed a chance to go back to his earliest specialty. Demolition. The explosion blew out most of the windows in the nearest office building.

Which happened to house the Internal Revenue Service.

Within twenty seconds, the voices in Adler's right ear exploded into pandemonium. The handful of uniformed cops standing near the corner in anticipation of the day's crowds clawed at their shoulder radios and began moving, slowly at first, in the direction of the explosion. The sound had been loud enough to be heard in the plaza, but as something distant and confusing. People looked around, slowly registering that something odd was happening, more from the actions of the cops than from what they had heard.

Lersch was five feet away now. He was standing near the curb, facing Oswald's window, still pointing at something. Adler slid through the crowd until he was standing immediately behind the man, and then keyed the second number.

This package was inside the big rolling suitcase standing against the floor-to-ceiling window in his hotel room. He'd built this one to be as loud as possible and to pour out a huge volume of smoke without actually starting a fire. In all of the plaza, his was the only head that didn't turn at the enormous *bang* to see black fumes billowing from a shattered window on an upper floor of the hotel.

The screams were immediate, from every direction. People began running, some toward the hotel, others away. Alex Lersch didn't scream or run, though. As he spun on his heel at the sound of the explosion, his chest met Adler's knife, coming in the opposite direction. Lersch's eyes widened. Adler put his left arm around the man's neck and pulled him close, the further movement of the knife masked by their two bodies, to all appearances just two men clinging to each other in the terror of the moment.

Many people nearby had fallen, either in shock or simply tripping out of panic. Lersch did not seem out of place as Adler eased him to the ground, on his stomach. There was no longer a cop in sight. He joined a knot of people moving north, away from what seemed to be the burning hotel, listening to the frantic voices in his ear coordinating the response to what looked very much like an organized attack.

His car was parked in the lot of an aquarium, half a mile away. On his way there, he ducked into the YMCA, where he'd left another set of clothes in a locker. He was changing when the voice in his ear started talking about a body in Dealey Plaza.

Ten minutes later, he was on the interstate, heading home.

* * *

"Not exactly stealthy," Melanie said when she brought the rest of his money a few weeks afterward.

Winter was slow in coming. There was beginning to be a bite in the air, but it was comfortable to sit out on the deck in light jackets.

Perfect bourbon weather, Adler thought. He poured another finger into his glass. "Stealthy was never an option," he said. "Not with what the client wanted."

"I guess not. But Christ, Adler, there's a damn federal task force on this now."

"Task forces aren't cops, kiddo." Adler sipped, feeling the warmth slip through him. "Task forces are politicians and press conferences and fourteen different three-letter organizations fighting over jurisdiction."

"You sound like Dad."

"There are worse ways to sound."

Adler was four years old when Kennedy got shot. Too young to really understand what was happening, but the memory was there, a dark time when every adult he knew suddenly seemed very angry and very, very scared. It must have been like that for Lersch, too. In that moment when Lersch turned into the blade, and his eyes widened, Adler saw the little boy who would spend a lifetime trying to understand.

"There are kids today," he said, not realizing he was going to speak out loud until he did. "Someday somebody will ask them what's the first big news story they really remember being aware of, and they'll say the explosions in Dallas."

"And this is a good thing?"

"Damned if I know," Adler said. "The mystery endures."

Melanie would stay in the extra room again. In the morning, he would make pancakes for her and tell her he was retiring. She would protest, but not much. After she drove away, he would untie his little boat, push off into the cold water, and try to decide if knowing why made any difference at all.

The Last Man in Lafarge

I walked into the High Street Tap at a little after three in the afternoon. Frank Alton had my drink ready: a large plastic cup, packed to the brim with crushed ice and Dr. Pepper, a cherry nestled into the top of the ice. He put it on a napkin in front of me as I sat down. "Anything happening, Sheriff Wright?" he asked.

I'd given up telling the man he can call me Cal. "Not a thing, Frank," I said. I tipped the cup back, let some of the ice rattle into my mouth along with the sweet, cold drink. As usual at this time of day, the dim room was almost empty. Reggie Crowe was sitting at a table by the side wall, drinking by himself, his right sleeve hanging empty after a decades-ago disagreement with an angry steer. I gave him a nod in the mirror, but he ignored me.

"Reggie's still angry that you yanked his license," Frank said.

"Reggie came into this world angry," I said. "Figure he'll leave that way." I took another long drink and asked the question I'd asked at least a hundred times before. "What brought you to Lafarge, Frank?"

"I'm glad you asked, Sheriff," Frank said. He polished the inside of a glass with a rag, cocking his hip against the bar. He was a big man, with a torso like a beer keg, long, muscular arms, and a shaved head tinted red by the neon sign behind him. "I used to be the captain of the Staten Island ferry," he said. "One day I got sick of it, so I locked the doors and took a boatload of pissed-off commuters under the Verrazano-Narrows Bridge into the open sea. Scuttled her off Red Hook. I'm number three on the Coast Guard's list of most wanted men." He set the glass down gently on the bar, near my elbow.

Lucy Tannen came out of the back room and began stacking bread. The Tap keeps a few shelves of necessities in the back of the barroom for folks who don't feel like driving two hours for diapers or aspirin. Lucy's father owned the place, though he hadn't set eyes on it in years. His was the only ranch in Stagg County where wells pumped oil, not dust. After his wife drank her way into an early grave a decade ago, Wayne Tannen took his two kids to Dallas. Lucy came back to Lafarge a year ago by herself. She wouldn't say why, but folks around here looked at the tattoos that twined around her arms and her shapely legs, the quarter-sized rings in her earlobes, the curves accentuated by her t-shirts, and figured she ran wild in the big city, and Wayne spanked her ass and sent her home. Me, I just think she seems sad.

I brought my attention back to Frank. "On the run from the Coast Guard," I said. "Well, I doubt they'll find you here."

"That's what I figured," Frank said. There was a dark, vaguely olive cast to his skin that could have been genetic or just the memory of a thousand tans. His accent was middle American, the featureless flat voice of a national news anchor. He might have been from anywhere in the world, which was what annoyed me.

I finished my drink and stood up, bracing for the blast oven outside the door. I did not pick up the glass, the one Frank always put in my reach, carrying his fingerprints. I decided long ago that sending the glass to the lab in Austin would be cheating, unless I thought Frank actually had broken the law. "Keep it cool, Frank," I said. He nodded. I turned to say something to Lucy, but she'd already disappeared into the back. I knew Reggie didn't want to hear anything from me. There was nothing to do but go back out to the cruiser to resume patrol.

* * *

Lafarge is the county seat of Stagg County, in western Texas. We've got just under two thousand people rattling around just over a thousand square miles, mostly on small farms and ranches. Around two hundred of them live in Lafarge, along a main road named High Street by some comedian. Across the whole county, there's about six inches of variation in elevation.

I've been the Sheriff here for seventeen years. I have an office, with my small apartment on one side and a couple of cells on the other. I have two part-time deputies. I have a cruiser that gets replaced every five years, $48,500 in annual salary, and full medical coverage, as long as I don't mind driving two and a half hours to the nearest hospital.

The way I figure it, I'm grossly overpaid. Stagg County is dying. The young people have nothing to stay for, and the old people are disappearing, as old people do. It's always been a miserable place, and lately, no amount of grumbling about liberal conspiracies can disguise the fact that the summers are becoming downright unlivable. I spend my days cruising the endless back roads—Stagg County doesn't have any other kind—thinking about the last guard who punched a clock at Alcatraz, the final soldier coming down off the Berlin Wall. My fellows in futility. Men fought wars for this land, and soon it will be empty.

I know every soul who lives in this county. Every single one of them grew up here, except one. Frank Alton. He showed up three years ago, driving a rusted-out VW Bug that clearly wasn't long for this world. He parked outside the Tap, went inside, and asked for a job. Old Will Packer hired him, mostly out of surprise. Packer left a few months later to live with his daughter in Santa Fe, but Frank is still here, apparently content in his tiny room behind the bar. The Bug is still parked where he left it.

It knocked me for a loop the first time I walked into the Tap and he asked what I wanted. A strange face around here is generally somebody's relative, or an oilman on the prowl, or a government agent of one kind or another with bad news. None of them serve drinks. He introduced himself and gave me the soda I ordered, and I asked him, for the first time, what brought him to town.

"I'm an animator," he said. "Disney is making a movie set in purgatory, so they sent me out here to get a feel for it." He looked at me with half a smile, daring me to challenge him. I kept my face still and nodded.

It's been three years, and the son of a bitch hasn't given me the same answer twice. What really gets me is that he never hesitates. He's always got the story ready.

"I'm an elephant trainer. We lost one off a truck out here, and in my spare time, I'm tracking him."

"My wife ran off about five years ago. She seemed determined to hit every bar in the world, so I figured I'd pick one and wait for her to show up."

"I used to be a college professor. Couldn't take the grading."

"I'm an Australian gone walkabout, mate."

"I came to Stagg County for the waters."

I damn sure wasn't going to rise to that one.

* * *

I spent the rest of the day circling the county, looking for wrecks, checking on some of the folks nobody else checks on. Once in a while, I find one of them dead. Sometimes they're just gone, note or no note, house left open. It's not an exciting job. Once, I stumbled across a brand-new pickup parked behind an abandoned house. There were two men in the bed, strangers to me, one white, one Hispanic, with their throats cut and silver dollars over their eyes. The Rangers came out with helicopters and an RV they called a mobile crime lab. By the end of the day, the truck and the bodies were gone. If they ever figured out who did it, they didn't bother to let me know. I guess that was just about the peak of my law enforcement career.

A little after nine o'clock, I got back to Lafarge and parked the cruiser behind what passed for the sheriff's office. The western sky was banded with orange and pink hues so deep and rich you could ignore the faded emptiness of the land beneath it. To the east, soft purple was deepening to black. I'd been planning to go inside to heat up a can of soup and flip on the TV, but I lingered, leaning back against the car. You look at a sky like that and understand why we've always assumed the gods live up there, not down here in the dust.

When the sun was all the way gone, I wasn't ready to close myself in for the night. I walked the couple of blocks over to the Tap.

Over the last several hours, there'd been a population explosion. Reggie Crowe was gone, but there were ten people sitting around the tables. Frank was still working, and Lucy Tannen was standing next to him, pouring a bag of pretzel sticks into bowls. The two TVs, one above the bar and the other across the room, had been turned on and were showing an Astros game.

"Sheriff Wright," Frank said, raising his voice above the announcers. "Another Dr. Pepper?"

"Shot of Jack," I said. I sat on the stool closest to the door, swiveling to survey the room. A few people nodded at me, and I nodded back, seeing none of the handful of Lafarge residents who lived in the bottle and might cause trouble on any given night. A few of the men in the room wore holsters, but this was, after all, Texas.

Frank brought a shot glass over and filled it. I picked it up and drained it in one motion, gestured for another. Lucy put one of the bowls of pretzels on the bar near me.

I didn't want to ask, but damned if I could think of anything else to say to the man. "What brought you to Lafarge, Frank?"

He smiled and poured. "I'm an FBI agent under deep cover, assigned to keep the communist party out of Stagg County."

I picked up the glass and shook my head. "Now I'm supposed to say, but we don't have any communists in Stagg County, and then you say." I drank.

"Sounds like I'm doing a hell of a job," Frank finished. He held up the bottle. I hesitated, then nodded, and as he tipped the bottle again, we all heard the heavy rumble of a big engine pulling up outside.

Everybody looked at the door. People in Lafarge just walk to the Tap, so this figured to be somebody coming in from one of the ranches. We heard a car door, and a moment later, a man stepped into the room.

It took me a minute to place him. I hadn't seen him in ten years, not since I used to roust him and his friends for setting fire to abandoned buildings and cutting fences. He was a scrawny teen back then, smirking at me as his daddy's money smoothed things over. He'd gotten taller and filled out into a trim, muscular man, and the way he wore his tight black t-shirt said that he wanted you to notice. He stood in the doorway, his eyes sweeping across the place, clearly relishing being the focus of everyone's attention.

"Lee Tannen," I said. His eyes snapped over to me, and there was a flicker of the old smirk.

"Cal Wright," he said. "I figured you would have retired by now."

"How the hell old do you think I am?" I asked, but his gaze had moved past me. I looked over my shoulder. Lucy Tannen was staring at her brother, her face pale. She'd forgotten all about the two glasses of beer she had been about to take out to a table. Frank gently took them out of her hands.

"Lee," she said. "What are you doing here?"

"Nice way to greet your brother," Lee said. He looked around, happy to see that everybody was still staring at him. Aside from his sister, everyone there was at least fifteen or twenty years older than him. We remembered him raising hell and pissing people off. The buddies he used to do it with were long gone, a couple of them, to my sure knowledge, in a federal pen. He turned sharply on his heel and ambled toward us, and every eye dropped to the shiny black leather boots he was wearing. Clearly, the Tannens hadn't gone broke.

He put his hands on the bar a couple of feet away from me. "How about a hug for your big brother, come all this way to see you?"

Lucy still looked dazed, but she leaned across the bar and put her arms around him awkwardly. He raised one hand and patted her shoulder, the other staying on the bar. He was looking at Frank now. "You, I don't remember," he said. "I'm Lee Tannen."

"I got that," Frank said. Without introducing himself, he walked around the end of the bar and took the beers he was holding to the table waiting on them.

Lucy pulled back. "Is Daddy here?" I couldn't tell what answer she was hoping for.

Lee was watching Frank in the mirror. "Nice hospitality," he said mildly.

"Lee," she said. She poked at his hand. "Is Daddy here, I said."

"No, kiddo," he said. He sat down on the stool next to mine, put one hand on hers. "That's what I came to tell you. Daddy's dead."

He hadn't lowered his voice a fraction, and the whole room went still, except for Sarah Cooper, sitting in the farthest corner with her husband Bill, both of them looking as ancient as wind-carved rock. Sarah pulled at Bill's shirt. "What did he say?" she asked.

"Said Wayne Tannen passed," Bill said. They probably thought they were whispering.

Lucy was even paler now, swaying slightly. Frank was back, standing just behind her, not touching her but clearly ready if she fell. "Lee," I said. "Maybe you want to take this somewhere private. Take her home." I wasn't real sure what I meant by that. The old Tannen ranch was a thirty-mile drive, and nobody had lived there for ten years. Lucy rented a house here in Lafarge, but as far as I knew, Lee had never been there.

Lee shrugged. "I count a building I own as private," he said. "Any y'all don't want to hear this can pay your tabs and leave."

"Dead," Lucy said. "When? How?"

"About a week ago," Lee said. "Car accident. A drunk ran a red and T-boned him."

"Jesus," I said. "Show some respect, son."

He looked at me, his nostrils flaring, but Lucy was clawing at his arm, odd high-pitched sounds coming from her throat. Frank's hand was on her shoulder. "A week?" she said. "You waited a week to tell me? A week?"

"I wanted to tell you in person," Lee said. "I got here as soon as I could. There's been a lot to deal with, what with the services and the will and all."

"Services," Lucy said. She sagged. Frank held her up, his powerful hands under her arms. He looked at me and nodded his head toward the middle of the room. I got up, took the nearest empty chair from a table, brought it back behind the bar, and together we steered her into it. She was shaking. "I missed the *funeral*?"

"Come on, Luce," he said. "With the way things were, you think he would have wanted you there?"

"That's enough now," I said. "Lee, I think you should come down to my office so we can talk this over." Behind Lee, some of the folks in the room were standing up now, milling uncertainly. I raised my voice and walked back out around the end of the bar. "Come on, folks. Let's let the young lady grieve in peace."

"Grieve," Lee said. I don't think I'd ever seen someone sneer in real life before. "My sister and father weren't really on speaking terms, Sheriff. I don't think there will be much grieving involved."

Frank stirred angrily, started to speak, but Lucy beat him to it. "Where's Alex?" she said. She was staring at her hands in her lap, speaking so quietly that I could just make out her words.

Lee cocked his head. "What's that?"

"Alex," Lucy said. She looked up at him. "Daddy said if I came back here, if I was good, that I could have him. Where is he?"

Lee smiled. I saw in his eyes that this was the moment he'd wanted, the reason he made the drive. "Alexander," he said, stretching the name out. "If you mean that little bastard you shamed us with, I have no idea. Wherever the orphanage sent him, I suppose." He leaned on the bar, getting closer to her frozen face. "You think Daddy was ever going to accept that child? He just sent you out here to make sure there'd only be one."

"Lord," somebody over by the tables said. Other than that, everybody in the room was still.

"It's time for you to go, Lee," I said.

His head snapped around to me. "I'll say it again, *Cal*. This is my place now, and if I decide to stand here, or bulldoze the place, or turn it into a damn Starbucks, you got nothing to say on the subject." He pulled himself up to his full height. "Daddy left every red cent and every foot of land to me. Not that I'm going to spend a single night in this godforsaken place. I'll probably just slap a padlock on it and never think about it again."

"*He's my child*," Lucy said. Her teeth were clenched, her hands clutching desperately at the edges of her chair. Frank hovered over her. "He's *your blood*."

I glanced at the small group now huddled together in the middle of the room. Most of them seemed more confused than anything, but a few were beginning to look at Lee in a way I understood but didn't like. They weren't all so old that they couldn't do some damage if they chose, and Stagg County has a way of carving the soft out of people. Maybe Lee had forgotten that.

"Okay," I said loudly. "This is over. Whoever's place this is, I am charged with keeping the peace, and we're shutting down for the night."

If anybody heard me, they certainly didn't pay any attention. Lee was opening his mouth to say something when Lucy screamed, wordless and high. Everybody in the room flinched, and she pitched forward and reached under the bar and came up with a gun.

They say things go into slow motion. I had time to think a lot of things as she was bringing the gun up. I had time to curse myself for not remembering that Will Packer had kept the gun there, like a lot of Texas bartenders, as a last resort against brawlers and bandits and drunken fools. I had time to drop my hand toward my own holster while realizing that in seventeen years I'd never drawn my gun except on the firing range. I had time to think about the fact that I really, really did not want to shoot Lucy and that I didn't see anything else I could do.

And Frank Alton had time to reach over Lucy's shoulder, as casually as he'd grab an empty from the bar, and pluck the gun from her shaking hand, at the same time putting his other arm around her waist and pulling her back against him. She yelled and sobbed, pounding on his arm with her fists, her face twisted and ugly, but he kept his hold on her. "You don't want to do that, girl," he said.

Time sped up again. Lee Tannen had stepped back from the bar, raising his hands as if to ward off a blow, and they started to come down. I felt the muscles that had tensed begin to relax, and my hand fell away from my holster.

"But, damn, I sure do," Frank said, and he shot Lee Tannen through his right eye.

* * *

A lot of things happened after that. I pulled my gun, but by the time it cleared the holster, Frank had set his piece on the bar. He eased Lucy to the floor and raised both his hands. There were screams and curses from the folks by the tables, some of whom had dropped to the floor when Lucy grabbed the gun. Bill Cooper, who was a medic in Korea, crawled over to Lee Tannen, old training overcoming arthritis and a weak heart, but I knew there was nothing to be done.

I think Lucy had fainted. Sarah Cooper and a couple of other women went around the bar and knelt by her, kneading her hands and getting something soft under her head. I used a couple of napkins to pick up the gun from the bar and took a step back, holstering mine. "You ladies okay to handle Lucy for a bit?" I asked.

One of them snorted, not bothering to answer. Between the three of them, the women with Lucy had gotten through close to two hundred years of everything from childbirth to sudden death with no help from anybody. Anything I did would just be getting in their way.

"I'm taking Frank to my office," I said to the room in general. "Unless you're helping with Lucy, go on home. Nobody touch the—nobody touch Lee." I looked at Frank. "Do I need to cuff you?"

He shook his head. "Ready when you are, Sheriff."

We went outside. The night was clear. A lot of the day's heat had bled off, and the buildings around us, most of them just low black shapes, were ugly mistakes that had nothing to do with the reality of the stars wheeling overhead and the ground under our feet. Neither of us said anything.

I put him in a cell. After I put the gun he used in an evidence box and locked it, I went back and stood at the door. "I've got to make some phone calls," I said. "Let me have your belt and shoelaces."

"There's no need for that, Cal," he said.

"I just let you kill a man standing two feet away from me," I said. "Let's not do anything else tonight that calls into question my basic competence."

He turned them over, and I went to the phone. After my calls, I got a couple of cans of Dr. Pepper from the refrigerator in my apartment. Frank was sitting on his bunk, his hands hanging between his knees. I passed one of the drinks through the bars, and he took it and rolled the cold can across his forehead like he was trying to erase something. I opened the door of the other cell and sat on that bunk, facing him through the iron as we both drank.

"Rangers will be here in a couple of hours," I said. "Don't know if they'll wait until morning to take you."

"Hardly matters," he said.

"I guess legally I should tell you that you don't have to talk to me," I said. "I'm just wondering if you knew Lucy had a baby."

He nodded. "We've gotten pretty close since she came back to town."

"Close as in…"

He chuckled. "Lord, no. Me and that little girl? I've got thirty years on her. She just didn't have anybody else to talk to." He opened the can and took a long drink. "All she wants in the world was to get that baby back. Her Daddy told her if she tried to keep the kid he'd cut her off without a dime, but if she came back here and proved she could behave, he'd reconsider."

I thought about Wayne Tannen, the way he acted when his wife was drinking herself to death. Like all he needed was popcorn to really enjoy the show. "I doubt he meant that."

He grunted. "At least now Lucy will have money. Maybe she can find the kid."

"Alex," I said. "What about the father?"

"Mexican," Frank said. "Why do you think Daddy was so pissed off?"

I hadn't turned the lights on in the cell room. A shaft of light cut across the space but Frank was in shadow, mostly an outline. He put the can on the floor and rolled onto his back, resting one big forearm across his eyes.

"Guess I'm finally going to find out where you're really from," I said.

"There's not all that much to find out," he said. "I'm just a man who got in his car one day and started driving. Every time I could turn onto a smaller road, I did. And I kept doing that until I got to a place that looked like the end of all the roads."

"Perceptive," I said. He didn't reply. I sat for a while, until it was clear he was either asleep or done talking. I was in some danger of falling asleep myself.

I went back into the office and then stepped out onto the porch and closed the door. In a few minutes I'd have to go check on Lucy. They probably had her in her own bed by now, the women clustered around her, the men in the next room leaning against the walls and waiting for instructions. I hoped she could find her son. I hoped she would use some of her money to get a good lawyer for Frank. Texas juries have been known to accept "he needed killing" as a defense. Most of all, I hoped she would get away from here and never come back.

Lafarge was dark and quiet. Pretty soon, I think, the day will come when the dark and the quiet is all there is here, except me, and then I'll get in my own car and start driving, and this little part of the world, at least, will be left to slowly erode the scars and the stains of our passing.

Everybody Pays a Tax

Jason, who gives me physical therapy three times a week, is probably in his late twenties, but I can't help thinking of him as a kid as he wheels me from my room—I'm sorry, my *suite*—to the big rec center, talking all the way. He's good at his job, cheerful, always polite, even when the exercises get me mad enough to curse him. He called me Mr. Harper for months, even after I told him anybody that familiar with my body can call me Toby.

Jason wears a bright little rainbow pin every day. Hanging in his office is a picture of him and his husband on a beach somewhere in Mexico, hoisting drinks the size of their heads. His husband. Right there on the wall, where everybody can see it. When I was his age, I couldn't have imagined the life he's leading.

But then, he probably can't imagine the life I led.

* * *

When I first got to this city, men were *everywhere*. Yearnings I'd barely had words for in the small town I came from could now be met as easily as picking up a loaf of bread. There were men cruising at the Y, men cruising in bookstores and libraries, men cruising in train station restrooms. Quiet men in understated three-piece suits, sitting in lounges with dark wood paneling, and the beautiful, dangerous street queens in their wigs and tied-off blouses. Burly dockworkers lingering near unused piers, and long-haired students sprawling on blankets in secluded nooks of the parks. There were bars where men could buy each other drinks and hold hands. There was a club where we could dance with each other.

Back home, I spent four years trying to concoct a reason to touch Robbie O'Neill, our high school's pretty basketball hero. I'd been in the city less than two days when Andy K took me behind some bushes, in the small park near my rattrap apartment, and became the first man to kiss me. I didn't even know his name yet. When he pulled my hand to the front of his pants and I hesitated, he laughed softly.

"Here's a rule I live by," he said. "It's the things you don't do that you end up regretting."

* * *

Most of the time, being in the city felt like I'd been set free. The times when it didn't feel that way were mostly because of the cops, who could be the ruin of one night if you were lucky, or a few weeks if you weren't. More than one shift commander padded his arrest stats by sending his best-looking young officer out in civilian clothes to collar any man who so much as winked at him. Andy K taught me things to look for. An undercover almost never had hair that looked right, and most of them rushed things, or used slang terms stiffly. Still, it was easy to get tripped up. You let a guy in a bar buy you a beer, or followed him into a bathroom stall, and next thing you know, he's slapping cuffs on you. There wasn't much you could do at that point. Hope you're not holding anything that will add to the charges. Hope Lily Law is just looking for the easy arrest, and you'll be out by breakfast. Hope you don't end up getting ground through the system for months, sharing cells with speed freak bikers who use you to kill the time.

Andy K called it the cost of doing business. Street theater, so the papers could say the city was safe for decent people. Some of the political types went to city council meetings and bitched about entrapment. You can guess how far they got. We hated the cops, but we could manage them. They'd raid a bar early in the evening, a little money would change hands under a table, and by midnight, it would be reopened, with the guys who got busted trickling back in as they posted bond. Mostly, cops were more an annoyance than a threat, and they didn't keep us from feeling like we had made the city ours.

But if a place feels like paradise, look around for the serpent. The snake in our garden was Lieutenant Francis Morelli, head of the city's Immorality and Indecency task force. Compared to the other cops, Morelli and his squad were very different beasts. Still pigs, but feral razorbacks. They didn't bother with entrapment, they didn't care about public relations, and they weren't just out to pad their numbers. Their game was catching gays in the act, and their goal was making anyone they got their hands on suffer.

I saw it for myself one night when they raided the empty trucks parked down by the docks. One minute, everything was peaceful, guys pairing off to melt into the shadows or climb up into the empty trailers. Somebody had a little portable radio, and a few guys were dancing, the thin sound from the cheap speaker drifting out over the river. Then there were shouts, and a flying wedge of cops, nightsticks slashing out in every direction, blocked the main route back out to the streets. Morelli was in the lead, yelling for everybody to sit their asses down and motivating the slow with blows to the head. I fell to the ground and rolled into the filthy space under a van parked against a wall. From my hidey hole, I watched feet scrambling around, listened to yells and curses.

A Hispanic man in a fringe vest fell to the asphalt ten feet away, bleeding from an ugly gash on the side of his head. His eyes were open and pointed right at me, but I didn't know if he was seeing anything. I thought about trying to pull him under the van, but before I could, Morelli himself was squatting by the man's head. Morelli was six and a half feet tall. The short sleeves of his uniform strained against his biceps. His round stomach hung out over his belt.

"Sally Ruiz," he said. "I thought I told you to get your faggot ass out of my city." He bounced his nightstick solidly off Ruiz's elbow. Ruiz bit his lip but didn't cry out. I was sure now that he saw me.

"You don't listen so good," Morelli went on. "Looks like you get to pay the queer tax tonight." He grabbed Ruiz's long black hair and pulled the man up as he stood. I watched as he half-marched, half-dragged him around the corner. I kept an eye out for Sally Ruiz after that. I never saw him again.

* * *

Like Andy K, Morelli had a rule: sooner or later, everybody pays a tax. Most of the gay men he and his crew picked up on any given night were just arrested, which was bad enough. It meant hours, possibly days, of being run through institutions designed at every point to make you feel dirty, and small, and worthless. It meant sitting behind bars, hoping your cellmates weren't in a dangerous mood, while the cops on the other side sneered and spat. Any cop in the city could make all that happen. When Morelli got you, though, merely being arrested felt lucky. It was better than paying a tax.

Morelli's queer tax took a few different forms. It *could* be financial, if you happened to have enough folding money in your pocket to catch his interest. More often, the queer tax meant that Morelli and his thugs with badges took you into an alley or some dark corner and went to work with sticks and fists and feet. Their reports would say you resisted arrest. When you paid the tax that way, you went to the hospital, not jail, and you were there for a while, pissing blood into a bedpan.

If you really annoyed Morelli, or he remembered you from one too many previous busts, or he was just in the wrong mood, you paid a different queer tax. He dragged you into that alley all by himself, shoved you to your knees, and lowered his pants. He held his service revolver alongside your head, to discourage any bright ideas about biting. When it was over, he slammed the gun butt into your temple and left you stunned on the ground.

* * *

"That fascist asshole is going to kill somebody," Andy K said.

I ran straight to his place after Morelli's crew cleared the docks, leaving me undiscovered under the van. Andy K's apartment was right across the street from mine, which was convenient, since he'd become my best friend.

We fell into bed together once in a while, but often just hung out or went to movies.

When he was in elementary school, there were five kids named Andy in his grade, so the teachers added last initials to call on them. In Andy K's case, it stuck. Even his severely uptight parents called him Andy K, when he called home once a week to mournfully report that he still hadn't met the girl of their dreams.

I shook as I talked about Morelli dragging Sally Ruiz away. Andy K gave me a joint, which didn't help much, and sat on the couch holding me, which helped some. For a couple of weeks after that, I went straight home after work and stayed away from all the popular pickup spots. I couldn't walk toward a corner without imagining that Morelli was just around it, waiting for me. When I did start going out again, I was perpetually on alert, ready to run at the first sign of a raid.

I only wish Andy K had been as careful.

* * *

I was out of the city the weekend it happened, back home for a cousin's wedding. After almost two years, seeing family members and friends from high school, some with their own spouses and wide-eyed pink babies, was surreal. I couldn't escape the feeling that everyone was wearing a mask. I wondered who and what they would be if they could really choose, as I had chosen. I couldn't wait to get back to my new life. My *real* life. I rehearsed in my head the report I would make to Andy K, the cutting lines I would use to preen about how completely I'd left that world behind.

But when I got back, Andy K was in the hospital. He was making out with an art student from Long Island, in that same little park where he and I first met, when Morelli and his crew swept through. Andy K was Morelli's choice to pay that night's queer tax.

I sat in a bright yellow plastic chair and held the hand that wasn't cuffed to the bed. There were four beds in the room, and the flimsy curtain pulled around us didn't allow me to forget the other patients and visitors. The way they had looked when I came in, their eyes flicking from me to Andy K. You could see them filing us away. Fruits. Faggots. Their faces were as cold as the cop guarding the door.

Andy K's eyes were swollen almost shut. He had a cast on one leg, and every move he made was stiff and slow. I brushed hair off his forehead and spoke softly. "Somebody said you took a swing at Morelli." I'd heard that but didn't believe it. Andy K weighed maybe a hundred and forty pounds.

He nodded. "Got him," he said. His voice was a rasp. I held a cup of ice water with a straw to his mouth. After he sipped, he sounded a little better. "Right on the chin. Best punch of my life."

"Why would you do that? You're lucky they didn't kill you."

His chest jumped a couple of times, like he was trying to laugh and couldn't. "Things you don't do, you regret," he managed.

When he was able to get out of bed, they sent him away for six months. He told his parents he'd won a grant to attend an intensive actors' retreat that allowed no contact with the outside world.

* * *

About a month after Andy K paid his tax, Morelli raided a bar I was at. I had no chance to run. His men sat me against the wall, lined up with a dozen others, under the watchful eyes of a couple of uniforms. In the severe glare of the overhead lights they turned on, the elegant martini-and-olive atmosphere dissolved into an ugly basement lined with stained curtains.

Morelli walked in front of us, looking closely at each face. He used his nightstick, not gently, to raise the chin of anybody who tried to keep their head down. When it was my turn, I managed to at least look him in the eye. I was terrified, but I owed Andy K that much.

The queers sat against the wall. The cops stood around, watching nothing and everything at the same time. We all waited to see if someone was going to pay the tax tonight.

The last guy in line, the bartender, was older than anybody else in the room. He stared at his feet, stretched out in front of him. Morelli slammed his stick into the wall, an inch over the bartender's head. The bartender didn't flinch. He sighed and looked up.

"I've seen you before," Morelli said. "Work a lot of fag joints, don't you?"

"Money's the same color as yours," the bartender said.

Morelli shook his head. "You're lucky I'm in a good mood, Pops. I could make this the worst night of your life."

He was turning away when the bartender spoke again. "You wouldn't make the top ten, you limp-dick pig motherfucker."

I think everybody in the room stopped breathing. Morelli stood still for a long minute. He didn't turn to look back at the bartender. When he finally spoke, his voice was quiet and carefully measured. "Bring him," he said. "Get the rest of these assholes in the wagon."

I never knew exactly what Morelli did to the bartender. Somebody told me he had to move to Florida, where he had a sister who could tend to him. They said that the sister, like the bartender, had a number tattooed on her arm.

* * *

Andy K was released from prison on a Saturday morning in April. A Department of Corrections van took him and a few others to a nearby train station, where he bought a ticket for the three-hour ride to the city. Then, ever playing the dutiful son, he called his parents. I don't know how long he talked to them. I know he tried to call me, afterwards, but I'd gone out for coffee and eggs. Andy K's call was answered by Miguel, a fantastically agile dancer I met the night before, brought home, and became so besotted with that I wanted to cook him breakfast.

I don't know what might have been different if I was there to answer.

Andy K asked Miguel to take a message. "Tell Toby that Morelli called my parents," he said. "Just that. He'll understand."

Then he hung up and walked onto the tracks, directly in front of an arriving train.

* * *

I spent a week in bed, unable to do almost anything but cry. Sometimes it was angry crying, and I threw things around and fantasized about burning Andy K's childhood home to ashes. Mostly, I just numbly stared at the wall as the tears came. I kept the blinds pulled down and the lights off. I barely ate. By the time I went back to work, I was so gaunt that nobody questioned all the days I called in sick.

I worked in customer service at one of the big downtown banks. I helped poor people open checking accounts and start quarter-a-week savings for their kids. I sent any customer with a more complex request, or seeming to have any significant money at all, to larger desks, manned by older men in better suits. It was dull, but most of the people I knew washed dishes or waited tables, so I didn't complain much.

About two weeks after I went back to work, I looked up and saw Morelli in the lobby. He was walking away from one of the teller windows, tucking an envelope into his breast pocket. He glanced in my direction, and I was too slow looking away. He saw the expression on my face. When I looked back, he was coming my way, grinning broadly. He stopped on the other side of my desk and looked down at me. "I know you," he said.

This time, I couldn't meet his eyes. I stared at his belt buckle. "I don't think so, sir."

"Sure I do." He rapped his knuckles on my desk. "That pansy joint in the basement, the one with the mouthy bartender. You were there. Never would have figured somebody like you worked in a classy place like this." He pointed at a desk a few yards behind mine. "That your boss?"

"No," I said.

"No, huh? Looks like a good conversationalist, anyway. You think I should go talk with him? Compare notes on mutual acquaintances?"

I didn't say anything.

"Gimme twenty dollars," Morelli said.

"What?"

"You heard me." He raised his voice a shade. "Give me twenty dollars."

My face felt warm. My jaw clenched so tightly I don't think I could have talked again. I took out my wallet and found two ten-dollar bills. Morelli held out his hand, but I put the bills down on the edge of the blotter. He chuckled and picked them up.

"That's okay," he said. "You'll put it right in my hand next time, pervert. Won't you?"

* * *

I like to think Andy K had something to do with what happened a few weeks after that. He was popular, and the way he checked out upset a lot of people. It's not like there was any shortage of other things to be upset about, though. Really, it was probably the heat as much as anything. It was the hottest summer anybody could remember, leaving everyone miserable and short-tempered. The city was in an ugly mood. It all boiled over one night when the cops raided our dance club, and the queers fought back.

I wish I could say I was there when it started. I've met a lot of guys over the years who claim they were. I doubt any of them were telling the truth.

My truth is that I was at a party Miguel was throwing, five or six blocks away from the club. I still wasn't in much of a party mood, but some friends got insistent, telling me I was letting Morelli win by wallowing in my room. I was half stoned when the phone rang. Miguel picked it up and waved at somebody to turn the music down. When they did, we heard what seemed like dozens of sirens outside. He listened, and got the kind of expression that makes everyone in the room freeze, waiting to hear what's happened.

"There's a fucking riot going on out there," he finally told us. He listened for another minute. "Reuben says the street queens are chasing cops around in the streets."

"Bullshit," somebody said.

"Maybe not," said a guy with John Lennon glasses. "I wouldn't cross those bitches. Every one of them goes around with a knife."

"Yeah, well, the cops go around with guns."

Miguel waved us to silence, his ear still to the phone. "Some kind of raid at that club across from the park," he said. "They're throwing rocks."

I stood up from the couch. "I wanna see."

Somebody tried to pull me back. "You don't want to be out there when the riot squads show up."

I shook them off and headed out the door, not waiting to see if anyone else followed. By the time I got to the street, I was running, heading in the direction of the sirens and the yells.

It was well past one in the morning, but the streets were alive. A lot of people were going the same direction I was. We passed people coming the other way, some of them bleeding or limping. Pretty soon, I could see that the street up ahead, between the club and the park, was thronged. A group on the sidewalk had their fists in the air, chanting something I'd never heard before: *gay power*. A police wagon halfway up on the curb was rocked back and forth by dozens of people, apparently intent on tipping it completely over. I skirted the edge of the park and grabbed somebody's arm. "Where are the cops?" I yelled over the racket.

"Pinned inside." He pointed at the club. The front door was closed. Some people were trying to break through the plywood the owners had put over the windows. Three guys ran right past me with a parking meter they'd somehow wrenched out of the ground and started pounding it against the doors.

It was already noisy as hell, then a bigger clamor broke out down the block. People on balconies pointed down and waved frantically. A couple of big police vans had pulled up at the edge of the crowd, and cops in heavy armor and helmets were pouring out, starting to swing their nightsticks. The crowd scattered, but didn't break. I watched from the park as a group of the street queens, terrifyingly young and small, mooned the cops, then ran. The cops gave chase, but they were slower, weighed down by their equipment. The street queens turned into side streets, went around the block, and came up behind their pursuers, singing taunting songs and throwing rocks. The cops spun and started after them, and the queens did the trick again.

I started to feel ashamed of myself for lurking behind a tree. I was looking around for a rock to throw when I saw Morelli. He was in uniform, but he'd lost his hat. His thinning hair pointed out wildly in every direction. He must have gotten separated from the rest of his men, somehow. He was running across the park, away from the club, being chased by a crowd of about ten gays, some of them street queens.

Without a thought, I ran after them.

Morelli was faster than I would have expected. Maybe sheer terror made him faster than he'd ever been before. The group after him obviously knew who he was, and the things they were shouting would have gotten anyone's adrenaline going. *Kill the pig! Fuck his fascist ass!*

They were out for blood, and gaining on him. He turned into an alley. The small mob followed, me about ten yards behind the others. I turned the corner into the alley and skidded to a halt. Morelli had stopped in front of a set of garbage cans twenty yards into the alley. His chest was heaving as he tried to catch his breath. He was turned to face us, and he had pulled his gun. The crowd chasing him stopped, halfway between me and him. I hovered at the mouth of the alley, waiting to see what would happen.

Morelli had his gun down by his side and his other hand up toward his pursuers. I think he was starting to say something, but before he could get it out, somebody threw a rock. Whoever it was should have tried out for the Yankees. The rock hit Morelli hard, directly in the forehead. He staggered back against the cans and fell. There was a victorious yell, and we all started for him again, but at that moment a police cruiser turned into the other end of the alley. The driver hit the siren and lights and came toward us, accelerating. The mob wavered, then broke, running past me back out onto the main street. I ducked back around the corner and flattened against the wall. In a few seconds, the cops came past me, turning to pursue the biggest group as they ran back toward the park. I doubt they'd even seen Morelli.

I went into the alley. Sirens and shouts from blocks away echoed strangely off the brick walls. There was nobody else around. I felt weirdly detached from myself as I walked toward Morelli. He was on his hands and knees, swaying a little as he tried to get up. From ten feet away, I could see his blood dripping onto the filthy pavement. His gun was on the ground where he had been standing. I picked it up.

I stood over Francis Morelli, one foot on either side of him, like I was going to sit on his back for a game of horsey. I clutched the back of his collar with my left hand and used the right to put the barrel of the gun against the base of his skull. He tried to reach back for me, but he was too weak and winded.

My father taught me about guns. One of his efforts to make a man out of me. "First lesson," he said. "You don't put your finger on the trigger unless you are going to shoot."

I tightened my grip on Morelli's collar and put my finger on the trigger.

It's the things you don't do that you end up regretting.

* * *

I look at the picture of Jason with his husband while he twists my body, trying to get my legs to hang onto whatever life they've got left. I guess I'm supposed to think it was all worth it, if it ends up with that picture on the wall. And I do. I just wish Andy K got to see it.

I don't have regrets. What I have are memories. Young people don't understand the weight memories carry. I didn't, until now, in this broken body, with so many friends gone. If everyone pays a tax, maybe mine is that weight, those fragments of a world I hope Jason never knows. In the middle of the night, I feel Andy K's delicate hand in mine. Rolling down the hall inch by inch, I see Miguel's lithe form spinning through the air. And sitting down to lunch, I hear the empty sack that had been Morelli, crumpling limply to the ground.

What They Say I Used to Be

"Heston says you used to be a cop."

It was the waitress, the new one. Lindsey. She'd been at the Blue Light for about two weeks and hadn't said a word to me until now. She sat across from me and put a glass next to the empty one my hand was still wrapped around.

"The good stuff," she said. "Heston says it's on the house just for listening to me."

Heston was leaning against the shelves behind the bar, looking at our table, his heavily inked arms crossed across his chest. I lifted the glass. A question. He nodded without really meeting my eye. An answer. Enough of one.

I took a sip. There are people who say booze is booze, that paying for top-shelf stuff is a sucker's game. After drinking well whiskey for a couple of years, though, just a taste of the good stuff felt like my sinuses opening up after days with a cold. I rolled it on my tongue, making it last.

"Yeah," I said, after I finally swallowed. "I was a cop. Detective, Major Crimes."

"What happened?" she said.

"I've been in here every night since you got hired. What do you think happened?"

She thought about getting up. Instead, she slid a picture across the table. It was her, a couple of years back. A posed shot, smiling against a black background. "Look at the necklace."

It was some kind of purple stone, about the size of a quarter, in an elaborate silver setting.

"It was stolen," she said. "I want it back."

"The city does have actual, currently employed cops," I said.

"They won't do anything. It's probably not worth a hundred bucks. Petty theft. But it was my grandmother's. It's all I have of her."

I allowed myself another sip. "You got money?"

She put a little stack of twenties next to the picture. I fanned them out. A hundred and forty bucks.

"This wouldn't buy a day's work from a real PI," I said.

"It's what I have," she said.

I thought about my half-pension, the tiny room I rented three blocks away, the five drinks a night I built my days around. I folded the bills and tucked them in a pocket.

"You know who took it?"

"Yeah," she said. "An asshole named Noah Flynn."

She told me the story, though she didn't want to. She met Noah at another bar a month ago. She was coming off a bad breakup and looking for something casual, something fun. Noah seemed that way in the bar. Once they were back at her place, he was different.

"I can't say it was rape," she said. "But it wasn't casual and fun, either." She looked at me, daring me to judge. "Some men like to hurt people," she said. "Like to hurt women. You know?"

I was a cop for better than twenty years before I found myself in a bottle with no way out. A wave of images and sounds crawled up from my memory, and I finished the drink to slam the lid back down on them. "Yeah. I know."

When he was done with her, Noah Flynn got up, turned on the light, and put on his clothes, whistling. He ignored Lindsey, curled up into herself against the headboard, watching him. Once he was dressed, he rummaged through the things on top of her dresser. She thought he was looking for his phone, but then he picked up the necklace.

"Put that back," she said.

He winked at her, stuck it in his pocket. "I always take a souvenir," he said. Before she could do anything else, he walked out.

"Seen him since?"

"I went back to the bar a few nights later. He was there. I think he runs the place. I told him I wanted the necklace back, and he laughed in my face. So I slapped him. And then a couple of other guys grabbed me and threw me out. Since then, they won't let me in, and I don't know where he lives."

I tapped the edge of the picture against the table. "The name Flynn mean anything to you?"

"No," she said. "Should it?"

*　*　*

Derek Bergman was my partner for the last seven years I was on the force. He was a captain now, so it took me the better part of an hour to get him on the phone the next day. The cops don't bother with hold music. I listened to a lot of dead air while I stared at a crack in the plaster above my bed and wondered if the guy upstairs was going to fall through the ceiling some night.

"Tim," he said when he finally came on the line. "You don't call, you don't write. Your mother and I worry."

Aside from thinking he's funny, Derek's okay. One of the few from my old life who will still talk to me.

"Noah Flynn," I said. "Younger guy. He part of the family?"

There's no such thing as the Irish mob in most of the US anymore. Like the Italians, they've been run out by Russians and Latin Americans who can draw on endless manpower. Our city is an exception. The Flynns have run things here for as long as there's been anything to run, and they still do.

"That little fucker," Derek said. "Yeah, he's Cillian's youngest. What I hear is that Cillian sent him to college, wanted him to make a clean living, but the kid couldn't hack it. There was some kind of trouble, and he got kicked out."

"What's he doing now?"

"Runs the Eightball, that dive the Flynns have owned forever. He's probably dealing, maybe running some girls, god knows what else. We'll get our hands on him at some point. I've never met him myself, but everybody who has says he's a cocky bastard without the brains to back it up."

"That college trouble," I said. "Anything to do with a woman?"

"I never heard any details." He got an edge in his voice. "What's this all about, Tim? You know something I ought to know?"

I hung up.

* * *

That night, I went to the Eightball instead of the Blue Light. The place looked the same as it had the dozens of times I'd been there flashing a badge: like someplace roaches would hang out if they were down on their luck. The night she met Noah was Lindsey's first visit, and she chose the place just because it was in her neighborhood. Bad luck.

I ordered a beer and put two of her twenties on the bar. "Noah around?"

The bartender looked at the edge of the bar between my hands. "Don't know anybody by that name, officer."

I grunted. "Good eye, but I'm retired. Tim Chadwick. Noah ought to know the name. Let him know I'm here." I took my drink to a table in the far corner and watched him.

They knew they could make me wait, so they did. There was a lot of that going around. At least in the bar, there was music to listen to. It was terrible music, but willing each song to end was something to do.

I didn't mind waiting. It gave me plenty of time to wonder why I was doing this. Since I left the force, I've been following rules I made for myself that keep me, just barely, hanging on to something I can call a life. I don't have more than five drinks a night, and nothing during the day. I don't buy bottles. I don't drink in my room or keep drinks there. I call somebody from my family once a week, though they usually hang up on me. And I don't get involved with anyone. I was breaking that rule. I couldn't afford to break any more.

After a little more than an hour, a door at the back of the place opened and a red-headed guy came out and sauntered toward me. His face was etched into a permanent smirk. He was about five foot four and couldn't have weighed more than a buck forty, but he walked like he thought he was King Shit. I assumed that everybody who worked for him had nightly fantasies of punching him out.

"Tim Chadwick," he said, standing over my table. "I don't think I want you in my fucking place. Didn't you put a couple of my uncles behind bars?"

"Don't forget the one I shot," I said. "Have a seat, Noah."

"I'll stand. You're not going to be here that long."

I shrugged and held up the picture. "You know her?"

He barely glanced at it. "Nice piece. She's not your daughter, is she? Or are you fucking her?" He cocked his head. "Maybe both?"

"You took her necklace. She wants it back. That's all this has to be."

"You're not a cop anymore, Chadwick. Way I hear it, you're just a drunk waiting around to die." He shook his head and turned to walk away. "You're still here in ten minutes, a couple of my boys are going to put a hurting on you, showing you out."

"Later on, remember I tried the easy way," I said to his back. He didn't slow or look around. I wouldn't have either.

* * *

At noon the next day, I was sitting at a coffee shop in the lobby of one of the big office buildings downtown. I was nursing a coffee that tasted a little better than the cardboard cup it was served in when the elevator doors opened, and Neil got out. He was wearing a nice-looking suit and talking on a cell phone. When he saw me, he stopped, looked at the door he'd been heading toward, looked back at me, shook his head, and came over, ending his call as he got to the table.

"Dad," he said. "What are you doing here?"

I was finding it a little tough to breathe. "I just need a couple of minutes, son. Take a seat?"

He looked at the door again, and I had a flash of Noah Flynn refusing to sit with me the night before. There was a feeling like a massive weight pressing down on my shoulders, but then he sighed, shook his head, and sat. I took

215

in a gallon of air.

"How's your mother?" I said.

"Don't," he said. "Let's not pretend like this is a small talk situation, okay? I haven't seen you in two years, and you just show up where I work?"

"I've done a lot of things wrong," I said. "I'm trying to maybe do something right."

"Jesus Christ," he said. "I thought you were going to ask for money. Is this one of those fucking AA things? Are you here to make amends?"

He put a lot of spin on the word.

"No," I said. "I need help."

"So, it is money."

I would die before I took money from my son. There was a time when he knew that.

"No," I said. I took the box out of my pocket and slid it across the table. A new smartphone. All of Lindsey's money and most of what I'd had squirreled away. "I need you to teach me how to work this."

He looked at it, confused. "What? You mean how to make calls?"

"Well," I said, "mostly the camera."

* * *

I called in a couple other favors. There was a landlord who owed me from back in the day, when I vouched for his kid at a parole hearing. He came up with an empty, furnished apartment I could use for two days. Then there was Flora. I gave her a couple of breaks when she was walking the streets. These days, she found her clients online, making a lot more money with a lot less risk. She was probably a little older than Noah Flynn usually aimed for, but I had a lot of faith in her experience at getting men to overrule their better judgment.

* * *

My faith was justified.

It was a little after ten, two nights later, when I heard the door to my borrowed apartment open. There was a murmur of voices, some laughter. I sat up straighter and got ready. Flora opened the door to the bedroom, came in, and immediately crossed to the bathroom door and closed it behind her. Noah came into the bedroom trailing her. He found the light switch and hit it, and was three paces into the room when he saw me sitting in a chair in the far corner, pointing a gun at him. He froze.

"Lace your fingers behind your head," I said. "Do it now."

His face was already beginning to match the vivid red of his hair. "Chadwick," he said. "You're out of your fucking mind."

"That's right. I might even be crazy enough to shoot you. Now put your hands behind your fucking head."

He didn't like it, but he did it.

"Okay," I said loudly. The bathroom door opened, and Flora came out carrying a pair of handcuffs. Noah was turning to try to see her as she came up behind him and snapped the cuffs on. "Hey," he said, but before he could get anything else out, she'd taken him by the elbow, turned him to face the bed, and shoved him so that he fell face-first across it, unable to break his fall. She put a knee in the small of his back, making him yelp, and attached the chain between his wrists to the one I'd already secured to the headrest. Then she rolled to the foot of the bed, pulled up the chains attached there, and used carabiners to attach them to his ankles. The whole operation took her about twenty seconds. He was a small guy, and she's had a lot of practice. You'd be surprised at the things some men will pay for.

"What the fuck," Noah yelled. He had to turn his head to the side to talk without being muffled by the pillows. "You're fucking dead, Chadwick. You think you can do this to me?"

"I think I can, yeah," I said. "Let's find out if I'm right."

Flora was back at the bedroom door. She gave me a salute and walked out, and a second later, I heard the apartment door close behind her. She'd given Noah a fake name, of course, and she lived miles away from here. I wasn't worried about him finding her.

"Just you and me now, Noah," I said. I stood up and put the gun on a side table. Noah was writhing and cursing. I ignored him. The phone was set up on a little tripod on the dresser. I'd tested it several times. The camera covered the whole bed, and it was plugged into a charger so I could take all the time I wanted. I turned it on.

I went over to the bed and started going through his pockets. He twisted and cursed, but I spent a lot of years frisking pissed-off people. He didn't have a gun, but there was a switchblade. I tossed it in the corner and flipped through his wallet. He had a few hundred bucks in cash. I tucked it into my pocket and dropped the wallet on the floor.

"One chance before we get started," I said. "You gonna give me the necklace?"

"Fuck you." He rolled as far to the side as he could manage, tried to spit at me.

"Okay," I said. I went around to where he could see me easily and knelt to pull out the box I'd put under the bed. Taking my time, I started putting things up on the nightstand, watching his eyes getting wide. A pair of garden shears. A set of brass knuckles. A short, brutal-looking club. A pair of pliers.

It was the power drill that broke him. "Jesus Christ," he said. "You win, Chadwick. You can have the fucking thing."

"I told you, Noah. One chance. The easy way's over." I stood up and stripped to my undershirt. "If I just take the necklace now, and let you go, every Flynn in this city will be taking shots at me by the end of the day tomorrow. And you'd probably go after Lindsey, too. So it's insurance time." I picked up a pair of heavy scissors. "Let's start by getting rid of those clothes."

My landlord friend had assured me these apartments had the best soundproofing in the city, so I wasn't worried when Noah started to scream.

* * *

Cillian Flynn has worked for years out of the back room of a moving company warehouse down near the river. The moving company itself is legitimate. Not much that happens in Cillian's office is.

At a little after three the next afternoon, I walked in and told my name to his receptionist. Five minutes later, I was ushered into the office, and the door closed behind me. Cillian was notably older than the last time I'd seen him. He'd put on twenty pounds and some wrinkles, and the famously blazing Flynn hair was just a red stubble on the back half of his head. His eyes hadn't changed, though. They burned when they looked at me.

"My youngest kid is missing," he said, "and out of the blue, fucking Tim Chadwick resurrects himself to appear in my life. I don't believe in coincidence."

"Me neither," I said. I put the phone down in the middle of his desk and sat. "Hit play."

He lasted three minutes before his finger shot out and hit pause. He was shaking. He looked at me with loathing and despair, and for one moment, I thought about Neil and almost felt sorry for him.

"You didn't even get to my favorite parts," I said. "About fifteen minutes in, he pisses himself. He spends a lot of time crying, of course. Then, for a while, he was offering to do anything I wanted him to do. *Anything*, Cillian, you understand me?" I leaned back in the chair. "Half an hour in, he says he'll tell me anything I want about every Flynn operation in town. Including yours."

"What the fuck do you think you're doing, Chadwick?" Cillian hissed. "You're not a cop anymore. You're barely a fucking man. What the hell do you want?"

"Noah knows what I want," I said. "In a couple of hours, I'm going to turn him loose. Then he's going to go get a necklace he stole from a woman I know, and he's going to return it to her."

He waited for more.

There wasn't any more.

"That's it?" he exploded. "You did—you did *that* to my boy over a fucking necklace?"

"I'm a little surprised myself," I said.

"Tell me one fucking reason not to kill you now," he said.

I laughed. "If you thought that was the only copy of that movie, I'd already be dead. Don't kid me, Cillian. You know why you can't kill me." I picked the phone up and leaned forward. "Here's the deal, Cillian. That kid of yours, he isn't right. He's not smart, and he likes hurting people too much. That's a bad combination. He's gonna end up inside, and you know it as well as I do."

I stood up. "If anything happens to me, or to anybody I'm even distantly related to, or to the woman he stole the necklace from, a copy of this goes to every cop and every Flynn foot soldier in the city. And then it goes out to every leader of the Aryan Brotherhood. What do you think Noah's life will be worth inside once they know how easy it is to break him?"

"Fucking Christ, Chadwick," Cillian said. He seemed to be shrinking down into his chair.

"Put a leash on the kid, Cillian," I said. "For everybody's good."

That seemed to be the moment to walk out. So I did.

* * *

The next night, Lindsey came into the Blue Light wearing the necklace. She brought a glass over to my table. "This is the first time you've been in since we talked," she said. "I thought you just took my money and blew me off."

"Maybe I did," I said.

"I don't think so," she said. "This was in my mailbox this morning with a little note that just said *tell Chadwick.*" She put the glass down. "The good stuff," she said. "On me this time."

She got to work, tending to the other drunks. I took my time with the drink and watched her moving around, touching the necklace every few minutes.

Cillian wouldn't be able to keep the leash on. I'd cut too deeply into Noah's pride. He would stew about it for a while, and lick his wounds, and sooner or later, he'd decide the only way to get back right with the world would be to come for me. I was looking forward to it. Maybe he'd put me out of my misery. Or maybe I'd find out if there's anything, anything at all, left of what they say I used to be.

In the meantime, I had another taste of the good stuff.

Filthy Looker

"Heston says you used to be a cop."

The speaker was a woman I'd seen around the bar a few times in recent weeks. She generally sat by herself, drinking bottles of Corona and scrolling on a phone propped up against a wadded napkin. From across the room, I would have guessed her at around fifty. Up close, I judged the number of years closer to forty, and the nature of the years difficult. She stood at the other side of my table, holding a glass with an alluring, dark amber glow.

"Heston has an underdeveloped sense of the value some attach to privacy," I said.

The woman put the glass down and pushed it toward me. "The good stuff," she said. "Heston says you can have it if you hear me out."

Heston was behind the bar polishing glasses, his heavily inked arms moving rhythmically. A slight dip of his chin when I looked over might conceivably have been meant as a nod.

I picked up the drink and let the aroma drift into my nose. The fifth and last drink of the night. Ending on a high note. "Sit," I said. "I'm Tim Chadwick."

"Andrea Court." She sat down. "So it's true you were a cop?"

"I was a detective in Major Crimes."

This was the point where people either asked what happened or made a conscious, visible decision not to. Andrea Court decided not to.

"I got this problem with my nephew Elway," she said instead.

"Family's always fun." I took a tiny sip. Pace it out. The longer this drink lasted, the longer I could put off the next one. Drunks have our own logic.

"He took something of mine. If you can get it back, it's worth something to me."

"You gone to the actual cops?"

"Elway's blood. I wasn't raised to call the cops on blood. Anyway, I don't think they'd care. We're not talking about much actual value."

"Something sentimental?" The hell with pacing. I threw most of the rest of the drink back and closed my eyes as it coated my throat and spread warmly down into my chest.

"It's a box about this big." Andrea ran her hands around an imaginary object the size of a car battery. "Made of cherry, with a brass catch and hinges. When you open it, there's a tray that nestles in the top. Underneath that, there's some coins, in those cardboard sleeves collectors use."

"They worth anything?"

"Not really. Collecting them was a hobby I had when I was a girl. I couldn't afford much. Some common silver dollars, stuff like that. The whole lot's probably just a couple hundred. It's the box I want back."

"Why?"

"My father made it," she said. Without warning, she stood and walked to the bar. Heston knocked the cap off a bottle, shoved a wedge of lime in the neck, and handed it to her. Coming back to her seat, she went on as though there'd been no interruption. "It's the only thing I have of him. The only thing I have that was made just for me. It's got my name etched on the bottom."

"Okay. You're sure Elroy took it?"

"It's Elway. My brother named him after some football player, and don't bother explaining who because I never cared, and I still don't. Anyway, he came over a couple of nights ago, trying to borrow money. Next morning, I noticed the box was gone."

"Why would he take it if the coins aren't worth much?"

She took a long swig of the beer. "It's been kind of a family joke for years, my coin collection. You know, making like it's a big deal, pretending I'm going to sell it and buy a luxury car or something. Elway's not bright. I don't think he got that we were joking."

"How much money did he want?"

"Five thousand dollars. I laughed my ass off."

"You got five thousand dollars?"

"Lord, no. If I did, I wouldn't give it to Elway. Might as well set fire to it." She rolled the bottle between her palms. "He means well, I think, but he's always in trouble. Mixing with the wrong kids, you know. Getting in fights, getting expelled, getting fired."

"He got a record?" My fingers itched to signal Heston for another drink, but that would be six. I folded my hands on the table and pretended they were glued there.

"He did a few months for shoplifting last year."

Nobody does a few months for shoplifting on their first fall. I didn't press the point. "If you're sure he took it, why not go get it back yourself?"

"I been down that road before." Andrea shook her head. "First, he'll deny it, get all defensive and hurt. Then he'll break out a sob story about why he needs the money. Then he'll come up with a reason why it's my fault he's so fucked up, or his mother's fault, or some teacher who flunked him on a science test ten years ago. Anybody but him. Then he'll start denying it all over again. Who needs it? You're a big guy, and you got that cop thing, the way you look. I figure if I send you, maybe this is the last time I have to deal with it."

"I'm not going to hurt him."

"Nobody's saying hurt. Scare, maybe." Andrea slid her hand across the table toward me. When she took it back, she left a small stack of tens. "A hundred now and a hundred if you get the box. That fair?"

* * *

Elway Court's small apartment was in a bad neighborhood, a couple of miles from the marginally better neighborhood of my small apartment. I could have taken a bus to see him the next morning, but walking it would stretch the chore out nicely. No rush. There was nothing else on my calendar for the day, or the month, except my nightly appointment with exactly five drinks. I'd been keeping that one for years, and there wasn't much danger of me breaking it now.

The night I would order a sixth drink was coming. The inevitable end, the final fall into the center of the whirlpool. The game was putting it off as long as I could.

The route was not scenic. I went through blocks of small houses built too close together, where crazed dogs paced tiny yards behind chain-link fences. I passed a couple of schools with bars over the windows, a dozen ugly apartment buildings charging by the week, and a ten-room motel charging by the hour. I passed blocks that were just rubble and weeds. At major traffic arteries, I passed fast food joints and half-empty strip malls.

There were usually a few young men at the edge of visibility, two or three blocks ahead, hanging out on street corners, lounging on front stoops, goofing around with skateboards. By the time I got within a block, they were always gone. The street didn't know anything about disciplinary hearings and suspensions and half pensions. The street still saw what Andrea called *that cop thing*.

Elway was in apartment 511 of a twelve-story cinderblock slab with the misleadingly genteel name Belvedere Tower. According to his aunt, Elway's parents paid the rent, more or less to keep him out of their house. She didn't know if he was working. Elway's employment history was spotty.

I'd been to the Bel several dozen times in my patrolman days, usually on domestic disturbance calls where the combatants stopped going after each other to turn on any uniform coming through the door. You hoped you weren't going to find a body or get on the wrong end of a pair of scissors. Some parts of being a cop are hard to miss. It was almost noon when I walked into the lobby and pushed the button to go up.

When it came, the elevator was just about filled by one of the largest men I'd ever seen in person. He was better than six and a half feet tall, wearing denim shorts and a sleeveless black t-shirt, and his arms and thighs bulged with muscle. His shaved head gleamed like he'd just put on a coat of wax. I stepped back from the door, partly to let him out and partly as a nod to the fight or flight sensors lighting up my central nervous system. The giant came out of the car, looked at me like I was a cockroach in his cereal bowl, and went past, making it a point to brush forcefully against me. I watched him walk to the main lobby doors and out into the glare of the day.

When I got off the elevator on five, I wasn't really surprised to find the door to 511 standing open several inches. I stood in the hallway, a few feet off, and thought about it. If I still had a badge, I could call for backup. And I'd have a gun. Mine was back at my place, since I didn't think I'd need it to take anything away from Elway. From the pictures on Andrea's phone, the kid weighed maybe one forty. He had the face of a dog that's been kicked its whole life and doesn't expect that to change.

Of course, I didn't have a badge, or a gun, or backup, or the 82nd Airborne standing by for my signal. I could go in, or I could walk back home.

I went in, recognizing the layout from the old days. A small living room, a postage stamp bedroom, a kitchenette barely big enough for a refrigerator and stove, and a bathroom barely big enough for a shower and john. A couple hundred square feet, all told. Elway Court was occupying about eight of them, curled up in a fetal position on the floor in front of the sagging couch. His hands were clutched tightly to his stomach, and he was making a keening sound between short, gasping breaths. Somebody had given him a good shot to the body, maybe several. His eyes widened at the sight of me, and he began trying to push himself toward the far wall with his legs. He didn't make much progress, and as a defensive strategy, it seemed short-sighted.

"Relax," I said. "I'm not here to hurt you."

Elway didn't seem convinced, but he stopped kicking at the floor and started trying to sit up. While he worked at it, I closed the door and glanced around the room. A dark wooden box rested on its side on the floor in front of the stove. A matching tray was on the floor next to it, the bottom cracked in half. I grunted and crouched to examine the box. Andrea Court's name was carved into the bottom, and a few dozen coins in cardboard sleeves rattled around inside. My years of experience as a detective enabled me to identify these as clues. The box was intact, though a big gouge on the back seemed fresh. The tray was a lost cause.

"Tha's mine," Elway rasped. He was propped up against a once-blue recliner that had surely come off a curb, one arm still clutched tight against his ribs.

"You don't look much like an Andrea." I stood and put the box on the kitchen counter. I managed to get the tray to rest in the depression that held it, but I didn't think it could be repaired. "You need me to call an ambulance, kid?"

The noise he made was forceful and negative.

"Suit yourself. I'm guessing the guy who tenderized you was bald? Looks like he makes his own weather patterns?"

"Talon," Elway said. His voice was starting to sound a little better, but he was wincing every time he breathed in. Probably a cracked rib or two.

"He calls himself *Talon*? Jesus Christ." I straddled the lone chair at the tiny linoleum table. "I ran into him downstairs. Business associate?"

"Who the hell are you?" Elway said. He tried to use his elbows to lever himself up into the chair, but came up short. "Why should I tell you shit?"

"No reason I can think of. I'm just a naturally curious guy. Your aunt sent me for the box."

"Take the fucking thing." This time, he managed to get into the seat, his face twisting with the effort. "Lot of good it did me."

"Let me take a stab at this," I said. "You owe Talon money. You tried to give him the coins, and he didn't bite."

"Man hardly looked at them." Elway's wariness of me was no match for his offended sense of justice. "Dropped the box on the floor and kicked it. Then he tuned me up. That fucker is jacked, man. I feel like a car fell on me."

"Sure you don't want an ambulance?"

"No way. Just end up owing *them* money." The kid seemed to feel a weird form of pride. "I been beat on before. Couple days, I'll be fine."

"Right." I knew I should just pick up the box and go. "Do I want to know how you're into Talon for five k?"

"Four," he said, then immediately snapped his mouth shut.

I smiled. "You asked your aunt for five. Trying to make a little profit on the deal? You're a piece of work."

"Yeah, what the fuck are you, then? You look like a damned cop. An old cop."

"Not anymore. I'm just doing Aunt Andrea a favor."

"Sure." Elway pulled himself a little straighter, grimacing. "I don't owe shit to Talon. I owe his boss, Henry T."

"Investing in an assembly line?"

"Huh?"

"Skip it."

"See, I hold things for Henry T sometimes. I got places to keep things, you know, hidey holes. Only last week he asked me to hold something, and I guess it wasn't as well hid as I thought."

"Got it. You let a stash get lifted, and now you're on the hook."

"See, this is my point," Elway said. He spread his hands in a gesture of innocence, but his face twisted, and he pulled the right arm back in. "It's the damn thief Henry T should be mad at, right?"

"Sure. You just keep explaining that to him, he's bound to come around." I stood and picked up the box. "Been a pleasure, Elway. Don't steal from your aunt again."

"Man, you think I'll ever have the chance? This was a warning. Next time, he kills me."

"Call the cops."

He laughed at that, his chest rattling. I could still hear it after I walked back out into the hallway, closed the door behind me, and rang for the elevator. The box was tucked under my arm. It wasn't heavy, but it was an awkward size for something I had to carry a couple of miles. Maybe I should have made the kid go to a doctor. Probably a moot point, since he'd be dead in a couple days, anyway. I went out the front door of the Bel and turned toward home, switching the box to my other arm. Maybe I could find a bag somewhere. Maybe Elway could come up with the cash he needed, or Henry T would decide another beating was enough punishment. Maybe the whole lot of them would find Jesus and start a choir together. It wasn't my problem.

I realized I'd been standing on the sidewalk outside the Bel for five or ten minutes, just staring down the road. I tried to make myself walk forward, but it wouldn't take.

"Well, fuck," I said out loud. I turned back to the building, and in under a minute, I was back at the door to 511. I'd closed it, but not locked it. Elway was still in the chair, pulling his shirt up to examine the purple marks already deepening on him. He yelped and cringed when I came back in.

"Where do I find Henry T?" I asked.

* * *

Henry T ran his operations out of his uncle's scrap metal yard, four blocks away from the Bel. According to Elway, nobody had seen the uncle that actually owned the place in a few years. I hid Andrea's box in a dense clutch of weeds behind an abandoned house half a block away before I walked in. The yard was bordered by a high chain-link fence topped with razor wire. Inside, a few dozen rusted-out car bodies were almost buried in towering stacks of old appliances, ragged sheets of siding, and the other detritus of modern life.

The only break in the fence was in the middle of the block on the east. A short gravel drive went through a five-slot parking lot and around the left side of an RV with an "OFFICE" sign tacked on the door. Where the drive petered out, at the rear corner of the RV, Talon was sitting on the end of a weight bench, doing curls with fifty-pound dumbbells. Other weights were scattered on the ground, a couple leaning against an old blue oil drum holding pipes of various lengths. Behind him, in the shade cast by the nearest mountain of rusting dishwaters, three men were playing cards at a folding table.

When he saw me coming, Talon put down the dumbbell and stood. He was wearing only gym shorts and blindingly white sneakers. A tattoo stretched across his entire, nearly hairless chest. In vivid color and detail, it showed an eagle's claw clutching the head of a cartoonishly stereotyped Orthodox rabbi. Blood, flowing from the head's severed neck and the places where the eagle's talons pierced it, pooled underneath to form the words YOU WILL

NOT REPLACE US.

"Charming tat," I said. "You think I could get that on some coasters, maybe a coffee mug?"

"Get lost, old man." There was something off about Talon's voice, like he was trying to pitch it deeper than was natural. He put one big fist in the other and cracked his knuckles.

"If I promise I'm impressed by how big and manly you are, can I get by?"

His eyes narrowed. "Fuck you say to me?"

"Step aside, junior. I've got business with your boss that's above your pay grade. Filthy lucre."

He stepped forward. "Say that again."

Before I could, one of the men at the table said, "Talon." He was the biggest and oldest of the three, which still put him closer to twenty than thirty.

Talon spun. "This old asshole called me a filthy looker, T."

"I heard what he said. Sit your roid ass down." Henry T nodded to me and gestured at the seat across from him. "Somebody wants to talk to me about money, I'm always willing to listen."

The two other men stood from the table and drifted away a few feet. I walked past Talon, resisting the impulse to stick out my tongue, and sat. Henry T was wearing a shirt with the logo of the scrap yard on one side of his chest and *Henry* on the other. He watched me with eyes that held nothing but a little amusement.

"I don't imagine you know who I am," I said.

"Haven't the faintest idea. Officer."

"Once upon a time. Detective Tim Chadwick." I nodded at his two sidekicks. "After I leave, one of these guys will call whoever it is you call and find out I got kicked out a few years back."

"That supposed to make me think you're not wired now?"

I stood and lifted my shirt, doing a slow pivot. "No wire. No gun. You need more?"

"All right. For now. So why should I care who you are?"

"I just wanted you to know who it's coming from, when I tell you what I came here to tell you."

"Man, you're really stretching this out. You got a point?"

"Elway Court is my point. He's off limits, as of today. You don't threaten him, you don't hurt him, you don't work with him, you don't sell to him, you don't talk to him. You're in McDonald's and he comes in, you best go out the door. The one on the other side of the building."

Henry T's eyes had lost some of their amusement. "I don't eat at fucking McDonald's. And Elway Court owes me money."

"Not anymore." I jerked my thumb at Talon. "Your man Godzilla here was offered payment. He declined. You got a problem, seems to me it's with him."

"That's bullshit, T," Talon said. "Court tried to give me some piece of shit box with a couple quarters and shit rattling around in it."

"Not sure I trust the big boy here on asset valuation," I said.

"Enough," Henry T cut in. "I don't want to hear this shit about coin collections. Do I look like I got time to run around trying to figure out who to sell coins to? I want my money, not a damn chore."

"Now you got neither. Elway's off limits."

Henry T stretched his neck slowly one way, then the other. "So why should I do anything you want, if you ain't even a cop anymore?"

"But I was," I said. "I was a cop for a good long time, and I made a lot of friends." I leaned back and made a show of looking around the yard. "Doing what you're doing, where you're doing it, you're kicking something up to the Flynns. Who is it you deal with? Ronan?"

Henry T was very still now. "I know Ronan Flynn. Am I supposed to believe he's one of your friends?"

"Hell, no. Ronan hates my guts. I put a couple of his uncles inside and shot another one."

"Then I'm not seeing the threat here, Tim."

One of the guys who'd been at the table took a knife out of his pocket and started casually trimming a fingernail with it.

"My friends work in places like the Narcotics department and the DA's office. I guess you know Ronan Flynn has friends in those places, too. So what do you think would happen if your name found its way onto, say, a list of confidential informants? Or even better, how about a witness list?"

Henry T's face didn't change, but I thought I saw his hands clench for a moment. "I'd just tell Ronan you set me up. I could tell him about this talk before you even could do it."

"Sure, you could do that. Assuming you think he's got so much faith in you that he'd bet a life sentence on you telling him the truth. You think he has that kind of faith, or do you think he'd kill you just to be on the safe side?"

Nobody said anything.

"There's a real easy way to find out. Just breathe in the general direction of Elway Court, and we'll all find out."

"So maybe I kill you."

I grinned. "Try it. See what kind of insurance I arranged before I walked in here." None, but Henry didn't need to know that.

"What's my alternative?" He had to force the words out.

"I already said. Leave Court alone. Write off the four K as an educational expense."

"That's it. Just steer clear of Court."

"That's it."

"You've met him, right? I've known Elway since third grade. He's got the worst luck of anybody I've ever met, and he does a lot of stupid shit around people with no tolerance for stupid shit. Somebody's gonna kill him sooner or later, even if we don't."

"Hope for later. Elway has a bad day, you're gonna have a bad day." I stood up. "I assume we have a deal."

"You listening to this bullshit, T?" Talon was standing again. His arms were crossed, and every muscle in them was tensed.

"Deal," Henry T said. "But I don't think you want to come around here again."

"I'll miss the hell out of it." I touched my finger to the brim of an imaginary hat. "You gentlemen have a good afternoon."

I headed back the way I came. As I passed Talon, he spit at my feet. "I'm gonna be coming for you, old man."

Without breaking stride, I pulled a four-foot length of iron pipe from the barrel, pivoted on one heel, and swung it with all the strength I could muster into the side of Talon's left knee. There was a crunching noise and a snap like a rifle shot as the knee bent sharply inward. Talon made a sound that had nothing human in it and dropped to the ground. The leg stayed bent at a sideways angle that made my stomach lurch. He reached for it, the high whines he was making not a lot different from the noises Elway Court was making when I first saw him.

"Thanks for the warning." I dropped the pipe on top of Talon. "I'll keep an eye out for a big motherfucker with a limp."

I didn't look at Henry T or his sidekicks. I turned and headed for the street. I waited for a shout or a shot. None came.

* * *

Andrea was good for the second hundred and didn't ask any questions when I dropped the box off. She told me I might not see much of her at the bar because she was trying to cut back. I told her that was a good idea. Then I headed straight for the bar myself.

If Talon was lucky, he might be walking without crutches in a couple of months. Henry T probably wouldn't be able to keep a leash on him after that. His injured pride would mean more to him than some deal his boss made. Maybe by then I'll have ordered that sixth drink, and I'll be past giving a damn.

Heston put a drink on the bar between my hands. First of the day. First of five. Probably.

Some Sunny Day, Baby

"Heston says you used to be a cop."

At the sound of the voice, I looked up into the face of Anson Brancato, a face I hadn't seen in six years. Heston stood behind the bar at the far end of the room, polishing a glass and looking not quite directly at us.

"He says that to everybody," I said. "I think he's trying to discourage the stickup punks."

"I could have told him you stopped being a cop a long time before you took off the badge."

"You still can," I said. "I don't think he'll much care."

"You gonna ask me to sit?"

I shrugged. Brancato worked himself into the chair across the small, scarred table. His middle had gotten thicker since I saw him last.

It was early yet, just a few other people in the place, none close enough to listen to us. I had just finished the first of my five nightly drinks.

"I been trying to find you all day," he said. He set his beer down. "Bergman finally told me to try coming here. Don't you have a cell?"

"Had one for a while," I said. "Didn't care for it. Just makes it easier for the assholes to find you."

Brancato flushed. He'd never been my kind of cop. A paper-pusher, a bureaucrat, a desk guy. Desk guys and street guys don't always have much to say to each other.

"I'm here doing you a favor," he said. "Christ knows why."

"Can't think of a thing I need from you, Brancato."

"So maybe I'm not doing you a favor. Maybe Carl Denham needs the favor. You want to listen or what?"

Hearing the name, I signaled Heston for a refill. Second of the five drinks I allow myself every night. "Carl sent you?"

"No." Brancato took a couple of swallows of beer. "But he fucked up, bad. Maybe you can do something about it."

Heston set a fresh glass in front of me and faded away. I let my fingers brush the smooth, cool glass, but didn't lift it yet. "You've got my attention."

Brancato hunched forward, dropping his voice. "So, I'm not in community relations anymore. I'm in the property room, the big one downtown. You been there."

"Sure." It took up most of a subbasement at Police HQ, shelf after shelf of seized goods and evidence behind a chain-link fence that went right up to the ceiling.

"I spend most of my time inside the cage," he said. "Pulling exhibits for trial, cataloging forensic samples, shit like that. You get to know where things are, right? It might look like a big mess to other people, but it makes sense in your head."

"Okay."

Brancato shot a look around the room, then took a deep breath and plunged ahead. "I'm in there this morning, and something don't look right. A box just a little out of place from the day before. Most people would never notice."

"I get it. You're fucking Sherlock Holmes. Where are we going with this?"

Brancato ignored me. "So I check it out. Chadwick, there's fifty grand missing."

I tilted my head. "Cash?"

He nodded. "Seized in a drug raid last year. Twenties and tens, rubber-banded into thousand-dollar rolls in a grocery sack. They told us to save it that way so the DA can put on a big show if it ever goes to trial."

I took a sip, letting the liquid fire slide down my throat. "I don't like where this is going."

"I checked the logs, looked at the tapes from the last couple days. Denham took it, late last night, when he was supposedly returning some cold case boxes he checked out a week ago."

"Denham's a lot of things," I said. "He's not dirty."

"That's what I thought," Brancato said. "That's why I haven't reported this yet. I know you don't like me, but I'm not looking to burn a cop who's one year away from a full pension."

"So why are you talking to me instead of him?"

Brancato took another drink and wiped his mouth with the back of his hand. "I'm not looking to burn myself, either. If Denham's into something and IA or the Feds or god knows who is working it, the last thing I need is to be on some surveillance tape knocking on his door."

I grunted. "Guess it's not just Denham's pension you're thinking about."

"Fuck you. I could have just reported this right away."

I held up a calming hand. "Okay. You're right. So you want me to talk to him."

"Yeah," Brancato finished his beer. "Look, maybe it was just an urge. It happens to everybody in the cage. You see a stack of money gathering dust, or a laptop your kid could use, or whatever. You stick it under your arm and don't really think about what you've done until you're in the car on the way home, right? If that's all, and he gives it back, like, *now*, this doesn't have to be anything."

"But you won't talk to him yourself, and you can't go to anybody who still has a badge, because there's no unringing the bell. So you dig up poor, disgraced Tim Chadwick to do your dirty work."

"Spin it how you want. I'd say I'm going to somebody who probably owes Denham something."

I couldn't hold back any longer. I picked up my glass and drained it. "How much time has he got?"

"End of the day tomorrow. If it's not back by then, I'll have to report it to cover my own ass, and don't try to make me feel bad about it. I got three kids, Chadwick, and twenty-nine months to retirement. I'm not going down for this."

I rolled the empty glass between my palms. Carl Denham was my first partner, back in the prehistoric days when I wore a uniform. He taught me most of what I knew about being a cop, saved my life once. After a couple of years, he got bumped up to Narcotics, where he spent months at a time undercover, and we didn't run into each other much. It didn't matter that I hadn't seen him in maybe a decade. When you owe somebody, you owe. Even Brancato knew that much.

I had three drinks left for the night. They were going to have to wait.

* * *

Denham lived in a one-story prefab home in the near suburbs, a neighborhood that had gone a little shabby without ever quite reaching run-down. I had more than one meal on the backyard deck he built with his own hands. Brancato, still seeing FBI agents behind every tree, dropped me two blocks away. I told him I'd walk the three miles back, or get Denham to give me a ride.

Dusk deepened as I walked, listening to the muffled hum of the Interstate half a mile away. A few people walked dogs, but mostly the streets were empty. It was a place long lived in, a place where most of the children have grown up and moved on, a place where some families still religiously mowed the lawn and brought in their trash cans, while other houses lost shingles and sprouted weeds. When I used to have dinner with Denham and his wife, there were always couples sitting out on their porches, waving to people passing by. Everybody was inside now, looking at screens that showed people out doing things.

It bothered me that I couldn't remember the name of Denham's wife. I should have asked Brancato.

The lights were on at Denham's place, but I couldn't see anything through the curtains. In the twilight, I wasn't sure if it had been painted since I was last there. My first knock was met with silence, but one of the things you learn as a cop is the difference between the silence of absence and the silence of waiting. I knocked again.

"Who is it?"

The voice from just inside the door was raspier than I remembered.

"It's Tim Chadwick," I said.

I felt surprise in the long moment of silence before a lock clicked and the door opened. The years since I had seen Carl Denham sat on him uneasily. He was thin to the point of being scrawny, and looked like he hadn't shaved in a week. His face was heavily lined, his gray hair hanging lank to his collar. He wore jeans and a blank, black t-shirt with a couple of small holes.

"What the fuck are you doing here?"

"Nice greeting," I said. "You want to let me in?"

He hesitated, but pushed open the screen door and gestured me inside. The door opened directly into the living room. The flatscreen TV was new, but I thought I recognized the carpet and the worn furniture. Hanging over the couch was a large, framed painting I definitely hadn't seen before. It showed four women in grass skirts, doing a hula dance on a beach of white sand, with palm trees and a mountain behind them.

Denham closed the door behind me. "It's good to see you, Tim, but this isn't a great time. I got to take off in an hour or so."

"I won't keep you," I said. "But we gotta talk."

He looked like he was going to argue, then shrugged. "Okay, I can kill twenty or thirty minutes. You want a beer?"

"No, thanks." I wasn't going to waste one of my five drinks on beer, especially since Denham favored cheap, stale-tasting brands. "Take a water, maybe."

When he came back from the kitchen with a glass, I was standing in front of the painting. "This is new," I said.

He handed me the water. "Alice found it at a garage sale," he said. Alice, that was it. "Fell in love with the damn thing. She used to stand right where you are and say *some sunny day it'll be you and me on that beach, baby.*" He ground to a stop and looked away.

"Where is Alice?" I asked. I wasn't finished saying her name before I saw the look on his face and wanted to take the question back.

"New Jersey," he said. "Her new husband is a lawyer."

"Fuck, Carl. I didn't know. I'm sorry."

Denham perched on the edge of a recliner. "Happened a few years ago. After you—after what happened to you."

I sat on the couch, facing him. "Anson Brancato came to see me."

"That SOB? What did he want?"

I raised my eyebrows. "I hope you aren't really planning to go with that line, Carl. You've been in my place too often to believe I want to listen to a lot of lies."

Denham's face hardened. "You wired, Tim?"

I laughed. "You know anybody in the city who would wire me up? You think I'd go along with it?" I spread my hands. "It's just me, man."

He held my eye for a minute and looked away. "I didn't think anybody'd notice so fast."

"Being a prick doesn't mean Brancato's bad at his job."

"I assume he wants me to bring the money back."

"By end of shift tomorrow, or he's turning you in. He could have done it already. You'd be in the box asking for a lawyer and a union rep."

"Yeah, well. I can't do it."

"He's serious, Carl. He's terrified of going down with you."

Denham snorted. "Asshole doesn't know what terrified means."

"You saying you're afraid of something? Is that what you need it for? Let me help you out. Talk to me."

Denham lurched from his chair and began pacing. "How's your kid, Tim?"

"Don't change the topic."

"We'll get there. Tell me about your kid." He pulled back an edge of the curtain and peered out. "Neil, right?"

"Yeah," I said. "Neil's okay. Working downtown, some kind of financial job I don't understand. I see him a couple times a year."

"That's good." He wasn't really listening. "Now you ask me about my kids."

"How are your kids, Carl?"

He turned from the window. "Randy's working with the EPA out west, cleaning up old mining sites. Always was a smart kid. Clint's in dental school."

"That's good. Real good."

"And Abby is dead."

The air in the room went still. I had a flash of memory. A little girl in this room, five or six years old, playing with dolls in a corner while I talked shop with her dad. Golden hair. Big, blue eyes. Carl Denham watched me and waited.

I let out a slow breath. "Jesus. I'm sorry, Carl."

"You're sorry," he said. "I'm sorry. Alice is sorry. Her asshole husband is probably sorry. Hell, Brancato is sorry. All the sorry in the world." He broke off and turned his back to me.

Cops give a lot of bad news. After a while, you realize there's not much to say that really helps. I watched his back and thought dirty, angry thoughts about Anson Brancato. I should have been back at Heston's. About now, I'd be finishing my fifth drink, and waiting to see if this was the night I ordered number six.

When I couldn't take the silence anymore, I spoke softly. "You saying that has something to do with the money?"

Denham turned sharply on his heel. "Wait here." He stalked out of the room. In a minute, he was back, carrying a big leather briefcase. He put it gently on the coffee table in the middle of the room, opened it, and spun it to face me. It was filled with packets of money, each banded in a strip of red paper.

"Took me most of the day to get it all out of the rubber bands and looking professional," he said.

I shook my head. "Brancato's going to be pissed. They're supposed to be keeping it as it was found for the DA."

"Brancato's never going to see this. I got plans for this money."

"We both know you're gonna tell me, man. Might as well tell me."

Denham sat down, again just at the edge of his chair. "Fifty thousand in cash gets me in a room with the guy who supplies the dealer Abby used."

I closed my eyes. "Abby OD'd."

"Three months ago," Denham said. "Her dealer's number was in her phone. I didn't give it to the guys working her case. The day after I buried her, I started working on getting next to the guy."

I opened my eyes. "Is he dead?"

"I didn't want him. I wanted his boss." Denham's face softened with a moment of pride. "It was beautiful, Tim. I used everything I knew from those years undercover. Took my time. Hung back at the right moments, pushed at the right moments. All leading to this. Tonight. They think I'm a player from out west looking for a new supplier. The fifty is my down payment."

"So it gets you in the room. It's not like they're gonna let you bring in a gun."

"I don't need a gun." For the first time that night, Denham smiled. "I mean, I have one, and I'll let them take it. Doesn't matter." Now he looked downright delighted with himself. "Maybe you don't know. I was still in Narcotics when you left, huh?"

"Yeah," I said. "Why, you somewhere else now?"

He nodded, his mouth grinning and his eyes dead. "I'm in my fifth year on the bomb squad."

My mouth went dry. I felt a ridiculous urge to edge away from the briefcase. "Jesus Christ, Carl. You're not serious."

"Serious," he said. "My little girl is in a hole in the ground." He looked at his watch. "Time's about up, Tim. I've got a meet to get to."

"You're not making sense." I clutched my fists. "You didn't want her dealer, right? You want the dealer's boss, the guy you're about to meet. Well, he has a boss too, right? And then that guy has a boss. Fuck, you know how this works. Why you stopping with this guy?"

"I can't kill them all," Denham said. The ghastly smile wasn't there anymore. He just looked old. "So I'll kill the ones who might have known her and did it anyway. The ones who had a hand in deciding what *exactly* would go into the little baggie they sold her."

"You know better than this. You're a cop."

"No, I'm not. When they send whoever they send to break down the door tomorrow, they'll find my badge and resignation in my nightstand. You can tell Brancato to relax. I make it very clear I didn't have any help."

"I don't think that will relax him. I can't let you do this, Carl."

"Nobody's asking your permission, Tim. You're not even on the job. You got nothing to do with this. You wouldn't be here if Brancato wasn't too big a pussy to come himself."

"I owe you. That's why I'm here."

"You bring a gun?"

"Of course not."

"Then I guess we're done talking." Denham put his hand into the side pocket of the recliner and brought out a big, ugly revolver. He held it casually, pointed at the floor between us. "Let's go to the kitchen."

I didn't move. "I don't believe you'd shoot me."

"I don't want to," he said. "But I'm also way past the point of giving a fuck. You try to stop me, I'll put one in your knee." He stood up. "On your feet. Into the kitchen."

I stayed where I was. Denham sighed and raised the gun, pointing it directly at my kneecap. The barrel looked huge. I stood. "Figuring it'll be easier to clean my blood off linoleum?"

Denham didn't answer. He stood back to give me a clear path and waggled the gun. I headed for the back of the house, feeling pins and needles all along my spine as he followed me. The kitchen hadn't changed any that I could see in the last twenty years. The refrigerator in the corner was a massive slab of stainless steel. One end of a pair of handcuffs was fastened to the handle, the other end hanging open.

"Guess you can figure this out," he said.

I closed the other bracelet around my right wrist.

"Don't treat me like a rookie," he said. "Let's hear a couple more clicks."

I grimaced and tightened the cuff. "If I can't talk you out of this, Carl, then let me come. Don't tell me you couldn't use backup."

"I don't think so," he said. He tucked the gun into his belt at the small of his back, staying several paces away from me.

"I do owe you," I said. "That apartment on Belmont. I haven't forgotten."

"I have." He sounded exhausted. "I've forgotten a lot of things. I don't think any of them matter now." He took a key out of his pocket and dropped it on the counter at the other end of the room. "You're a clever guy. I'm sure you'll figure a way to be out of here by the time anyone comes looking."

"Don't do this, Carl. For the love of Christ, think of your sons."

He was starting out of the room, but at that, he turned back. "I've tried to, Tim. I can't even remember what they look like. I can't remember what Abby looked like, either. All I can see is the space where she used to be. All I can see is what's gone."

He left the room. I yelled after him, yanked on the cuff, but it was no good. I heard, sharp and clear, the two latches on the briefcase closing. I had time to yell his name twice more before I heard the front door open and close and knew I was alone.

* * *

It took me most of an hour to get free. The broom leaning against the wall was six inches too short to reach the key. I tried pulling the fridge itself out from the wall, but with only one arm to work with, I couldn't get any leverage. Eventually, I opened the fridge, found a stick of butter, and smeared it all over my wrist and hand. It made a hell of a mess and took off a fair amount of skin, but finally I managed to slide my hand through, cursing a blue streak the whole time.

I cleaned up as best I could, got the key, and took the cuffs with me. There'd be a crime scene unit going over this house soon. I could explain my fingerprints in an old partner's house. I couldn't explain my blood and skin on a pair of cuffs.

It was a long walk back to Heston's. I figured later that I was about halfway there at the moment when the explosion tore through an abandoned warehouse near the docks.

* * *

It was a week before they released the identities of the four bodies inside: a veteran police officer with years of honorable service, and three career criminals known to be involved in the local drug trade. I sat at Heston's, watching the mayor and the police commissioner tell a room full of reporters that Carl Denham was a hero who lost his life in the line of duty. It made for a better story than a rogue cop. I figured Brancato was safe. They couldn't burn him without burning their cover. I flexed my hand, feeling the healing skin stretch and crack.

It was months before I stopped dreaming every night of that briefcase, blooming in an instant with the fire and light of the sun, leaving nothing but ash behind.

Making the Bad Guys Nervous

"Heston says you used to be a cop."

The stocky man didn't wait for a response or invitation. He put his beer on my table with a substantial thump and dropped into the chair facing me. I shot a look across the room at Heston. He pretended to be too absorbed in carding some college kids to notice.

"Bartenders are supposed to listen, not talk," I said. "But, yeah, I was a cop."

"And now you ain't. Pulled over the mayor's nephew or something, I bet."

I looked at him, tapping the scarred wood with my now-empty fifth drink. I have five drinks every night. The night I order a sixth will be the start of the end for me. Tonight, what came after the fifth drink, reliable as sunset, was a curdled self-disgust that turns against others very easily.

My new companion was oblivious to my mood. "Thought you could help me with something." He held out his hand. "I'm Gabe Lawson."

After a beat, I took the hand. "Tim Chadwick."

"I'll tell you the problem I'm having, Tim." Lawson took a cardboard coaster off the table and started absently shredding it. "My mother lives in Applebrook. You know it?"

Applebrook was a suburb west of the city. Affluent, but not wealthy. "I've been there."

"Her neighborhood's getting hit hard by porch pirates. Two, three times a week, she hears about somebody getting a package stolen. She's lost a couple herself. Always somebody in shades and a hoodie, so cameras aren't much good. You know anything about the lowlifes who do this?"

"Some," I said. "Wasn't my division, but you hear things. Usually it's an impulse, just somebody who sees a chance to run off with something."

"It's happening way too often for that."

"You do get organized rings sometimes, but they're still amateurs. Pros aren't interested in a package that might be granola bars and a six-pack of deodorant."

"Some of her neighbors called the cops. They say they'll patrol more, but that never lasts more than a day or two."

"Sure. It's nonviolent crime, usually petty theft. Most people don't even call the police."

The table in front of Lawson was covered with tiny scraps of damp cardboard. He swept them onto the floor with the back of his hand and picked up another coaster. "I want it stopped before these punks step up to break-ins and hurt somebody. Like my mother."

"Tried going private?"

"I called one agency. They just about hung up on me. Said it wasn't serious enough for the time and manpower it would take." Half the second coaster was gone. "I was crying in my beer about it, and Heston said maybe you could help."

"I'm only one man, Mr. Lawson."

"Gabe."

"I don't have an agency. I don't even have a license."

"All I'm asking is, go see what you can see. Show Mom I'm doing something. I'd do it, if I could get off work. I can handle myself. I boxed, back in the day."

"I can tell. You're sheer hell on coasters."

"Look, tomorrow's Monday. Go talk to Mom, drive around, hang out until five. The bastards always hit during the day. Take one week. Catch them or scare them off, I don't care which."

"And if I don't come up with anything?"

"You go your way, I go mine, God bless."

I looked at my empty glass. "Two hundred a day. In advance."

"A grand for the week?" Lawson got out his phone. "No problem. What do you take? PayPal? Venmo?"

"Cash."

He looked like I'd asked the way to the nearest malt shop. "Cash?"

"Legal tender for all debts, public and private."

"Man, I haven't carried cash in years."

"There's an ATM by the restrooms."

He stood, then hesitated. "Think you can be out there by eight, put in a full day?"

"Let's say ten. Most thieves sleep in."

* * *

I don't have a car anymore. I don't have much of anything except a rented room, five drinks a night, and regrets. And now, I guess, a job.

I caught a bus and was in Applebrook by nine the next morning. I spent an hour walking the streets in a grid pattern, working towards Mrs. Lawson's address.

The houses in her development were thirty or forty years old, and bigger than they should have been for the lots they squeezed onto. Most were two stories, and some had walk-out basements. Aside from a few dogwalkers and joggers, nobody was on foot. It was early summer, but there were no bikes on their sides in front lawns, no crudely chalked hopscotch patterns on the driveways, no basketball hoops mounted above garage doors. The childhood I remembered might have happened on a different planet.

It was ten on the dot when I rang the bell of a blue house in the middle of the block. A tall, gangly woman, somewhere in her upper sixties, opened the door. The hair pulled back into a gray ponytail had apparently never been dyed. She wore a checkered work shirt with rolled sleeves and streaks of paint across the front.

"Mrs. Lawson? My name is Tim Chadwick. Your son hired me to look into the package thefts around here."

"Well, I didn't do it," she said. "You can search the place." Seeing my expression, she smiled. "I'm kidding. He called me. Do you have ID?"

246

I showed her. She nodded without really looking and stepped aside to let me in. "No car?"

"Strange car in your drive might make the bad guys nervous," I said. "I'll try not to get in your way. All I need is a room where I can watch the street. I'll probably walk around the neighborhood a few times a day."

The living room she led me to had the comfortable air of a space that saw a lot of use. The furniture was well broken in, and books and magazines were scattered over every flat surface. An upright piano in one corner had piles of sheet music stacked on top. The big window looked out over the street. "This will be fine, Mrs. Lawson."

"Call me Sandy. I should have gotten rid of that wretched name when Gabe's father ran out on us."

"What's your maiden name?"

"Windkloppel. Just sings, doesn't it? Would you like some coffee?"

"If it's no trouble. Sandy."

I moved one of the smaller chairs to see as much of the street as possible, while staying mostly hidden behind the blinds. When Sandy came back with a cup of coffee, I put it on a small table by my elbow, along with a notepad and a pen.

"What's your plan?" she asked.

"*Plan* is a generous word." I crossed my legs. "The first day or two, I'll mostly watch, try to get a sense of patterns. Look for cars or people who seem out of place, or go up and down the street too often. See how the delivery people operate. I figure I'll sit for a few hours, take a walk, rinse and repeat."

"It seems like you're counting on luck."

"Not much more I can do solo. If I was doing this right, I'd have two or three people in unmarked cars and surveillance cameras at every corner. We'd be working with the delivery companies, putting out fake packages with trackers."

"That sounds expensive."

"And that's why you get one guy counting on luck."

"I hope you have it. Did you want me to stay with you? I was painting, on the back porch. The morning light is perfect there."

"Pretend I'm not here. I'll let you know if I go out."

* * *

Watching—*really* watching—takes practice, patience, and attention. Most people these days can't do it. Five minutes in, they need to get out their little external brain to check email or see what Harry Styles is up to or throw birds at pigs or some damn thing. I get a phone sometimes, when it's a real necessity for a job, then ditch it as soon as I can.

I took notes on every vehicle and pedestrian I saw. There weren't many. Sandy Lawson lived on one of the main arteries of the subdivision, but often four or five minutes would go by with nobody at all passing. I figured by Wednesday afternoon I'd be bored enough to start taking notes on the squirrels.

At half past eleven, a woman in her early twenties, wearing yoga pants and a crop top, came out of the house next door. I observed her closely as she stretched and set off jogging. I saw no indication that she was intending to steal packages, but it's important not to eliminate suspects prematurely.

Ten minutes later, the garage door across the street opened. A man in khaki shorts, black socks, and Birkenstock sandals came out with a leaf blower. He spent fifteen minutes meticulously working over his front lawn, blasting every fallen leaf and loose blade of grass into the street or a neighboring yard. The machine's whine set my teeth on edge, and I was glad when he went back inside.

The first delivery truck went by just before noon. FedEx. It didn't stop on Sandy's block.

At twelve thirty, the jogger returned, shiny with sweat. She slowed to a walk in the driveway, arching her back and stretching her arms. She didn't have any packages. I'm pretty sure she didn't have any loose change or pocket lint, either.

Sandy carried in a tray with sandwiches, bags of chips, and cans of soft drink a little after one. "Lunch?"

"That's nice of you."

She put half of the food on my table and took hers to a chair beside the window. "Can I sit here and eat with you, or would that make the bad guys nervous?"

"I'm pretty sure the bad guys are otherwise occupied. I've had three delivery trucks, sixteen cars, and four pedestrians."

"Sounds riveting."

"You could sell tickets." The sandwich was ham and cheddar. "Have you lived here long?"

"Since it was built."

"Changed much?"

"Just the way everything has, I expect. I used to know everyone within three blocks of here, but they died or moved. Most of the new people I only know to wave at."

"People fall away," I said. "It's the curse of aging."

"One of the curses." Sandy washed down a bite of her sandwich. "I Googled you."

"That's never good news. Should I leave?"

"I try not to judge, Tim. You've had your troubles. We all do."

I was spared answering by a piercing sound from outside. Khaki shorts was back, sweeping his noisemaker across his grass, though there didn't seem to be a single illicit leaf on it. "That's odd," I said. "He just did that about an hour ago."

Sandy leaned forward to look around the edge of the window. "That's Carl Levy. He grew up here, but his parents are gone now. He's been working from home since the pandemic." She leaned back. "Sometimes I think he has OCD. He spends hours working on the garden in back, then he's out front waking the dead with that thing five or six times a day. It's maddening, until you get used to it."

"How long does that take?"

"I'll let you know when it happens."

* * *

I went for a walk after lunch and tried to look like I was jotting down snatches of poetic inspiration, as opposed to license plate numbers. When I got back, I found a paper plate with three cookies on my table. Sandy was at the piano, energetically tackling a series of Elton John tunes. I watched the road, nibbled, and listened. I don't know enough about music to put a name to what she was doing wrong, but she was doing a lot of it. The notes were mostly correct, but each one seemed either far too long or way too short, giving the music the jerky cadence of a sputtering engine.

After twenty minutes, she spun to face me. "Terrible, right?"

"Better than I could do."

"I never touched a key until about three years ago. I was thinking how I'd always wanted to play an instrument, so I decided to go ahead and play one."

"Beats staring at a TV all day."

"I started painting landscapes at the same time. I'm even worse at that."

Carl Levy's leaf blower started up again. "Christ," I said. "Play as bad as you want if it'll drown that out."

* * *

Carl was at it again when I got to Sandy's house Tuesday morning. She had coffee ready, and we watched together as he dealt severely with purely hypothetical leaves.

"Were his folks like this?" I asked.

"Not in the slightest. That yard used to be a real eyesore. His father was a gearhead, always taking a car apart in the drive. Carl doesn't even own one."

"Sounds like Carl needs to work some things out."

"Don't we all?" She looked at me. "So what would you say you accomplished your first day?"

"Not much." I sat and flipped to a fresh page in my notebook. "I have the start of a rough list of vehicles that belong in the neighborhood. I saw several delivery people leaving stuff on porches, and none of them seemed like they were paying attention to anything around them. They most likely wouldn't notice being followed or watched by anybody halfway competent."

Sandy sat in her corner chair. It was too cloudy for painting, she said, so she'd keep me company for a bit. "I imagine they're on too tight a schedule to be that attentive."

"Sure. I'm more interested in something that didn't happen."

"What's that?"

"I walked around this neighborhood several times yesterday, looking closely at homes and cars, writing things down. Nobody challenged me or asked what I was doing. Nobody called the cops. As far as I could see, nobody noticed me at all."

For lunch, Sandy went, as she said, Full Retro Suburban: frozen fish sticks. Afterward, she started in on a batch of John Mellencamp tunes. I went out for one of my recon walks when she hit what I think was the second verse of "Jack and Diane."

Aside from the overcast sky, I might have been walking through a rerun of the day before.

Sandy spent much of the day reading in her corner. We didn't talk much, but I didn't mind having her there.

At a quarter to five, she put her book down and rolled her shoulders. "Another day passes," she said. "It's really nothing like TV, is it?"

"What's that?"

"What you're doing. Police work, I guess. A stakeout." She had trouble saying the word with a straight face.

"No, it's not much like TV. A lot of it is paperwork and politics. A good chunk of the rest is trying not to fall asleep."

"Why did you want to do it?"

I took my time answering. "My dad was a cop," I finally said. "I never really thought about being anything else."

"Do you miss it?"

That, I didn't have an answer for.

Across the street, Carl Levy started his fifth session of the day with the leaf blower.

* * *

Wednesday was sunny again. Sandy spent some time painting on the back porch, but she wandered into the living room once in a while. She was there a little before noon, asking if I had any requests for lunch, when I cocked my head and held up my hand for silence.

Sirens. Nothing unusual in that, but these were coming closer. A lot closer.

"That's at least two cruisers," I said. "Ambulance too, I think."

"Car wreck?"

"Maybe." Neither of us believed it. The sirens cut out with a squawk, and I stood up. "That wasn't more than a couple blocks away. I'm going to check it out."

"I have an impulse to say *be careful*," Sandy said. "I can't imagine why, except that's what the woman would say right now in a movie."

I turned right out of Sandy's front door and walked past four houses to the corner. Halfway up the cross street, three cruisers and an ambulance were parked at different angles in front of a white house. Two paramedics on the porch were strapping a man in an oxygen mask onto a gurney. A couple of uniforms strung yellow tape from the corners of the porch out into the yard. Neighbors stood in their yards, trying to watch without seeming like ghouls. It was the most people I'd seen in Applebrook at one time.

An unmarked car whipped around the corner and stopped at the curb with a screech of brakes. The driver had the build of a featherweight boxer, the nervous energy of a chihuahua, and a full head of hair the color of crude oil. He was halfway to the house before his car stopped rocking on its springs. He grabbed the elbow of the first uniform he came to and started barking orders, somehow pointing in several directions at once.

I leaned against the back fender of the nearest cruiser and crossed my arms, watching as the man practically bounced through the front door.

One of the uniforms came over. "Please step away from the car, sir."

"Herzog told me to wait here," I said.

She put her thumbs in her belt. "You didn't speak to Lieutenant Herzog, sir."

"How long has he been out here? Last I knew, he was downtown working robbery."

The woman's expression didn't change. "Lieutenant Herzog has been assigned to the local precinct for eight months. Sir."

"That must make the bad guys nervous. Is he as popular here as he was downtown?"

"I really couldn't speak to the Lieutenant's personal reputation. Please step away from the car."

Apparently, she'd given up on *sir*.

"I bet he is," I said. I glanced at her nametag. "Officer Petty, what would you say if I told you that coming out of that house and seeing me is guaranteed to make Herzog's day worse?"

Petty breathed in through her nose, then very slowly out.

"I'd say have a nice day, sir." She walked off toward the house. I decided not to push my luck by asking her what happened here.

Twenty-three minutes later, Herzog came out onto the front steps, yelling into his cell phone. Petty touched his arm and pointed in my direction. When Herzog looked, I waved cheerfully. He stared for a second, gave me the finger, and turned back to Petty, but it was a struggle to argue with her and the person on the phone simultaneously. Finally, he threw up his hands, shoved the phone in a pocket, and stalked over to me.

"What the hell are you doing here, Chadwick?"

"Just an innocent bystander, Loo. Got family in the neighborhood."

"Sure you do. I should cuff you for interfering with a crime scene."

"Maybe I should cuff you for assaulting Mother Nature. What is that in your hair? Shoe polish?"

His face turned crimson. "Get lost, Chadwick." He started back toward the house.

"Ben," I said.

He shook his head, but turned.

"It's just a reflex," I said. "I'm sorry. Look, seriously, I've got an elderly aunt a block and a half from here. Just tell me if I need to be worried."

Herzog rubbed his eyes, shook his head again, and took a few steps closer. "Somebody was lifting a package off the porch. Homeowner sees it on the doorbell camera, decides he's a cowboy, grabs his gun, and goes out after him. But he gets too close, the perp grabs at him, they wrestle, and of course it's the idiot cowboy who ends up getting shot."

"Dead?"

"Hip. He won't be dancing for a while. Bad guy runs off, cowboy hears but didn't see his car. We'll do roadblocks, but you know how that is. Gotta figure he's twenty miles away by now."

"Get much of a description?"

"Skinny white guy in a hoodie. Whoever he is, he won't be back here for a while. Your aunt's fine." Herzog took another step forward. "Now that's all you get, Chadwick. I swear, in five minutes, if I can see you, I'm arresting you."

I nodded and walked off in the opposite direction from Sandy's, mostly to confuse the issue if Herzog decided to look for my aunt.

Did I have any reason, now, to come back for the next two days? Herzog was right. This particular porch pirate, anyway, would be steering clear of Applebrook for a while. The shooting was going to make the news, which meant the department would step up patrols for real, at least for a while. It looked like my job was over.

On the other hand, if I didn't put in the full week, Gabe Lawson might want some of his money back. And what would I do instead? My days were spent waiting for the moment when I could order my first drink. I might as well wait someplace nice.

I passed a brown minivan with a flat front passenger tire. I walked another ten feet, stopped, and went back. It was an ugly vehicle, a little older and dirtier than most of the cars in the neighborhood. The doors were locked. I pressed my forehead against the glass. A blanket was draped over a shapeless mass in the rear footwell. Could well have been, say, a bunch of cardboard boxes.

I looked at the license plate, then crouched to look closer. It was a dummy. Somebody had cut two plates in half, then welded them together to create a new number.

The minivan was parked at the curb in front of a house with a slightly shaggy yard and a realty company's sign. I went up the driveway and walked around the building, checking doors and windows. It seemed secure, and there was no sign of any life inside.

Okay. Mr. Pirate jumps in his car, adrenaline pumping, makes it around a couple corners before he notices the flat. He's probably hearing sirens by the time he gets out. Hardly a situation where he wants to stand around waiting for an Uber. He has to get away on foot.

Or find someplace to hole up.

I didn't run back to Sandy's. I'm too old and tired. But I didn't amble, either.

I heard the piano as soon as I let myself in the front door. I let out a breath and went into the living room. "Is that Springsteen?"

"If you're feeling generous." She looked up at me. "What happened?"

I gave her the headlines while I flipped through my notebook. "Looks like I saw that minivan once on Monday and twice yesterday. All three times within ten minutes of a delivery truck going by."

"Are you going to tell that man you talked to with the ridiculous hair?"

"Herzog?" I looked at her. "Did you follow me?"

"I'm sorry. Was I meant to put on a gingham bonnet and get to work in the kitchen?"

"I'm just surprised. I usually know when I'm being followed."

"Not to judge by the available evidence. Quit getting sidetracked. Are you going to tell him?"

"He's left the scene by now, and I doubt he'd answer a call from me. I could try calling the local precinct and hope I get the attention of somebody who knows what they're doing." I rubbed the back of my neck. "There's not a big overlap between the people who will still talk to me and people who are on good terms with Herzog."

"Tim," she said, "I hate to say it, but I'm noticing something that isn't happening."

"What's that?"

"It's been quite a while since I heard a leaf blower."

We both looked out the window. Carl Levy's house stood silent, the windows blank. For a long moment, nothing happened.

"Well, hell. I don't suppose you have a gun in the house."

"Don't you have one?"

"Not with me."

"We've never had guns."

"Okay. I'm going out like I'm walking around the block again, then I'll cut through backyards. Stand where you can see that corner of his yard. If you see me there and I wave one arm, everything's okay. If I wave two arms, or if you haven't seen me at all thirty minutes from now, call the police."

It took me less time than I expected to work my way between two houses around the corner and back to Carl's place. Sandy mentioned his gardens casually, but the neatly trimmed flowerbeds took up most of the backyard and were already showing vibrant color. There were no fences, but a row of short evergreens marked the boundary between the Levy property and his neighbor to one side. I used it for cover and duck-walked the last several feet to the house, plastering myself against the siding. I took a couple of long, quiet breaths, eased my way to the nearest window, and with infinite patience slid my eye to the corner of the glass.

A spare bedroom, the floor stacked with laundry baskets and assorted detritus. Carl was obsessively neat with the outside of the house and a slob inside. Useful material for his therapist, but of limited utility right now. I moved silently to the next window.

They were in the dining room at the rear of the house. Carl Levy sat in a wooden chair with his back to the window. Metallic silver tape had been wound a few dozen times around his body and the chair. His head was slumped to his chest, and I couldn't tell if he was conscious. A scrawny man, with a patchy beard and a blue hoodie, was pacing madly back and forth, ranting as he shook the gun he'd taken away from Herzog's cowboy. I could only hear him faintly through the glass, but he was enraged, sometimes at Levy and sometimes at the world in general. I could only guess what he might have taken to deal with the shakes that came after the fight on the cowboy's porch. He slapped the bound man's face, then held the gun against his temple. Carl shrank away, which at least told me he was awake and alive.

The back door was a dozen feet farther on. I covered the distance as quickly as I could without making noise and, holding my breath, turned the knob gently. I didn't expect it to be locked, and it wasn't. Not many people are paranoid enough to consistently lock a door they go in and out of a dozen times a day.

I was in Carl's garage. Like the other interior spaces I'd glimpsed, it was a mess. Utility shelves overflowed with lawn and garden equipment, and the air was heavy with the smells of earth and fertilizer. Two steps led up to a little mudroom, beyond which a half-open door went into the rest of the house.

I could hear Blue Hoodie yelling. Now he was saying that Levy was lying about being alone in the house, and that if he didn't start telling the truth, Hoodie would start cutting off Levy's fingers.

It took me a few minutes to find what I was looking for: rope. Actually twine, but close enough. I used my pocketknife to cut several long sections from the coil and made a tripwire across the mudroom doorway, tying it off to the legs of the big shelving units.

Then I stood to the side of the door and turned on the leaf blower.

It was hard to be sure, since being right next to the damn thing was like standing near a jet engine, but I thought I heard a yell from inside the house. I know I felt, through the wall at my back, the quick, heavy steps as he came running through the kitchen. He was going fast when he hit the rope. As I was hoping, he flew into the middle of the room, the gun knocked from his hand as he hit the hard concrete floor. What I wasn't expecting was that the shelves weren't as well anchored as I thought. The one on the other side of the doorway, yanked forward by the sudden impact on the rope, teetered, spun slightly, and fell, an assortment of tools and supplies bouncing off the fallen man.

I turned off the blower. Blue Hoodie wasn't moving. His feet had ended up pointing in my direction, out from under the shelf. I knelt and used part of the rope to tie his ankles together. He started to stir feebly, but there wasn't much to it. I moved up and pushed the shelf aside to tie his hands behind his back. As a final touch, I ran a taut line between the ankle and wrist bonds and anchored him to the shelf.

When I was satisfied he wasn't going anywhere, I found the button to open the garage door. Sandy was on the porch across the street. I waved both arms at her.

"They're on the way," she yelled.

I nodded and went into the house. Carl had a piece of the silver tape across his mouth. "Police are on the way, Mr. Levy," I said. He flinched when I took out my pocketknife, then relaxed when I began cutting through the tape. As soon as he had an arm free, he reached up and slowly peeled the tape off his face.

"He wanted a car," he said. "I don't have a car. He kept screaming at me that I was lying."

"I know," I said. I heard sirens, getting closer again. I expected I'd be spending several hours in a box with Herzog. I hoped he'd let me go in time for my first drink.

"I don't even know who you are," Carl said. "What can I do to thank you?"

I closed the knife and stood up as the first uniforms came through the door. "I guess there's one thing," I said. "Buy a damn rake."

Kindling Delight

"Look around you," the little Asian lady on TV said. "Contemplate each object in your space carefully. Does it kindle delight? If not, why not set it free?"

I blinked. It was all the answer I could manage.

"Your home is beautiful," the Asian lady told a family, standing in front of a five-foot pile of clothing they'd dragged from every room in the house. "But it has become a place where you merely store things, not a place where you live. By ridding yourself of all that does not kindle delight, you will create space to breathe and be content."

That sounded nice.

I was on the couch in the middle of the morning, my eyes fixed on the big TV mounted on the wall. I was hyperattentive, but completely incapable of movement. Aftereffects of whatever brew of booze and pills and pot I'd subjected myself to in the last twenty-four hours. During a commercial break, I thought hard about my left hand, but couldn't get it to budge.

Uncle Chad had been over the previous night with a bunch of his crew. You don't say no when Uncle Chad offers you a pill, even if you don't know what it is. The last thing I remembered was a couple of his guys getting in a fistfight over a poker game. Seemed like I just blinked and here I was, alone as far as I could tell, captive to the screen.

It was tuned to a cable channel showing a marathon of *Kindling Delight*. In every episode, the woman, Sakura, visited three families who had lost control of the sheer volume of stuff in their homes. One of the couples was always gay or interracial. Sometimes both. Sakura solved their problems, basically, by making them throw a lot of shit out, but before they could toss anything, they had to hold onto it, think about it, and see if it kindled delight. Then, at the very end, Sakura went back to each family a month or two later, to bask as they thanked her for changing their lives.

At first, I was annoyed by the people Sakura visited. They all lived in beautiful homes, homes like I only saw in real life if I broke in while the owners were on vacation, but they would be in tears about a little clutter. I mean, I'm supposed to feel sorry for you because you have too much crap?

I'll be damned, though, if I *didn't* start feeling a little sorry for them by the third episode, and even happy when they felt better. It was the way they acted like completely different people as they stood in emptied-out rooms, marveling at their sense of inner peace. They looked like actual weight had been lifted off them. Hell, they looked younger.

After several hours of Sakura, I couldn't help thinking about the stuff I was surrounded by all the time. Like, take the big cardboard box in the corner to the side of the TV. Uncle Chad stuck it there years ago to throw beer cans into, so they wouldn't be rolling around on the floor. That worked great, except nobody ever cleared out the box. Actually, you couldn't even see the box anymore, but I was pretty sure it was down there, in the base of the mountain of sour-smelling, sticky beer cans crawling up the walls where they met. I didn't think the box kindled delight. It wouldn't have kindled delight even if I could still see it. So I found a roll of trash bags and started shoveling the cans in. I was on the fifth bag before I realized I wasn't paralyzed anymore.

I kept it up for the next few days. Uncle Chad was on a trip down south for some business he didn't tell me about, and nobody else had any reason to come by with him gone. Uncle Chad installed me in the house three or four years ago to keep an eye on the trailhead, at the back of the property, leading to the cabins where his guys cooked. I got to be Uncle Chad's problem when my daddy, his brother, was killed by some Oklahoma bikers who objected to Uncle Chad moving product under their noses.

Sometimes days or weeks passed without anybody coming to the house. Sometimes Uncle Chad stashed stuff there. Sometimes he came by with members of his crew and some women and partied. Sometimes he showed up in the middle of the night and dragged me out to unload a hijacked truck or help beat the shit out of a guy who came up short on a bet.

Uncle Chad dabbled in a lot of lines of work.

The house never really felt like home, so I never really took care of it. Now I did, applying Sakura's test to everything. Aside from some of my clothes, the TV, and my supply of weed, hardly anything in the house kindled delight. I hauled bag after bag out to the side of the road to wait for trash day. I couldn't do anything about the broken-down furniture, and I knew better than to mess with Uncle Chad's stuff. He had a big safe in a back room that I didn't have the combination for, several loaded handguns and shotguns hidden under old blankets in the front closet, and a go-bag behind a false back in a kitchen cabinet.

Even leaving all that stuff alone, I got the place looking a lot better pretty quickly.

Smelling better, too. I started to understand the way the people on Sakura's show felt, like I could breathe easier. It was nice to walk from one room into another without immediately seeing some huge mess that would never be taken care of.

That's when I really got to thinking.

If I could make the house better, could I make myself better?

Could *I* kindle delight?

I remembered Uncle Chad at the card table in the dining room, sharpening a knife and smoking a cigar-sized joint, telling a bunch of us about a high school girl who OD'd on some of his junk. Good news, though, he said. She paid upfront.

Everybody laughed.

I laughed.

I remembered Uncle Chad smashing a guy's fingers in a car door for looking the wrong way at the wrong woman in the wrong bar.

I remembered the way I felt when I visited a guy who owed Uncle Chad money and drove my fist, again and again and again, into the middle of his face.

None of those memories kindled delight. I couldn't think of any that did.

"It's never too late," Sakura always told her families. "The life you want is already here, if you carve away the things you don't."

I was a week into my project when I came back from a walk in the woods and found Uncle Chad on the back deck. He sat in a chair with his long legs stretched out in front of him and watched me come across the yard.

He wasn't drinking or smoking, which was a bad sign.

"What the fuck you done to this place?" he asked when I got close.

I stepped up onto the deck. "Nothing. Cleaning up a little."

"There must be fifty sacks out there by the road. You trying to draw attention?"

"Just got tired of living in filth. That's all."

"That's all, huh?"

"Actually, no." I perched on the arm of the chair facing his. "I'm gonna get my GED. Maybe go to college."

"College." Uncle Chad said the word flatly.

"I can't live like this anymore. I want a real life, a straight life. I want to kindle delight."

Uncle Chad could be hellishly fast. I didn't see him move, just felt the back of his hand whip across my face. My head snapped to the side, and I went sprawling to the deck. I might have passed out for a second. When I was fully aware again, I was propped up on my elbows, and my head felt like the inside of an alarm bell. Uncle Chad was in his chair, still leaning back as if nothing had happened.

"You ever talk like that again, I'll tie you to a wall and let the boys take turns beating on you."

I didn't answer. I was moving my jaw gingerly back and forth.

"Now, speaking of college, there's a couple boys been dealing at frat parties without paying tax. You and me are dropping by tonight to show them the error of their ways. So go wash the blood off your nose, and don't give me no more shit about *delight*."

I picked myself up and went inside. I went straight to the front closet and pushed aside the blankets on the shelf. All the guns were loaded. I picked one up at random.

Even a worthless old asshole like Uncle Chad could be turned around, I figured. Even he could kindle delight. All I had to do was turn him into fertilizer.

Flowers kindle delight. I'd plant some beauties on top of him.

A Note from the Author

We live in a time when reading of any kind seems endangered by our collapsing attention spans and the gaudy attractions of our various digital playgrounds. Short stories in particular often struggle to find readers—but I believe reading is vitally important to our future, and vitally important in developing the empathy and understanding so often missing from the world. The editors and publishers of the magazines and anthologies where these stories appeared are doing heroic work in keeping the short crime story alive, and it's my hope that every reader of these pages will support them. Subscribe to a magazine; buy an anthology from a small press; seek out more work by the writers you enjoy. Long live the short story!

Original Publication Information

- "Etta at the End of the World." *Alfred Hitchcock's Mystery Magazine.* May/June 2020
- "Bonus Round." *Alfred Hitchcock's Mystery Magazine.* May/June 2019
- "And Now, An Inspiring Story of Tragedy Overcome." *Three Strikes—You're Dead!* Ed. Donna Andrews, Barb Goffman, and Marcia Talley. Wildside Press, 2024
- "Give or Take a Quarter Inch." *Tough.* Toughcrime.com. July 5, 2021
- "Chasing Diamonds." *Ellery Queen's Mystery Magazine.* September/October 2020
- "Wednesdays at Ten." *Alfred Hitchcock's Mystery Magazine.* May/June 2021
- "Awaiting The Hour." *Day of the Dark: Stories of Eclipse.* Ed. Kaye George. Wildside Press, 2017
- "Haven." *Seascape: The Best New England Crime Stories 2019.* Ed. Verona Rose, Harriette Sacker and Shawn Reilly Simmons. Level Best Books, 2019
- "Golden Lives." *Mystery Weekly.* September 2020
- "Mercy." *Peace, Love, and Crime: Crime Fiction Inspired by the Songs of the '60s.* Ed. Sandra Murphy. Untreed Reads, 2020
- "Pillbug." *Alfred Hitchcock's Mystery Magazine.* March 2015.
- "Herb Ecks Goes Underground." *Bloodroot: The Best New England Crime Stories 2021.* Ed. Susan Oleksiw, Ang Pompano and Leslie Wheeler. Crime Spell Books, 2021
- "Crime Scene." *Malice in Dallas: Metroplex Mysteries Volume One.* Ed. Barb Goffman. Sisters in Crime North Dallas, 2022

- "The Last Man in Lafarge." *Ellery Queen's Mystery Magazine.* July/August 2021
- "Everybody Pays a Tax." *Under the Thumb: Stories of Police Oppression.* Ed. S. A. Cosby and Paul Garth. Rock and a Hard Place Press, 2021
- "What They Say I Used To Be." *Hoosier Noir Two.* First City Books, 2020
- "Filthy Looker." *Mystery Magazine,* May 2022.
- "Some Sunny Day, Baby." *Guilty Crime Story Magazine* #6 (Fall 2022)
- "Making the Bad Guys Nervous." *Black Cat Weekly* #102 (August 13, 2023)
- "Kindling Delight." *Stone's Throw: A Rock and a Hard Place Publication.* January 2023

Acknowledgments

Writing is a lonely act, but no writer succeeds without the support and belief of people around them. I've been lucky to have a number of people in my life who pushed me to get beyond my insecurities, and my tendency to dismiss writing as nothing more than a self-indulgent hobby. My wife, Mary, is first on the list; she might not have understood *why* I wanted to do this, but she never doubted that I could, and didn't let me doubt it either. My thanks to my parents, who always indulged my hunger for reading. My thanks to the friends who were always excited to hear about a new story coming out: Eric, Leslie, Angel, Penny, Brian, and Deep.

These stories appeared in a variety of anthologies and magazines, and I owe a great deal to the editors of those publications. They invariably made the stories better, and working with them has made me a better writer. Often they've also become close friends. A special tip of the cap to Michael Bracken, Barb Goffman, Josh Pachter, Linda Landrigan, Janet Hutchings, Rusty Barnes, and Kaye George.

About the Author

Joseph S. Walker is the author of more than a hundred published crime and mystery stories, which have appeared in various magazines and anthologies (including four editions of *Best Mystery Stories of the Year*). He has been a finalist for the Edgar, Derringer, Shamus, and Thriller awards and is a two-time winner of the Al Blanchard Award. From 2024 to 2026, he served as the president of the Short Mystery Fiction Society. He lives in Indiana.

AUTHOR WEBSITE:
   https://jswalkerauthor.com/